USA TODAY BESTSELLING AUTHOR

M. ROBINSON

Connect with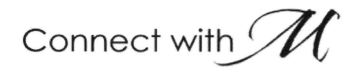

[WEBSITE](#)

[FACEBOOK](#)

[INSTAGRAM](#)

[TWITTER](#)

[AMAZON PAGE](#)

[VIP READER GROUP](#)

[NEWSLETTER](#)

[EMAIL ADDRESS](#)

MORE BOOKS BY M

All FREE WITH KINDLE UNLIMITED

EROTIC ROMANCE

VIP (The VIP Trilogy Book One)

THE MADAM (The VIP Trilogy Book Two)

MVP (The VIP Trilogy Book Three)

TEMPTING BAD (The VIP Spin-Off)

TWO SIDES GIANNA (Standalone)

CONTEMPORARY/NEW ADULT

THE GOOD OL' BOYS STANDALONE SERIES

COMPLICATE ME

FORBID ME

UNDO ME

CRAVE ME

EL DIABLO (THE DEVIL)

ROAD TO NOWHERE

ACKNOWLEDGMENTS

Dedication
Heather Moss & My Betas

Thank you for everything you ladies have done!

Yoda I couldn't have done this without you! I love you!

Betas: Thank you for your feedback and your boo boos. I love
you, too!

Boss man: Words cannot describe how much I love you. Thank you for ALWAYS being my best friend. I couldn't do this without you.

Dad: Thank you for always showing me what hard work is and what it can accomplish. For always telling me that I can do anything I put my mind to.

Mom: Thank you for ALWAYS being there for me no matter what. You are my best friend.

Julissa Rios: I love you and I am proud of you. Thank you for being a pain in my ass and for being my sister. I know you are always there for me when I need you.

Ysabelle & Gianna: Love you my babies.

Rebecca Marie: THANK YOU for an AMAZING cover. I wouldn't know what to do without you and your fabulous creativity.

Heather Moss: Thank you for everything that you do!! I wouldn't know what to do without you! You're. The. Best. PA. Ever!! You're NEVER leaving me!! XO

Silla Webb: Thank you so much for your edits and formatting! I love it and you!

Erin Noelle: Thank you for everything you do!

Michelle Tan: Best beta ever! **Argie Sokoli:** I couldn't do this without you. You're my chosen person. **Tammy McGowan:** Thank you for all your support, feedback, and boo boo's you find! I'm happy I made you cry. **Michele Henderson McMullen:** LOVE LOVE LOVE you!! **Rebeka Christine Perales:** You always make me smile. **Alison Evan-Maxwell:** Thank you for coming in last minute and getting it done like a boss. **Mary Jo Toth:** Your boo-boos are always great! Thank you for everything you do in VIP! **Ella**

Gram: You're such a sweet and amazing person! Thank you for your kindness. **Kimmie Lewis:** Your friendship means everything to me. **Tricia Bartley:** Your comments and voice always make me smile! **Kristi Lynn:** Thanks for all your honesty and for joining team M. **Pam Batchelor:** Thanks for all your suggestions. **Jenn Hazen:** Thank you for everything! **Laura Hansen:** I. Love. You. **Patti Correa:** You're amazing! Thank you for everything! **Jennifer Pon:** Thank you for all your feedback and suggestions! You're amazing! **Michelle Kubik Follis:** Welcome back! I missed you too! **Deborah E Shipuleski:** Thank you for all your quick honest feedback! **Kaye Blanchard:** Thank you for wanting to join team M! **Beth Morton Conley:** Thank you for everything! **KR Nadelson:** I love you! **Bri Partin:** Thank you for everything you do! **Mary Grzeszak:** Thanks for all the military info! You're amazing! **Patti McDaniel Adams:** Thanks for all the MC information! You're awesome! **Danielle Stewart:** Thanks for coming in late and helping! **Mel LuvstooRead:** Thank you so much for everything! You helped so much! **Lily Garcia:** I love you! **Allison East:** Thank you! **Louisa Brandenburger Michelle Chambers, Aidee Cruz, Bernadett Lankovits, Colleen Egger, Sheila Marie, Leeann Kidson Van Rensburg: THANK YOU! Emma Louise: Thank you for the graphics! BOOM Street Team: Thank you for all your hard work promoting. I love you!**

ALL MY VIPS!!!

Wander Aguiar: Thank you so much for doing a photo-shoot for me and being amazing. Wander Book Club

Marshall Perrin: Thank you for the amazing cover photo! You make the perfect Creed. Marshall Perrin

To all my author buddies:

Jettie Woodruff: You complete me.

Erin Noelle: I. Love. You!

To all the bloggers:

A HUGE THANK YOU for all the love and support you have shown me. I have made some amazing friendships with you that I hold dear to my heart. I know that without you I would be nothing!! I cannot THANK YOU enough!! Special thanks to Like A Boss Book Promotions for hosting my tours!

Last but not least.

YOU.

My readers.

THANK YOU!!

Without you…

I would be nothing..

PROLOGUE

Mia

I watched with stone cold eyes as the shiny white casket was lowered into the earth's soil. The heavens were weeping right along with me, raindrops seeping into my black jacket.

Burning my core.

Little by little.

Deeper and deeper.

Until darkness surrounded me, until all eyes were only staring at me, I could feel their eagerness, like a noose around my neck. Waiting for me to react, waiting for me to breakdown, just waiting for me to do something.

Anything.

It could have been one minute, two hours, or three days that had passed in front of my swollen eyes. I truthfully couldn't say how long I'd been standing there. If my puffy eyes and shivering body were any indications, I would have guessed a few hours. Time just seemed to stand still while my whole world shattered all around me.

Piece by piece.

One by one.

Now there would be nothing left of me. Not the girl everyone wanted me to be. Not the girl everyone remembered. The old Mia. All they saw was a hollow shell of a person they used to know, holding onto the hope that she was still somewhere deep inside of me. Not the girl…

Who had ceased to exist.

Except I tried to pretend I wasn't there. I tried to imagine that my life hadn't been changed in a matter of seconds. That my world hadn't been turned upside down in the span of a few hours. That everything I wanted to believe in wasn't truly…

A lie.

Life was about choices...

Good ones.

Bad ones.

It was the butterfly effect. Every action had a reaction. Once something was changed, you couldn't stop the chain of events following. One simple decision could be the catalyst of chaos.

One minuscule second.

One life-altering moment.

Set the tracks in motion.

It was what made the world go around. It allowed you to see glimpses of what could have been if you made a different choice. There were no do-overs, no matter how much you tried to reach those invisible lines and put them back in order, fixing what was broken. It would tease you, showing you the possibilities of a different outcome, but then it would laugh in your face like a cruel entity telling you it would never be.

Not now.

Not *ever*.

Except this decision wasn't my own. I didn't choose this. I didn't want this. I never prayed for this. My worst nightmare became my reality. In the end, it didn't matter.

Because this decision not only changed me, but my entire future.

It also cost me the love of my life. The person I watched being buried deep into the ground, six feet under, where I would never see them again.

Not one smile.

Not one I love you.

Not *one*…

Not *one*…

Not *one*…

I tightly shut my eyes, listening to the rain pelt the concrete and the ratchet noise of the hoist taking everything away from me. And then, I suddenly felt him behind me.

Everything about him hurt.

His scent, his aura, especially his love for me.

For us.

"I'm sorry. I'm so fuckin' sorry," he voiced in a tone that was filled with nothing but pain and remorse. His guilt was so thick, so consuming, I could feel it engulfing me, making it hard to breathe.

Hard to think.

Hard to feel.

Right now, at this moment.

My life ended before it ever even had a chance…

To begin.

While I stared at the gray granite tombstone, etched with the last name…

Jameson.

My eyes fluttered open just slightly, only to be met with nothing but darkness. A thick piece of fabric obstructing my view. I tried to get my arms to move, to take off the offending object, but it was no use. I was too weak. I opened my mouth to say something, but I couldn't get the words to come out. My lips were too dry, my throat was raw and burning, making it hard to swallow, let alone speak. I tried to process what was going on, what had happened, how long I had been out, but I couldn't push through the haze. I was so tired, so dizzy, so out of it that panic couldn't even set in.

My head pounded heavily as if it weighed a thousand pounds. Sensing as though it was lying on someone's lap, the rough material of my abductors pants, scraped against my cheek. All I could hear was the rumbling of a loud engine while a cool breeze swept across my face, neck, and hair. My body was warm which made me think a blanket was wrapped around me, but I was numb. All I could feel was the vibration from the uneven ground we must have been driving on.

The vehicle felt like it never stopped climbing and turning. Right, left then right again, over and over, throwing me off course. There was no way I could keep up with the twists and turns. My sense of direction was long gone. Nothing seemed familiar, not the sounds and not the scents. I was too drowsy to function. My body continued to be jostled from the fast movements. The roads were coarse and jagged, making the ride extremely uncomfortable and unpleasant. The sound of the wind whistled in my ears as we whipped through what I thought might have been a forest because tree branches snapped under the weight of the tires. I could occasionally hear branches scraping against the roof of the car.

They were driving so fast, as if they were getting away from someone. I couldn't fathom why I was there, what my role was in all of this and before I could give it another thought, I blacked out again.

My head fell back against the headrest in my Jeep, staring at the house out in front of me.

Creed and Noah's house.

The irony was not lost on me. Although, I couldn't possibly complain, it wouldn't be fair to Noah if I did. He had stepped up in every way possible when it came to the baby girl that grew inside of me. In the process of it all, I don't know how it happened, but we started to become close friends. I couldn't help it. I had spent more time with Noah than I ever had with Creed, in the past seven years. Ever since I first laid eyes on his tortured soul, it had always been a game of push and pull. Even just thinking about him made me smile. I sat there contemplating, trying to convince myself to walk into his childhood home for the very first time.

Except it wouldn't be his warm welcoming arms that wrapped around me, engulfing me with his comforting musky scent that I loved more than anything.

It would be his brother's.

My baby's father.

The man that shouldn't be looking at me like I was the one he'd been waiting for all his life. I'd often catch glimpses of Noah staring at me adoringly during our many doctor visits. He didn't even try to hide it. Noah wanted our unborn child. He wanted to be a part of this journey. He wanted it all.

A future.

A life.

A forever...

Possibly with me.

If I knew the truth, there was no way in hell Creed didn't. The thought alone sent shivers down my spine, making the ends of my hair stand straight up. Feeling the consequences of what hadn't happened yet, but would eventually come.

The inevitable.

A battle.

For my heart.

I learned pretty quickly that Noah was just as lost as his brother, if not more. His eyes held the same sadness that Creed's carried all his life. A burden I could never understand or contemplate. I didn't know anything about the Vice Prez of Devil's Rejects, other than what his eyes always showed me. What his sullen presence provided me, or what his strong, callused hands and fervent, burning lips promised me.

His love.

Noah was a lot like his older brother, but at the same time, they couldn't have been more different. Like night and day, and oil and water. The more time I spent with Noah, the easier it was for me to see a side of him that I wished Creed would show me after all these years.

His heart.

Creed was still guarded, broody, and temperamental, and those were some of his best qualities. All I could hope for was that eventually he would open up, show me the man I knew was behind his cut all along. The man who I'd loved since I was nine years old.

I shook off the sentiment, taking in a deep breath, closing my eyes, and placing my hand on my swollen belly. Imagining a breathtakingly beautiful baby with bright blue eyes and dark brown hair, smiling back up at me. An expression on her face that looked exactly like her father's. A smile I couldn't help but love. Much like Creed's.

"Jesus, Mia, get your shit together," I whispered to myself, wishing more than anything it was Creed's baby girl I was carrying.

I sighed, chastising myself. Creed's priority was the MC, which I'd known since day one. It was more so now than ever before, or so I thought. He was traveling all over the place, day in and day out. I barely kept up with where he was, or what he was getting involved in. All I knew was he had to go whether he liked it or not. Everything changed so quickly and so suddenly.

I never stopped thinking about him.

I never stopped praying that he stayed safe.
I never stopped...
Loving him.
I couldn't. He was a part of me in more ways than one. He always had been. Yet to this day, I didn't know why. It was one of those unexplainable things, a powerful magnetic pull that only he held over me.
And he knew it.
Using it to push me away every chance he got.
I took one last deep breath to steady my nerves, opened the Jeep's door, and hopped out, straightening my dress before I made my way to their front porch.
The sonogram picture of our baby girl held tightly in my grasp. Noah wanted a girl and had been beyond excited since they told us that afternoon. He wanted to tell the world or at least his mom. He'd been inviting me over to his house for the last several months, but I kept making excuses as to why I couldn't come. I guess now was as good of a time as any to finally meet her. Secretly wishing Creed had been the one to invite me to meet his mother and not his brother.
Noah wanted me to be a part of his world, and I think Creed only wanted to be a part of mine, if that made any sense.
I knocked on the door and waited while looking around the front yard. Memories of the last time I was here instantly assaulted every last fiber of my being, witnessing the fallout between Creed and my father all over again. Thinking how things had changed in just four short months. At least between Noah and me. My dad still hated the boys, and felt the need to remind me often that they were nothing but biker trash, even though he knew his words hurt me. He still couldn't look me in the eyes, and I hated that more than anything.
"Hey, pretty girl," Noah greeted, pulling me back to reality, moving aside to let me in.
I shyly smiled, looking down at the ground as I walked by him.
"I like your dress," he added, grinning. Eyeing me up and down, taking in my white flowy maxi dress.
I swallowed hard, locking eyes with him. The familiar mischievous spark glimmered right back at me.
"Thanks," I replied.
"You get dressed up for me, Mia?"

I smirked. "Don't flatter yourself, Rebel." I never called him Noah, I only knew him as Rebel. "I wanted to look nice for your momma."

"Don't need to put on a dress to accomplish that."

I shyly smiled again, my cheeks flushing. "Are you going to show me around or just stand there and flirt with me?"

"It ain't flirtin' if you've already slept with the girl." He put his hand on my belly, proving his point.

I stepped into the foyer a little further, putting some distance between us. He smiled, shaking his head, pulling the screen door shut, but leaving the other open to allow the evening summer breeze to flow in.

"Come on." He grabbed my hand, leading the way around his parents' house.

Showing me all the rooms, including his, which was just how I imagined it. A typical guy's room complete with a big screen T.V. and PlayStation. A black bedspread ruffled on his mattress, and laundry piling up in the corner.

He continued, walking past a closed door that I assumed was Creed's room, not stopping to show me, much to my disappointment. It was the room I wanted to see the most, hoping it would give me more answers about the man I loved. Instead, I took the opportunity to look at all the pictures of Creed throughout the years on the walls. He was the cutest baby and little boy, looking so sweet and innocent, but I knew otherwise. Already sporting tattoos from such a young age, and a cigarette in his mouth in almost every picture shortly after.

"This house is beautiful. Your momma did a great job making it feel so homey and loving."

He narrowed his eyes at me as if what I'd just said had been anything but the truth.

"Oh my God, Noah, is this you?" I pointed to the baby boy straddling a mini-motorcycle. Creed stood next to the bike, holding another little boy that looked a few years younger in a headlock.

"Who is this?" I pointed to the mystery boy, noticing another picture of him on the wall with a rosary hanging from the frame.

"Our brother, Luke." Noah simply stated, not elaborating.

Ends Here

"I didn't know you guys had another brother." I glanced over at him dumbfounded.

"We don't. Not anymore."

"Mia!" A woman's voice, who I assumed was their mother's, echoed down the long narrow hallway into the living room where we stood. She immediately pulled me into a tight hug. "So nice to officially meet you, honey. I've heard so much about you and your family, I feel like I already know you."

I hugged her back, pushing back the thoughts of the Jameson boy I didn't even know existed. Making a mental note to ask Creed about it later.

"I've heard a lot about you, too. But please don't believe everything you hear from Creed, he—"

"Creed?" She pulled away, cocking her head to the side. "You mean Noah?"

I shook my head. "Right." Playing it off like I said the wrong name, trying to hide the hurt expression on my face. "I mean, don't believe everything Noah has told you. He—"

"Hasn't said anything but the truth. You're perfect, Mia. Couldn't ask for a better girl."

I smiled again, ignoring the sentiment in his tone. Handing his momma the sonogram picture in my hand. "Congratulations, Grandma. It's a girl!"

She beamed, staring down at the photo with the same expression my mom had when she saw it earlier that day. Her eyes welled up with unshed tears. Before I could give it too much thought, Noah tugged me into the nook of his arm, close to the side of his body. My hand subconsciously connected with his firm, muscular chest. Steadying myself.

From an outsider looking in, we probably appeared to be a couple. I nervously laughed. Silently thanking God that Creed wasn't there to witness this particular scene playing out. He would flip his shit if he saw—

I jolted awake from the unexpected bump we hit on the road, followed by a strong hand placed on my head in a comforting gesture, pulling me away from the day that was supposed to be nothing but happiness.

"Fuck! She's waking up! Fucking hell, just keep her quiet," I heard a male's voice I didn't recognize, shouting from behind me.

We weren't alone.

I opened my mouth to scream, but quickly shut it when I felt a needle poke my thigh, and warmth spread throughout my entire core in a matter of seconds.

"Heeellllp me," I whispered as loud as I could to no avail.

"Shhh…" the voice of the person who was rubbing my head coaxed near my face.

I couldn't keep my eyes open any longer to care, closing on their own. My body instantly went lax as sleep took over once again.

All eyes turned to him, stepping inside the house in that Creed sort of way. Dominant and overbearing, demanding that his presence be acknowledged by all.

Especially me.

"Creed, honey, what are you doing here?" his mom greeted him with a smile.

"Since when do I need an invitation to come home? I interruptin' somethin', Noah?" he snapped. His eyes burned holes into his brother's arm that was still placed around me, which only provoked Noah to hold me tighter.

I warily smiled at Creed, casually stepping away from Noah. I didn't want to hurt Noah's feelings. I tried to gauge Creed's reaction as to how I should proceed. My heart was beating out of my chest so hard. I swear he could hear it.

"Of course you don't," their mom chimed in. "I just assumed you'd be at the club, honey, since you just got back this afternoon. Oh, you have to see this!" she yelped in excitement, rushing over to him. Things couldn't have gotten worse than they were at that exact moment. "Mia brought this over with her. Look, honey! It's a girl! We're having a girl!"

He grabbed the photo out of her hand, looking down at my baby girl in his grasp. I wanted him to love her. I wanted him to love her just as much as I did without even having met her yet. The desire seeped out of my pores. He wasn't the father, but it didn't mean that

19

I didn't want him to feel protective over her like she was his own. She was still a part of him. My uncles may not be blood-related to me, but I loved them all like second fathers, and I prayed it would be the same for my baby girl and Creed, too.

There were no words to describe what I felt while the love of my life held my heart in his hands. His eyes scanned the sonogram picture, mesmerized by the tiny being, and for a moment I thought I saw everything I'd been hoping for since the second I found out I was pregnant.

It was my turn to beam.

He finally peered back up at me with daunting eyes. Breaking his silence, he spewed, "Your phone broke, Pippin? Was workin' last night when you told me you missed me. Funny how those things work, yeah?"

My hopefulness quickly faded, not expecting his response. I stepped forward, roughly taking my baby girl's first photo out of his hands.

"Bro, don't see the reason why she has to call ya, you ain't the father," Noah snidely replied, making matters worse.

"Boys…" their mom warned, looking back and forth between them. "Mia came over with some great news. You both check your testosterone at the door. You hear me? Not tonight. Dinner's going to be a while. Behave. I'm going to call Stacey and Laura and tell them we're having a girl."

She gave both of them one last stern look and left, walking into the kitchen. Noah's phone rang as soon as she left, breaking the uncomfortable silence between us all.

"Yeah," Noah answered, walking out of the room.

As soon as he was no longer in sight, Creed grabbed my hand, taking me by surprise. He rushed me into his room, shutting the door behind him. Not wasting any time, he leaned up against it and folded his arms over his broad chest.

I sighed, taking a seat on the edge of his bed. Mentally preparing myself for his wrath that I knew was about to be unleashed. Not getting the chance I'd been waiting for to look around his room even just for a second.

"Creed…" I coaxed just above a whisper.

He put his hand up in the air, stopping me, cocking his head to the side. "You got one minute to fuckin' explain what the fuck was that?" He sternly pointed to the door behind him. "Before I lose my shit. Don't got any patience left for fuckin' bullshit tonight, Pippin. Fuckin' exhausted, been on my bike all goddamn day to come home to you. Only to find you at my Ma's house with my brother's arm around you like you're his fuckin' property. When you're mine," he gritted out, emphasizing the last word.

I acted fast, kicking off my wedges and sitting up on my knees in the center of his bed. Gazing adoringly up at him through my lashes, biting my bottom lip for good measure. I picked up the sides of my dress, swaying it side-to-side. Giving him that look which he was more than familiar with.

"Do you like my dress? It's new..." I smirked, batting my lashes at him. "I bought it just for you, babe. I know how you love the color white on me."

"Is that right?" He grinned, pushing off the door. Walking over to me, each stride more confident than the last. My heart sped up, as my breathing quickened. In a few short seconds, he would be over to me, and all would be right with my world.

All I needed was Creed.

I fervently nodded with nothing but mischief in my eyes. I wanted him to hold me, kiss me, and tell me he loved me. I hadn't seen him in weeks, but it felt like no time had passed between us, exactly how it always did. It never mattered how much time went by until we saw each other again. Our connection was always alive and thriving, beating right in front of us.

I slowly licked my lips. "Do you have any idea how hard it is to find a dress that's still small, but will fit my..." I glided my fingers along the top of my ample cleavage that was popping at the seams. I knew he loved my breasts that were bigger now from my pregnancy. "They're huge, right?" I leaned forward, slightly pushing them together, baiting him. Luring him in to love me again, and not be mad at me anymore.

He sat on the edge of the bed, immediately reaching over to bring me onto his lap, to straddle his thighs.

A much better position, I thought.

He softly, tenderly pecked my lips. Assaulting me with his peppermint and cigarette breath, making me quiver from that alone. His lips skimmed my neck then down to my breasts, which had doubled in size since he'd last seen me. I was so overly sensitive to everything, particularly his touch. He was taking his time with me, nice and slow like he knew I loved. His hands roamed while his tongue ran along the seam of my white dress, causing my head to fall back, and a soft moan to escape my lips.

"Pippin?" he said in between kissing me. "As much as I'd like to titty fuck you and come on these right now. Asked ya a question, expectin' a fuckin' answer." He pulled away, lying back on his bed with his hands under his head.

Leaving me wanting more.

Wanting everything.

Him.

"Didn't you miss me?" I pouted, swaying my hips on his hard cock, causing him to chuckle. I wasn't about to give up without a fight. I was relentless. I was getting my way, plain and simple.

Besides, he couldn't stay mad at me. He never could.

"Creed? Mia?" Noah's voice resonated through the door. "What the fuck are you doin'?" He loudly knocked.

"Fuck off! We're busy!" Creed roared, never taking his eyes off me.

I shook my head, leaning forward to kiss him, but he stopped me, putting his index finger to my lips. "Not gonna ask you again, Mia."

I sighed. I couldn't explain my relationship with Noah as much as I couldn't explain my relationship with him.

It was all so complicated.

So I simply stated, "Noah was just excited about finding out we're having a girl. He got carried away. It doesn't matter. Don't you trust me?"

In one swift movement, he was on top of me, closing me in with his strong muscular arms. "How often does that little shit get carried away? I saw him eyein' your tits. He get carried away with them, too? Don't fuckin' like it."

"It's not like that. I love you."

"You love me so fuckin' much, I'm the last to find out you're havin' a baby girl?"

"That's not fair. My appointment was this afternoon. I knew you were riding home. Not like you could have come... Besides, you wouldn't have heard my call anyway."

He arched an eyebrow, calling my bluff. "Phone's always on vibrate. Try again."

I didn't hesitate, blurting out, "I don't know how all this works, Creed," I honestly spoke for the first time, needing him to hear me and understand. "It's new territory for me, too. I want my baby to have a father, and Noah has been there for all my appointments, he knows everything that's going on. He seems invested in being a part of helping me raise her. We're just getting to know each other so we can be the best parents to our baby. That's all."

"I respect the hell out of both of ya for that. But I'm gonna be just as much, if not more, a part of this baby girl's life as he is. Ya feel me?"

I nodded, hearing him say that gave me the courage to ask what I needed to know the most. "I know you said you're claiming me, but I don't entirely understand what that means. Are you my boyfriend? Are we together?"

He kissed my lips, murmuring, "Not fuckin' anyone else, Pippin. Haven't in a while. Who's my girl?"

I resisted the urge to roll my eyes. He was always so crass and vulgar, but those were some of the things I loved the most about him. He spoke his mind, no matter what.

"I want to hear you say it. Not going to ask you again, Creed," I mocked. Making him smile while he ran his nose from my chin to my collarbone, kissing all over my tender breasts.

"How you smell so fuckin' good all the time? You're my girl," he reassured me, pulling down the front of my dress. "I lov—"

"Oh my God, babe! She just kicked," I shouted, cutting him off. "Give me your hand. You need to feel this." I grabbed ahold of his hand, placing it on my belly. "Say something, I think she likes your voice."

My baby girl already loved him as much as I did.

He instantly looked up, glaring at something out in front of him, not paying me any mind. "Fuck!" he seethed, his demeanor quickly changing into the man who hid behind his cut.

I opened my mouth to say something but sounds of rapid-fire echoed all around the room, rendering me speechless. The glass windows shattered as each bullet ricocheted off the walls, landing on the ground below us. Within seconds, Creed sprang into action, rolling us off his bed while tucking my head against his chest. Trying to break our fall as he threw me onto the wood floor. Immediately shielding my body with his.

Shots continued to fill the air throughout their house, bullet casings falling all around us. I was terrified, I had never been so scared, but not for my life.

For my baby's.

I gasped, finding it hard to breathe. How long was I out for this time? I was no longer in a moving vehicle, but in sturdy arms that were now carrying me to the unknown.

"No!" I yelled, trying to fight, but it came out more like a soft murmur.

"I'm not going to tell you again. Shut the bitch up!"

"Shhh…" the man carrying me repeated in the same tone as before. Calm and collected.

"Please, please let me go. I promise, I promise I won't—" They were laying me down on what felt like a mattress and I instinctively, exhaustingly fought to get free. Kicking my legs, flailing my arms, clawing to escape from the men who were probably preparing to rape me.

Or worse, kill me.

"Enough," a stern tone demanded, holding back my hands and pinning me to the bed. Slits of light shined through the blindfold that was still securely placed around my eyes.

"Please don't hurt me. I'm pregna—" the familiar pain of a needle poking my thigh rendered me speechless. Tears ran down my heated cheeks as darkness took a hold of me all over again.

I clutched onto my stomach, screaming and crying out in agony. Convulsing in his arms. Something was wrong. The pain was blinding. I couldn't think, I couldn't see, all I could do was feel the excruciating stabs all over my abdomen. Crippling me in ways I never thought possible.

Creed pulled out his gun, sat up and returned fire.

"Ahhh!" I cried out, rolling over into a fetal position, my arms tightly wrapped around my baby.

Chaos erupted all around me, yet all I could comprehend and wrap my mind around was my baby was in danger.

I was there but I wasn't.

It felt as though hours had gone by. The pain was getting more and more unbearable. Every last part of my body hurt, suffocating me and making it hard to breathe. I choked on my words, overcome by fear of what was happening.

Was I losing my baby?

"Fuck! Baby, you okay?" I heard Creed yell out from above me. Pure panic laced in his tone.

"Creed, I can't... she's... it hurts..." I whimpered, barely speaking through the pain.

His bedroom door was suddenly kicked open, slamming against the adjacent wall. It vibrated deep within my core. For a split second, I thought this was how my life was going to end. The baby and I were going to die right here on the floor with Creed's arms *wrapped around us. I couldn't help but think about all the times he told me to stay away from him.*

That he was no good for me.

I breathed out a sigh of relief when I heard Noah's voice fill the small room, "Boys are coming! Ma's in the steel pantry, she's safe! Give her to me, Creed! I'll take her to the basement!"

"The fuck you will! Cover me!" Creed picked me up off the floor, cradling me in his arms. I cringed from the sudden movement, on the verge of passing out. The pain was too excruciating to bear. Mentally begging him to stop. Pleading with him to leave me there.

I closed my eyes, coming in and out of consciousness until Creed gently laid me down onto a hard, cold surface. I slowly opened my eyes, seeing boxes all around me with a single name written on them all. Luke. A damp, stale smell assaulted my senses, causing a sudden wave of bile to rise in my throat.

"I'll be right back. Do not move!" Creed demanded in a harsh stern tone.

"Creed... please..." I bellowed, shaking so damn hard. "Don't leave me... please... please, I need you!"

I caught the panicked expression on his face. It was the first time I had ever seen worry radiate off his eyes and sear into my skin. He wasn't even trying to hide it from me.

"Mia, you need to stay here. Protect our little girl, alright," Noah chimed in, making me look over at him. It was only then I realized he was there too.

"Promise, baby. Be right back." Creed kissed my forehead. Letting his lips linger there for a minute before releasing me. He stood up, taking his warmth with him.

The sound of bullets decorating their house echoed in the distance. They stood there, listening intently to all the rounds going off. One right after the other sounded with no pause in between.

"Stay with Mia—"

"Fuck you!" Noah interrupted. "You're not goin' up there alone. We can take them all out. The boys are on their way. Won't be long."

"Noah—"

"Wasting fuckin' time! Let's go!"

Creed took one last look at me before returning to the violence that had always been his life. I understood it now more than ever. Everything he warned me about, all those times he pushed me away, his words repeating themselves over and over in my mind like a broken record.

I watched them leave with hooded eyes as they ascended back up the stairs, locking me in.

Where was I?

My grip tightened on my stomach, trying to steady the stabbing pain coursing throughout my entire abdomen. The pressure intensified with each second that passed, lying curled up on the concrete floor. Not only was my baby girl's future hanging on the line, her daddy's was too. Along with the man I couldn't live without. All I could hear above were sounds of rapid gunfire, bodies hitting the floor with a thud, bullet casings littering the ground, and loud voices echoed in the air vents above, but I couldn't make out what they were saying. My heart beat uncontrollably in my ears. Pounding against my chest, taking over every last inch of my body.

I don't know how much time went by when I felt a sudden rush of warmth seep beneath my dress, in between my legs.

I sucked in air until there was none left for the taking. My lungs feeling as though they were collapsing. There were no more tears for me to shed, no more prayers for me to plea, there was nothing left but darkness.

I didn't know how long I was out when my eyes flickered open. The pain returned with a vengeance as I was being carried away.

"Creed?" I softly spoke, blinking away the haze and tears. Willing my eyes to stay open. "Please... save... her..." was the last thing I said.

I swear I could hear Creed yelling, he was coming for me, closing the space that separated us. It's only then that I realized the strong arms that were holding me weren't familiar. They weren't Creed's.

I couldn't fight.

I couldn't move.

I couldn't speak.

Everything just faded to black.

I jerked awake, sitting straight up in the bed gasping for air. Immediately gripping my head between my hands, noticing the blindfold was no longer in place. I closed my eyes, desperately trying to catch my bearings. The dizziness had washed over me. Where was I? Who had taken me? Creed and Noah never talked to me about the MC, why was I dragged into something that had nothing to do with me?

The questions were endless.

I protectively placed my arms around my baby girl, when the realization hit me like a ton of bricks, I didn't feel any pain like I had before. It was gone, replaced by my body's own drowsiness holding me down. How much time had gone by since they took me? Was my baby okay now?

Nothing made sense.

As if sensing my panic, she kicked making her presence known, and I breathed out a huge sigh of relief as I stared around the bedroom. Taking in my surroundings, thinking I would find the answers written on the walls or something. There were two black nightstands, one on each side of the bed with a lamp placed on top. A long dresser in the corner of the room, and a chair strategically placed by my bed as if someone had been sitting there, waiting for me to wake up.

An eerie feeling swept through my body, like a cold gush of water hitting my overly-frenzied skin. I swallowed hard, continuing to let my eyes wander. The black curtains were closed, keeping the light from shining through, making the room have a soft, dim glow. It was easier on my eyes to get accustomed to the brightness, and for some reason, I knew someone had done that on purpose.

There wasn't anything hanging on the white walls other than the flat screen TV in front of my bed. The room was small, but not entirely unpleasant. Under any other circumstances, I probably would have loved it in here. It reminded me of a bed and breakfast I'd seen in movies.

I shook off the thoughts, peering down at the bed, feeling the plush fabric of the duvet comforter under my fingertips, and comfy sheets beneath me. Pushing through the lightheadedness, I guided my legs to hang off the side of the bed. Setting my feet on the cold wood floor, I slowly stood, holding onto the bed as I made my way toward the door. I knew it wouldn't be open, but it didn't hurt to at least try. I turned the knob back and forth, wiggling it and just as I presumed, it was locked. I made my way over to the window next. Pulling back the curtains, causing the vivid sunlight to shine in, assaulting my sensitive eyes.

The windows were locked as well, with steel bars secured all around them. There was no way in hell I was getting out of this room unless they allowed it. That realization was the hardest pill to swallow.

Out of the corner of my eye, I noticed another door slightly ajar. Making my way over to it, I slowly pushed it open, revealing an en suite bathroom. Complete with all the toiletries I would need, laid out on the counter. I didn't think twice about it, I rushed in, roughly tearing through the cabinets and under the sink, needing to find anything I could use to protect myself.

It was fight or flight time, and I refused to be a victim in this situation. I had to try to save my life and most importantly the life of my unborn child. It wasn't just me anymore. I had to protect her at any cost.

"Yes!" I breathed out when I found a pair of scissors behind the toilet paper.

They were a bit rusted and not as sharp as I would have wanted, but they would do. I securely placed them in the back pocket of my jeans, noticing for the first time that someone had changed my clothes. I was wearing a tan, wool sweater with a white tank top underneath it. My jeans fit perfectly, accommodating my swollen belly.

I abruptly stood up on trembling legs, confused by the turn of events. Taking a good hard look at myself in the mirror in front of me. Turning my head side to side preparing myself for the worst. To my surprise, there were no bruises on my face, neck, or chest. I ran my hands through my hair and took a closer look at my face. I was paler than usual, but I didn't look any different than before. The fact that no one had harmed me was mind-blowing and too much for me to take in at that moment, but I continued to stare at the girl in the mirror.

Me.

I splashed some cold water on my face, brushed my teeth and took one last look at myself before I went back to bed. I couldn't mentally or physically do a damn thing about the situation, but at least I was prepared to fight back when the time came.

So, I allowed my eyes to close and my body to sink into the mattress, aware of the cold metal on my back. Welcoming the darkness with open arms, allowing myself to slip back into dreams of the man I knew in my heart, would come and save me.

He grabbed my ankle, tugging me back toward him. Making me squeal. "Babe, if I want in. I'm gettin' in," Creed rasped, flipping me over in one quick, sudden motion. Kneeling on his bed, he hovered above me, locking my arms above my head. Holding me in place, he peered deep into my eyes and spoke with conviction, "This is how it's gonna go down. I'm gonna angry fuck you now, and then you're gonna beg me to make you come with that saucy, little mouth that never seems to know when to shut the fuck up. Yeah?"

"You wouldn't dare," I offered in a shaky voice, mostly because I wanted everything he just said.

"Try me."

I smiled, cocking my head to the side, provoking him even more. "I'm sorry, but visiting hours are over. I'm afraid you will have to come back later when you can be a gentleman."

He grinned, arching an eyebrow. Getting closer to my face, he started to kiss his way from the corner of my lips, down to my chin and neck. Working his way toward my breasts that were just as eager for his touch.

"Oh, I will be comin', question is... will I let you."

I smiled, feeling the stubble on his face all over the cleavage of my breasts.

"Creed," I giggled, loving the feel of him against me.

"I need to check her heart rate," someone said, bringing my attention to the man holding a small monitor in his hands.

"What?" I replied but no one responded. When I looked back in front of me Creed was gone, no longer above me, loving on me. He was standing in the corner of the room with the same worry in his eyes when I last saw him. Sinking further and further away until he was gone. "What's going on? Where am I?"

I was talking but no one could hear me. My lips weren't moving, there were no sounds coming from my mouth, yet I could hear myself. Were those my thoughts?

"Mia, babe, you're gonna be alright, so is our baby. I promise," Noah said, standing above me.

"Noah?" *I shook my head, looking up at his face. Peering from him to Creed. Squinting my eyes, everything was so bright. Where was that light coming from?*

There were so many people in the room. Why was everyone shouting?

"I don't feel anything abnormal anymore," *the same man from my left said, pressing on my stomach.* "Don't touch me! Get your hands off me!" *I screamed, repeatedly thrashing around, but still, no one heard me. Still, no one sees me fighting.*

No one does anything.

Not Creed.

Not Noah.

Not anyone.

And then they were gone. No one was with me. I was alone. Scared and cold. So damn tired. My eyes inadvertently shut, taking me under. Spiraling into the dark corners of my mind.

"You nervous, Mia?" *Creed murmured in my ear, making me smile again.*

I opened my eyes and he was hovering above me, exactly the way he was before. "Yes…" *I whispered as if nothing had happened.*

"Why?"

"Because it's you," *I simply stated.*

"I make you nervous?"

"Sometimes."

"Why do ya think that is?"

"I don't know."

"Yes, you fuckin' do," *he growled, his lips were on mine before he got the last word out, attacking every last fiber in my being. Feeling his love. His protection. His warmth all over me.*

The hard, jagged footsteps descending down the hall startled me awake. Boots pounding onto the wood floors, vibrated through the space between us, getting louder and louder with each passing minute. I looked over my shoulder slightly, peering around the room

31

that was now pitch black. I couldn't even see an inch in front of me. Nightfall had taken over. It took me a moment to remember where I was and what had happened.

My mind was still groggy and filled with unanswered questions which never seemed to stop. I grabbed the scissors from the back of my jeans, clutching them tightly in my grasp, almost to the point of pain. Bringing them close to my chest. My hand was shaking uncontrollably as I thought about the consequences of what this would bring. What did I have to lose at this point? Nothing.

I waited, steadying my quivering breath. Praying he didn't hear my heart that was beating out of my chest. I felt it ringing through my ears, hammering against my skin. I tightly shut my eyes when I heard the lock on the door click over, opening mere seconds later.

I just laid there on my side facing the window in a state of shock, trying not to think about what I was about to do. In the forefront of my mind, I kept contemplating that maybe this wasn't a good idea, but each time the thought circled back around, I pushed it away. Knowing this would be my only chance to get free, I wouldn't be able to catch him by surprise again.

It was now…

Or never.

The soft translucent lighting from the hallway entered the room, but it wasn't enough to see more than a few inches in front of you. I silently prayed he wouldn't turn on the light. He would just leave it somewhat dark not wanting to wake me. He obviously cared enough to close the curtains earlier in the day. I figured this was the same concept.

I pretended as best as I could to be asleep, having years of practice with my parents coming in my room. Making sure I wasn't up when I was supposed to be sleeping. The thought of my parents made my heart ache, thinking of what they must be going through made my eyes well up with tears. I knew they'd be searching for me. I knew they would never give up till they found me.

Dead.

Or alive.

I pushed away those thoughts as well, knowing it wouldn't do me any good to think about things I couldn't change. I needed to stay in the here and now. In the present so I could have a future.

His footsteps got closer and closer to my bed until there were no more steps for him to take. Until he was standing right next to me, hovering above my side. Waiting, like I was waiting for him.

I knew he was staring at me, contemplating what to do next. He pulled back the comforter and sheets from my body, taking away my false security. I felt the edge of the bed dip. His knee touching my back.

Was he getting into bed with me?

He leaned forward, brushing the hair away from my face. Letting his fingers linger for what felt like forever. I resisted the urge to throw up, bile rose in the back of my throat. My rapid, erratic heartbeat ready to betray me. The flats of his fingers glided from my cheek down to my neck, gripping onto my shoulder. He started to turn me onto my back as I used his same momentum against him. Whipping around, I slightly opened my eyes, stabbing the scissors as hard and as deep as I could into his thigh.

"Fuck!" he groaned out in pain and I sprang into action.

I hauled ass off the bed, ignoring the unsteadiness of my body and mind, and rushed out of the room. Slamming the door behind me, peering down to see if there was a lock on the outside to lock him in with.

"Shit!" I panicked. I needed a key.

He still had the damn key.

So I ran. I ran as fast as I could down the narrow hallway, my bare feet pounding into the floor. Hoping it would lead to the front door or anywhere else I could escape from.

"HELP! SOMEBODY HELP ME! PLEASE!" I screamed through the sting of my already burning throat. "HELP!" I ran as fast as I could through the vaguely lit hallway, only stopping to check the few doors that lined the walls. Trying the handles, banging my fists, hoping with some sort of miracle, one would open. Freeing me. "HELP! PLEASE, PLEASE HELP ME!"

I heard the door to the room I was being held in open down the hall, and the sound of boots dragging on the wood. He was coming for me. Panic set in again, and I took off running, looking back, making sure he wasn't behind me, not paying attention to where I was going. Before I knew it, I slammed into what felt like a brick wall, abruptly falling to the ground with a hard thud. My body collided with the hardwood, knocking the wind completely out of me.

I wheezed for air, urgently trying to get to my knees, crawling away from the tall muscular frame that was looming over me.

"Mia!" he called out, catching me by surprise.

I immediately looked up, recognizing the tone of voice.

Never in a million years expecting to see the person who was standing above me.

"Mia!" I called out again, desperately waiting to hear her voice, assuring me she was okay. Terrified when I realized the basement was silent.

No screaming.

No crying.

Blood.

"The fuck..."

I thought I had experienced every loss I could in my life. Felt every form of pain, every form of agony and hurt known to fucking man. I was wrong. Nothing could compare to the moment I walked back to where I left my girl safely.

Where I left Mia...

And she wasn't fucking there.

"MIA!" I growled, searching for her all over the basement. Not giving a fuck that I was knocking over boxes, which I knew held Luke's belongings.

I needed to find her. Silently praying for the first time, in I don't know how long, that she was just hiding. Cowering in a crevice of the murky concrete cellar. Scared, and in shock from everything that just went down. I never wanted her to see this part of my life. I never meant for any of this to happen.

The last thing I ever wanted to do was fuck up her life by bringing her into mine.

"MIA! BABY, PLEASE!" I pleaded, tearing apart the basement like a rabid fucking dog, leaving no box unturned no door unopened.

I wouldn't stop till I knew she was safe. Till she was in my arms where she always belonged. It tore my fucking heart out hearing her pleas to not leave her down there earlier.

"Creed… please… Don't leave me… please… please, I need you!" Her words would forever be etched into my conscience.

I would have given my soul to the devil to find her, to see her smiling face, to hear her laughing. To feel her brush up against me in the way only Mia ever could. It was as if she was there in spirit. Exactly where she had been since the moment she handed me her first patch.

"Baby, please give me a sign. Please…" I crouched down, ignoring the pain in my leg where I had been shot in the crossfire. Letting the blood drip onto the ground, mixing with Mia's. Running my hands roughly through my hair.

On the verge of rage.

Hanging on by a fucking thread.

Memories of our time together attacked my mind, one right after the other. Twisting and turning, not letting up, not giving a fuck she wasn't there. That she had been taken, right from under me.

I couldn't find her.

I didn't save her.

This was my entire fucking fault.

"MIA!" I yelled out for the last time, destroying every corner of the dark, cold open space until there was nothing but destruction left in its wake.

I rushed back up the stairs, taking three of them at a time. Ignoring the blood gushing from the bullet hole in my thigh.

"Honey, you've been hit—"

I assaulted my baby brother before Ma could get another word out. Roughly gripping onto the front of his cut, slamming his back against the nearest wall, causing our childhood pictures to rattle and fall on the ground. Adding to the rest of the debris.

"Where the fuck is she?!" I seethed, barely holding onto the last bit of my temper.

All I could see was red.

Bright. Blinding. Fucking red.

"The fuck?" Noah jerked forward, trying to break loose from my tight hold.

I didn't give him any leeway, I held him tighter. "Where. Is. She? Not gonna ask again, you little shit!" I shoved him into the wall with more force, jolting his body forward again. Not giving a flying fuck he was my blood.

"Creed! What's gotten into you? Let go of him! He's your brother!" Ma demanded with a shriek, grabbing ahold of my arm.

I pushed her away. I was a crazed man. No one would be able to stop me.

Not even my family.

"I've been with you, motherfucker! Fightin' by your side. If Mia ain't down there, it ain't cuz of me. You took her to the basement! You left her down there! If she's fuckin' missin', it's on you," he gritted out through a clenched jaw, trying to gain his bearings. Eyeing me up and down.

I let him go with a hard shove. Pacing the living room, kicking bullet shells around with my boots.

This house was a fucking disaster.

Reflecting how shitty my life had always been.

"Jesus Christ! You think I'd hurt my kid? You think I'd hurt my girl?"

I lunged at him, but Diesel held me back. "She ain't your girl. You understand me? Don't ever let me hear those words out of your goddamn mouth again. I'll lay you the fuck out. Don't give a shit who ya are to me!"

"Boys! Stop it! We need to find Mia! You fighting won't make that happen any faster. We're losing time!" Ma chimed in, looking back and forth between us.

I pushed Diesel off of me, glaring at him for holding me down.

He put his hands up in the air in a surrendering gesture. "Calm the fuck down. We'll find her," Diesel rasped. "But this don't make any fuckin' sense. Prez said we ain't got beef with the Sinners no more. Who the fuck just started a war?" He pulled out his cellphone from his pocket, walking away. Needing to make the necessary phone calls, before I truly lost my shit.

I glared around the room with a primal regard, seeing all of my brothers standing around. Knowing they would have reacted the same, had it been one of their old ladies. Ignoring the same looming questions, I'd been asking myself since the first bullet rang out.

Ma breathed out a sigh of relief, stepping out in front of me. Peering down at the blood pooling at my feet. "Look at me."

I did.

"We will find her. Now let me fix your leg before you get an infection."

"I'm fine."

"Creed, you're no good to anyone hurt. Let alone dead. Let me—"

"I said I was fine!" I got up in her face, but she didn't cower down. She was used to our tempers, having battled the Jameson men all her life.

"Goddamn it! You boys are so stubborn, just like your father." She glanced around the living room, searching for the prick. "Speaking of him, where is he?"

I followed her stare, checking out all the faces. Noticing, he really was missing. Through my fury, I hadn't realized that before. I knew he would've been here. No matter what, he would have fucking been here.

My eyes widened and my heart dropped. All the blood drained from my face. "Son of a bitch!" I snapped, running out the front door that was hanging on its hinges before I got the last word out.

"Creed! Creed! Wait up!" I heard some brothers say from behind me, but it was too late. I was already on my bike, speeding the fuck out of there as fast as the old girl could go. Leaving nothing but dust in my wake.

It didn't take long till I was pulling into the compound, engaging the kickstand, jumping off my bike before I even turned off the engine. In a blink of an eye, I was in the clubhouse.

"Creed, you—"

I grabbed a hold of my old man's throat, slamming him up against the nearest wall, much like I had just done to Noah. He gasped, his hands latching onto my strangling grip.

"Only gonna ask you one fuckin' time. Where is she?" I scoffed, loosening my hold enough for him to reply.

"Who?" Pops choked out, slowly grinning.

I was about to wipe the fucking smug look off his face when I felt the cool metal graze the back of my head. I didn't have to turn around to know what it was.

"Ain't that fuckin' cute, you gotta guard dog," I snarled, cocking my head to the side.

"Let him go," the voice from behind me ordered in a tone I didn't appreciate.

"Fuckin' A," I breathed out. In one swift, sudden motion I released my pop's throat, sending him to the ground and had the gun out of the Prospect's grasp in a matter of seconds. Drop kicking him to the floor, making him kneel in front of me in pain. "I'm your VP, you stupid fuck."

"Shit! I'm sorry. I'm new, I didn't—"

I pistol-whipped him in the side of his head, knocking him unconscious. His body went limp on the floor with a thud. He was lucky I didn't put him to ground. I quickly turned back around, pointing the gun in the middle of pop's forehead.

"Gonna answer my question? Or you wanna test the last bit of my fuckin' patience," I warned, narrowing my eyes at him.

"You'd shoot your old man for some goddamn pussy? The fuckin' bitch is pregnant with your baby brother's seed. Didn't seem to give a fuck about you when she spread her legs for Rebel in your bed, now did she? She ain't any better than the club whores around here. Fuckin' easy lay if you ask me."

I didn't think twice about it, I lowered the gun to my side and I punched him in the face. Cold clocked him right in the nose. His body whooshed sideways, knocking him back into the wall from the unexpected blow.

"She ain't nothin' like the cunts that parade their pussy around here. Call her a whore again, and I'll put you to ground. That ain't a threat, it's a fuckin' promise."

He regained his footing, standing upright, shaking away the haze until we locked eyes. Blood flooded from his nose, drenching his white shirt. I aimed the gun to his leg and pulled the trigger.

"What the fuck?" he snarled, grabbing onto his leg with one hand. Almost falling to the floor. He wiped his crimson face with the back of his other, spitting blood on the ground.

"Next shot will be at your cock, you miserable fuck," I warned through clenched teeth.

The sound of motorcycles, entering the compound, vibrated throughout the entire foyer where we were at a standoff. The house would soon be filled with brothers witnessing the Prez versus Vice Prez, father versus son altercation. I pushed the gun deeper into his forehead, my steady finger on the trigger.

He beamed, his eyes filled with pride. "I raised you right, boy. Defend what's yours. It's in the Jameson blood."

"Cut the shit and tell me where she is! NOW!"

The brothers quickly filled the empty space, all shocked from the unexpected scene unfolding in front of them.

"Creed, drop—"

"Mind your fuckin' business, Diesel." I pulled the slide back, clutching the grip in one hand. Cocking the gun to the side.

Pops cunningly smiled, placing his hands up in the air in a mocking gesture. Arching an eyebrow, he stated, "She's in your fuckin' room. You're welcome."

I didn't hesitate.

I pulled the fucking trigger.

"Rebel?" I gasped, confused. Locking eyes with him while I was still on the ground. "What's the meaning of all of this? You orchestrated this shit show?"

He shook his head no, reaching his hand down for me to take.

I knocked it away. "Fuck you!"

He didn't pay me any mind. "Mia, it ain't what it looks like," he stated, grabbing my upper arm. Tugging me up to his chest, much to my disapproval.

I hastily shook off his hold and pushed him away. Placing my hand out in front of me, to stop him from coming any closer.

He raised his hands up in the air in front of him where I could see them. "Ain't gonna hurt you, pretty girl. You're carryin' my baby. You know you can trust me. Calm down and let—"

"Always thought it'd be a bullet I'd take for you. Never imagined it'd be a pair of fuckin' scissors."

"Oh my God!" I drawled out, recognizing his voice instantly. Placing my hand over my heart, I turned around, coming face to face with none other than Creed. I didn't know whether to run and tackle him, or run away from both of them.

My heart was telling me to go to the man I loved, though my mind wanted me to check out, not knowing what either of their involvement was in all this. In the end, my heart won over my mind. My feet moved on their own accord as if being pulled by a string he held, closing the distance between us. My small frame hit his tall, stalky, muscular body with a thud, as I wrapped my arms securely around his neck. Causing him to stumble back a little from the startling impact. Even he was surprised by the sentiment pouring out of me.

Fresh tears started to flow down my cheeks, but I didn't bother wiping them away. A whirlwind of emotions hit me all at once while I held onto his broad frame tighter. Always feeling so tiny against him. His arms snaked around my lower back, holding me closer, but not close enough.

I pulled back. My wide, tear-filled eyes instantly went to his right thigh where his jeans were soaked in blood. "What the hell is going on?"

"The fuck it look like, Pippin? You stabbed me in the leg."

I pushed him. I shoved him as hard as I could and he barely wavered. I knew the slight movement was only a reaction from his injured leg. I vigorously shook my head, unable to control the surging hormones taking over my body.

"Now is not the time for your smart-ass mouth! Do you have any idea what I've been through? Any idea what I'm going through, right now? Do you even care? I thought you were going to rape me! I didn't know who was getting into my bed! What did you expect me to do, lay there and take it?"

He limped into the adjacent room, and sat on the couch, facing me. Placing his wounded leg up on the coffee table. The loud clunk from his heavy boot, making me jump. My adrenaline overly heightened.

"Was comin' to wake you up. Guess you had other plans. Don't know whether to be pissed at ya or proud as fuck you defended yourself." He arched his eyebrow, nodding, "Ask me again in the mornin'."

Noah had the nerve to chuckle as he took a seat in the armchair.

"One of you needs to explain what the hell is going on? Right now!"

Creed peered up at me through the slits of his eyes, ripping open his jeans to inspect where I stabbed him. He hissed as he tore away the fabric, exposing the nasty wound. Leaning forward, he pulled his shirt off over his head, wrapping it around his thigh. Using it as a tourniquet.

"Fuck!" he gritted, tying it tight around his wound, trying to stop the bleeding.

I stood there, impatiently waiting with my arms crossed over my chest, fuming.

He finally peered back up at me. "Just got this stitched up." He nodded to it. "You sliced it open again."

I jerked back, dumbfounded. "Again?"

"You gone through a lot. It's why we kept you sedated. It was easier that way," he replied, peering straight into my eyes. Ignoring my question.

"By kidnapping me?"

"We didn't kidnap you, Mia," Noah interrupted, bringing my attention over to him. "Our old man took you from the basement, he—"

"That was your father?"

"Yeah." Noah nodded. "You were bleedin' out. He brought you back to the clubhouse during the shootout."

I placed a protective hand over my stomach. "Our baby—"

"She's fine. Doc was already in Creed's room lookin' you over when it was all said and done."

I glanced back at Creed, who was still sitting on the couch, only staring at me. Trying to gauge my reactions. It felt as though they were leaving a lot out, which added fuel to my already burning fire.

"What happened? Why was I bleeding?" I asked only looking at Creed.

"Some shit about your placenta havin' a minor detachment from your uterus." I could hear the shudder in Noah's voice, even though he was trying to keep his tone neutral. As if he was reliving it all over again. "We had you moved to Doc's house with Ma, you stayed there for a few days, he was checkin' your vital signs, monitorin' our baby. He kept you sedated, sayin' it was for the best. He didn't give ya anythin' that would harm our baby. So don't worry. What you witnessed was traumatic enough. You needed to rest as much as possible, and regain your strength so we could bring you here, to our safe house. You just gotta take it easy for the rest of your pregnancy. And no sex for at least four weeks," he glanced over at Creed warning him, not me. "He'll come and check on you while you're—"

I peered over at Noah, taken aback. "How long exactly am I staying here?"

"As long as it takes," Creed chimed in, eyeing me with a look I'd never seen before.

"For what?"

"The less you know, the better, Pippin."

"For you?"

"No." He stood, speaking with conviction, "For you."

"So that's it? This is all the information I get? Am I supposed to say thank you now? Sit and stay like your damn dog?"

"You're safe, aren't you?"

"Where am I?"

"Where I need you to be."

"That's pretty vague even for you, Creed. This is bullshit. I have a right to know what's going on! You can't just take someone and hide them away from everyone."

"I already did."

I stepped toward him, getting close to his face. The smell of cigarettes and mint assaulted my senses. "Why? What's going on?" I repeated in a demanding tone.

Our eyes stayed connected for what felt like forever. Dark pools barred into mine, warning me to back off. This was the Creed that broke my heart on the balcony at Giselle's apartment. Saying it was for my own good, he wouldn't tell me the truth even if I begged him for it. It was useless to try to reason with him in this state. His guard was up, and nothing could bring it down, not even his weakness. Me. The tension was so thick between us, there was no way Noah didn't feel it clear across the room.

Creed took one last look at me, narrowing his eyes, deeply thinking about what to say next. His gaze never wavered. Our intense stares were locked together, but he was the first to break our connection when he turned his back on me. I watched him leave, limping to the back of the house. Hearing a door slam moments later.

I took a deep breath before facing Noah, contemplating what I could say to make him tell me the truth. He was gazing off in the direction his brother had just left.

I opened my mouth to say something, but shut it just as quickly, when I heard the word, "Don't," harshly leave his lips.

"You can't possibly think this is okay? I'm carrying your child. It's not safe for me to be here," I honestly spoke, hoping he would be on my side.

"This is the safest place for you to be, Mia. Open your goddamn eyes, and take a look around." He spread his arms wide, pointing around the open space. Walking over to the nearest wall, he knocked on it, showing me it was made of concrete.

I looked around the room for the first time, seeing the bars that lined every dark, tinted window. Making it impossible to see in. My intuition told me the glass was bulletproof, too. Nothing could enter this place.

My eyes proceeded to wander over to the far corner of the room, where a large wrought iron front door stood, complete with several sets of steel locks you'd need a key for it to open. It was then I realized this house was like a prison. Locked down like Fort Bragg. If there was no way of getting in, then again there was also no way of getting out. And for some reason this epiphany didn't scare me, it did the opposite.

It gave me comfort.

I glanced back at Noah. "Then tell me what's going on. Help me understand."

"I can't."

"Can't or won't?"

"It don't matter."

"It does to me."

He glanced over my shoulder, looking down the narrow hallway again. I stepped out in front of him, blocking his view. Reaching up, placing my hands on his vast shoulders. "Please," I added with a sincere expression written all over my face.

I could see it in his eyes he wanted to tell me, maybe not everything, but some of the truth at least. I patiently waited, hoping I would be able to get through to one brother. Silently pleading for him to break.

Never expecting what he would say next.

"The first time I saw the reality of *my* world, I was eleven years old. It came out of the hands of Creed, and it was nothin' compared to what I've seen and done, since. From an outsider's perspective, he ain't a man to be fucked with, much like our father. I can take them, but a little girl like you should think twice before pushin' buttons and steppin' on fuckin toes. Jesus Christ, just last week, Creed pulled the trigger on our pops for shits and giggles. Shooting him in the leg, then near his head, missin'. Just to prove a fuckin' point." He shrugged off my hands like what he told me was perfectly normal. "It's a fucked up way of life, but we don't know any different." He brushed his calloused thumb across my cheek. "Be a good girl and stay put, Mia. It's for your own good. I promise."

With that he turned and left, leaving me with more questions than I had before.

I reluctantly left her in the living room with Noah. I hated seeing her so fucking upset, but there wasn't a damn thing I could do about it. My hands were tied. This was how it had to be, end of fucking story. I was beyond exhausted, barely having slept since shit hit the fucking fan. Between worrying about Mia, and getting her here safely without anyone knowing our involvement, proved to be a pain in the fucking ass. Plus, dealing with the fallout of the shootings and her supposed kidnapping, it seemed to be one thing after a fucking another.

Not to mention Martinez was fucking gunned down, murdered at his place in New York around the same day as the shootout. It was just another reason why we had to put Mia into hiding. Nothing made fucking sense.

It took less than twenty-four hours for Noah and me to be taken into custody by Detective McGraw. Mia's mom and dad were there, along with her aunt and uncle. Her mom sat in a chair, hysterically crying, sorting through pictures to give to the police. While her aunt tried to comfort her the best she could. Her dad spotted us as we walked past them, lunging at the glass window, screaming obscenities. Calling us every name in the book as her uncle held him back. It took everything in me not to fucking flip him off. Knowing they were hurting, too.

We were questioned for hours on end about our connection with her disappearance. McGraw even got a warrant to search our house and the clubhouse, coming up empty. The fucking pigs ripped our compound apart trying to find her. At the time, I already had her moved. She was hiding out with Ma and Doc at his place, further south. Accompanied by a few brothers, watching their every move.

Each member of the MC was taken into custody for questioning, including our old man. It wasn't any different from any other time they called us into the station, needing answers.

Mia was mine.

Which meant she was family.

And we protected our own.

McGraw probably knew we were full of shit, but couldn't prove we were guilty without any fucking evidence. If there was one thing our MC knew how to do well, it was cover our tracks. Our only saving grace was the fact that Mia didn't tell her parents she was coming over to our house that evening. Before anyone realized Mia was missing, a few brothers waited till dusk and drove her Jeep to the nearest train station. Leaving it in the overnight, unguarded parking lot. The same tracks I spent most of my adolescence at, daydreaming of running away.

The irony was not fucking lost on me.

I hoped that staging her car at the station would provide her family with some peace of mind. That maybe Mia didn't get kidnapped, but she ran away on her own. The brothers were extra cautious, making sure they didn't leave behind any fingerprints or DNA behind that could jeopardize our club. Destroying her cell phone so it couldn't be tracked, discarding anything that pointed fingers to Devil's Rejects. Our involvement with her disappearance needed to stay non-existent.

It didn't matter, though, none of it did. Her old man and his boys were tearing apart Oak Island trying to find her. Not that I could blame them, I would have been doing the same fucking shit if I hadn't found her first.

I heard Mia's soft, subtle footsteps descending down the hall. I would be lying if I said I wasn't shocked as shit when she knocked on my bedroom door. Opening it shortly after. I didn't pay her any mind, staring at the muted television while she watched me from the doorframe. Staying as far away from me as possible.

I wanted to touch her, pull her into my lap, and never fucking let her go. But I allowed her the distance for the time being, knowing she was pissed at me. Her guard securely in place for the first time since I met her, where it should have been all along. Instead, she was now tainted by my life, exactly the way I never wanted her to be.

It was too late for that now and there was no going back for either of us. This was our life.

I took a few more swigs from the bottle of Jack and placed it back on the nightstand, gearing to stitch up my leg. Grabbing the first aid kit the doc left behind for us, I threaded the nylon through the needle hole. Taking a lighter to the end to sterilize it.

Mia gasped when I punctured my injured skin, causing me to look back up at her with a questioning regard. She bit her lip for a few seconds, clearly struggling with an internal battle, evident on her face. She suddenly moved one foot in front of the other, making her way over to me in three strides. Wanting to get to me as quickly as possible, just in case she changed her mind.

"You're doing it all wrong," she muttered, sitting beside me on the bed, taking the needle out of my hand.

"You know a lot about stitchin' up stab wounds, Pippin?" I teased, reaching up to lazily twirl a strand of hair around my finger.

She rolled her eyes, pulling her head away. "My papa is a doctor. I've seen him stitch up Mason and Bo in our house, more times than I care to remember."

I nodded, leaning back against the headboard. Thankful as fuck I didn't have to do this on my own.

Her face frowned, thinking about her family. She was too wound up before, needing answers from me on what was going on, to remember them. It was funny what the mind was capable of doing when put under a strenuous situation. Mia was no different.

I swept the hair away from her face, grabbing hold of her chin to look at me.

Her breathing hitched. "They don't know where I am, do they?" she whispered loud enough for me to hear. A pained expression crossed her face.

I shook my head no.

She grimaced, even though my response was expected.

"It's for your own good. And theirs," I coaxed, knowing it wouldn't do any damn good.

"They must be freaking out. I can't even imagine what they're going through. My momma has to be worried sick. Mason is deployed with no word on his safety, and now this. Her poor heart is breaking, Creed."

I just sat there, looking at her not knowing what else to say.

"Can I call—"

"No," I interrupted, already knowing what she was going to ask. I'd been expecting it all fucking night.

"I won't tell them where I—"

"No."

"Please, Creed. Just so they know I'm oka—"

"Mia!" I snapped in a harsh tone. "No!"

She scowled, grabbing the bottle of peroxide from the first aid kit, preparing the cotton swab to clean and disinfect my wound. "This is going to hurt," she stated in an irritated tone.

I narrowed my eyes at her. "Can't hurt any more than you stabbin' me." Before I knew what was happening, the little minx poured the peroxide on my gash, instead. "Motherfucker!" I roared, throwing my head back, clenching my fists in the sheets.

"Thought you said it wouldn't hurt more than me stabbing you in the leg. What did we learn, Creed? Hmmm… That you're not always right? So maybe I can call my par—"

"When ya gonna get it through your thick fuckin' head, huh? You're a smart girl, Pippin. Shouldn't haveta spell it out for ya. Callin' your parents will only get you killed. I'm tryin' to save your life. Not fuckin' end it. All this questionin' ends here!"

Patience was never one of my goddamn virtues and it wasn't about to start now. This was one of the reasons we kept her sedated and blindfolded, while we brought her up here in the middle of nowhere. No one could get to this place unless they knew the woods just outside the door. You needed a side-by-side vehicle just to get here. As much as I hated having her unconscious, I didn't trust her enough to not call her family and tell them where she was. I couldn't blame her for that. Anyone would call home the first chance they got.

"This is far from over," she mumbled under her breath, sticking the needle into my leg a little harder than necessary.

I groaned, grabbing the bottle of Jack from the nightstand, chugging it down till I no longer felt the searing burn from my nerve endings. Letting out a grumbling sound from deep within my throat, I threw the empty bottle on the floor next to me, watching it shatter on impact. Gesturing to my leg for her to finish stitching me up.

It all happened so damn fast. One minute she was tying off my stitch and the next my phone pinged with a new text message. Both our eyes simultaneously darted to my phone that was lying in the middle of the bed, like it was wired with explosives, ready to fucking detonate.

Without giving it a second thought, she lunged over my leg, scraping my wound to grab the phone. Snatching it before I could, clutching it tightly in her greedy little hands. She propelled off the edge of the bed so fucking fast as if her body was set on fire. Taking off toward the adjacent bathroom in the corner of my room.

She never had a chance.

I caught her by the back of her sweater as she rounded the bed, thrusting her backward with my staggering hold. There was no way I could grab a hold of her securely without hurting her or the baby, and she knew it. My arm wrapped around her upper ribcage, tugging her into my lap, trying like hell to reach the phone. She twisted and turned, huffing and puffing until she weaseled her way out of her sweater. Hauling ass into the bathroom, slamming the door behind her. I heard the lock snap into place seconds after.

"Fuckin' A," I clenched out. Throwing my injured leg off the bed, I stood, making my way over to the door. "Mia! Open the fuckin' door!" I pounded my fists on the wood.

There was a jarring commotion, followed by a loud scraping noise, coming from the bathroom. I knew she was barricading herself in, moving furniture up against the door to keep me out.

"Mia! Open it or I will!"

"NO!" she screamed, not backing down. "I'm calling my parents! I can't do this to them! I can't believe you're making me! This is all your fault! Now go away!" Her voice echoed away from the door like she was standing in the shower, far away from me.

"Jesus Christ!" I took a step back, ramming my foot against the door. Forcefully kicking it open, breaking it off the hinges and taking the frame along with it. Causing pieces of the linen cabinet she blocked the door with, to smash right along with it.

Her eyes widened in shock. I didn't fucking hesitate, stomping over to her in three, hard strides. Making her retract until her back hit the shower wall. I loomed over her small frame with a menacing regard, getting right up in her face. Her bright blue eyes wide and anxious.

Here I was trying to save her life and keep her safe, and she was about to jeopardize everything. The thought alone made my blood boil, frustration erupting from deep within my core. My hands balled into fists, my chest heaved, reaching my breaking point very fucking quickly. I was at my wits end. I couldn't go to war with everyone, plus *her*. Fighting a battle with a full-grown woman constantly throwing tantrums when she didn't get her way.

We had to be on the same page.

No more fighting.

I needed to get my point across, and it needed to happen right fucking now.

"Didn't I tell you to open the fuckin' door?"

"I-I-I—" she sputtered, her demeanor quickly changing.

"Didn't I just say you couldn't call your fuckin' parents?"

"Y-yy-ees…" She nodded, offering me my phone back. I crudely knocked her hand away, sending the device crashing to the tile floor.

I didn't waver, I grabbed her upper arm and held her in place. This would be the second time I ever manhandled her this way. I wasn't trying to scare her. I needed her to listen and understand. This was not a fucking game. This was about her surviving through a shit storm. Our way of life was cruel, I'd lived it my entire life. Mia, on the other hand, was privileged, a fuckin' princess that had no clue and needed a reality check. It was my duty to protect her from unseen enemies, and rules had to be fucking obeyed. She was testing me, making me have to put her in her goddamn place.

Bottom line, she needed to fucking listen to me.

"You don't run away from me. Ever!"

She jolted. "You're scaring me." Her lips started to tremble.

"Is that right?" I rasped, leaning down close to her lips. "This ain't nothin' compared to what our enemies would do if they found you. They'd rape you. Beat you, and then fuckin' kill you when they had enough. That what you want?"

"No," she breathed out, tears forming in her eyes.

"I ain't got time for your childish, bullshit. I'm tryin' to protect you, Mia. What part of that is so goddamn hard for you to understand?"

"I just want to tell them I'm oka—"

My fist slammed into the shower wall behind her, causing her to duck and scream. Tile cracked beneath my knuckles. "Fuck!" I growled, backing away from her, knowing I was doing exactly what I said I wouldn't.

I was scaring her and that wasn't my intention, I was fucking this up real quick.

How the fuck do I get her to respect my rules and trust me?

I shook my head, disappointed mostly with myself.

"Just go, Mia. Just go to your room and stay there, yeah? You think you can fuckin' do that?"

She didn't have to be told twice. She cautiously made her way around me before running from the room, crying. I resisted the urge to go after her and pull her into my arms. Apologize for my behavior.

I let her go.

Even though…

It was the last thing I wanted to fucking do.

I ran back to my room down the hall from Creed's, slamming the thick wood behind me. Leaning my back against it, I slid down to the floor as I pulled my knees into my chest. Letting all the emotions from the past week drain out of my exhausted body. Questioning everything I had ever felt.

When did my life come to this? How could I be so blind?

I missed my mom and dad, my brothers, my home. Mine and Creed's relationship before the MC came in between us. I don't know how long I sat there, letting my thoughts race before I crawled over to the bed in the center of the room. Not bothering to change my clothes, I hid under the sheets, letting the tears flow freely. Crying myself to sleep.

My body stirred when I felt a strong arm wrap around my waist later in the night. Pulling me against him, engulfing me with nothing but his warmth and scent.

"Stop," Creed ordered in a low tone near my ear when I tried to move away. "Please," he added when I continued to squirm.

I stilled, going lax against his hold. He placed his other arm under my pillow, holding me as close to him as possible.

"Babe, I fucked up. I'm sorry."

I didn't say a word. A part of me was convinced I was dreaming.

"I love you, Pippin. I've loved you before I even knew I fuckin' loved you," he paused to let his words sink in. "When I went back down to the basement to get you, and you weren't there. I thought… I mean… it was… shit… I'm no good at this."

I turned around in his arms to face him, looking deep into his eyes through the dim light of the moon. "You thought what?"

"I thought I'd lost you. Ain't ever been so scared in all my life. I know I'm all wrong for you. I know you deserve better. I know there a million reasons why we shouldn't be together, but it don't matter anymore. You're fuckin' mine. You been mine since you gave me that first patch, bouncin' around, wearin' pigtails, actin' like you grown," he laughed with a gleam in his eyes, remembering me as a child. "Even back then you were a pain in the ass. The baby girl who filled my heart with hope and love. Got me through the fuckin' war with your letters, knowin' someone back home was thinkin' 'bout me. Worryin' 'bout me, prayin' for me. Lovin' me."

I smirked, my anger gradually dissipating while hearing his confession.

"Everything that ever mattered to me don't matter no more. Devil's Rejects, my brothers, my fuckin' life. I'd do whatever it takes to protect you. Ya feel me?"

"Yes."

"I know what I'm doin'. I know it may not seem that way, but I need you to trust me. Yeah?"

"Okay."

"I promise I'm doin' my part on gettin' you home… safely."

I snuggled closer to him. "I trust you, but I'll have your balls if you don't find a way… fast," I teased, trying to lighten the mood. Sensing he was uncomfortable with expressing his feelings. As if it was the first time he'd ever done so.

"You can start right now." He rubbed his dick against my leg, making me laugh.

"I love you, too."

He kissed my forehead, letting his lips linger. "Now that. That I always knew."

It had been three weeks since Mia woke up at the safe house in the woods. Getting settled in to a new routine, knowing she may be there a while. Giving Noah and me a list of essentials she'd need us to bring back, including clothes, books on pregnancy, chick-flicks, a guitar and a supply of her favorite ice cream and pickles. Spending her days following Doc's orders, staying in bed, watching mindless movies and reading to the baby girl in her stomach. Saying some shit about giving her a head start in literacy. I knew it was because she wanted her to be educated, unlike Noah and me.

Doc came by at least once a week to check on her and the baby. Bringing a portable ultrasound machine so Mia could see that her unborn child truly was okay and that her own body was also healing, well. He even cleared her to resume sexual activity, which was music to my fucking ears.

Mia was still worried about baby girl, and it seemed to get worse as the days went by. On one of the visits from Doc, I pulled him aside and asked him if there was anything I could do to ease her worry. He said he could leave a Doppler, a handheld device with a little wand that Mia could use anytime she wanted. Not only to check the baby's heart rate but hear it, too.

I surprised her with it one night while we were lying in bed relaxing.

"Babe, pull 'em panties down, lift your shirt, and close your eyes."

She turned her head, giving me a questioning look. "Again? You're insatiable."

"Ain't gonna tell ya again, Pippin."

She slipped her panties down and lifted her tank. "I am yours to do with as you please."

"Now be a good girl and close 'em eyes."

When she did, I reached over, opening the drawer in the nightstand and took out the monitor and gel. Squeezing a small amount on the wand.

"Are you up to no good?"

"Always," I chuckled, placing the tip of the probe on the lower right area of her stomach. Spreading the gel out, making her jump from the cold contact.

"Are you putting lotion on me?"

"Shhh… listen."

Seconds later, baby girl's heartbeat filled the room after I located it. Just like Doc had shown me. Mia's eyes fluttered open as soon as she realized what was going on. Bursting into tears when the strong beat sounded. Not going to lie, it was the most amazing sound I'd ever heard. I hadn't met baby girl, yet, but she had already melted and owned my fucking heart.

"Oh my God, Creed. How… I mean… when…" She couldn't get the words out, sobbing so hard. A constant stream of tears falling to the sheets beneath her.

"I know how worried you've been. I asked Doc the last time he was here, what I could do to ease that. He left me this Doppler and said the best thing for you is to hear your baby's heart beatin' whenever you wanted. Some shit about it bein' soothin' for the mother. He showed me how to use it and here we are."

"This is the best gift anyone has ever given me. I can't even begin to tell you how much this means to me. I love you so much.

"I fuckin' love you. Now dry those tears, listen to our baby girl growing inside you. That there is a Jameson heart. Strong and unbreakable. She's already proven that once," I reminded, leaning over and placing a kiss on her forehead. Reminding her that I would always do anything for her.

No matter what.

She hadn't made any other attempts to call her parents since I showed her a glimpse of the man she wanted. She even gave up on asking any more questions. Content with what she knew for now. She was following the rules and listening to me for the most part, but she was still Mia. Stubborn to a fucking fault. I knew she was getting restless in the house. Mia had always been an active person, and being cooped up like that was beginning to take a toll on her, especially since Noah and I couldn't stay with her every night. She was never alone, though. I didn't trust any of the Prospects. It was always Diesel or one of the other brothers who took shifts, staying with her. Pops kept his distance after the drop-off at the safe house, wanting nothing more to do with the situation.

Ma begged me a few times to let her come stay with Mia. Saying she wanted to help during her pregnancy. Some shit about needing a woman around and not all us men hovering over her. I told her that right now wasn't a good time. Mia was overwhelmed enough as it was, she didn't need another person on her ass. She was disappointed but settled for making her some homemade meals for me to take back to the house to help out.

I tried to be there as much as I could, but I was still VP of Devil's Rejects and needed to know what the fuck was going on back in the real world. Keeping a close eye on the Sinner's and any other enemy lurking the streets. The constant surveillance we had to dodge in order to drive to the safe house wasn't making things any easier. Fucking McGraw had us on watch, day in and day out. Noah stayed behind at the clubhouse for the most part, which I preferred. I didn't want that little shit near my girl, especially by himself.

It had become a fucking waiting game, finding out who was behind the shootout at our house. We were running in circles with no end in sight. Chasing our fucking tails. We had words with allies and suppliers. Paying unexpected visits to every son of a bitch we could think of. Getting our hands dirty with more blood and lives. Some corrupt. Some innocent, caught in the crossfire. Every ride out we did, we came up empty. Not one fucking answer to all the relentless questions.

To make matters worse, I had Mia's old man, his boys, and McGraw on my ass constantly. There was no staying away from daily life for too long, they were already suspicious of our behavior.

I had to fly under the radar and play nice for the time being. Even offering to help, but that didn't go over very well. Words like low-life and piece of fucking trash were thrown in my face. None of it fazed me. I knew what I looked like in their eyes. I'd never be their prodigal son, who'd be welcomed into the family with open fucking arms.

So, I pretended like nothing had changed when everything had. Noah would come and go as he pleased, but he was in the same boat I was. Plain and simple, they were waiting for one of us to slip up. We had to stay one step ahead of them at all times.

I cut the engine to the side-by-side, parking it at the back of the house along with the others. Completely out of sight. I couldn't fucking wait to see Pippin. Take her in my fucking arms and straight to bed. It had been at least twenty-four hours since I had slept, exhaustion beginning to set in. I'd been sleeping like shit at the clubhouse, wishing I were somewhere else. It was crazy how fast I'd gotten used to sharing a bed with Mia in my arms or on my chest. Always needing to have some part of her touching me. It was new, considering I'd never shared a bed with anyone before her.

I smiled just thinking about how someone so tiny could take up so much space. Hogging the entire bed. I woke up every morning on the edge of the king-sized mattress. No matter what, half of her body was always lying on top of me, using my torso like a body pillow. Baby girl seemed to like it, too. She'd kick inside Mia's stomach in the middle of the night all the time, waking me up.

I unlocked the front door, stopping dead in my tracks when I heard Mia giggling like a fucking schoolgirl on the other side.

"The fuck?" I muttered to myself, barging inside. Jerking back from the scene unfolding in front of me.

Mia was on the couch with Noah kneeling in front of her on the floor. His body in between her legs with his head resting on her stomach while his hands stroked her bare skin as he whispered shit to the baby. They both glanced over in my direction when they heard me walk in. Mia warily smiled, slowly moving away from Noah, who didn't bother getting up. She nonchalantly stood, pulling her shirt down over her belly. Making her way over to me on unsteady legs.

Standing on the tips of her toes, she kissed me. "I missed you," she coaxed against my lips.

"Shouldn't you be in my bed?" I questioned, grabbing underneath her chin so she'd look at me.

"Waiting on you." She shyly smiled, her cheeks turning a soft shade of red.

I don't know what came over me, maybe it was the fact I hadn't seen her in a few days, or maybe it was from seeing Noah's hands all over her stomach. Or it could have just been the fact that I hadn't been inside of her in God knows how fucking long. I gripped onto the back of her neck, tugging her pouty fucking lips toward me.

Kissing her.

Fucking devouring her.

Clutching onto the side of her face with one hand, while taking her bottom lip between my teeth. Sucking it hard. Causing a soft moan to escape her lips.

My cock twitched, aching to be inside of her.

Suddenly, my hands fell to her luscious ass, unable to control myself. Gripping on tight, I carried her up in one swift motion, so she could straddle my waist. Wrapping her long legs around my hips as I kicked the front door shut, never breaking our intense kiss. Noah cleared his throat, but we were too far gone to give a fuck, wrapped up in each other's love. I walked us back to my room, making sure to flip Noah off as we strode past him.

Crossing the threshold into my room, I used my boot to close the bedroom door behind us, needing some privacy with my girl. I never stopped kissing her as we made our way over to the bed. Gently laying her down on the mattress, hovering above her heady frame. Causing her breathing to escalate when she realized she was now beneath me.

I kissed along her jaw, murmuring, "The fuck was that out there?" Continuing to lick and kiss down to her ample tits. I yanked down her flimsy cotton tank top, exposing a nipple, sucking the round pebble into my mouth.

"Ahhh…" Her back arched off the bed, only encouraging me to keep going.

I couldn't help myself.

I never fucking could when it came to her.

"Asked you a question, sweetheart. Expectin' a fuckin' answer, unless you want me to stop," I warned, sucking on her other nipple while my hands roamed, fondling her breasts.

She moaned again, her hands fisting my hair. Mia had always been sensitive to my touch, but pregnancy heightened that tenfold. She could feel me all over with a simple touch or flick of my tongue, exactly how I wanted her to.

"Creed…" she panted. "Please don't stop."

I grinned. "You want some of me? Then answer my fuckin' question."

She bucked her hips, tilting her head back, giving my lips more access to her flushed skin.

"Can you just—"

"Not till you answer."

"It was nothing. Why are you worrying yourself over this? I'm yours."

I growled, kissing her more aggressively than before. Crashing our lips together, brushing my cock against her thigh. I rasped, "Prove it," in between kisses.

"What? What can I do to make you happy?"

I pulled away, causing her to whimper from the loss of my heat. Eyeing her up and down with a predatory regard, I replied, "You can let me fuck you in the ass."

She sucked in air, sitting up slightly, startled by what I had just requested. Her wide eyes searched my face for any sign of humor.

I wasn't fucking laughing.

I pushed her back down and took what I wanted. Thrusting my tongue into her mouth, seeking hers out. Reassuring her with my lips, my taste, my scent, and my love. Reminding her who she fucking belonged to. I pecked her one last time before settling my forehead on hers.

We locked eyes.

She swallowed hard, taking a deep breath. "My ass? Like my ass, ass? You're kidding, right? Look, if this is about Noah—"

"Mia, even when I fuck you. I'm makin' love to you," I honestly spoke, kissing her lips, beckoning them to open for me. "Now spread those legs like you know I fuckin' love." She did, and I placed my body in between her thighs, caging her in with my arms, holding my own weight. "I was the first man to kiss you, to touch you, woulda been the first to fuckin' claim you, but I fucked that up. Biggest regret of my life, babe. I'll never hurt you again," I whispered close enough to her mouth that I could feel her breath against mine. I brought one hand down, touching along her stomach as I continued confessing, "This baby girl inside you shoulda been mine, but it don't matter cuz I'll love her just the same."

She beamed, smiling so big against my mouth. "Is that why you want to—"

"Fuck yes. Give it to me. It belongs to me."

"Will it hur—" I placed my hand under her skirt, skimming my fingers along the seam of her panties. Sliding them over. Rendering her speechless.

She was already so fucking wet. It was one of the things I craved the most. Her body's natural response to my touch.

Mia was made for me.

"Need to hear the words, babe," I urged, rubbing my fingers along her slit. Working them up to her clit, drawing slow, torturous circles and spreading her moisture.

Getting her ready to take my cock.

"Ah… yes… I'm yours…"

I smiled. "Fuckin' love you," I declared, kissing all along her face and back down the side of her neck. Where I knew it drove her crazy with need. With want.

I licked from her collarbone to her breasts, sucking her nipples into my mouth. Working my fingers on her clit as she swayed her hips, riding and guiding them to grind against her nub. Harder and faster until I pushed two fingers inside her pussy, still using the palm of my hand to rub her swollen clit.

"Your pussy is so fuckin' tight. That's right, just like that, baby. Fuck my fingers, ride them like you would my fuckin' cock."

Her body arched, her eyes rolled to the back of her head, and her hands balled up, on the edge of release. I didn't let up, moving my fingers so fast, so deep inside her, wanting her to come apart so fucking hard. Still not stopping until she screamed out my fucking name. Her body shook, trembled, and quivered, barely able to come any longer. I allowed her some mercy, letting her catch her breath and steady her heart.

I had her clothes off in a matter of seconds. Yanking my shirt over my head, throwing it to the ground with hers. Gripping onto her legs, I didn't hesitate, placing my face between her goddamn thighs.

Needing to taste her.

I ate her pussy until I had her come dripping down my chin, onto my chest. My rough, callused hands sought out her breasts. Kneading her tits, pulling at her nipples, and making her come undone with my tongue. I slid my hands to her hips, holding on, rotating them to follow the rhythm of my lips. It had been so long since I made her fuck my face.

Sucking.

Licking.

Fucking her with my mouth, bringing her on the verge of shuddering. Wanting her to come again, needing her to fucking come again. I kicked off my boots, unzipped my jeans, and pulled out my cock. Gripping my shaft, working myself over, all while lapping at her sweet pussy.

Taking the time to slowly rim my finger around her asshole. "Gonna let me in, babe?" I drawled out, gently pushing my middle finger inside.

Her body locked up, but only for a second. My mouth became more urgent, more demanding, sending her spiraling into a frantic frenzy. Her legs shook, her core vibrated. Her ass took my finger in like I knew it would, once I got her to focus on the pleasure, sliding in and out of her. Stroking the back of her g-spot through the walls of her asshole.

"Holy shit," she panted in a heady tone, not expecting how good I could make her feel.

"Here, baby... Like it here...yeah?" I taunted. "My finger is fuckin' your ass, Pippin. Now tell me you want my cock," I groaned, watching her come so fucking hard as I stretched her as best as I could. Never letting up on my dick with my other hand. Gripping it tighter, imagining it was her tight little cunt wrapped around me. Working my shaft the only way her pussy knew how.

I sat up, wanting to take a good look at her perfect fucking physique for what felt like the first time in over a month.

Vulnerable.

Exposed.

She was goddamn perfection.

So fucking beautiful. She peered up at me through hooded eyes, so dark and dilated. Watching me stroke my dick. Jerking off harder from the sight of her.

"Want my cock?"

She nodded as she continued to watch me with a fascinated regard. I chuckled while licking her come off my lips, wiping the rest of it off with the back of my hand as I crawled my way up her body. Positioning the head of my cock at the entrance of her pussy, thrusting right in.

"So fuckin' good," I growled, feeling the warmth of her wetness, her pussy squeezing my cock. I roughly gripped onto her ass, groaning. Moving in and out of her, loving the way her skin felt beneath mine. I could no longer restrain myself, she felt too fucking good. The smell of her engulfed me. Attacking my senses all at once.

I claimed her mouth, wanting to taste her. Enjoying the push and pull of our kiss, both of us taking what the other wanted. I reached down to her overly sensitive clit, massaging it till I felt her on the verge of coming.

"The next time you come it will be from my cock in your ass," I groaned, sliding my cock out of her pussy, before slowly, gently thrusting it into her ass.

She gasped, holding her breath. Waiting for the pain, the discomfort, the ache to subside.

"Breathe, baby," I murmured close to her ear. "Relax, let me in. Won't hurt you. Won't ever fuckin' hurt you."

Her mouth parted, getting used to the unfamiliar sensation that my cock stirred in her ass. I never stopped my assault on her clit, knowing it would ease the distress. The desire making it much easier for her to give me what I wanted.

"So fuckin' tight, so fuckin' wet, so fuckin' perfect." I breathed out, almost balls deep inside of her.

A little deeper.

A little harder.

I kissed her again, resting my forehead on hers, picking up the pace. It didn't take long for her body to relax, becoming accustomed to my size. The pressure from the tip of my cock hit her g-spot from inside of her ass like my fingers did moments ago. Her legs widened, allowing me to ease two fingers into her pussy. My hips simultaneously moved with my hand.

"Creed, I can't... oh my God... it's too much... I can—"

"You can... you will."

My movements became harder and rougher, responding to everything I was giving her.

Everything I was taking...

She came over and over again as I fucked both her holes. The palm of my hand still controlling her clit.

I didn't think she would ever stop coming.

Looking deep into her eyes, I spoke with conviction, "Your ass, your pussy, your fuckin' heart... it all belongs to me. I own you. Every last fuckin' part of you... is mine."

And I meant every word.

***

I waited until Mia was passed out in my arms before slowly slipping out of her grasp, the red digital numbers read two o'clock in the morning. She moaned, feeling my absence, even in her sleep. Her breathing calmed, shallowing out, exhausted from the night's activities. I covered her up with the blankets, captivated by how fucking gorgeous she truly was.

Her messy hair partially covered her face, spreading out on the pillow and down her back. Her skin looked as silky and as inviting as it felt. Her pouty, perfect lips perched out and adorable. Even with her baby bump growing, she looked even sexier than she did before. She was glowing from the inside out.

I was a lucky fucking bastard.

I didn't deserve her.

Not her love.

Not her body.

Not her heart.

Not one damn thing.

But I'd never let her go.

I threw on my jeans, not bothering with a shirt, grabbed a cigarette from the half empty pack on the dresser, and made my way outside. Making sure to close the door behind me. I walked through the house to the front door, finding Noah out on the porch, a bottle of Jack firmly in his grasp. The light from the moon illuminated his profile. He looked lost in his own thoughts, staring off into the woods. Not saying a word when I stepped outside, leaning against the post as I lit my cigarette.

I stood there quiet, allowing myself a moment of normalcy. Looking over at Noah, seeing the little boy who once upon a time used to look up to me instead of a fucking biker who had knocked up my girl.

"You're drinkin' too much," I muffled through the smoke of my cig. Blowing it up into the night's warm air.

"Naw." He took another big swig. "Not nearly enough." Pointing the bottle to the door, he added, "This place is bulletproof, not fuckin' soundproof. I forgot how loud Mia could be."

I wasn't surprised he was throwing that shit in my face, but that didn't stop the anger his words emanated. I was fucking counting on her being loud. I even provoked it to be honest just to prove a point to him. Noah knew how to push my fucking buttons. He had done so since he was a kid. Part of me knew he was still pissed I went into the military, leaving him to deal with our old man on his own. Noah was always used to me protecting him, especially after I killed Luke.

I often wondered if that was why he wanted Mia. To get back at me. Make me hurt the way I made him hurt. Payback was a brutal cunt, but the eye for an eye mentality was all we'd ever known.

"Those are fightin' words, baby brother. Tread fuckin' carefully." I took another drag, letting the nicotine course through me. Hoping it would calm the rage stirring inside of me.

He snidely chuckled, nodding. "Don't change the fact I had her first, and she's carryin' my kid to fuckin' prove it."

I was in his face, yanking him up off the chair by his cut, but he shoved me off. "Truth hurts don't it, motherfucker."

I shook my head, scoffing out, "No one asked you to be here! Don't know what you think you're doin', but you need to stand the fuck down. Mia ain't your concern. She's mine. Knockin' her up don't fuckin' change that."

He shrugged, not missing a beat. "Then what you worryin' about?

"Don't fuck with me, Noah. I gotta enough fuckin' bullshit to deal with. Don't need your shit, too."

"Tell me, Creed... she's yours right?" he questioned, narrowing his eyes at me. "Then what's her favorite color?"

I jerked back like he had hit me. Knowing exactly where he was going with this.

"Time's up. It's pink. How about her middle name? Don't remember?" he mocked, cocking his head to the side. "They wanted to name her Savannah after her grandmother who died of cancer. She never even got to meet her. But instead, it's Alexandra, after her momma. Why don't you tell me her favorite thing to eat? Or drink? Favorite book? Or movie? How about you tell me anythin' that doesn't include what she sounds like when she's fuckin' gettin' off?"

"You little shit! Congrats, Noah, on knowin' some trivial bullshit. I know what shes's feelin' by just lookin' at her. I know what she's thinkin' without her sayin' one goddamn word to me. And fuck yeah, I know how she likes to be touched, kissed, fucked and I'd rather be the man who knows all that, plus how to fuckin' get her off," I snarled, stepping up to him again. He didn't cower, if anything he stood taller. "Who the fuck you think you are, Noah?"

"The *right* man for her, that's who."

"Is that right? So what, you tellin' me you love her? You love Mia?"

There was no hesitation with his response when he clearly replied with, "Yeah, Creed. I fuckin' do."

"Don't start a war you can't fuckin' win, baby brother."

"Consider this my breach."

I nodded slowly, backing away. Taking everything in while battling the urge to lay him the fuck out.

The lines were drawn now. Each of us on the opposite side for the first time in all our lives, but if there was anyone I would go to hell and back for it was Mia Ryder. Even if it meant going to war with...

My fucking brother.

I was getting agitated in the house, being locked up all day, especially since I hadn't seen Creed for a few days. I had been here for a month now, and there was only so much I could do behind these concrete walls, not being allowed to step foot outside. I missed the sun, the fresh air, and the grass beneath my bare feet. I'd give anything just to feel the hot rays on my face, even if it was for five minutes. Often thinking about sneaking out to the porch while the boys were away, but I was never alone.

They always had someone with me. Men they considered brothers, part of their MC family. They didn't talk much, going about their own business and making sure I was safe. Taking post at the front door to make sure no one unauthorized stepped foot in the house. I had a feeling Creed ordered them to not speak to me or something, since they never uttered more than a few words in my direction.

The smell of bacon and eggs filled my room, waking me up early Saturday morning, or maybe it was Sunday. I started to lose track of the days.

A woman's voice sounded from the kitchen, singing "American Pie." Bringing back memories of the night I met Noah. *Was I dreaming?*

I got out of bed, wrapping the silk robe Noah had brought back for me around myself. Cautiously peering out my door before padding down the hallway toward the smell of heaven. Rounding the corner, I stopped dead in my tracks, seeing Creed's momma in the kitchen. Singing and dancing around while she cooked breakfast.

"Oh hey, sweetheart. Did I wake you?"

"Oh my God, what are you doing here?" I smiled, walking over to her. Giving her a big hug.

"Didn't the boys tell you? I have been begging Creed to let me come up here and spoil you. He finally agreed. Mentioning how close you are with your family. I figured you'd be missing your momma by now. I'm not her, and I know it's not the same, but I'm here to keep you company for a bit. Gonna cook you up some dinners to freeze, too. I know how you love my apple pie. Got a few of those already waiting for you in the fridge."

The mere mention of my mom brought back the heartache I kept buried deep inside me, but I shook it off as best as I could, smiling at Diane. Grateful to have her here nonetheless.

"Well, this is the best surprise. Thank you."

"Take a seat, breakfast is just about ready," she informed, walking back over to the stove to prepare me a plate.

"So, Mrs. Jameson—"

"Darlin', you can call me Diane. You are carrying my grandbaby."

"Okay. Can I ask you a question, Diane?"

"Of course," she replied, setting my plate in front of me and taking a seat beside me. "What's on your mind?"

"Does Creed talk about me much? I mean... has he told you anything?" I asked, eating a piece of bacon.

"Well, I would say more now than ever. Noah was usually the one who wouldn't shut up about you."

I sighed, needing to address the questions she probably has been asking herself often. "I know what this may look like to you. Pregnant with one son's baby and in love with the other. But Noah and I were never together," I confessed, calling Rebel, Noah since that was what his mom was referring to him as. I needed her to understand what happened that night and what had been going on ever since. She took a hold of my hand. Encouraging me to continue. "It was one night. I went to the clubhouse with a friend. I didn't even know it was Creed's MC until we got there and I recognized their cuts. I would have never... I mean I didn't know Noah was Creed's

69

brother. Creed doesn't talk much about his life. In fact, I didn't even know he had a brother until the day I went back to the clubhouse to tell Noah I was pregnant."

"Creed has always been my quiet boy. Even when he was just a little guy, he was a man of few words. But when he does speak, his words carry a strong meaning behind them. They always have. Creed is so damn smart, he could have done anything with his life. Been something really important, like a lawyer or a builder. He's good with his hands, and I don't have to tell you how much he loves to argue. The man thinks he's never wrong," she laughed. "It's one of my biggest regrets, letting both of them drop out of school. Most of the time I felt like I was a single parent and the only one who cared about essential things, like an education. All Jameson ever cared about was the club and having his boys be a part of it."

This was more than I ever thought she'd share with me. I took in everything she was saying, wanting to soak up as much information as I could when it came to Creed.

"I tried to do the best I could with raising them right when all they saw was wrongdoings. I hated every time I had to clean blood off their clothes. As they became older it became more relevant. Jameson was teaching the boys to shoot guns and fight, drink and smoke cigarettes. He should have been teaching them how to ride bikes and play ball. So, I just made sure they knew how to respect a woman, how to wrap it up, and how to protect and provide for their families."

"You did the best you could under the circumstances. Creed and Noah are strong, confident men. They love with all their hearts. You did good, Diane."

"Thank you. It's nice to hear that. I was able to have more time with Creed, but with Noah and Luke…" She peered down at her lap, her demeanor quickly changing. "Well… I just made some bad choices. Noah was the one who suffered the most because of it. With Luke… I failed him. And it took a very long time to accept that and move on. Be there for my boys who needed me."

"What happened to Luk—"

"Anyhow, this isn't about me. I want to know about you. The boys have filled me in but they're men—they hardly understand anything."

I nodded, allowing her to change the subject. She already told me so much, I didn't want to cause her any more pain than what she obviously carried.

I smiled, easing her anxiety. "My family is really strict. I'm the baby and the only girl. I have two older brothers who watch me like guard dogs, exactly how my dad trained them to. From what my papa has told me, my dad was a handful growing up. Put my mom through a lot in their adolescent years. I think he's just making sure I don't go through what she did. I don't know… it makes no sense."

"You're his baby girl. I often wonder if it would have been different had I given Jameson a girl. Your daddy is just protective over you. And sweetheart, I can almost guarantee Noah will be worse with her. Not to mention poor baby girl's got Creed, too."

I chuckled, "Yeah…" Placing my hand on my belly, knowing what she said couldn't have been more accurate. "The night I went to the clubhouse, I just wanted a night to be normal. Have fun and not worry about who I was disappointing… or what my parents' wanted me to do. Noah was charming, handsome, funny… he was what I needed that night. One thing led to another and we made this baby girl." I gestured to my belly. "Noah was my first… I hadn't ever… and we used protection… but Creed and I weren't together. I promise."

"How did you meet Creed? You guys are nine years apart, right?"

I nervously laughed, breathing out, "Yes."

She shrugged, relieving my worry. "Age is just a number. Jameson is a lot older than I am, too. I was eleven when I fell in love with him, and he was nowhere near my age. Didn't stop him from claiming me when I was fifteen."

"Huh, I guess it was something like that for Creed and me, too. Except, he pushed me away every chance he got, constantly telling me he was no good. When all I wanted was to be his friend. He always looked like he needed one of those."

"Creed is his own worst enemy. My boy has been through so much, and I'm to blame for a lot of it. It took me a long time to accept that as well."

"I met him in the parking lot of my momma's restaurant when I was nine years old, but he was friends with my older brother, Mason.

They actually went into the military together. Mason is still there. Over the years, I just saw him in passing. Until one night everything changed, and it kind of turned into a domino effect. Now… here we are… I needed you to know all this. The last thing I want is for you to think I'm some sort of hussy," I divulged, feeling a huge weight lifted off my shoulders.

She lovingly smiled at me, seeming as though what I had shared didn't faze her. Not any of it. She squeezed my hand in reassurance. "Listen, sweetheart. I'm no one to judge. Hell, I even know what it's like to be torn between two men. I'm not a saint, not even close. You are far from a hussy, darlin', and I knew that the first time I saw your innocent face." She reached up and grabbed under my chin, speaking with conviction, "I have never seen my boys this happy, and I have you to thank for that. I couldn't have asked for a better woman to have walked into both of their lives. Regardless of the circumstances and situation y'all are in. We're all family now, and one day, I know I will be proud to call you my daughter. I am over the moon you are carrying my grandbaby." She stood, kissing the top of my head. Leaving me to finish eating my breakfast.

We spent the rest of the morning sitting on the couch, getting to know each other. Giving me a little insight to her and the boys' life. Telling me how she was a recovering alcoholic, and how she felt like the worst mother in the world for the longest time, but had spent every day since trying to make up for her past mistakes. It broke my heart hearing how Creed and Noah grew up, getting a small glimpse into their world, making me even more thankful I didn't come from a broken family.

"You know, I always wanted a baby girl," she admitted, grabbing my foot to paint my toenails.

My belly was becoming an obstacle these days. It was nice to be pampered for the afternoon, bonding with Diane. Having some much-needed girl time. Don't get me wrong, I loved having the boys around, but I couldn't imagine asking Creed to do this. I laughed to myself picturing my tattooed, alpha male biker, painting my nails pink.

"Oh yeah?"

"I even had a name picked out. Madison, which means a gift from God. We would have called her Maddie for short."

"Oh! I love that! Madison Jameson. Well, now you will have a grandbaby girl to spoil and do all sorts of girly stuff with."

She smiled, thinking about the possibilities. I could barely keep my eyes open as the afternoon kicked in, usually taking a nap around this time.

"Oh sweetheart, why don't you head to bed and get some rest. I'm going to finish the laundry, cook you some dinner, and head out for the night. Diesel's supposed to take me back soon."

"You promise to come back, right?" I asked, dragging myself off the couch.

"Of course. I had such a great time with you today. Now you go take a nap."

"Thanks so much, Diane. For everything." I gave her a hug goodbye and went to lay down on Creed's bed. Passing out as soon as my head hit the pillow.

By the time I woke up, Diane was gone. I spent the rest of the day by myself, dozing off sometime in the evening. When I woke up again, I yawned, stretching my arms above my head, craning my neck to see the time on the alarm clock. It was almost midnight and still no sign of Creed. Most of the time I would just lie in his bed, reading or watching movies. Snuggling up with his pillow that smelled like him, making me feel less alone. Waiting anxiously for him to return to the place I now called home. I hadn't seen him in a few days, and I missed him terribly.

Time just seemed to drag on when he wasn't around.

I took a hot shower and changed into some cotton shorts and a tank. The only time I ever wore revealing clothing these days was when I was going to sleep. There were too many men walking in and out of the house, day and night. The last thing I wanted was to start problems, knowing it wouldn't end well with my boyfriend. Creed preferred my clingy fuckin' clothes, as he called them. He said he loved the way I felt when he would slip into bed with me in the middle of the night when he made it back. Always coming home in the darkness, making me often wonder if returning so late had something to do with my family. Maybe it was easier to leave during the night, unnoticed.

I shook off the thought. Brushed my teeth, getting ready for bed, when my stomach began to rumble. After finishing my nightly routine, I walked down to the kitchen for a late-night snack. Baby girl wanted some ice cream like she did almost every night.

"Diesel, did you eat all my mint chocolate chip ice cream? I see you eyeing it every time I'm eating," I giggled, hearing his loud, clanking boots descending down the hallway.

He didn't answer. No surprise there. I closed the freezer door and started rummaging through the cabinets instead. When I suddenly felt his presence close behind me. The smell of alcohol muffled by the stench of a woman's cheap perfume assaulted my senses. My breathing hitched when the warmth of his chest pressed against my bare back, my eyes falling to his hands resting against the counter at my sides.

"You wear that little get up for me, pretty girl?" Rebel reached up, skimming my shoulder to grab the box of Cheerios. Setting it on the granite surface in front of me, he leaned in close to my ear. His breath hit the side of my neck, causing shivers to course through my entire body. "I'm hungry, Mia. You gonna feed me?" he rasped, softly caressing along my arm, leaving goose bumps in his wake. A groan escaped his lips, igniting a tingling feeling deep within my belly.

Where did that come from?

I abruptly turned around, causing him to move away from me rather quickly. Taking the box of cereal with him. Our eyes connected. He sucked in his lower lip, tugging it between his teeth, looking me up and down with a mischievous gleam in his eyes. Grinning as he popped pieces of Cheerios in his mouth, slowly chewing in a way only Noah could make look sensual. He'd never been this forward with me before, but I knew it was the alcohol talking.

"You look good, Mia."

I nodded, smiling. "I feel good."

"I know." He winked. "I remember."

"When did you get back?" I asked, ignoring his last remark.

"About an hour ago. Thought you were sleepin', didn't want to wake you."

"Were you with a girl?" I blurted, mentally kicking myself for it.

He arrogantly smiled. "What if I was? It bother you?"

"No."

"No, huh?"

"What you do with your personal life, Rebel, is none of my business."

His glossy eyes zoned in on me, trying to see if I was lying. "You're awful cute when you're jealous. Even if I was, it don't matter. She ain't the one I want."

I didn't have to ask whom he wanted. I knew he was referring to me. "Rebel, you can't—"

He was in my face, pushing me further into the counter. Caging me in with his arms, a little too close for comfort. "What, Mia? What can't I fuckin' do?"

"You're drunk. Go to bed and sleep it off."

"Only if you tuck me in."

"Reb—"

"You ever think about that night? The night I made you mine. I was the first man to ever make you come... wanna know how I could tell? Cuz of the way your tight pussy squeezed the fuck out of my fingers. You'd been waitin' for it. Fuckin' cravin' it. You always remember your first, Mia," he stated in a low, raspy tone. Brushing his fingers along my belly. "I'm already inside of you, sweetheart."

The same unfamiliar feeling resurfaced again, deep within my core. I should have moved or pushed him away, but I couldn't get my arms or feet to move. It was as if I was watching a train wreck right in front of me, unable to look away. His touch seemed so familiar, and that confused me more than anything. There was something about him in that moment that captivated me, drawing me into his hypnotic pull.

His lips pursed together like he knew what I was thinking, what I was feeling. An internal struggle he was causing.

"I'm Creed's," I simply stated, for I don't know who in particular.

"We'll see." With that, he pushed away from the counter, backing up. Never taking his eyes off me until he had to, leaving me with nothing but unease.

I spent the rest of the night tossing and turning. Thinking about what the meaning of his last words could have meant. They lingered all night, along with the feeling he stirred inside of me. I guess it would be normal to have some feelings for the father of my child, but it wasn't only that.

I admired Noah.

I liked having him around. I enjoyed talking to him, even though it was always a one-sided conversation. He never answered any of my questions about his life, only wanting to know about mine. He listened when I spoke, and not in that *I have to be polite* kind of way. He really wanted to know as much as he could about me.

At first, I thought he felt obligated since I was the mother of his baby, but tonight proved to be something else entirely. I mean, I allowed him to touch my belly all the time. It wasn't anything new. He would do it every chance he got, saying he was talking to his baby girl. Forming a bond before she came into the world. She even started responding to the sound of his voice by kicking or moving around when he spoke. I didn't think anything of it at first. He was the father. *Her* father. Touching her, not me. At least that was the way I saw it, though now I wasn't so sure.

Whatever it was, I needed to put a stop to it. At the end of the day, I loved Creed. I'd always loved Creed.

He had my heart.

I woke up the next morning by myself in a haze from the lack of sleep. Reaching over, feeling the cold sheets beside me. Wanting nothing more than Creed's arms holding me close. The warmth he radiated, to cover me like a blanket, barricading me with his love. I laid there staring at the speckled ceiling, coming to the decision to not tell him about what happened between Noah and me, the night before. It was pointless. It wouldn't do any good, and the last thing I wanted was to come between two brothers.

I needed to clear the air with Noah. Make it known that we were just friends. Close friends. And that we had a baby girl to raise together, that was it. Last night couldn't happen again. I thought about it all morning, going about my normal rituals—eating breakfast, lounging on the couch, reading a book, getting lost in a captivating story, while I waited for Noah to wake up. It was well into the afternoon by the time he finally came out of his room. Part of me thought he might have been avoiding me. Although, I hoped it was just from him being too hungover and needing to sleep a good part of the day away.

He froze in the doorway when he saw me sprawled out on the couch, glancing up from my book. Trying to keep his emotions in check as he stood there in nothing but a pair of gym shorts, hanging low on his hips. His muscular arms crossed over his chest, his body already covered in tattoos, much like his brother's. He started rubbing the back of his head like he was lost in thought, peering all over the room looking for answers. A few awkward seconds passed by before he finally made his way over to me, still not uttering a word.

I threw my book on the coffee table, turning to sit sideways to look at him, tucking my legs underneath me as he took a seat beside me.

"Mia, I-I-I..." he stammered, figuring out what to say first. Struggling to gather his thoughts. He shook his head, locking eyes with me, sighing, "I was drunk. I know that's no fuckin' excuse, but it's all I got."

"I know."

"No you don't. Not even fuckin' close."

"Rebel, you can't—"

"I know what it's like growin' up in a broken home. I know violence, and I know blood. That's it," he said out of nowhere, pausing to allow his words to sink in. "Never met anyone like you. I was drawn to you the second your pretty face walked into the clubhouse that night. Stickin' out like a sore fuckin' thumb. You didn't belong there. Not in that life. I knew it wouldn't take long for one of the brothers to come at you, you're fuckin' beautiful. The club whores I grew up around, don't hold a fuckin' flame to you. I couldn't ask for a better girl to be carryin' my kid. I don't regret that night, cuz you're the one fuckin' thing I've ever done right."

I took a deep breath, overwhelmed by his confession.

"Can't believe that's a surprise to you. You're fuckin' perfect, Mia. The more I'm around you, the more I want to be around you. Don't give a fuck if this makes me sound like a pussy, cuz you're worth it."

"Jesus, Noah."

"I know it's a lot to take in. Been keepin' that shit bottled up for so fuckin' long. You needed to hear it, and I needed to fuckin' say it to you."

"Broken home?" I found myself asking. Thinking back on what Diane had told me the day before.

He shook his head, huffing out, "You don't know a damn thing about Creed, do you? Cuz if you did, you'd know how we grew up."

"That's not fair."

"No shit. Life ain't fair. If it were, you'd be mine right now. Not with Creed. He knows nothin' about you. You're just playin' fuckin' house."

"Rebel, I'm your brother's girl. End of story. I don't want to come between the two of you. But to be fair, you don't tell me anything about your life, either. So if you're going to throw damn stones, it's best not to live in a glass house," I sincerely spoke, causing his expression to harden right before my eyes. "Creed loves me."

"You'd be hard to not love, pretty girl." He leaned over, placing a loose strand of hair behind my ear.

I jerked back, moving away from him. "You can't say shit like that to me. It's not right."

"Right for who? Creed? He ain't here now, is he? I am. Sittin' in front of you. Tellin' you I want you on the back of my fuckin' bike. I had you first, Mia, and I know you may not love me, but you sure as fuck have feelings for me. Try to deny it, I fuckin' dare you."

I sighed, dumbfounded by the turn of events. I would be lying if I said I didn't care about Noah. I did, very much so. He was the father of my unborn baby, how could I not. "Rebel, I know you're going to be an amazing daddy, and I can't tell you how grateful and lucky I am that you want to do right by her, but—"

"I wanna do right by you, too."

"Then back off," I let out harshly. My emotions started to get the best of me.

"What if I don't? Huh? What are you gonna do? I'm the father of your child. We made a baby, I ain't goin' anywhere. I owe it to our girl to fight for her momma, and not even you can fuckin' stop me."

I tried to remain calm, remembering the Jameson men were as stubborn as mules. "Listen, okay? I care about you a lot. I will admit that. And maybe in a way, I do have feelings for you, but it's nowhere near what I feel for Creed. Do you understand that? Maybe in another life or another time, it would have been different, but in this life, in this time… I'm your brother's. And I'm not going to apologize for that." The air grew so thick between us. I was surprised I could still see him through the dense fog filling the small space. I didn't want to hurt him. That was the last thing I wanted to do. I reached over and grabbed his hand, placing it on my belly. "We're both in this for the long run." Gesturing toward my stomach. "No one is ever going to take that away from you. You're her father. Always and forever. I'll never keep her from you. I promise you that. I give you my word."

As if on cue, baby girl kicked, making Noah and me laugh. I was glad she chose that moment to break up the tension that filled the entire room. There were no more words to be had after that, when there were probably hundreds that should have been spoken. We spent the rest of the afternoon watching movies on the couch, laughing and eating popcorn, but my thoughts never drifted far from Creed. And as much as I wanted to pretend that this was the end of our compromising situation. I knew Noah's mind never drifted far from…

Me.

M. Robinson

I took one last drag of my cigarette, stubbing it out on the side of the safe house, flicking it out to the front yard. Mia told me some shit about always making sure I put out my cigs before throwing them into the woods. Rambling on about needing to prevent forest fires. A fucking bear named Smokey taught her that in school when she was younger. I looked at her like she was fucking crazy, reminding her that bears didn't talk.

I don't know where she came up with half the shit that left her mouth, but I loved her nonetheless. I chuckled to myself, remembering the morning I was teasing her about sleeping on me instead of on the bed. She responded with some more shit about us being fucking lobsters. Mating for life. Trying to convince me that was how they slept. Saying her Aunt Lily had been telling her that story all her life, and that she needed to find her own lobster one day.

So, I guess I was her fucking lobster. Whatever the hell that was supposed to mean.

I nodded over at the two brothers who were standing guard outside, before opening the front door to the safe house.

"Hey!" Mia called out from the couch when she saw me walking in. "You actually came back during daylight. This is new. I was beginning to think you were only nocturnal." She smiled, walking over to where I stood. Rising up on the tips of her toes to kiss me. "I like it."

"I fuckin' missed you."

"I missed you, too."

I hadn't seen her in a few days, too many for my liking.

It had been well over a month and a half since she'd gone missing. Nothing had changed back at the clubhouse, same ol' shit different day. We continued to run in circles, heading down the same road to nowhere. Watching over our shoulders everywhere we went, just waiting for more bullshit to occur.

I kept thinking about the cryptic text message Martinez had sent me the day he died. But to be honest, I was so consumed with the situation at hand that I had no time to actually put any effort into it. As soon as I knew Mia was out of harm's way, you best believe I'd be getting to the fucking bottom of it. There was a reason he sent me that compromising photo of my ma. I just needed to take some time and look at the disc he gave me. I had a feeling I wasn't going to fucking like what I saw.

Mia's parents' still held onto the hope that their baby girl would be found, safe and sound. Organizing search parties, holding town meetings, and spreading missing person signs up all over the nearby counties.

I hated walking into the convenience stores, seeing Mia's face plastered all over the registers. Only reminding me she didn't deserve this. Detective McGraw was more relentless than ever, still sticking his nose where it didn't fucking belong. If it wasn't for Mia considering him as family, I would have put him to ground already. He was a cocky son of a bitch who rubbed me the wrong way one too many times. The more time I spent at the clubhouse, the more I realized this was no fucking place for Mia to be hanging out.

Especially with a baby girl.

The club's normal activities were worse now than ever. The boys were getting restless, their minds focused solely on figuring out what the hell was going on and who wanted our fucking turf. Club whores, drugs, and booze were the only way we'd ever blown off steam. I never stayed more than I had to anymore. Foregoing the festivities. Taking care of club business and coming back to Mia was the only thing on my mind these days.

"I'm fuckin' filthy. Need a shower, babe. Don't get too close."

"I don't care. I'll take you any way I can, Creed Jameson. I'll even join you in the shower."

"Is that right? You like it when I make you nice and dirty, Mia Savannah Ryder?"

She gave me a questioning look. "How did you know my midd—"

I kissed her, throwing my backpack to the ground, picking her up by her ass so she could straddle my waist. "Pippin, how you smell so fuckin' good all the time?" She giggled in that cute-as-shit sort of way when I started to rub my facial hair all over her neck. I hadn't been shaving lately, no time. "Who's my girl?"

She melted in my arms as I carried her back to my room, spending the rest of the morning proving to her that she was. Not giving a damn about what Noah said on the porch. She was *my* girl, and I wanted to fuck her.

So, I did.

"I was going to do my laundry today. I don't have any more clean clothes here," Mia informed, coming out of the bathroom. Walking around my room with a towel wrapped around her, while I threw on a pair of clean jeans.

Foregoing a shirt.

"Grab one of my shirts from the dresser and meet me in the kitchen so you can make me a sandwich."

"Excuse me, I didn't hear a please in that sentence."

I grinned, pecking her lips. "If I was gonna say please, might as well do it myself." I spanked her ass, and she yelped. "Feed your man, he's fuckin' starvin'."

"Okay." She nodded, side stepping me. "I'll go find him."

I chuckled, gripping onto the back of her towel. Tugging her against my chest, I wrapped my arms around her from behind. "You mad cuz I didn't say yeah?"

"Yeah isn't a please," she sassed, trying to block off my attempt to tickle her neck with my beard.

"But look at ya. Already barefoot and pregnant, just how I want you. Now make me a fuckin' sandwich, *yeah*?"

"You're such a barbarian!" she laughed, swatting me away. Her weak efforts to get free were no match for me.

I spanked her ass again, letting her go. "And it's why you fuckin' love me."

She rolled her eyes, shaking her head as she walked over to my dresser. I left to go wait for my sandwich in the kitchen. It didn't take long for her to find me sitting at the island, looking sexy as sin with my shirt on. Her perky tits showing through the white fabric that fell just above her knees. I made a mental note to have her wear my clothes more often.

"What's this?" she asked, trying to hide her amused expression. Throwing a bunch of baby magazines on the counter, right in front of where I sat. "Found them in your drawer when I was grabbing one of your shirts."

"Brought these back for us. Thought we could find some baby shit together."

She smiled wide, her face beaming. "I'd love that. I'll go make you your sandwich first." Stepping in between my legs, she threw her arms around my neck and whispered against my lips, "I'll even throw in some French fries and a milkshake."

I kissed her. "Good to know ya came to your senses and realized your place, woman," I joked.

But not really.

I swear he loved trying to get a rise out of me. Although he was right, I did love him, barbarian and all. There was something about his way with words that I found sexy. He was crude, vulgar, and said what he felt or thought, no matter what.

But he was one hell of a man.

My man.

I made him lunch, deciding to make some for myself, as well. Baby girl was starving. She had the appetite of her daddy and Creed. Most of the food would always be gone because of them, even though they weren't around every day like I was. They reminded me a lot of Mason and Bo. Momma was constantly stocking our cabinets, yelling about them eating us out of house and home.

I set the knife down on the counter, feeling a sharp pain in my chest. My heart breaking into a million pieces at the mere thought of my family, again. I missed them so much, and each day away from them became far worse than the day before. It didn't help that I knew they were worried sick. No parent should ever have to go through this.

I placed my hand on my belly, imagining myself in their shoes. How awful it would be to lose a child and not have any idea where they were or how to find them. How to bring them back home safely. I prayed every night that they still felt my presence, knowing I was still alive and not dead in a ditch somewhere. Hoping it would at least give them some peace when there wasn't any to be had.

I shook off the haunting thoughts and pain in my heart, focusing on lunch. Trying to suppress the ache as best as I could. It probably didn't help that Noah hadn't been coming around as often as before, either. I knew he was trying to keep his distance from me like I requested. But I didn't mean for him to not come around at all. It made me sad just thinking about it. I didn't like being the cause of another person's pain.

"Pippin, why don't ya tell me some of your favorite things so I can try to bring 'em back for you," Creed remarked, pulling me away from yet another plaguing thought.

I spun around, glancing back at him from the stove. He was looking down at one of the baby magazines, flipping the pages with a marker in his hand.

"What?" I questioned, caught off guard by what he was doing.

"You heard me," he simply stated, flipping another page.

"What kind of things?"

"Just some of your favorite shit." He shrugged, still not looking up at me, marking something down on one of the pages in the magazine.

What was he doing? "Like what? Give me some direction."

"Favorite books, movies, food, lotion for your belly—shit like that. Anythin' to make the time go by faster for you and baby girl. Know you been gettin' restless and don't fuckin' blame ya."

"Lotion for my belly? How do you know about pregnant women putting lotion on their bellies?"

"Read it in one of these magazines."

"You read that tidbit right now?"

"Ain't got all fuckin' day, Pippin, out with it," he asserted in a neutral tone, ignoring my question.

"Okay…" I grabbed our food off the counter, setting his plate in front of him. He didn't waste any time, picking up his sandwich and taking a huge bite. His eyes never wavered from the pages of the magazine.

I finished preparing our milkshakes, deciding to stay standing on the other side of the island to eat. So I could nonchalantly get a better look at what he was doing. "My favorite books are anything in the romance genre, pretty much, especially historical romances. I guess you could say I love the old-school heroes who were in charge of everything. Alpha male types who were dominant and demanding. Kind of assholes with hearts of gold, which is all that matters."

He hid his grin, placing the straw between his lips and sucking down his milkshake.

"The Bronze Horseman are my all-time favorite books, they're a trilogy… but uh… do you like to read?" I casually asked. Noah's words echoed in my mind about not knowing a thing about him. Silently hoping he would answer my question and not disregard it again.

"When it interests me."

Out of the corner of my eye, the Parenting 101 magazine beside him, caught my attention. My stare wandered from one magazine to the next, noticing for the first time that all the bindings were worn, and the pages were somewhat crinkled.

I bit down on my lower lip, suppressing a squeal. Excitement bubbled from deep within me. About to erupt like an active volcano. These weren't new, at least not for him. He'd read them before bringing them to me. My eyes immediately went back to the magazine lying open in front of him, finally realizing what he was jotting down. It wasn't a magazine he was gazing at this whole time. It was a Babies R Us catalog. He was circling the things he liked—furniture, toys, and anything else that interested him.

My heart melted at the sight of him. The initiative he had, planning for baby girl's arrival. I wanted to go over to him and tackle him to the ground. But I stayed put, mentally biting my tongue. If I called him out on it, he would stop. I'd embarrass him.

He was trying to play it off like it wasn't a big deal. As if what he was doing didn't mean anything to me.

When it meant everything.

"So, what other shit you like to do, besides surfin'?"

"Oh! I love that crib!" I blurted after he circled it.

He nodded, not paying me any mind. "Figured you would since your favorite color is pink. Baby girl will prolly love pink, too. Just keep it in her room, yeah? Don't want our place to turn into a fuckin' playroom."

I jerked back, confused. "Our place?"

He set the marker down, leaned back on the barstool, and pulled something shiny out of his jean pocket. "Come here," he ordered, finally peering up at me with an expression I couldn't read.

I did, rounding the island till I was close enough for him to grab my hand. He pulled me in between his legs, caging me with his arms placed on the granite behind me.

"The clubhouse ain't no place for a baby girl to be runnin' around. Screamin', hollerin', fuckin' playin'. Ma's house will always be my home, but it ain't ours. Ya feel me?"

"Yes."

"Good." He softly kissed me. "Got us a place, a house on the water so you can surf whenever you want. It's near your parents' place, but not too close that they become a bigger pain in my ass. Hoping maybe one day they will accept me, but don't hold it against them if they never do. I wouldn't want my baby girl with a fuckin' biker, either. But I'm tryin', Mia. Wanna change for you, have changed for you. Time to start a life with you and baby girl. I know I ain't the biological father, but it don't matter. She's mine, too. Already love her like she's my own. I wanna be the man you deserve, babe."

My eyes watered with tears.

"I know you're young, but from the second I met you, you've been wiser beyond your years. Often puttin' me in my place, only person I ever let do that," he chuckled, rubbing the tip of his nose back and forth on mine before he pulled away, staring me deep in the eyes. "You got your whole life ahead of ya, and if you'll take me, I'll spend each one of those fuckin' days by your side. Protectin' you, cherishin' you, and lovin' you. Grateful as fuck you let me."

"Oh my God, Creed, are you propos—"

"No, I'm doin' somethin' that means more to me than that. Somethin' I never thought I'd fuckin' do," he interrupted, reaching around to grab his cut from the back of the barstool. Handing it to me with a huge grin on his face.

I took it in my hands, noticing it was much smaller than the one he wore. My eyes widened as soon as I took in the embroidered stitching on the back.

"Property of Creed," I read out loud, locking eyes with him.

"This is *your* cut. You wear this and everyone knows you're mine. No one fucks with you, unless they wanna fuck with me. And trust me, babe, no one wants to fuck with me." He grabbed the black leather from me, turned it around, and laid it on the counter. Nodding to the front side. "Added some patches, too."

"Love the life you live. Live the life you love," I recited one of them, moving onto the next. "Despite the look on my face, you're still talking," I laughed, while he wiped away some of my happy tears. "La la la I'm not listening." He grinned when he saw me eyeing the last few. "A women's place is on her man's face," I huffed, shaking my head, moving on to another. "Don't mess with a biker's old lady, unless you want to die."

He smiled wide. "That one's my favorite."

"Of course it would be," I giggled, reading the last patch. "Don't even look at me. My biker is VP."

There were no words to express how I felt in that moment, especially when I read the patch *Pippin* where my name should be. My mind drifted to the night I went to the party at the clubhouse, remembering how I saw some women wearing cuts. Never imagining I would be one of them in my lifetime. I now understood why none of the brothers were looking at them the way they did with the other women. They were already taken.

This was the MC's wedding ring.

"So this means you're officially claimin' me?"

"Baby, I claimed you the day you were born. You were made for me."

I threw my arms around him, kissing all over his face. His words hit me in the feels, consuming every fiber of my being. I couldn't believe this was happening. It was all I ever wanted, for as long as I could remember.

He abruptly stood, taking me with him. Lifting me up like I weighed nothing, wrapping my legs around his waist. Walking us back to his room.

"I like to be outside, feel the sun, the breeze, the air all around me. It's what I like to do other than surfing," I answered his question from earlier in between kissing his face. "What about you? What's your favorite thing to do?"

He kicked the door shut behind him, laying me down on the bed and hovered above me. Looking deep into my eyes, he said, "You, Mia. Bein' with you is my favorite fuckin' thing to do."

And with that, he handed me the key to the new house that he bought for us, so I would love him more than I already did.

Mia was now in her third trimester, seven months pregnant and popping. It was like baby girl decided to grow double in size in only a few weeks time. I left for a few days and came back to a very pregnant Mia. She was still cute-as-shit, fucking adorable, walking around with this basketball under her shirt, or at least that's what it looked like to me. Mia was all belly. You couldn't even tell she was pregnant unless she turned to the side.

The season changed over to fall, and it began to get a little colder outside some days. Her clothes were no longer fitting as comfortably as they were before, and I couldn't take her shopping to see what fit, so we made due. She just started wearing my sweatshirt or long sleeved shirts. It wasn't like she had anywhere to go or anyone to impress.

She drowned in my clothes, barely being able to tell she was even pregnant anymore. I fucking loved it. Seeing her waddling around, wearing my things. I always made sure I took something with me when I left, so I'd have something to remind me of her since her addicting scent lingered in the fabric. Offering time and time again to try and bring her back some maternity clothes when I left, but she refused, saying my things were perfect. All she wanted was for me to come back home to her safely.

I hated that she started to think of this place as her home. Especially because of the reason she was there in the first place, for the last two months. I let it slide, playing it off when I was around her. Not wanting to add to the grief that I knew she already carried.

"Hey," Diesel greeted, standing guard outside the safe house. Watching me walk up. "You're here early."

I nodded to him. "Why don't you and Taz take off for a while. Got some business to handle with Mia."

"Everything alright?"

"I'd tell you if it wasn't."

"Alright. We'll be back later tonight. After dark enough time for you to handle your woman?"

"Should be. I'll let ya know otherwise if anythin' changes."

"Alright. Be gentle, bro." He winked, nudging my shoulder as he walked away with Taz.

I took a deep breath, standing on the porch, staring at the front door after they left. Trying to gather my thoughts before entering the safe house. This relationship shit was such new territory for me, but I wanted to make Mia happy. She was such an amazing woman and deserved a man who could put his pride and ego aside. Even if it was only for a few hours, just to give her what she obviously craved.

Women always said men were complicated, but they couldn't have been more fucking wrong. Men were easy—we wanted to be fed and we wanted pussy, that's it. As long as our woman kept our stomach's full and our ball's empty, we were fucking golden. Everything else was just an added bonus.

Women were a fucking paradox of contradictions. Mia's hormones were all over the place. One minute she was happy and the next she was crying over the stupidest shit, like a commercial on TV or a line she read in one of her books. Her emotions were a roller coaster and I was riding along, holding on for dear fucking life. Sometimes I could barely keep up.

I used to laugh at the brothers when it came to their old ladies. Badass bikers turned into pussy-whipped bitches, and here I was doing whatever it took to make Mia smile. To make her laugh. To make her happy.

To keep her in love with me.

She glanced up from her book when she heard me walk in. "Have I told you how much I love you coming back early?"

I set some bags down on the coffee table and took a seat beside her, pulling her onto my lap. She came effortlessly, straddling my waist, leaving enough room for her growing belly. I grabbed her chin, bringing her pouty lips over to meet mine, kissing her like I hadn't seen her in months. She moaned, reaching for my belt buckle.

But I caught her wrist at the last second, softly pecking her lips one last time. "Got plenty of time for that later."

"You're passing up sex? Creed Jameson, are you feeling okay?" she giggled as she pulled away, sitting up straight. "What's in there?" she questioned, pointing over her shoulder at the shopping bags. "Your momma make me some more food? Baby girl has been feigning for her apple pie."

"I bought you a lil' somethin'."

"Oh yeah?"

"Grab the gray bag."

She reached behind her, picking up the lightweight bag, and placed it in between the baby and me. Her eyes glazed over when she pulled out the cream dress.

"Thought of you when I rode past a mannequin, wearin' it in the window at one of those fancy shops downtown."

"It's beautiful. I can't wait to wear it when we can go out some day. Thank you, I love it."

"Wear it for me."

"Now?" she asked, confused. Looking around the room.

"Yeah, babe. Go get all dolled up for me."

She smirked, placing the dress back into the bag. "I can do that."

I watched her prance out of the living room, waiting till she was out of sight before grabbing the rest of the bags. Getting started on what I had to do. Thinking how fucking perfect Mia was going to look the entire time I was working. She had no clue that I hid makeup in the bottom of the bag, as well. Not that she needed it. She was flawless, naturally beautiful, but I knew she missed all that girly shit. Dressing up in something other than my clothes. Doing her hair and makeup for the first time in months, making her feel somewhat human again.

I spent most of my morning at the department store, trying to figure out what the hell was on the displays. There was too much to choose from. Silently questioning if women really used this much shit on their faces. No wonder it took them so fucking long to get ready. Thank God for the older lady behind the counter, who noticed I was getting frustrated with the endless supply of who the fuck knows what.

Finally, walking out with just the basics.

After spending thirty minutes, getting everything set for Mia, I spent another thirty minutes on the couch, waiting for her to emerge. I knew girls took fucking forever to get ready, but this was getting ridiculous. I waited another twenty minutes. Flipping through some of her gossip magazines she had laying around before I decided to forego this waiting bullshit. Walking back to my bedroom to see what the hold-up was all about, instead.

"Mia!" I called out, knocking on the bathroom door. "Everythin' alright in there?"

"Yeah! Just… Just…" She sounded like she was crying. "Give me a few more minutes!"

"Babe, I'm—" I started opening the door.

"NO! Don't come in here!"

"The fuck?" I whispered to myself, opening the door anyway. Completely caught off guard by what I walked in on.

She was soaking wet, standing naked in the bathtub. Her legs covered in shaving cream and a razor in her hand. "I told you not to come in here," she choked out, instantly covering her tits with her arms.

"Pippin, ain't nothin' new. I've seen them," I said, gesturing to her breasts.

She blushed, her eyes watering with fresh tears. "I didn't want you to see me like this."

"Mia, what's goin' on?"

She sank back into the bathtub, fidgeting with the razor in her hands, not looking at me. "I just can't…" she whispered out the rest of her sentence so low, I couldn't hear what she said.

"Gotta speak up, babe, can't read lips."

She sighed with tears streaming down her pretty face. "I can't shave … by myself, anymore. I'm too big… It's too hard… My belly won't… it won't let me bend over…" she let it out, speaking in

the saddest voice I'd ever heard. "I'm sorry. I know this isn't sexy…
I just wanted to look perfect for you… but I'm fat…"

It broke my heart seeing her so weak over something so
unimportant to me. I knew it was against her nature. Mia was one of
the strongest women I'd ever met.

She'd have to be, to put up with me.

I was over to her in three steady strides, grabbing the razor out of
her hand and helping her up out of the water. "Park that sweet little
ass of yours on the back ledge of the tub for me, babe."

She sniffled, wiping away her tears with the back of her hand.
Doing what she was told. I crouched down at the side of the tub and
reached into the soapy bath water, grabbing her foot. Propping it up
on the edge in front of me. She watched with curious eyes, as I
gathered suds from the water in my hands and slid them down her
soft, silky skin. Getting her leg prepped, again.

Her lips parted, sucking in air, when I placed the razor to her
ankle, gently gliding it up to her knee. Being careful not to cut her.

"Only gonna say this one fuckin' time." I stopped shaving her
leg so I could look at her. "You're perfect, Mia. Always have been,
always will be. I'm here for you no matter what… To shave you,
bathe you, or fuck you," I paused, smiling. Trying to get her to
laugh, earning me a smirk, instead. I leaned forward, grinning
against her mouth, rasping, "And just so you know… I'm hard as
fuck right now. Been hard since I saw you standin' there wet,
glowin', all fuckin' delicious. Don't ever let me hear you say your
fat, again. I'll take ya over my knee and spank that little fuckin' ass.
You're the sexiest woman I ever laid eyes on, big belly and all. Ya
feel me?"

She bit her lip, nodding. More tears falling down her cheeks.
This time I wiped them away with my thumbs. "I ask myself every
fuckin' day how I got so goddamn lucky. You're my everythin',
babe. Can't imagine my life without you in it. I love you."

I kissed her and went back to my task at hand. Mia blushed the
entire time, and I couldn't help but love being able to do this for her.
Feeling as though I was a part of her pregnancy, if that made any
sense. When I was done shaving her all over, I spread her legs open
and ate her pussy like a starving fucking man, unable to resist her

naked body any longer. It helped, making Mia more comfortable and relaxed again. My touch consistently had that effect on her.

I would always take care of my girl.

In every sense of the word.

Creed helped me out of the tub after he finished giving me a mind-blowing orgasm with his mouth. Wrapping a towel around my shivering body to warm me up. He offered to dress me, too, but I declined. Telling him I could handle it. Truth be told, I really just needed a few minutes to myself. I couldn't believe what he'd done for me. It was more intimate than anything we'd ever shared together, more than anything I'd ever shared with anyone. I always knew there were several sides to him. Though I never imagined, he could be like this…

With me.

There were no words to express how I felt in that moment, in that second, in that instant…

With him.

There were never any gray areas with Creed. No maybes. It was either black or white, yes or no. It took me until that day to realize I was his gray area. I was the maybe. He really would do anything for me, and I didn't understand why it took something so minuscule to prove it. He had been showing me since the first day I met him and every day after.

Pushing me away, time and time again.

Having to say goodbye before he went into the military, and taking my courage patch with him.

Talking to me at the lake, when I needed a friend.

Giving me my first kiss.

And every other time that followed…

His actions always contradicted his words. And now his words belonged to me. I think this was the turning point in our relationship, where I truly knew he was mine.

He'd always been mine.

He was leaning against the front door with his arms crossed over his chest, when I walked into the living room. Fully dressed for him with my hair and makeup all done up. He looked me up and down, taking in every last inch of my body, from head to toe. Staring at me, igniting a feeling deep within my body, the only way Creed ever could.

"There's my girl," he declared, reaching his hand out for me to take.

"How did you know my size?" I asked, referring to the dress that fit me perfect. I grabbed a hold of his hand and he instantly twirled me around in a circle, like one of those ballerinas in a jewelry box. Looking at me in a way I had never witnessed before. "Are we dancing? You taking me dancing?"

"Don't dance, Pippin," he gruffed out, continuing to twirl me around, pulling me back and spinning then forward. The look on his face as he watched me never changed, if anything it got more intense.

"You're dancing right now."

"*You're* dancin' right now."

I rolled my eyes. "And the makeup? That must have been quite a sight. Big badass biker, shopping around for me. The women in the boutique must have loved that."

He shrugged it off. "Babe, I was like one of those fuckin' heroes in the smut books you read. Jaws dropped and panties melted." He tugged me into his torso and kissed my lips. "Now close your eyes."

"It's not smut if it has a storyline." I cunningly smiled against his lips. "You're not going to kidnap me again, are you?"

"Can't kidnap what's already yours."

I laughed, closing my eyes. Impatiently waiting for what was to come. I heard the front door open as he took my hand, guiding me to walk forward. Following as close as I could to his warm body. Overthinking the possibilities of what he had planned in my mind when I suddenly felt him shift. He let go of my hand, moving to stand behind me, wrapping his arms around my shoulders, and pulling me close to his chest.

"Open them," he whispered close to my ear.

My eyes fluttered open, adjusting to the bright light. We were outside, the fresh air and cold breeze hit all my senses. It had been

95

months since I felt the outdoors. The sun on my face. The grass beneath my feet. Creed had made a picnic outside of the safe house, in the woods. Overlooking the gorgeous sun and riverbank situated out in front of us. The breathtaking greenery, the autumn colors, and leaves that were now falling from the trees. The view looked like a postcard.

"I can't believe you did all this," I said, trying to hold back the tears.

"Consider this our first date." He kissed my neck, leaving me in shock to go sit on the blanket.

I stood there dumbfounded for I don't know how long, taking in my surroundings before sitting down next to him. Noticing all my favorite foods, desserts and even my favorite thing to drink, lined the center of our blanket. My guitar leaning up against a tree. I had mentioned I missed playing it.

"I have no words, Creed. You have officially outdone yourself."

"You can thank me later." He winked, throwing a chocolate covered strawberry in his mouth. "It's a nice fall day. Didn't want to waste it."

"It feels amazing to be outside. God, it feels like forever since I felt the sun on my skin."

"When this all blows over, you can lay out naked by the pool at our house, for as long as you want. It can be my new favorite thing."

I chuckled, resisting the urge to ask him how much longer he planned to keep me captive. I didn't want to ruin the moment. He had put a lot of thought and effort into this date, and I couldn't have been more grateful.

We spent the next few hours eating, laughing, talking about anything and everything. Learning all sorts of new things about each other. At one point he handed me my guitar. He asked me to play for him, he knew that I never played for people, blame it on stage fright, he said he wanted a part of me that nobody had before. I grabbed it and started to strum the strings to the melody of "Foolish Games," by Jewel. A song that made me thing of him through the years. He sat there watching me with a fascinated look in his eyes, as I poured my heart out to him through the lyrics. Knowing I had never played for anyone before.

Time just flew by, and before I knew it, I was leaning against his chest, watching the sunset behind the trees.

"I talked to Mason," he said out of nowhere.

I abruptly turned around to face him. "What do you mean? When? He's alright then?"

"Yeah, Pippin, he's fine. He was just sent on a mission off the grid. Ain't too fuckin' happy with me, though," he scoffed, taking a swig of his beer.

"Why? You didn't do anything."

"Didn't watch out for you."

I jerked back. "What?"

"Promised him I'd watch out for you, after I was discharged."

"You did?"

He nodded, drinking again.

"But I... Noah and I... I mean... you were still in the military."

"Ain't got shit to do with you and Noah, but he ain't too fuckin' thrilled about that situation either." He looked me over. "You forget you're missin', Mia?"

"Oh... So, he knows I'm pregnant?"

"Yes. It's aiight. I can handle Mason. Just wanted you to know he's safe."

"And... my parents'? Did he say anything about them? How are they doing?" I coaxed in a gentle tone.

"How you think? Hmm?" he countered, tugging on the ends of my hair.

"Yeah..." I breathed out, finally mustering up the courage to ask, "What's going to happen when I go home, Creed? What am I supposed to tell my family? The cops? Everyone is going to want to know where I've been for the last... however long I end up staying here."

"You don't think I know that? What did you want me to do? Leave ya there. Back in Oak Island, let you be a sittin' fuckin' duck? An easy fuckin' target? Couldn't do it, babe. Against my fuckin' nature, ta not protect the ones I love. It's who I am. Knowin' that your family could fuckin' hate me cuz of this, well it was a risk I was more than willin' to fuckin' take. In fact, I'd do it again if I had to."

"They won't hate you."

97

"Yeah? You sure about that? They already think I'm fuckin' biker trash. A low life piece of shit from the wrong side of the tracks. Don't blame them either. Like I said before, I wouldn't want my baby girl with the likes of me either. But can't let you go, Mia. As you know... I've already fuckin' tried," he reminded me, taking another swig of his beer.

I smiled, sitting up on my knees in front of him, grabbing the beer out of his hand and placing it on the ground beside us. Throwing my arms around his neck for support as I straddled his waist. His legs went lax under me to allow more room for my belly. I snuggled my face close to his for a few seconds, resting my forehead against his when I was done.

"No one is going to hate you, because I won't let them. And you know how persuasive I can be. I always get what I want, or else you wouldn't be mine now."

He smiled, wrapping his arms around me. Pulling me closer. "See... that's where you're fuckin' wrong, Pippin, cuz I've always been yours."

And for the first time since I met him.

I knew his words were true.

"Baby girl is measurin' right at thirty-two weeks. She's approximately three and a half pounds right now," Doc informed, measuring from the top of my belly to my pelvic area. Then proceeded to push all around, making the baby wiggle inside me. "She's completely flipped, head's down going into your birth canal."

"Oh! That's why her feet are always in my ribs," I replied, looking over at Noah.

Creed was leaning against the doorframe to his room, allowing Noah to stand beside me. I was lying on the bed, while Doc examined my growing belly. I knew Creed wanted to be the one by my side, but he was respecting Noah and our situation. Noah had been coming around more often, now that I was closer to my due date. Acting as if nothing had happened between us, all the tension magically disappearing. We went back to being friends, talking about how we were going to make this work. Wanting to be the best parents we could to our child.

"Baby girl is growin' fast, Mia. Only about eight weeks to go, maybe sooner. You guys think of a name for her, yet?" Doc questioned, looking from me to Noah, and back to me again.

"I have a name in mind. Actually, it was your momma who gave it to me," I informed Noah. "What do you think about Madison? Can we call her Maddie for short? It means gift of God."

Noah sat on the bed, placing his hand over my bare stomach, gently rubbing it all around. I didn't have to look over at Creed to see the sad expression that would be staring back at me. I could feel it.

"What do you think, baby girl?" Noah leaned in, placing his lips close to my belly. "You like the name, Madison?"

As if on cue, she kicked Noah, making us both laugh. She was already so smart. He smiled, looking down at my belly with nothing but a loving look in his eyes.

"I think that was a yes."

"Madison it is then. I can't wait to meet you, hold you, and be your daddy," Noah addressed, talking to her. Following her movement with his hands.

He crouched down further, leaning in closer, with his lips inches away from my skin. His breath stirring the same emotions inside of me as he did that night. I swallowed hard, overcome by the sentiment from his simple touch. Fully aware we weren't alone this time. Something made me peer back at Creed.

We locked eyes.

Knowing he could feel it, too. He knew.

"You're the best thing that's ever happened to me, Maddie," Noah added, bringing my attention back to him. "You and your momma." With that he kissed my stomach, allowing his lips to linger for a few moments. "I already love you, so much," he murmured to my belly before he pulled away, standing up beside me again. His eyes were glossy with tears, but he quickly blinked them away. Shaking his head and clearing his throat.

The room fell silent for what felt like forever. Suddenly there was a huge elephant in the room, no one was going to address.

Especially me.

Doc pulled my shirt back down when he was done. "Pregnancy suits you, Mia. There are very few women who are still glowin' at this point. It's a good sign, means Madison won't be too much trouble. Which is surprisin' considering her bloodlines," he joked, trying to break the strain in the room.

I couldn't have been more appreciative of him for that.

"It's been easy for the most part," I sincerely answered, caressing my belly. "Other than being a little more tired than usual, she's been good to me. I'm going to miss having her in my belly, though. Feeling her kicking inside me, flipping around. It's the most amazing sensation."

"Just means I gotta knock you up again, Pippin," Creed vowed, speaking for the first time since my check-up started.

Noah narrowed his eyes at him, earning him a grin in return.

"How about we let Mia get dressed," Doc ordered, winking at me. He gathered up his things and placed them in the black doctor bag by his side he always brought with him.

Since I was in my last trimester, he started stocking up the safe house with everything he'd need to deliver the baby. Including medications, fluids, and a bunch of weird looking instruments.

The boys nodded, walking toward the door and following Doc out. I closed my eyes, taking a deep breath when I heard the door close behind them.

"Penny for your thoughts?"

My eyes flew open, startled by Creed's voice. Instantly looking in the direction it came from. He was leaning against the closed door, his arms folded over his chest. Eyeing me with a broody regard. I sat up, flinging the sheet off my body, reaching to grab my panties and yoga pants off the dresser.

He pushed off the door, walking over to me. Snatching my clothes before I could, he kneeled down in front of me and took a hold of my foot. I smiled as he helped me get dressed, knowing I was getting too big to do so by myself.

"Thank you," I let out when he was finished. Standing face to face.

He grabbed my chin, making me look up at him. "Asked you a question, expectin' an answer."

"Sounded more like a statement to me."

"Mia…"

I pulled away. "I have to take the chicken out of the oven before it burns. Doc is staying for dinner, and I told your brothers they could come inside to eat, too. I don't want to feed ten people burnt food. And since you like to remind me that my place is in the kitchen, cooking your meals, then you should probably let me go do that," I stated, giving him a curt nod. Sidestepping him to leave, but he caught my arm.

"This ain't over."

"I wouldn't dream of it." He let go but spanked my ass hard as I walked by, causing me to yelp.

We all sat around the dining room table, eating dinner together, for the first time since I had been there. It was a nice change from dining alone most nights at the kitchen island. Creed and his brothers, including Noah, had such a family dynamic to them. Reminding me so much of my own, making me miss them even more. He once told me that the MC was considered a brotherhood. They looked out for each other. Had one another's backs, no matter what. Reminding me often, I was a part of their family now, because I was his woman.

And they protected their own.

I could finally see what he meant just by watching them together, and this was only a few of the brothers. I couldn't even imagine what it would be like to have the whole club in the same room.

Diesel cleared his throat, bringing everyone's attention to him. Raising his beer in the air, uttering, "I'd like to make a toast to Mia. For puttin' up with us foul-mouthed bikers, makin' this kickass fuckin' meal, and for handlin' this situation like a fuckin' pro. Not being a little bitch or a pain in our fuckin' asses."

I laughed, smiling wide. "And here I thought you didn't know my name."

He knowingly nodded, giving Creed a smart-ass look. "We were told to treat you like a lady, and even God understands, none of us know what the fuck that is. So, we decided to keep our mouths shut, instead. Wouldn't want to piss off lover boy over here."

Creed flipped him off.

They spent the next hour, telling me funny stories about the club, shooting the shit, and filling me in on the good times and fond memories. It was one of the best nights I had in the last two and a half months. I loved every second of it and was sad when it came to an end.

They all thanked me for the amazing home cooked meal when we were finished. Shocked when they started to help me clean up, loading their dirty dishes in the dishwasher and wiping down the table. Grabbing their beers and cigarettes, excusing themselves to go outside. Creed said something about them needing to have a word, whatever the hell that meant. He kissed me before he followed them out to the porch. I put away the leftovers, even though I knew they wouldn't last long. Not with Creed and Noah both in the house.

I sighed, smiling when I realized Doc had left his take-out bag that I made for him, on the counter. For the life of me, I couldn't figure out why he was still single. He was such a sweet man, had been since the day I met him. I had grown close to him in the last few months, he felt like an uncle.

I opened the front door and called out, "Hey, Doc! You forget something?" Holding up the food.

He laughed me off, setting his black bag in the side-by-side, and jogging toward me. I stepped off the porch on the side of the house so I could meet him half way.

"Man would forget his own head if it wasn't attached to his goddamn body," Diesel shouted from behind me.

"It's okay, I'm forgetful too." I handed him his bag. "I'm actually glad I have a second alone with you," I whispered loud enough for him to hear, even though the boys were several feet away from us, in front of the safe house. "I just wanted to thank you. You have no idea how much of a relief it's been to have you come by as much as you do. I will never be able to repay you for the peace of mind you have given me with my baby girl."

He placed his hand on my stomach. "Mia, for the first time in I don't know how long, I'm actually doin' somethin' good. It's been an honor to be part of your journey with Maddie. I can't wait to help you brin' her into this world."

I nodded, pulling him into a hug. He froze, not expecting my gesture.

"Doc, your old ass tryin' to hit on my girl?"

"Don't listen to him. He's just being Creed."

He finally relaxed, and I felt the tension release from his biceps as he hugged me back. "You better go inside, before you catch a cold," he murmured, reminding me of something my dad would say.

My momma always told me I had the ability to make people smile, to make them laugh. To make them feel whole when they might have been broken. She called it my special gift. Saying the world was surrounded by too much devastation, destruction, and despair—where bad things happened to good people every single day.

To people who didn't deserve it.

To people who didn't expect it.

And to some people…

Who did.

I refused to ever think like that. I wouldn't let evil taint me. Take me under. Allow it to consume my mind, my body, and especially my heart.

But I couldn't have been more wrong.

This would be the moment in my life where evil would win. It would prevail and destroy, conquer and succeed, setting the tracks in motion for the collision courses to hit head on.

My mind would be forever changed.

My body forever damaged.

My heart eternally broken.

As soon as I pulled away, I turned around, locking eyes with Creed. Except, this time he wasn't smiling back at me. He wasn't laughing. He was no longer the man I made whole. The man I spent years loving, praying he'd love me back, was gone. There was nothing but his regrets in between us, his truths bleeding out for all to see. It was the expression on his face that would forever haunt me. I'd never forget the look in his eyes, the moment he realized…

He was going to die.

The next few seconds played out in slow motion, as if this was just a figment of my imagination and not my reality of what loving a Jameson man would bring.

His world collided with mine, leaving nothing but destruction in its wake.

Where neither one of us would make it out, alive.

"NO!" Creed shouted with everything he had in him. "MIA, RUN!" he roared, an ear-piercing sound that resonated deep within his lungs, echoing off the trees and into the woods as he simultaneously pulled out his gun from the back of his jeans. Aiming it right for me, he didn't hesitate, pulling the trigger.

"Cree—" I stumbled forward, trying to remain upright.

I couldn't move.

I couldn't breathe.

More gunshots, more bullets, more chaos erupted all around me. Time stood still, or maybe it moved faster. Everything blended together. Nothing made sense.

I was there, but I wasn't.

My trembling hands moved down to my chest and stomach, shielding myself as best as I could while I staggered on my feet. Trying to regain my balance, swaying all over, on the verge of becoming one with the ground. My eyes blurred, my vision tunneled, darkness drew me in and out.

"GET HER OUT OF HERE!" I heard Noah scream, or it could have been Creed.

It all sounded the same—the panic, the voices, the lives that were being taken, collapsing to the ground. I made one last attempt, willing my feet to run. Gasping for air, struggling to stay standing, all while shades of copper flew inches away from my body. From my face.

From my life.

And my baby's.

"Cre-ed... He-ee-lllp m-eee..." I managed to sputter, reaching my hand out to no one. I suddenly fell backward as strong arms caught me in their grasp. Bringing my limp body to the hard ground with them. I thought they were Doc's.

"Baby, baby, baby... no, no, no..." he stammered, close to my face. "Stay with me. You fuckin' stay wit' me."

Through hooded eyes, I saw Creed above me. Covered in blood, in anguish, in hatred and despair.

It was only then I finally realized...

I'd been shot.

"What the fuck?" Diesel snapped, his eyes focusing on something behind me.

I spun around, following his stare. Narrowing my eyes, searching the dense woods just beyond Mia and Doc. Trying to locate what he saw. Never expecting what stared back at me.

Choices…

Everyone had them. Especially me.

Good.

Bad.

Right.

Wrong.

They were one in the same. I couldn't tell them apart anymore or maybe…

I never could.

My life had been defined by decisions. Most of which cost me my morality, and a man without a conscience was capable of anything.

Now.

Forever.

And every day in between.

I thought my life was forever fucking gone the moment that I killed Luke. Brutally ripping away everything I wanted to believe in. Everything I prayed to be true.

Violence was all I ever knew.

The blood on my hands was so fucking thick, it became part of my skin. Engrained so far deep into my pores that I was drenched in nothing but the lives I had taken.

Until I met Mia Ryder.

She was a woman to love. To cherish. To fucking claim.

She was mine.

I wanted to be a part of her world. Never wanting to bring her into ours. Trying so damn hard to separate the two, but failing fucking miserably. This was the moment life had fucking saved just for me.

It. Ended. Here.

What started with her.

Ended with her.

My heart dropped, my chest seized, and all the blood drained from my face when I saw the barrel of the rifle peering from behind the tree. Giving me no time to react, I was driven on pure instinct.

My past and my present collided, leaving no road for the future.

Mia turned around as if she felt my pain.

My agony.

My heart bleeding out for her.

"NO!" I yelled out as loud as I could, pulling out my gun from the back of my jeans. The desperation in my voice echoed through the woods, vibrating against my core. I screamed till nothing came out, my chest aching. Instantly tearing up my throat. "MIA, RUN!" I roared, lifting my gun, aiming it right in her path. Not thinking twice about pulling the fucking trigger as a shot simultaneously fired from the rifle in the woods.

I would never forget the look on her face when she saw the bullet leave the barrel of my gun, never hearing the shots fired from behind her.

"Cree—" Her whole body flew forward from the unexpected blow.

I froze, not believing the scene unfolding in front of me as casings continued to fly. For a second, it wasn't Mia's petrified expression staring back at me. Desperately penetrating my eyes. Searching for answers. Looking for help.

They were Luke's.

My chest heaved, unable to hold back my hammering heart any longer. I could hear the drone in my ears, loud and clear. Memories of that night came flooding back, attacking my mind and assaulting my senses. Making me feel as if I was still in the clubhouse.

Where I just murdered my brother.

"GET HER OUT OF HERE!" I heard Noah scream, pulling me back to reality, back to the safe house in the woods, where Mia was the one who had just been shot. This was far worse than the place my mind had wandered. Bullets were flying in every direction. All hell had broken loose, and war was upon us once again.

I ran.

I ran as fast as I fucking could to my girl.

Sprinting to get to her. Immediately opening fire, lacing anyone who crossed me. Bullets recoiled off the trees, where men were trying to take cover, including Doc. Shielding themselves as best as they could, returning fire. I felt a burning sting graze my shoulder, and then again at the side of my stomach. Blood flew everywhere, not knowing if it was theirs or mine. I didn't let that slow me down. An endless stream of bullets continued to fill the night air. Brothers running alongside me, trying to cover me so I could get to her. Knowing I only had one end in sight.

Adrenaline coursed through my veins, throbbing through my bloodstream. Taking over every last inch of my body. My heart continued to pound against my chest. My vision tunneled, watching as Mia's quivering hands protectively went straight to her chest and stomach. She lost her footing, trying to take a step toward me. Not noticing she wasn't going anywhere but side to side. Stumbling all over while blood continued to gush out of her pink shirt.

"Cre-ed... He-ee-lllp m-eee..." she faintly muttered, reaching out her hand as her body fell backward, her legs unable to hold her up any longer.

My arms went around her, catching her limp body before she fell to the hard ground. I laid her down in between my legs, holding her head in the crook of my arm. Rotating her toward me, immediately applying pressure to the middle of her back where she'd been shot. Blood gushed through her shirt, soaking my fingers. No matter how hard I tried, there was no fucking stopping it.

"Baby, baby, baby… no, no, no…" I stammered, close to her face. Finding it hard to breathe. Struggling to keep going. "Stay with me. You fuckin' stay wit' me."

She peered up through clouded eyes. Her stare focused only for a few seconds, seeing all the blood on my chest and neck. Her eyes unconsciously traveled down to my bloody hands.

She sucked in air, realizing for the first time she'd been shot. "Creed… I can't… I can't… please… Mad…deee…"

"It's okay, Pippin, I'm here. I'm right fuckin' here. But goddamn it, you stay wit' me! Ya hear me? Keep your eyes open, baby. Just keep your eyes fuckin' open for me!"

She heaved, trying to answer. Wanting to say something, needing me to understand, but she was suffocating from her own pain.

"FUCK! MIA! DOC!" Noah yelled from above me.

I gently wrapped my arms under her upper torso and legs, carrying her up against my chest. Shielding her from stray bullets. Being careful not to cause her any more distress. An unceasing amount of blood poured from her back. Seeping into every last fiber of my being.

"I got you! We got you! Get her fuckin' inside!" Noah shouted. "Doc will be right behind us! GO!"

I hauled ass with Noah and Diesel by my side, guns drawn, taking out the motherfuckers who did this. Covering me so I could get Mia to safety. I'd never been more fucking grateful for them in all my life. My world was caving in on me, my walls crumbling down. The floor felt like it was swallowing me whole as I ran into the safe house with Mia in my arms.

My guilt fucking eating me alive.

I cradled her to my chest, feeling her shaking so hard. "Mia, babe, I'm gonna lay you on the couch, okay? I gotta look at you. I need to stop the bleedin'."

"Madd—"

"I know, baby, I know. Maddie's gonna be okay. She's gonna be just fine. I promise. Nothin' gonna happen to baby girl," I murmured, trying to keep my voice from breaking. Holding back the emotions that were threatening to erupt, needing to stay fucking strong for her, for the baby, for my fucking brother.

My body shuddered, shaking as profusely as hers. I held her so tight, so close to my fucking heart. Needing to feel hers beat against mine. Reminding me she was still alive. I kissed her forehead, gently laying her on her side, her back facing the front of the couch. Propping her head up with a pillow, causing her to whimper from the sudden movement.

"Fuck, Creed! She looks—"

"Shut the fuck up! Don't you even fuckin' say it!" I snarled to Noah, who was pacing the room, raking his hands through his hair. Looking at me like his whole fucking world was held in my tight grasp.

"Shit! Man! Brothers are comin'! But we gotta get these motherfuckers before they haul fuckin' ass! They gotta fuckin' pay for this! I won't stop until I've put a fuckin' hole in each one of their goddamn heads!" Diesel seethed, keeping an eye out the window. "Doc's comin'!"

He opened the door as Doc backed up into the safe house, not ceasing fire until he was past the threshold. "Jesus fuckin' Christ!" he scoffed, slamming the door behind him. "What the fuck is goin' on? How do they know about this place? It's been your family's safe house for fuckin' decades. This is bullshit! And I smell a fuckin' traitor!"

"Doc!" I called out, bringing his attention to me. His eyes immediately shifted to Mia, convulsing on the couch. She was sweating profusely, her skin drenched and fucking pale. Turning bluer with every second that passed.

"Move!" Doc sprang into action, pushing me out of the way. His black medical bag was firmly placed in his hand. It was then I realized he went back for it, knowing I had seen him place it in his side-by-side before he walked to Mia.

Risking his own fucking life to save hers.

I moved out of his way, sitting near Mia's head. Placing it on my lap, wanting to provide her with any comfort I could.

"Doc's here, baby, he's gonna make you all better," I reassured with trembling lips, caressing her cheek with my knuckles. My eyes blurred with unshed tears, barely able to see the side of her beautiful face.

"Creeeed… pleeeaa—"

"Shhh... Mia, you need to save your strength, sweetheart. Madison needs you," Doc interrupted, cutting up the middle of her blood-soaked shirt with scissors.

My chest locked up when I took in the gaping bullet hole in the middle of her back, praying it didn't hit her spine. Doc quickly worked, checking her vitals, placing a cuff on her arm that inflated every few minutes to monitor her blood pressure. He then prepared a syringe, injecting the needle near the open wound. Immediately locking eyes with me when he was done, conscious of the fact that I knew what came next. His fingers dug into her flesh, looking for the bullet. Mia's back arched as she screamed out in pain.

The numbing medicine not being nearly enough.

"Shhh... baby, you're such a good girl. Such a good fuckin' girl," I soothed, hoping it didn't take long for him to find the metal.

We all waited on pins and needles until we finally heard Doc say, "Got it!" he celebrated, throwing it on the coffee table.

"Shit! They're runnin' for the woods!" Diesel informed, making me peer over at him. He eyed Noah and then me, waiting for me to make the call.

"You do what ya need to, but you fuckin' drag them back here. We need answers, and we need them right fuckin' now," I demanded, nodding to Noah to go with him.

He fervently shook his head no. Rage radiating off his body, matching my own. "Ain't leavin' her."

"You want 'em to get away with this?" I asked, gesturing to Mia. "Look at me, Noah!"

He reluctantly did.

"You're no good to her here. Go get the motherfuckers who did this, yeah? You do it for Mia. You fuckin' do it for your daughter!"

I could see him battling, struggling with an internal conflict within himself.

"Please..." I choked out, fighting with my own urge. I wouldn't leave my fucking girl, but that didn't stop the desire to make the motherfuckers pay, wreaking havoc on my soul.

Noah crouched down beside Mia, sweeping her hair away from her face, whispering near her ear. "You fight, Mia. You fuckin' fight for our baby girl, and I'm gonna go fight for you." Kissing her cheek, he stood. Staring at me with dark, dilated eyes, silently answering my plea. "Creed, I love he—"

"I know," I interrupted, not wanting to hear him say he loved her.

It was just too much to fucking bear right then and there.

Diesel ran back into the room with more artillery, throwing Noah a rifle. He caught it in the air, taking one last look at Mia before turning to leave. Following Diesel out. I didn't waver, gently placing Mia's head back on the pillow. Needing to deadbolt the door, using every goddamn lock. No one was getting in here, not unless it was over my dead fucking body.

Mia sucked in a few breaths, gasping for more air. Her chest heaved uncontrollably, seizing as her eyes began to flutter.

I rushed over to her. "Fuck, Doc!"

He finished the last suture, closing up her wound. Taping a large gauze pad in place over it. All of a sudden, a rush of blood flooded the couch from in between her legs. He immediately flipped her over onto her back, his hands dropped to the sides of her stomach. Instantly feeling around.

"Pleeeaassee, saaave herr… saaave… Madd…" Mia slurred.

Her eyes rolled to the back of her head.

Her body went lax.

And her head fell to the side.

Taking every last part of me…

With her.

"Bab—"

"Creed, it's alright. She just passed out. Her blood pressure and pulse are strong, but her injuries are fuckin' serious. Far worse than I fuckin' thought. She needs a hospital!"

"Hospital?! Have you taken a fuckin' look around? Brothers are still fuckin' dyin' out there! Even if they weren't, she'd die in the time it'd take to get there! You're all she fuckin' has!"

"FUCK!" Doc roared, peering back down at Mia, knowing I was right. He looked deep into my eyes. "I need you to get me the brightest fuckin' lamp in this place. Get me some fuckin' blankets, towels and boil some water, too."

"The fuc—"

"NOW!"

I ran down the narrow hallway and into my room. Rummaging in the bathroom for every towel I could find, snatching the lamp off my nightstand, and grabbing the throw blankets off my bed. Hurrying back to the living room where Doc now had Mia in his arms.

"Table!" he shouted, carrying her into the dining room.

I set the lamp down and threw the blankets and towels on a chair. Clearing the contents off the table with one swipe of my arm. Mia's glass vase shattered at my feet. The flowers I brought to her, which made her smile so fucking wide, flew in every direction.

Hurting my fucking heart even more.

Doc set her down on the hard wood, while I rushed around turning on all the lights, plugging the extra lamp into the wall. When I looked up, he was pouring alcohol all over her stomach. Getting her fucking ready for I don't know what. He changed into a fresh pair of gloves, pulling out all sorts of instruments from his bag. Drawing up a couple more syringes, injecting them all into her stomach. I watched with wide eyes as he grabbed the scalpel, placing it right against her lower abdomen.

"Doc…"

He locked eyes with me. "I need to get Maddie out. She's in distress. Grab the lamp and hold it up as close as you can to me. I'm gonna need all the fuckin' light I can get."

"Fuck," I breathed out, doing what I was told.

My fear and worry bled out of me in unforgiving waves. My stomach dropped. My heart was now in my fucking throat. Bile rising, but I swallowed it back down. Remembering she needed me to stay strong.

For her.

I watched, taking in the gruesome scene happening in front of me, as Doc made a clean cut across Mia's stomach. Setting the scalpel to the side, he grabbed what looked like a clamping device. He inserted it, opening her insides up to get a better visual.

"I need more light over here! Gotta be careful not to puncture her bladder."

Setting the lamp down, I ran into the kitchen, grabbing one of the industrial size flashlights. Hauling ass back to Doc, who was checking her vitals before he continued, saying, "She's doin' fine. I'm gonna need your help, though. Shine the light right here, and don't fuckin' move," he ordered, pointing the scalpel where I needed to be.

I tried to steady my shaking hands, my overly beating heart, and my mind from losing control. Pushing through the pain of my own goddamn wounds. Doc made another cut, deeper this time. Making her blood ooze out everywhere.

"Listen to me, we need to move fast. I need to break her water to get the baby out. I need you to grab the towels and one of the blankets."

I readily grabbed them as he picked up another instrument that had a sharp end. Inserting it into the opening he had just created. Seconds later, green fluid leaked out of Mia's stomach in spurts.

"FUCK! Just what I thought!"

"What? What's goin' on, Doc? She okay?"

"The amniotic fluid is supposed to be clear. I need to get the baby out, and I need to do it fast," he snapped, grabbing a bunch of supplies from his bag. "Creed, spread a towel out over Mia's stomach, and get the blanket ready in your hands. As soon as I pull her out, I'm gonna need you to follow my instructions, we clear?"

I nodded, placing the towel on her, grabbing the blanket next to me. Holding my breath, not knowing what to expect or what was about to come. I would be lying if I said I wasn't fucking terrified, none of this was normal. Especially, having my girl bleeding out on the table in front of me. Doc's calm expression was the only thing keeping me from flipping the fuck out. I never imagined I would be the one standing next to Mia, waiting to see her baby girl being born.

As much as I tried to push away the guilt that Noah wasn't here, it lingered in the forefront of my mind. He wasn't going to be the one witnessing the birth of his daughter.

I was.

It wasn't right, but that didn't stop me from feeling honored as fuck that I was there and he wasn't. I had witnessed so many people being brutally ripped away from this cruel world. Never thinking I would have the privilege to see an innocent life being born into it.

It was one of the best moments of my life.

It didn't take long until Doc was pulling out this tiny baby girl by her head and shoulders. She was covered in blood and God knows what else. He placed her on the towel on top of Mia's stomach, clamped down on the cord, and cut it. Taking another towel, he quickly wiped her face and eyes.

I had never seen anything more beautiful, more breathtaking in all my life. She was already so fucking perfect.

She had a full head of dark black hair, reminding me so much of Noah when he was born. I counted her ten toes and ten fingers, making sure they were all there. She had these pouty pink lips, almost too big for her little face. Just like her momma.

Before I knew it, a huge smile spread across my face, watching her curl up in a little ball, like she was still inside Mia's stomach. Not realizing she'd made her grand entrance into the world so early. A sense of pride washed over me as Doc worked diligently, suctioning the gross shit out of Maddie's mouth and nose. Disturbing her peace.

After a few moments, the space filled with the weakest little gasps and squeals. Her teeny arms and legs flailed, pissed off and cold. Tears began to form in my eyes, thinking about what her momma was missing. She would never get to hear her first cry, be the first to hold her in her arms. And tell her that she loved her more than anything in this world.

I kneeled down, brushing Mia's hair away from her face, pleading for her to wake up. Whispering what I was seeing and feeling in her ear. Hoping she could at least hear me, or maybe even feel the overwhelming love pouring out of me.

"Baby, you did so fuckin' good. I'm so fuckin' proud of you. She's beautiful," I murmured, caressing the side of her face with my thumb. "Can't believe you made her in your stomach… Jesus, Mia, I can't believe I got to witness such a fuckin' miracle. I will never be able to thank ya enough for givin' me such a special gift. She may not be mine, but that don't matter. She's all that matters now." I leaned my forehead against her cheek, blinking away the tears. "I'm so sorry, Pippin, I promise I'll make this up to you, even if it takes the rest of my life. I love you so much," I choked out, my emotions getting the best of me.

"Creed, I need you to take off your shirt, wrap the baby up tight in the blanket, and hold her close to your chest. Her temperature is droppin', which ain't good. The heat from your skin will help. I gotta finish up with Mia."

I kissed her forehead, wiping away the tears that escaped from my eyes with the back of my hand. Clearing my throat, I stood while pulling my shirt over my head. Wincing when it scraped over the gash in my side and arm. I dropped the blood-soaked cotton on the floor and walked over to Doc. Holding my arms open, not knowing what the hell I was doing. He placed Maddie in the crook of my arm, telling me to support her neck, with my other hand securely placed under her small frame. She fit perfectly in the palm of my hand as I cradled her close to my chest, just like Doc had said.

My heart instantly melted, I was so fucked. This little bundle of joy would be the death of me, or maybe she would be my new beginning. Already having me wrapped around her tiny little finger. I walked around the room with her, holding her as close to my heart as I possibly could. Loving the way she felt up against me.

The sounds she made.

The way she curled up into my body as if she was molding herself to my chest, like she did in Mia's stomach. Lightly gripping onto my finger.

The smell of her.

The feel of her soft baby skin.

Loving every last thing about her, from the top of her head to the tips of her toes. She was my Godsend, my angel, the only thing that made sense anymore.

Her and her momma…

Were now my entire fucking world.

"Baby girl, I love you so much. I need you to know that I may not be your daddy, but I will always love you like my own," I stifled, barely able to get the words out. This was such an overwhelming moment, one I never thought I'd experience. "Your real daddy would be here, but he's fightin' for you. For your momma. He may not be here right now, but he's gonna have so many more memories with you. The first time you talk and walk. The first time he has to break a boy's fingers for lookin' at you. And I'm gonna be right there with him, Maddie," I chuckled, thinking about it. "Right by his side, raisin' you right."

She cooed, stirring in my arms as if she understood everything I was promising. I rocked her, trying to soothe her as I walked back over to Mia. Knowing in my heart that Maddie wanted and needed her momma. I crouched down beside Mia's face again, kissing her cheek.

"Baby, you gotta wake up. Someone is needin' to meet you. Open them pretty eyes, so you can see your beautiful daughter."

She didn't even stir. I glanced at Doc, gesturing toward Mia, and he nodded his head, silently giving me the approval for what I wanted to do. Thinking it might help. Maybe feeling the warmth of the life she created would make her regain consciousness. I placed Maddie on Mia's chest, holding her securely in place with my hand on her back, just in case she moved around.

I knew Mia would have a hard time, forgiving herself for not being awake when she was born. She spent her entire pregnancy telling me how she couldn't wait to meet her, hold her, snuggle her. Be the first person to tell her she loved her.

There wasn't a damn thing I could do to make this easier on my girl, make it right, other than to make a memory of it for her to look back on later. Hoping it would give her peace of mind that she was still one of the first people to hold her, even though she wasn't awake. I pulled my phone out from the back of my jeans, set it on camera mode, and took a picture. Both their faces were turned toward the camera, looking like they were sleeping peacefully. Both perfectly content and happy in each other's arms where they were meant to be.

Words couldn't explain how I felt in that moment, seeing them like this. It took my fucking breath away. I wiped my tears, leaned forward, and kissed my girls. Letting my lips linger on Maddie's soft skin, that I couldn't seem to get enough of. It was then I noticed she felt cool and damp when minutes ago she didn't.

I leaned back to take a look at her, making sure she was all right. My heart dropped and my smile faded, replaced with yet another image that would forever fucking haunt me. Silently praying, my mind was playing tricks on me.

Something…

Anything…

Other than what was actually happening.

"Doc!" I called out, instinctively reaching for Maddie. Placing her in my arms. "Doc! She's turnin' fuckin' blue!"

He didn't answer.

"Doc! Did you hear me?! Maddie is turnin' fuckin' blue!" I turned my head, prying my eyes off her, even though it was the last thing I wanted to do.

Doc's face was as white as a ghost, staring down at Mia, wide-eyed. "FUCK!" he shouted out of nowhere.

It was the first time all night I had seen the look of pure panic on his face. My eyes immediately followed the path of his petrified expression, rendering me fucking speechless. There was blood pouring out from in between Mia's legs again. Except this time, it wouldn't fucking stop.

"She's hemorrhaging, I need to get the placenta out! Now!"

"Doc, Maddie... what do I do? You take care of Mia! Just tell me what to do? What do I do with Maddie?!" I panicked, staring at him with pleading eyes.

My heart beat louder and louder with every second that passed. Trying to keep calm when all I really wanted to do was fucking lose my shit.

How could this be fucking happening? She was a good girl. They both were. They didn't fucking deserve any of this, but here they were getting punished for who I was. For what I represented.

For what I am.

I looked back and forth between Mia and Maddie, torn between who needed me the most. Desperately trying to tune out the turmoil in my mind, feeling so fucking helpless with wanting to fall apart.

"Grab another blanket, and place Maddie on the table!"

I didn't waver, gently laying her tiny frame down near the edge.

"I need you to grab the bulb syringe over here by me," he instructed, while he worked on Mia. "It's the blue thing you saw me use on her after I took her out. Squeeze the bulb, and insert it into her mouth to suction out any left over secretions. Do the same in her nose just like I did before. You need to clear her airways, fast!"

I grabbed the bulb, working on baby girl. Tears suddenly ran down my face, one right after the other, falling onto her lifeless body. "Come on, Maddie! Don't do this, don't do this to us!" I begged, my eyes blurring with nothing but fucking pain.

"Gentle, her bones are very fragile, you don't wanna break anything!"

I nodded, continuing to do exactly what I was told.

"Is she breathin'?"

"No! Fuck, Doc! She's turnin' bluer!"

"Feel the cord, is it pulsing? Does it feel like a heartbeat?"

I frantically shook my head as he peered back at me. The expression on his face told me everything I didn't want to fucking hear. I swear I could see him silently praying in the back of his mind like he knew the end was here.

"You need to start compressions! Hold her around her torso with your thumbs right in the middle of her chest. Support her head with your hands and start pressin' down with your thumbs on her rib cage. Not too hard, but enough to apply pressure. We need to see if we can get her blood movin'."

I nodded, my lips trembling.

"Creed! Do you understand me?"

"Yeah," I breathed out, getting right to work. "One, two, three, four…" I huffed, pressing down on her. Counting to myself.

Nothing.

"Is she breathin'?"

"Fuck!" I tried again, a little harder this time. "Goddamn it! Don't you do this to me! Don't you fuckin' do this to me!" I yelled, cursing fucking God.

"Place your mouth over her lips and her nose, and give her a few quick breaths. If her skin's gotten colder, then use two fingers to give compressions this time!"

Seconds turned into minutes and minutes turned into hours, but I couldn't just stop trying. I couldn't just let her die. When everything in my body was telling me that it didn't matter because this still wasn't going to end well. We didn't have the proper equipment. All we had was God. Hoping he'd be on my side for once in my sorry excuse of a fucking life.

Without thinking twice about it, I breathed into her tiny body, watching her chest heave from my air, but I felt nothing from her little nose. I don't know how much time went by, but I never stopped alternating breaths and compressions. Determined to get her little heart beating again. Not matter what.

Beep... Beep... Beep...

I instantly looked up when I heard the device that was taking Mia's blood pressure go off. The numbers drastically started to drop to dangerous lows. The dinging echoed through my ears and right into my fucking heart.

"Doc..."

"FUCK! We're losin' her!"

"NO!"

I couldn't breathe...

I couldn't fucking breathe.

"I almost got her placenta out! It's fuckin' stuck! Her body is goin' into shock!" I watched him move as fast as he could, from one thing to another. Using instrument after instrument to pinpoint the obstruction. Frantically trying to see through all the blood. "Need to get the bleeding under control or she'll fuckin' die!" He grabbed another two syringes and filled them with something I didn't recognize, rapidly jabbing one into her open abdomen and the other into her arm. Ripping open the IV kit with his teeth, he prepped her vein next and started a line.

I stood there, fucking frozen in place. Strangled by nothing but fear, crippling me in ways I never believed possible. Unshed tears pooled in my eyes, looking back from Mia's lax body, over to Maddie's lifeless one. "Doc... please... Maddie... she's still... not fuckin' breathin'."

He abruptly turned around, only looking at me. Like he had already given up on the baby girl who was still locked in my tight grasp. Peering deep into my eyes, he spoke with conviction, "It's either Mia or Maddie! I can't save both! Choose!"

I shut my eyes just for a second, fighting an internal battle I couldn't fucking win.

All I could see was blood, so much fucking blood.

All I could hear were the alarms on Mia's machines on the verge of flat-lining.

All I could feel was Maddie's cold skin under my fingertips as if she was never warm to begin with.

"Creed… Creed… Creed… please help me… if you ever loved me… you would find me… please help me… I'm scared, Creed… I'm so scared…" With Luke's voice from my nightmares tangled in between.

I hadn't heard his voice in years.

It brought me to my knees, pulling me fucking under. The pain and guilt consumed me, eating me alive. My legs couldn't hold up my misery and devastation any longer. I fell to the floor with Maddie in my arms. Shards of glass sliced into my legs, beneath me. I welcomed the fucking sting with open arms, wanting to feel anything other than my heart being torn in two.

"Goddamn it, Creed! Who's it gonna be?" Doc demanded, his voice muffled in the distance.

"Don't make me fuckin' do this! Don't make me fuckin' choose!" I shouted for I don't know whom.

"We're runnin' out of time!"

I blinked once then twice, seeing Autumn's face flash in front of my eyes *"Please… please… help me…"* her voice droned in and out. *"I… love… you… always."* Reminding me that everyone I ever loved begged for me to save them.

To help them.

Pleaded for their fucking lives.

When all I did was fail them. Exactly like I failed Mia and her baby girl.

I held Maddie so fucking tight against my heart, rocking her back and forth, feeling my future slip away. Knowing in the forefront of my mind, Mia would never forgive me for this.

But it wouldn't fucking matter, she'd be alive.

All I could think about was how could this be happening again. Praying it was all a nightmare I would soon wake up from, in bed with my girl, alive and breathing with baby girl still safely inside of her.

Conscious of the fact I was never that fucking lucky.

I wanted nothing more than to save both of them, even if it meant with my own life. If I didn't make a decision, they were both going to die. I don't know which punishment would be worse.

Taking both their lives.

Or just taking one of them.

"I'm so fuckin' sorry, Maddie. Please… know that I'm so fuckin' sorry… I tried…" I bawled, tears streaming down my face. Locking eyes with Doc, I nodded, muttering, "Mia, Doc. Save Mia."

Aware this would be the end of us…

When it should have been the beginning.

Mia's blood pressure beeped over and over again, signaling a weak pulse. Doc was right—we were out of time. I knew he wanted to fall apart like I was, I knew he was just trying to keep it together for her. Pushing on, doing everything possible to keep her here.

With us.

His silence was as painful as the pleas coming out of my mouth for him to save her.

It became a fucking waiting game.

Time seemed to stand still as my life slowly played out in front of me. Trying to balance somewhere in between the light and the darkness, when all I could see was gray.

I picked myself up off the ground, making my way over to Mia. My feet moved on their own accord, each stride more painful than the last. Until there were no steps to take, no more emotions to pull, no more sorrow to drown. Until there was nothing but my reality and truths staring back at me.

My stomach churned and my mind reeled. I couldn't move. I couldn't feel. I couldn't talk.

I was numb.

The darkness settled in all around me. Memories of Mia and I came flooding into my mind. From the first time we ever met, to this point in time and every day in between. I stood there, hovering above her with baby girl still in my arms, unable to let either of them go.

Watching Doc with dead eyes as he dislodged her placenta and removed it. Finding the source of the bleed and clamping it off. He grabbed the blood bags from the fridge, and fluids from the cabinet, hooking them up to her IV. Her new source of life was transferred into her veins, into her bloodstream, where I would forever be a part of her.

Whether she wanted me to be or not.

Her pulse grew stronger every minute after, her blood pressure steadying. A huge sigh of relief escaped Doc's lips as he wiped the sweat from his forehead with the back of his arm, peering over at me with hope in his eyes.

"She's stable. Not in the clear… but she's fuckin' stable."

I nodded, unable to form words of what I felt in my mind, in my heart, in my fucking soul.

Waiting…

For what was still to come.

My feet were glued to the goddamn floor that was cracking beneath me, ready to cave in. I felt Noah's presence in the archway before he even said a word.

"Creed," he whispered in an eerie tone. Cautiously walking around me. Dreading the inevitable. His eyes took in the scene in front of him, from all the blood to Mia to Doc, finally settling on me.

I mouthed, "I'm sorry," needing for him to hear it.

His eyes widened, his mouth dropped, and all the life drained from his body. "No," he breathed out, violently shaking his head. His lips quivered and his core shuddered as he peered down at his daughter in my arms. "NOOOOO!" he shouted, an ear-piercing scream that resonated deep in my bones. Where it would be eternally etched in my mind. Tears swelled up in his eyes as his chest heaved and his body trembled. "Give her to me!"

He stepped toward me, but I stepped back. Profusely shaking my head no with fresh tears rolling down the sides of my face. "Noah… please…"

"GIVE HER TO ME!" he yelled loud enough to break fucking glass. It echoed around the room, lingering in my ears. He attempted to reach for her again, causing me to take another step back. Trying to salvage what was left of his heart, protecting my baby brother. Knowing holding her would completely destroy him.

It wouldn't change the outcome. Letting him see her. Feel her. Fucking love her.

"Noah, we did everythin' we could. I swear to you. Mia is still hangin' on by a thread," I uttered in a voice I didn't recognize, nodding to her. Already aware of what Noah was thinking.

What he was feeling.

What he blamed me for.

"Fuck you!" he seethed through gritted teeth. Glaring at me. It was the first time I had ever seen him look at me with such hatred in his eyes. He lunged forward, roughly ripping her out of my grasp. Cradling her in his hands, he immediately unwrapped the blanket from her face. "NO! NO! NO! PLEASE! PLEASE! DOC, DO SOMETHIN'! PLEASE FUCKIN' DO SOMETHIN'!" he bellowed, holding onto his daughter for dear life. He fell to his knees, placing her on the floor in front of him. "It's okay, baby girl. It's okay, daddy's here... I'm here now... Everythin' is gonna be fine. I'm gonna make it all better. It's okay," he choked on his words, hands shaking over her, not knowing what to do. Desperately wanting to resuscitate her. "Please... Maddie... please... don't do this to me... please don't fuckin' do this to me... I can't lose you... you're all I ever wanted... please..."

The back of my arm went to my mouth, feeling as though I was dying right along with him. Forcing myself to not look away.

"Why are you just fuckin' standin' there?! Why isn't anyone doin' anythin'?! PLEASE! FUCKIN' HELP ME!" He sucked in air, hyperventilating, his heart visually fucking breaking into pieces. "How could you let this happen?! I shouldn't have fuckin' left! She would be alive if I hadn't fuckin' left!" Grabbing ahold of her, he took her in his arms, pressing her up against his face. "I'm sorry, Maddie... I'm fuckin' sorry I failed you... Please... please... baby girl... forgive me... I love you more than anything... I'm sorry," he repeated over and over again, kissing all over her face, her arms, and her chest.

I made my eyes stay open. I made my body stay in place. I made myself take in every tear that fell from my brother's face, every word that flew out of his mouth, every last emotion that bled out of his broken soul.

His body hunched over from crying so fucking hard. Losing the battle he never had the chance of winning. All that could be heard was Noah's sorrowful screams and tears piercing out into the night.

After this day, our lives would be forever changed. There was no coming back from this. Noah and Mia were now going to be living in my nightmare, along with me.

This was my punishment for trying to bring good into my life. Knowing deep in my fucking gut that this wouldn't have ever happened.

If it wasn't for me.

15

CREED

We all watched in silence as Noah struggled to hand Maddie over to Doc. Needing to hold onto his daughter for a few more minutes, wanting to hold her for as long as he could. Having a hard time with letting her go. He couldn't do it, he couldn't say goodbye to his baby girl.

Not now.

Not ever.

He hunched over her tiny body, mourning her death. The life she should have had. The happiness she should have brought into this world.

Not the devastation that occurred.

He cried into the nook of her neck and broke down. Whispering his apologies in her ear before turning his face away, unable to look at her any longer. Doc aided by grabbing ahold of her and gently pulling her out of his tight grasp. Causing Noah to reluctantly let her go from his arms.

"I know, man… I know…" Doc grieved with him, letting Noah hold onto his shoulder for support.

He could barely fucking stand.

Seeing all my darkest secrets. All the pain I inflicted. All the love he still held onto for her.

He pushed off Doc, needing the momentum to keep moving, keep going…

Keep fucking living.

Only stopping when he was standing beside Mia, looking down at her with glazed, broken eyes. A shell of the man he used to be. No longer full of life, no longer full of love, or fucking hope.

No longer full of anything.

He leaned forward, placing a kiss on her forehead. Letting his lips linger on her skin. "I'm so sorry, Mia," he whispered, brushing her hair away from her pale face. Staring at her adoringly, trying like hell to hold it together. He kissed her one last time, before pushing off the table. Walking away from what was supposed to be his future.

"Noah!" I called out after him as he made his way for the front door.

He didn't answer or stop, not that I expected him to. I rushed over, grabbing a hold of his shoulder and turned him to face me. Only to be met with the barrel of his gun, firmly pressed against my chest. Digging right into my heart.

I jerked back, my eyes widening. Never fucking expecting that.

"If you know what's good for you, you'll let me walk out of here. I've killed men for far fuckin' less than what you just did in there, Creed," he gritted out, glaring straight into my eyes.

I was no longer his brother standing in front of him.

His family. His blood.

I was just the man who killed his daughter.

Taking away his whole fucking world.

His finger didn't move from the trigger as he cocked his gun to the side. "But you ain't worth the blood. You ain't worth the fuckin' effort. Bein' a part of your life is a guaranteed fuckin' death sentence." He adamantly nodded behind me. "Maddie's death… her blood… it's on you. You're the reason she's dead."

The sincerity of his words were like taking bullet after bullet, after fucking bullet to my heart.

He backed away, still aiming his gun at my chest. Took one last look at me with disgust and hatred evident in his eyes, turned and left. Slamming the door behind him.

I watched my baby brother leave, knowing he had just turned his back on me.

"Fuck, brother," Diesel breathed out, walking up beside me and grabbing ahold of my shoulder. I shoved his hand away, not needing his condolences or his fucking pity.

"Where are they?"

He took a deep breath, fully aware of who I was referring to. "I'm sorry, man. They got away."

I didn't think twice about it. I spun around grabbing the armchair, chucking it across the room. Watching as the frame shattered against the wall, falling into shards on the hardwood floor. My body couldn't move fast enough around the open space, pushing over everything that was in my immediate path. Throwing and swinging at anything I could find. Growling, fucking seething, needing to hurt something.

Anything.

"GODDAMN IT!" I screamed, throwing one thing after another across the room. Not giving a flying fuck I was destroying the place. "The fuck you mean they got away?! I told you to bring those motherfuckers back here! And you're gonna stand there and tell me you fuckin' failed!" I picked up the lamp beside me, ready to heave it at the fucking door.

Diesel stepped out in front of me, blocking my way. "We'll find them. I fuckin' promise you. I give you my word that we will fuckin' find the motherfuckers who did this and make them pay!"

I looked around the room, trying to catch my breath from the rage coursing through my veins. Seeing the rest of the brothers who weren't put to ground for the first time. All nodding along with Diesel's words, silently assuring me what he was saying was true. Giving me the only comfort I did want.

Fucking revenge.

"Creed! We need to call an ambulance. Mia is stable, but she needs to get to a hospital," Doc announced, walking into the living room. Removing another pair of blood-soaked gloves.

"We're out in the middle of fuckin' nowhere, you already know that. An ambulance couldn't even find this place if we painted them a fuckin' map. Can't even drive a car through those woods, it's why we been fuckin' drivin' side-by-sides," I replied, pacing the room, kicking shit out of my way. Raking my hands through my hair, needing one goddamn second to think.

Just *one* goddamn second.

"We take her! We take her right fuckin' now!" I tried to sidestep Diesel, but he firmly grabbed my arm before I got the last word out.

"Need to get our story straight. Cops are gonna be swarmin' when you show up with her at the hospital. Did you fuckin' forget she's missin'? I know you gotta protect your girl, but you also gotta protect your club, *VP*," Diesel stated, emphasizing the last two letters.

I tore my arm away, looking him dead in the eyes. "You do whatever the fuck you gotta do or say… but you got an hour to get me a fuckin' cargo van. Need to get Mia to the hospital as comfortably as possible. She's already been through enough. Have it meet us at the end of the road just out of the woods." I cocked my head to the side, adding, "And you prolly got less than twenty-four hours to handle this shit and take care of business. Yeah?"

He nodded, pulling out his phone to make the necessary calls to save our asses. Except, I was the only one who didn't give a fuck about my future anymore. I was already living in Hell. Prison wouldn't be any different.

All that mattered to me was getting Mia safely to the hospital.

My eyes fluttered open, or maybe they were still closed. Darkness clouded my vision, making it hard to decipher between the two. I tried again, blinking a few times, willing them to focus, but I was so drowsy and tired. My body was so stiff and sore. It felt like it weighed a thousand pounds, sinking into the blankets on the hard surface beneath me.

I groaned, moving my head side-to-side, nestling in my aching body. Pain radiated from the middle of my back, wrapping around my abdomen. Hugging me tight like a vise. I couldn't comprehend if I was awake or asleep at that point. Feeling as though I was in a moving vehicle.

"It's okay, baby," I heard Creed coax from above me. Instantly feeling a warm sensation course through my body. The pain almost immediately subsided into a hazy bliss. The familiar smell of cigarettes and his musky, masculine scent aided in keeping me content.

"Water," I mumbled, feeling like I hadn't drank anything in forever. He placed a straw at my lips and I greedily sucked it down. Trying to quench my thirst.

"Easy, babe, gonna make yourself sick."

I nodded, slowing down my pace. Wondering why the hell I was so thirsty and disoriented. Waiting for Creed to tell me what was going on, but he didn't say anything. I turned my head away when I had my fill of the water, trying to gather my rambling thoughts and adjust to my surroundings.

The space was darker than I initially thought. My eyes finally adapted to the soft light coming from what looked like a lantern down by my feet, and a few overhead lights the driver must have turned on. My gaze slowly moved around the closed space, realizing I was right. We were in a moving cargo van.

My eyes immediately landed on Creed. His body was hunched over, leaning up against the metal steel with his elbows on his knees, but that wasn't what caught my attention. It was the fact that he looked like he hadn't slept in days.

Even through the dim lighting, I could see that his cheeks were sunken in and his skin was pale. His hair was all disheveled and messy as if he'd been yanking at it. A few strands had fallen around his gaze, only accentuating the dark, puffy circles under his eyes, which were also bloodshot red. His bright blue irises that I could never get enough of appeared almost translucent and white. They were void of any emotions, empty pools, no feeling pouring out of them whatsoever. His expression was vacant and hard. I've never wanted to know what he was thinking, more than I did in that second.

The more I looked at him, the more I realized the man I loved with all my heart was now a blank canvas. A mere illusion of the person I used to know.

My heart started urgently pounding against my chest. An unsettling feeling churned deep within my stomach. There was something in the way he was looking at me that left me breathless, and more confused. I wanted to ask him what happened, but I couldn't find my voice. Suddenly terrified to know the answer. I wanted to look around, but I couldn't will myself to look away from him. Our gazes were locked. Neither one of us willing to break the intensity of our stares as my emotions continued to run wild.

He narrowed his eyes, looking at me with a visible yearning. Showing me a glimpse of the man I've known and loved.

The same man I knew that loved me back.

The thought alone calmed me.

His eyes searched my face for I don't know what, eyeing me up and down. Fighting an internal battle that was clearly raging war inside of him. Unfolding right in front of me. He was the first to break our connection, unable to look at me any longer. His face dropped to his boots as his hands dug into his hair, tugging at it like I imagined he'd been doing all night. His mood shifted into a cluster of emotions. So contradicting to the man he had just shown me.

He was bracing himself for something I had yet to grasp or understand.

You know how people say your mind could protect itself from anything it thought could hurt them… I never understood that statement until right then and there. For some reason, I instinctively narrowed in on his nails, noticing for the first time there was dried up blood caked under them.

Which was all it took to set the tracks in motion…

"What do you think baby girl? You like the name, Madison?"

Blink.

"This ain't over."

"I wouldn't dream of it."

Blink.

"I'd like to make a toast to Mia. For puttin' up with us foul-mouthed bikers, makin' this kickass fuckin' meal, and for handlin' this situation like a fuckin' pro. Not being a little bitch or a pain in our fuckin' asses."

"And here I thought you didn't know my name."

Blink.

"Hey, Doc! You forget something?"

Blink.

"Mia, for the first time in I don't know how long, I'm actually doin' somethin' good. It's been an honor to be part of your journey with Maddie. I can't wait to help you brin' her into this world."

Blink.

"NO! MIA, RUN!"

Blink.

"GET HER OUT OF HERE!"

Blink.

"Stay with me. You fuckin' stay with me."

Blink.

"You fight, Mia. You fuckin' fight for our baby girl and I'm gonna go fight for you."

Blink.

"Pleeeaassee, saaave herr... saaave... Madd..."

Shouting...

Crying....

Blood...

Pain...

Pain...

Pain...

Nothing. But. Pain.

My eyes filled with tears, suddenly finding it hard to breathe. "Creed..."

It felt like an eternity before he finally glanced up, looking at me through the slits of his eyes. His stare, his demeanor, his aura all mirrored mine.

My lips parted taking a deep breath. Letting it wheeze out as my hand slowly, intuitively moved from the side of my body, toward the center of my belly. Though my gaze never shifted from his.

I sucked in air, my body seizing completely. "Where is she?" I whispered so low as soon as my hand felt my non-existing stomach.

He didn't move or say anything. He didn't even blink.

My heart sped up, beating a mile a minute. I swear he could hear it. There was no way he couldn't have, it echoed throughout the space between us.

"Is she with Noah? Is my baby girl with her daddy? Is she in the front passenger seat with Noah?"

Silence. Nothing. Not one reaction.

Each second that passed between us, felt like hours had gone by.

"Is she with Doc? Does he have her? Are you taking us to the hospital?" I couldn't get my questions out fast enough.

Silence.

I began nodding uncontrollably like I was answering my own questions. Biting down on my bottom lip, to the point of pain. "Where is she? She needs her momma! I'm her momma, Creed! She needs me!"

His expression never once wavered from a deep stillness and penetrating stare. Glaring at me as if I was asking questions that didn't make any sense. His silence was deafening, like an array of tiny razor blades cutting into every last inch of my skin.

I could feel him everywhere and all at once, even though he wasn't touching me.

"Why are you just sitting there?!" I shouted, becoming angry from his lack of response. "Where is Maddie?! Where is my daughter?!"

He shut his eyes just for a second murmuring, "I'm so fuckin' sorry, Mia." Bowing his head in shame.

I placed my shaking hand over my heart, trying to steady my breathing. The space was caving in on me. My vision blurred, clouding everything around my vicinity, including him. My lips started to quiver, my chest started to heave. Unleashed tears from my swollen eyes immediately streamed down the sides of my face.

"For what, Creed?! What the hell are you sorry for?!" I yelled, my body trembling uncontrollably.

He just shook his head back and forth. "Baby, I—" Looking back up at me with torment in his eyes.

"Answer my fucking question!" I ripped the blanket back, ignoring the wires and tubes pulling at my skin. Swiftly sitting up. Groaning out in immediate pain.

He was in my face trying to get me to lie back down. "Mia, stop! You're gonna hurt yourself!"

I shoved him away, but he didn't budge. "What are you sorry for?! What did you do, Creed?!" My hands connected with his chest with a loud thud, repeatedly pounding into him. Weakly struggling against his body and the machines that held me back. "Where is Madison?!"

"Pippin, calm the fuck down! Let me explain! I'm sorr—"

"Calm down?! You want me to calm down?! Tell me where my baby is!"

He tried to wrestle me into his arms, wanting and needing to hold me. Trying to control me.

"Let go of me!" I shouted, trying to shake loose from his hold. Ignoring the pain cycling my entire body. Roughly clawing at his hands, his arms, trying to pry them off of me. Only making him hold me tighter.

"Babe, I'm hangin' on by a fuckin' thread here... Please..." he pleaded as I continued to struggle against him. "We did everythin' we could, but she was just so fuckin' small, Mia. Her lungs..."

"NO! NO! NO!" I hysterically ranted, thrashing and whipping my body all around. Excruciating pain tore through my body this time, but I couldn't stop. Ripping the IV line out of my hand as my fists beat into his chest harder with each punch.

He took every blow as if he knew he deserved it.

I wanted him to hurt.

I needed to fucking hurt him.

He caught my wrists mid-hit, tugging me toward his body. Holding me against his chest, against his heart. Against the agony and grief that would always live inside of him.

"You're lying! You're fucking lying! You did this! Why?! Why would you do this to me?! I thought you loved me! I thought you loved her! You wanted this, didn't you?! Why you fucking bastard?! Because you weren't the fucking father?! Let go of me! All of this is your fault! I should have never been there! She would be alive if you didn't fucking bring me to that goddamn house! For what?! My safety?! Look how well that turned out, you fucking murderer!" I sobbed violently, desperately trying to push him off of me.

Melting down.

Losing all my strength.

My strength to fight, my strength to live and most of all my strength to fucking love him.

"Baby, I'm so fuckin' sorry... I loved her... I love you... you know that, Mia... you fuckin' know that... if I could switch places wit' her, I would... please... baby... please... I can't lose you, too."

His words felt like acid on my skin as I stared into his sorrowful eyes. Silently pleading for my forgiveness. "You killed her! You killed my baby! I hate you! Do you hear me?! I fucking hate you!" I spewed, meaning every word.

"Fuck, Pippin! You're bleedin' again! Please, baby, calm down!"

The harder he held me, the more I wanted to hurt him. The more I wanted to break him. The more I wanted to die. The next thing I knew the back doors to the van roughly slammed open and Doc came into focus. I hadn't even realized we'd stopped.

"Doc! Where is she?! Please… let me hold her… let me touch her… please, Doc… please give her to me…" I begged, reaching for him.

Needing him to understand.

"Shhh…" he soothed in a gentle tone, stepping into the van, making his way toward me. "It's okay, sweetheart. It's alright," he coaxed, caressing the side of my face as he sat down beside me. Wiping away my sweat and tears. Nodding to Creed to let me go.

Reluctantly, he finally did.

I narrowed my eyes at Doc, trying to take him in. Something wasn't right, something felt off. It was then I saw the syringe hiding behind his back.

"No… No… No…" I panicked, vigorously shaking my head. Scooting back as far away as I could from the both of them. Hugging my knees to my chest. Looking down at the blood on the blankets but not caring it was coming from me. My head continued to rapidly shake. "No, no, no, no, no, no," I chanted over and over again, rocking back and forth. Mumbling incoherently. Trying to comfort myself as best as I could.

"Mia," Doc murmured, touching me.

I swatted his hand away, covering my ears. "No! No! No! No!" I endlessly screamed. Tucking my head in my knees, curling up in a ball. Hands touched me everywhere and all at once, causing me to fight harder. Pain coursed through my entire body, my head throbbed, and my vision twisted.

"Mia! Fuckin' stop!" Creed yelled from above me. "You're only hurtin' yourself!"

"She's in shock!" I heard Doc say. "Her body's in fight or flight mode! Her pain doesn't even matter at this point. Her body's just movin' on autopilot mode!"

"Nooooo!" I cried out. "No… no… no… no… no…" I sobbed, my body shaking uncontrollably. Convulsing to the point of pain.

"Mia, sweetheart, you need to stay with me. You need to calm down," Doc added as I shoved their hands away. Pushing at the grips they both had on me. Flailing my arms.

"Don't touch me! Don't fucking touch me!" I screamed, violently lashing out. Causing even more pain to wreak havoc on my entire body. The sounds of the machines beeping all around me were ear-piercing. "Don't fucking touch me!" I repeated, yelling bloody murder.

"Grab her legs!" Doc demanded from beside me. "Help me grab her arms!"

"No! No! No! No!" I whipped around every which way, but they were too strong for me. "Please... please... please..." I bawled like a baby, my emotions overtaking me. Smothering me in nothing but a sea of loneliness and despair.

A sharp prick entered my bicep. My body fell slack, heavy, and foreign as soon as a familiar warm sensation began surging through me from my head down to my toes. Creed's strong arms circled my body, engulfing me in his scent. Pulling me to lie on his chest.

"Shhh... go to sleep. Close your eyes and go to sleep, Pippin..." I heard him faintly say, his voice an echo in the distance.

I did as I was told, unable to fight even if I wanted to. Letting the darkness take over. I prayed I would never wake up.

Dying right along with Maddie.

My baby girl I never even got to meet.

I sat in the waiting room area, leaning back into the chair with my head against the wall. My legs spread out in front of me, and my arms crossed over my chest. Doing exactly that.

Fucking waiting.

The chain of events in the last few months led up to this place in time. And soon the moment of truth would be knocking at my door, ready to let itself right fucking in.

Doc, Diesel, and I brought Mia into the ER to be admitted. Along with Maddie's body, Doc had wrapped up and placed in a wooden box to be taken to the hospital morgue. I let them handle the staff, answering the necessary questions. Following whatever fucking protocol was needed, including calling her parents and the cops. Reporting that the missing girl from Oak Island had finally been found alive.

Diesel and Doc stayed by my side in the waiting room, knowing I'd need some back-up from the impending shit storm that was about to erupt. I came to the decision that I wouldn't lie to Mia's family, at least not anymore. Extinguishing the fire that protected all my secrets. Airing them out if it meant saving her. The staff wouldn't allow me into her room, informing me I wasn't immediate family. Saying some shit about having to wait until her parents' showed up to grant me permission, even though I was the one who brought her in.

The staff wouldn't tell us one damn thing about her medical condition. In spite of the fact that all we had done since we stepped foot into the ER was cooperate with anything they needed or wanted. They wouldn't even tell us if she had woken up, or if she was going to be all right. Looking at us the same way this entire fucking town always had.

Like we were nothing but pieces of shit, biker trash.

It never used to bother me until I met Mia. She was the only person who ever looked at me like I was someone special to be looked at. Like I mattered in this fucked up world and deserved to be respected.

I took a deep breath, watching as pictures of Mia took center stage on the flat screen TV hanging on the wall in front of me. Images of her pretty face scrolled across the screen with headlines that read, "After months, missing Oak Island native Mia Ryder found alive." Showing live coverage just outside the hospital doors. Only a few yards away from where I sat. It wouldn't take long for the press to find out about our involvement, and all hell would break fucking loose by morning. Our club spent decades trying to keep our names out of the papers, and in a few short hours we'd be front-page news.

Which was the least of my fucking worries.

Soon Mia's family would make their grand entrance, cutting off any ties that their daughter and I had. I'd lose her for good. Completely conscious of the fact that I didn't deserve to have her to begin with.

I'd be lucky if they didn't throw my ass behind bars before the end of the day.

No good would come of this.

No good would have ever come from us, and I knew that since day one.

My entire life flashed before my eyes like a goddamn movie reel that I couldn't pause or fucking stop. It felt like I'd been sitting there for days, but in reality, it was only a few hours. Thinking about what went down in the van, repeatedly playing it over in my mind. I would never be able to forget the words she spewed, the way she hit me, and especially the look on her face when I told her Maddie had died.

"You killed her! You killed my baby! I hate you! Do you hear me?! I fucking hate you!"

One word stuck out among the rest. *"Murderer!"*

I got out of my chair a few times, pacing the room. Shaking off my demons that plagued my mind. Randomly wandering over to the double doors to look out into the hallway where Mia was taken back.

My mind raced with thoughts, with guilt, with shame from all the shit I put the people that I love the most through. All the memories faded when I heard loud, rumbling footsteps coming down the hall. I didn't have to wonder who they belonged to.

"You son of a bitch!" Mia's old man called out, making me look up from my chair. Moving in an autopilot state of mind, I stood. Watching as he and McGraw came barreling through the same double doors where Mia was wheeled back.

They must have been in to see her already, giving me a sliver of hope that maybe she was awake again and well. As well as she could be at least. The nurses must have told them we were waiting around since we brought her in.

"I'm going to fucking kill you!" His fist collided with my jaw before he got the last word out. My head whooshed back, taking half of my body with it. I stumbled, trying to shake it off. He didn't waver, gripping onto the front of my cut, and slammed my back up against the wall. I hit it with a hard thud, knocking the wind out of me for a second.

I never took my eyes off of his while he laid into me, but I knew Doc and Diesel were standing there twitching to interfere. As soon as we sat in the waiting room, I had warned them to mind their own fucking business when it came to her family and me.

Her old man could do whatever the fuck he wanted. I deserved every blow to my body, every punch to my face, every wound he wanted to inflict. No damage could ever compare to what their daughter had been through. Or what she had lost.

Because of me.

"You motherfucking piece of shit!" he snarled, punching me in the stomach and then again in the ribs. Grazing my wound from being shot at. "I knew you had her this whole fucking time, you fucking liar! Didn't you?!" Another hit to the side of my face. An uppercut to the jaw, making me instantly taste blood. "Answer me, you son of a bitch!" he screamed, hurling my body across the room. I knocked over a few vacant chairs, leaving nothing but destruction in my path. "Why aren't you fighting back?! Huh?! Where's your pussy ass brother who knocked her up?!"

I staggered to my feet, wiping the blood off my face with the back of my arm. Watching with hooded eyes as hospital security abruptly rushed into where we were. McGraw put his hand up, stopping them dead in their tracks. Showing them his badge, and nodding to Lucas to keep going.

That was all it took for him to be over to me in two strides, punching me in the face again. "Prison is too fucking good for you!" Hitting me in the side of my stomach. "I knew you and that piece of shit club were behind this! For what?!" he growled, throwing a few more blows to my ribs.

I peeled over, gasping for air when he picked me up, slamming me against the drywall. Causing it to crack and fall beneath me. He immediately held up my lax body, shoving me harder against the adjacent wall.

"Dad! Stop!" I heard Mason shout from down the hall. Bringing his father's attention to him as he ran into what was left of the waiting room. Mason booked it over to us, grabbing ahold of his dad. Trying to pull him off me. "He didn't do this! You guys didn't even let the doctor finish before you hauled ass out of the room! They saved her!" Mason gestured to all of us. "They found her during a shootout! She's alive because of them!"

Lucas jerked back, stunned by Mason's revelation. McGraw stood there like he already knew that fact.

Fucker.

It was then I realized this was the alibi Diesel and the club must have come up with to save my sorry ass.

"What?" his dad clenched out, completely caught off guard. His chest heaved from the adrenaline that was throbbing full force through his veins.

"You should be thanking him, not trying to kill him," Mason added, shaking his head. Trying to pry him off me.

I didn't know what to say to them, so I didn't fucking say anything at all.

Diesel stepped forward as if reading my mind, knowing I wouldn't lie to them. "Yeah, it's fuckin' true," he stated, answering for me. "We've been tellin' you since she went missin', we were doin' everything we could to help. Well, we fuckin' found her, deep in the woods. Creed was the one who said to take Doc with us not knowin' what condition she'd be in. He's a jack of all fuckin' trades in the medical field. So why don't you folks back the fuck off! You should be kissin' Creed's ass instead of ridiculing him. He saved your daughter's life!"

Diesel wouldn't look me in the eyes, knowing exactly what he would fucking see. Doc stepped beside him, clearing his throat. Bringing everyone's attention over to him. He stated, "I can only imagine what you've all gone through. We are more than willin' to come down to the station and answer any questions you may have. We want to find the motherfuckers who did this to her as much as you do."

I swallowed hard. At least that part was true.

"I'm just sorry I couldn't save the baby," Doc apologized in a sincere tone as if he'd wanted to say it since the moment she turned blue. "I did everythin' I could with Creed's help. There was a shootout... Mia got caught in the crossfire and was shot in the back. We had to move fast. There was no time. Like Diesel said, they had her in the middle of nowhere. Mia was bleedin' out... I did what I had to do, but we rushed her to this hospital as soon as I was able to get her stable."

All eyes were focused on him as he continued to fill them in on what he could divulge. Some of it was bullshit and some of it was true. I turned my head, shutting my eyes, trying not to relive it all over again. Her father's grip loosened slightly, allowing me to take a deep breath and slowly let the air escape from my lips. I opened my eyes, seeing each one of them observing me.

Mason let go of his dad, and his dad finally let go of me, backing away. But not before punching me one last time in the fucking face, and spitting on me for good measure.

"I don't give a shit what they're claiming you did! I won't believe it until it comes out of Mia's mouth. And even then, if it's true... you will stay the fuck away from my daughter! You, your pussy ass, brother and your fucking club! I will kill you if you come near her again! And that's not a threat, you piece of shit, that's a fucking promise! Now get the fuck out of this hospital before I have you thrown the fuck out!"

"Dad, that's not fair," Mason spoke, looking over at me.

"Don't," I demanded in a stern tone, eyeing their father. "Your old man's right. Just please tell me how's she's doin', is she up? She okay? That's all I wanna know."

He scoffed out, shaking his head and left. McGraw pointed at me with a menacing regard.

"This is far from fuckin' over. You better pray their stories add up to what Mia says. Or I'll make sure your new best fuckin' friends are cellmates who'll love to make you their bitch. That's if I don't encourage a lifer to bleed your body out in your cell," he sincerely stated, nodding toward the exit. "You got one fuckin' minute to see your ass out. Or I'll personally escort you myself, and trust me, motherfucker, I want nothin' more than to take your ass out."

I knew he meant every word. I would be lying if I said I wasn't fucking tempted to let him follow through on every threat he'd made. The only reason I didn't was to find out the truth and make the motherfuckers pay.

I owed it to Maddie.

Noah.

And especially to Mia.

Diesel and Doc followed me out of the back entrance of the hospital to avoid the press. We headed over to my bike that was in the back parking lot, hidden from the main street. Sitting pretty next to Diesel's bike and Doc's car. They must have had prospects drive them over.

The cargo van was nowhere to be found, not that I expected it to.

"Fuck, never thought I'd see the day you'd get your ass kicked like that," Diesel chuckled, walking beside me. "Better yet, never thought you'd let someone kick your ass like that."

I pulled out a cigarette, lighting it up as soon as I got to the old girl. Inhaling half the filter in one long, hard drag, letting the smoke seep from my busted up lips and nose. "Ain't nothin' I didn't deserve," I reminded, spitting a mouthful of blood on the pavement, ignoring the sting in my lungs from Mia's father's assault. I took a seat on the curb, mentally and physically fucking exhausted from all the bullshit that had gone down. Allowing the nicotine to course through me, hoping it would calm my nerves the way it always had.

"Creed, you're bleedin' all over the fuckin' place," Doc stated the obvious, grabbing some alcohol swabs and gauze pads from the back seat of his car. "This may sting," he informed, swiping the alcohol pad over the gash above my eye.

"The fuck?" I winced, turning my head away.

"It's deep, but not deep enough for stitches. I'll butterfly it to stop the bleeding and clean up your fuckin' ugly mug."

I nodded. Too tired to argue.

"You know Mia will back us up, Creed. She won't say a word till she speaks to one of us. She's a good fuckin' girl," Diesel said out of nowhere as if he thought that was what I needed to hear.

"Let's get one thing clear, yeah? I don't give a fuck what Mia tells them. Truth, lies, it's all the same. All I want is ta' put fuckin' holes in whoever's heads are behind this. Ya feel me?"

He nodded.

"Ain't too fuckin' happy about the bullshit lies you told in there, though."

"What did you want us to say, Creed? Huh? It's not just about you. We were all in involved in some way or another. Besides, it's not that far from the truth. You did save her. Can't hold yourself responsible for her baby—"

"Don't even fuckin' say it! You say it, and we ain't brothers no more." I took another long drag, cocking my head to the side, looking him over.

"Jesus Christ, man. You're your own worst enemy, Creed. One day I hope you fuckin' realize that. You did what you had to do! End of fuckin' story. I'll meet you back at the club, Prez called in church."

"Ain't leavin' till I know she's alright. You tell Prez he can take it up with me later."

"What are you gonna do, Creed? Sneak into her room?" Doc questioned, looking at me like I was fucking crazy.

"If that's what it takes."

"Creed!" Mason hollered, interrupting us. Running through the parking lot, over to where we were.

Doc nodded goodbye, taking off. Diesel lingered for a few seconds before jumping on his bike and speeding off toward the clubhouse. Waving at Mason as he rode by.

I flicked my cig into the bushes, lighting another one as he walked up. "Look at you," I breathed out through the smoke, eyeing him up and down. "All decked out in your fatigues. Boots still pinch like a motherfucker?"

He chuckled, knowing I was just trying to make light of the situation. "I was back at Fort Bragg when my parents' called, saying Mia had been found. Been back in the states since the last time we talked. I jumped on the first plane I could out of Afghanistan after finding out she was missing. Wanting to be as close to home and my family as possible to help find my sister."

I resisted the urge to ask him how he was doing as he took a seat beside me. Resting his elbows on his knees and signaling for my cigarette, instantly reminding me of old times.

Mason never smoked unless we were in the middle of a shit storm overseas. I guess this situation could be comparable to that.

He took a few drags, peering over at me. "I'm sorry about my dad, man. He… just… just give him some time. The last few months have been pure hell for them. I don't think they've slept for more than an hour, here and there. Terrified they'd miss something. Focusing solely on trying to find her. I swear they've aged ten years since Mia went missing. My Aunt Lily has been running my mom's restaurant, and my dad has his employees running jobs. Bo's been a fucking wreck… Fuck, bro, my whole family has. Nobody had given up hope that we'd find her alive, and I think that's the only reason we're all still standing."

Bile rose in my throat, but I pushed it back down. It was one thing to assume they were going through hell, it was another thing entirely to fucking hear it. I didn't think I could feel like any more of a piece of shit than I already did, but I was wrong.

Yet again.

"He's grateful you found her, I swear," he reassured, even though I knew he was full of shit.

We sat there for I don't how long, passing the cigarette back and forth. Exactly how we used to. There were times when all I looked forward to was doing this with him, mindful that we were both going through the same shit. Fully aware that we might not make it out alive. War didn't even come fucking close to what I knew we were both going through right now.

Except they got Mia back.

And I just fucking lost her.

"Fuck… bro… if you… I mean… if you hadn't… found her… she could of…" Mason stammered, unable to say what he was thinking, not realizing how close she was to exactly that.

Death.

"You got no idea..." I whispered under my breath. "Your old man may be grateful she's back, but not wit' my involvement in it. He made that very fuckin' clear. Don't hold it against him either, if my baby girl was missin' and then turned up lyin' in a hospital bed," I paused, shaking my head. "The motherfucker responsible would be dead." Stubbing out my cigarette with my boot, I stood. Not wanting to have this conversation any longer.

"Do you know who did this?" he asked, looking up at me. "What fucking happened out there, Creed? How did you find her?"

I walked over to my bike blowing off his interrogation, removing my cut and draping it over my seat. Waiting for what I knew he'd say next.

"What the fuck, man?! If you know who is responsible for this, I want to help take the fuckers down!"

We locked eyes.

"You wanna help me? Then I need ya to do me a favor."

Mason didn't bat one eye when I asked him for his uniform. He was fully aware of why I needed it. I think it was his way of thanking me for bringing his sister back home. This was the only way I could get past security and anyone else who stood in my way. After we exchanged clothes, he took off saying he'd be back later. Something about needing to go find Giselle, she'd been ignoring his calls since he came home. He was going to drive over to her apartment and tell her Mia had been found.

Shortly after midnight, I walked through the double doors of the hospital like a man on a fucking mission. Praying I could pull it off and see my girl. I spent hours outside waiting for the right moment, hiding in the fucking shadows watching people come and go. Eventually spotting Mia's dad leaving just after eleven-thirty. Minus Detective McGraw. When he got into his car and sped off, I knew I didn't have much time.

But it was now or never.

I walked in like I knew where I was going. Hanging my head, hiding under the brim of Mason's military hat as I made my way down the now dim hallway. Heading straight toward Mia's room. There were three police officers right outside her door, just as I expected there would be. McGraw's back was turned to me, talking to one of the cops by the nurse's station. I approached with caution, my heart beating out of my fucking chest the closer I got to see her. I saw McGraw abruptly turn out the corner of my eye as I passed by.

"Hey, Mason," he called out.

I didn't stop. I didn't turn. I just raised my hand, making sure the cuff on his crew was pulled down past the tattoos on my hand. Giving him a wave as I approached the guards.

Nodding to them before I reached for the handle and quickly walked into the room, closing the door behind me.

"Shit," I groaned, faltering against the door. Even through the soft lighting of the hospital room, I could still see Mia's mom sitting beside her on the bed, holding onto Mia's hand.

Not saying a word, she eyed me up and down, taking in Mason's military fatigues and badge. Letting out a loud, long breath when she was done.

I removed my hat, giving her the only respect I could. "No disrespect, ma'am. I just wanna see her and make sure she's all right," I coaxed, needing her to know.

She glanced back down at Mia who was hooked up to all sorts of machines. I recognized some of them which were similar to what Doc had used. Though most I didn't know what the fuck they were for. She stood, wiping the tears from her cheeks with a tissue, and adjusted Mia's blankets to tuck her in. Reminding me how she came from such a loving family. Breaking my heart even more that I was also responsible for this woman's pain. She leaned over and placed a kiss on her daughter's forehead, murmuring something in her ear I couldn't make out.

"You got twenty minutes," her mom whispered, peering up at me, catching me completely off guard. Never expecting her to say that. "I need some coffee." With that, I moved away from the door, letting her pass by.

I walked over to Mia and stood at the foot of her bed. Watching my world, my girl, my life, fight for hers.

"She hasn't woken up yet, but the doctors think that she's going to be just fine. Physically that is… the rest will take time to heal," she shared, bringing my attention back to her. She was almost the spitting image of Mia, except for the brown eyes. "Mia has always been a very happy girl, and it breaks my heart that losing her baby… that… this…" Her eyes welled up with tears, struggling to keep going. "But Mia's a fighter. She's always been this stubborn, strong-willed, determined girl. Even as a baby there was no telling her no. If Mia put her mind to something then she would do it. I know she will get through this, we all will. Even her father."

"Why are you lettin' me stay?" I questioned, yearning to know.

"Because if my son can you give you the benefit of the doubt then I can, too. But please do me a favor. Be gone before I get back."

I nodded as she turned around and left.

The beeping sound of Mia's heart monitor brought my eyes back to her. The rhythmic hissing sound of the ventilator echoed all around me. Filling me with some sort of hope. I pulled up a chair next to her bed to get a closer look at her beautiful face. Reaching for her hand, I lifted it and placed it in my tight grasp. Hoping that she could feel my presence, my heart, and my love for her.

I leaned forward, bowing my head in shame over her broken, bruised, cut up body. Laying my forehead on our joined hands. Needing to feel her soft skin against mine, I kissed along her pulse.

It felt like only seconds had gone by, but my time was starting to run out with her. I didn't know when I would be able to see her again.

Hold her.

Feel her.

Love her.

"I'm so fuckin' sorry, Pippin," I choked out, praying she could hear me.

She could feel me.

She could possibly still love me.

Her hand stirred, and I immediately looked up, narrowing my eyes. I was so fucking exhausted, I couldn't even see straight. I blinked away the haze, thinking my mind was playing tricks on me, but it wasn't. Big, bright blue eyes stared back at me, void of any reaction. Dazed and confused. She searched my face for I don't know how long before she blinked, showing me she was really awake. As if she could read my mind.

"Oh my god, baby, you're awake." I jumped out of my seat, getting close to her face just so I could feel my lips against her skin. "Jesus Christ, Pippin… I love you so fuckin' much… I'm so fuckin' sorry, babe. I'll do whatever it takes… please… please… fuckin' forgive me..." I urged, kissing all over her face. Unable to get enough of her. Wanting her to feel my love, hear the sincerity in my voice. The desperation in my touch. So fucking thankful she was awake.

I leaned back, taking her face in my hands to look into her eyes. Ready to get on my knees and beg her for forgiveness. Do whatever it took to make her mine again.

Her eyes widened and her skin suddenly paled, making my heart suddenly drop.

"Fuck... baby, you okay? Tell me you're okay..."

She stared right into my eyes and softly muttered,

"Who are you?"

"*Mia is experiencing situation-specific amnesia. It's a psychogenic amnesia that can occur in distressed patients as a result of a severely stressful situation they have experienced. It can also be brought on by post-traumatic stress disorder. In her case, we think it's the result of being shot in the back and/or losing the baby. She has no recollection of either incident, the shootout or even being pregnant, to begin with. It could also possibly stem from what she saw while being held captive. At this point, it could be a number of different factors. Although, like I said before, her body has no trauma other than the bullet wound and the incision from the emergency C-section that was performed. Her mind shut down to protect itself. As far as I can tell, there were no signs of negligence nor physical or sexual abuse.*"

The doctor's words played over and over in my mind, set on repeat with no end in sight.

According to the therapist I met with at the hospital, the violent experiences I endured caused my brain to go into emotional shock. My head was hoarding said traumatic events as a way to protect my mind from itself. As far as I knew, nothing ever happened. The potentially harmful memories were blocked out. Stuck in the unconscious purgatory of my brain where they would remain until I was willing to free them.

What if I didn't want to free them?

I knew I was Mia Ryder, daughter of Lucas and Alexandra Ryder. Sister of Mason and Bo Ryder. My memory wasn't completely lost. There were some key moments I still recalled, like the first time I rode a bike and my first day of preschool. Even the time I jumped into the pool and landed wrong, fracturing my arm. But I couldn't remember what my favorite food was, or my favorite color, or the first time I was even kissed. It was as if there were holes in my memory... I knew where I lived, but not what my room looked like. I recognized my uncles, aunts, and cousins, but confused their names.

The list of what I did and didn't remember grew with each passing day. It was an endless scroll of paper I couldn't keep up with.

We hadn't discussed the bullet wound in my back or the scar from my pregnancy. I was told that I was missing for several months, but no one bothered to talk about the details or mention how I was found. Everything remained a mystery that I was too exhausted to solve. We also didn't talk about the man who got kicked out of my hospital room by my Uncle Dylan after I woke up.

Nothing.

Maybe it was because I hadn't asked, or it could have been that they didn't want to divulge the truth. I figured it was probably a little bit of both. My therapy sessions were starting in a week, and I assumed the truth would eventually reveal itself behind those closed doors.

To be honest...

It was just another thing I didn't want to know. If my mind blocked out the traumatic memories, why would I want to remember them? It would only lead to more harm for *me* and my family.

It was so overwhelming not knowing who I was, how I was supposed to act, what to say and not to say. Especially when everyone around me looked at me with such fondness and love. They waited months for me to be found, never giving up hope that I was alive. And I couldn't even remember I was missing to begin with. No amount of words could describe how deeply it hurt my heart to see the struggle in my family's eyes. Looking at me, desperately searching for the girl they anxiously prayed for to return.

Mia Ryder.

The exact same girl…

I prayed would never be found.

The day had come to lay my baby girl to rest, an event that no parent should ever have to endure, but here I was doing exactly that. The only difference was I didn't feel the tragedy like most would. I spent the whole morning laying in bed, blankly staring at the ceiling, conjuring up excuses to why I wouldn't be able to attend the funeral.

What was wrong with me? Was I always this heartless? Why couldn't I mourn my baby?

One question after another plagued my mind till I found myself out of bed. Standing in front of the full-length mirror in my bedroom, in nothing but my bra and panties. Lightly tracing my finger along my C-section scar. Lazily tilting my head to the side, watching the motion through my reflection. While a voice in the back of my head screamed at me to dig deep, try to push through the murky waters separating me from the truth.

It was like I was having an out of body experience. A battle between the conscious me and the unconscious me. I watched from afar as a girl who looked like me stood there in a trance-like state. Going through the motions of life, feeling absolutely nothing but guilt that she couldn't remember her own flesh and blood.

Then there was me, yelling at my conscious self to snap out of it. Willing her to remember what she once loved more than anything in this world. Breathing life into her to feel, to mourn. To honor a life that was so cruelly ripped away from her. Trying to break through the wall my own mind built, so I could feel whole again.

And not this girl who didn't feel anything at all.

"You ready, sweetheart?" Mom asked in a gentle lull, walking up behind me later that morning.

I was once again standing there, staring at myself in the full-length mirror in my room, only this time I was clothed. Taking in the black dress and cardigan I was wearing, along with a pair of black heels I had slipped on to complete my outfit for the funeral. My dark hair was down, cascading along the sides of my pale face, a face I no longer recognized. My once bright blue eyes were now empty of any life. They held no emotion. They were just dark pools, hollow caves staring back at us.

You'd think that would be enough of an answer for her.

It wasn't.

It never was.

Not for any of them.

I didn't answer her question, preferring to stay silent instead. I wasn't ready. I would never be ready for this. I learned rather quickly, once I was released from the hospital a few days after I woke up. It was better to just stay quiet and not say anything than to say something wrong.

She gazed at my reflection in the mirror with the same familiar longing I'd come to expect. She hesitantly reached up to sweep my hair back away from my face, placing the loose strands behind my ears. Wanting to get a better look at her broken daughter. Not grasping the fact that I was intentionally trying to hide.

"You look beautiful, Mia Pia," she whispered, silently hoping the term of endearment would stir a memory inside of me.

It didn't.

My whole family did this, more times than I cared to count. Thinking it would jolt my memories free from the black hole in my brain. All it did was the exact opposite, making me feel more frustrated and alone.

"Thank you," I simply stated, turning my face away to avoid the disappointment in her eyes.

"No matter what. I'm always here for you. Please tell me you know that, sweetie?"

I nodded, knowing she was being sincere.

She spun me to face her, taking hold of my chin to make me look at her. "You don't have to do this. No one expects you to be there if you can't, Mia. The last thing we want is to cause you any more distress."

"If that were the case, all of you would have to stop looking at me or talking to me," I blurted, regretting my words immediately. Causing her to jerk back and let go. "I'm sorry, Momma, that wasn't fair."

"I know…" she paused taking a deep breath, her eyes welling up with tears. "It's only been a week since you were discharged from the hospital. This whole situation is new for all of us. We are learning together how to cope. I look at you and see my daughter, the Mia I remember… the happy little spitfire, the one I know will come back to us. It's just going to take some time. I'm doing the best I can as your mother to protect you, help you get over this hurdle life pushed in your path. We need to take this one day at a time, sweetheart. I'm just so thankful you're home." She pulled me into a tight hug. "I love you, baby. I love you so much."

"I love you, too."

She whispered all sorts of reassuring things to me before we left my bedroom together. I barely remember any of it, choosing to tune her out. It was easier than pretending to be someone I no longer was. My dad was waiting for us at the bottom of the stairs, taking me into his arms when we reached him. Holding onto me for dear life before pulling away and kissing my cheek. Not saying a word as he gave my hand a reassuring squeeze. He escorted me out to the town car, never once letting go of my hand as if he was terrified I'd disappear again.

I blankly stared out the window the entire drive, watching cars blur by. The rain coming down from the heavens, mimicking the tears I knew I'd shed. It felt like all I did was blink and I was walking up to my baby's closed casket at the front of the church. Feeling random arms wrapping me in their embrace, offering condolences I didn't want to hear. While tears streamed down their faces, breaking down, bringing me right along with them. I couldn't tell if I was mourning the death of the baby I knew nothing about, or if it was just the whole situation becoming too much for my emotions to overcome.

It was one thing right after the other.

I blinked a few more times, going through the motions when I suddenly felt the cool wood of the pew hit my skin as I sat between Mason and Bo for the service. My parents' sat to our right, my mom breaking down in my dad's arms. My aunts, uncles, and cousins filled the rows behind us.

I looked around noticing some unfamiliar faces scattered throughout the church. I assumed they were extended family or close friends of my parents'. I just didn't recognize them. My eyes continued to roam while the priest went on about the baby going up to the good Lord. Reading verse after verse from his Bible, muffling the sounds of the sobs echoing off the vaulted ceiling.

I continued looking around the open space when a woman dressed in all black, sitting in the last pew on the opposite side of the church, caught my attention. She was the furthest away from us as if she was trying to blend in or hide. Sitting by herself with what looked like a rosary in her grasp, her head bowed like she was deep in prayer. At one point she looked over at me with tears streaming down her face, giving me a slight smile. I wasn't sure who she was, but something about her presence gave me a strange sense of comfort. I made a mental note to ask my mom who she was after the funeral.

For most of the service I sat there in a trance-like state, feeling as though my entire family's eyes were focused solely on me.

Waiting for I don't know what to happen.

My parents' kept the service small, not wanting to overwhelm me. They had yet to understand that anything and everything overwhelmed me, no matter how big or small. During one of the readings the priest quoted Helen Keller, *"The best and most beautiful things in the world cannot be seen or even touched. They must be felt with the heart."* For some reason, his words pulled at my core and brought tears to my eyes. I needed to get some air. I was suffocating in a sea of everyone else's despair, about to drown in my own. I excused myself to use the restroom, holding back the tears that threatened at the surface. Surprised when no one followed me out, but grateful nonetheless.

I made my way outside instead, craving to feel the sunshine on my face and the fresh air in my lungs. It seemed to be the only things that calmed me these days.

I pushed through the heavy wooden doors, hearing a loud thud on the other side. Followed by a man's voice, rasping, "Oh, shit."

Blocking out the sun with the back of my hand, I immediately looked up, blurting, "I'm so sor—" His eyes bared into mine, rendering me speechless. Locking me in place, I couldn't move even if I wanted to, and for the first time since seeing yet another unfamiliar face, I didn't want to.

His tall, muscular body towered over my small frame, looking down at me with the same longing in his solemn expression that my family wore every day. There was something about him, I couldn't tear my gaze away from. A magnetic pull I was instantly drawn to.

As if he could read my mind, he murmured, "Mia..." just loud enough for me to hear.

I cocked my head to the side, narrowing my eyes, feeling as though I knew him. It evidently wasn't from him knowing who I was.

It was from something deeper.

More meaningful.

A connection I couldn't explain was happening. It was as though we had a link that was severed and one look was all it took to start mending it. The familiarity in his intense gaze made me weak in the knees. I hoped he didn't notice, although he seemed like the type of guy who would notice everything. Neither one of us said a word, but it didn't matter. Our eyes spoke volumes on their own.

"Yeah... that's me," I nervously stated, stepping further outside, wiping away the one tear that had escaped from my eye. Allowing the door to shut behind me. "I umm... I don't know... I mean... I don't remember who you..." I loudly sighed, giving up. Showing him I was getting frustrated. "I don't have the best memory these days."

He smiled, chuckling, "I know, pretty girl." Setting me at ease.

I genuinely smiled back for what felt like the first time since I'd woken up in the hospital. Maybe it was the light blue shade in his eyes that was so damn enticing, or his smile that lured me right in. He was extremely handsome in that rugged, hard edge kind of way.

I took in his black suit, questioning, "Are you here for the funeral?"

His smile abruptly faded, making my stomach drop right along with it. Thinking I had just said something wrong once again. I hated that feeling. Especially knowing I was the reason for the hasty look that pushed away his beautiful features. Replacing them with the same pained expression I seem to cause everyone anytime I open my mouth.

He peered down at the ground, kicking the dirt around with his shoes like he was contemplating what to say next. Finally, he faintly nodded his head. Silently answering my question, but he still didn't look me in the eyes.

"You're not like my brother from another mother, right? Because I guess I already have one of those," I shyly laughed, trying to lighten the mood again. Hoping it would work.

He grinned, glancing back up at me through the slits of his eyes with a certain gleam hiding behind them. "I look like someone who could be related to you?"

My gaze shot to the tattoos taking over his neck, peeking out through the collar of his black button-down shirt. Continuing down to his hands, quickly realizing his body was probably covered in ink.

Making my stomach flutter for entirely different reasons.

I needed to change the subject, so I asked, "What's your name?" Wanting to know who he was.

He arched an eyebrow, wavering for a few seconds before he responded with, "Noah. But you used to call me Rebel."

"How do we—" The double doors to the church flew open, cutting me off. Both of us came face to face with my parents' as they walked out of the service, followed by my family. They stopped abruptly when they saw us together. Peering from me to Noah and back to me again, as if their eyes couldn't settle on one of us for very long.

Except my father's, his never shifted. They stayed murderously narrowed in on Noah.

"You little sh—"

"Lucas!" Mom interrupted in a harsh, demanding tone, grabbing hold of him. Stopping him dead in his tracks from stepping any closer to Noah. "This is not the time, nor the place!"

"Half-Pint—"

"Don't you Half-Pint me! You calm yourself down, now! Unless you want to take it up with me later!"

My eyes widened, taken aback by my dad's actions. Confused by the turn in events. Wondering why he wanted to go after Noah in the first place? Where did all this unexpected hostility stem from? I was more in shock by the fact that my dad reluctantly listened to my mom. Causing her to let out a sigh of relief.

I was about to ask why he was behaving that way. Anxiously needing to know the answers to all the questions that were suddenly plaguing my mind. But the clicking sound of heels came up from behind me, pulling my attention to the same woman who was sitting on the other end of the church. She walked right up and stood beside Noah.

At least one of my questions was finally revealed, I no longer had to wonder who she was. It was obvious she was his mother, they had the same piercing blue eyes.

She didn't waver. "I read in the paper that the service for the baby was being held today. I apologize if our presence has caused you anymore grief, Mr. and Mrs. Ryder," his mom sincerely expressed in a sad tone, making me even more confused by what the hell was going on. She looked over at me with the same comforting smile her son had shown me minutes ago. "It wasn't our intention to hurt you either, Mia. I'm sorry if we did."

"Not at all," I reassuringly replied, still completely caught off guard. "I was actually enjoying Noah's company."

"Sweetie, do you remember him?" my mom questioned, bringing our attention to her.

I hesitantly shook my head no, knowing Noah was staring right at me.

"It's alright, Mia," Noah chimed in. "Just means we gotta make all new memories. That's if it's alright with your parents', of course."

Before I could give what he was saying too much thought, his mom added, "That's why Noah chose to stay outside while I paid respects for the both of us. I wanted to at least be able to say goodbye for him. He didn't mean any disrespect."

"It's okay, Mrs. Jameson. Noah has a right to be here. You both do," my mom interjected, pausing to let her words sink in. "You are welcome to come to the burial service, too. We will be heading over to the Oakdale Cemetery over on North Fifteenth Street in a few minutes." She stepped forward, standing directly in front of Noah. Her face frowned, taking him in for a few seconds before she softly said, "I'm so sorry, Noah. I know you're hurting. The baby was just as much a part of you as she was of Mia. It wouldn't be right to keep you from finding your peace as well."

I jerked back, my eyes widening. Finding it hard to breathe, feeling as though my chest was caving in on me. "Oh my God..."

Noah and I locked eyes as if we were the only two people standing there. Everyone else just faded into the background. Out of sight. Out of mind.

Uncovering the one answer I wanted to know the most all this time.

It all made sense now. The expression on my family's faces when they saw us together. The look that was still in my father's eyes, glaring at him. The way his mom provided me immediate comfort when we were inside of the church.

Especially, the instant connection I felt with him. The second we laid eyes on each other.

Every last look.

Every last feeling.

Every last emotion he pulled out of me.

"It's you..." I finally breathed out, breaking the silence between us. Never realizing I was standing with...

The father of my baby this entire time.

Ends Here

"Missing Oak Island native, Mia Ryder, who was found two weeks ago will be laying her newborn baby to rest this Saturday at the Oakdale Cemetery at noon..."

Now the day had come to lay Madison to rest. At the exact same cemetery where Autumn's memorial was located. The irony was not fucking lost on me. I hadn't slept all night, staring at the obituary I held tightly in my goddamn grasp. Spending the entire evening at the clubhouse in the darkness of my room, drowning my fucking regrets in a bottle of Jack. I knew they'd eventually say their final goodbyes to baby girl, but what bothered me the most about that obituary, was that no one knew she had a name.

Not even her mother.

I spent all morning telling myself I'd pay my respects to Maddie after the funeral, when everyone was gone. When it was just her and I, but the heart wants what it fucking wants. For hours I battled my own worst enemy inside, wanting to be there for Mia. Needing to be there for Mia, even if she didn't remember what I meant to her.

I remembered.

"Who are you?"

"Pippin, what do you mean who am I?" I questioned, thinking this couldn't be fucking happening.

She weakly shoved her hands onto my chest, trying to push me away. Shaking her head to break free from my hands that were still placed on the sides of her face. "Pippin? Who's Pippin?"

Before I knew what I was doing, I found myself pulling up to the cemetery just after one with a new set of fucking demons strapped firmly on my back. Failing miserably at keeping my shit together. I parked my bike as close as possible to where the burial was being held, still trying to stay out of sight, though. The last thing I wanted was to fuck up any more of Mia's life, but I needed to see her at least.

It had been too fucking long since I last laid eyes on my girl in her hospital bed, two weeks ago. Picturing nothing but her face as I backed away from her without even putting up a fight. McGraw had kicked me the fuck out of her room, having one of the officer's escort me out of the hospital, threatening me to stay the fuck away from her.

Or else.

I jumped on my bike and left, even though it took everything in me not to haul ass back into her room and make her remember who I was.

It took McGraw less than a day to call the MC into the police station for questioning, after Mia woke up. I walked in with the club's lawyer, refusing to answer one goddamn question. That's what I was paying Leo a fuck load of money for. He was Martinez's bitch when he was alive, and if he could get him acquitted for all his bullshit, our case should be a breeze. Leo could lie to them all he wanted, but I refused to do it anymore.

Trust me, McGraw wasn't fucking thrilled about it, but he was aware I knew the law as much as he did. I had every right to let my lawyer speak for me. Especially, since none of us were under arrest or detained for anything. We were just there as law abiding citizens, doing our part to solve the case in Mia's disappearance.

Much to McGraw's fucking disapproval.

By the time I made it to the funeral that afternoon, the parking lot was empty. Most of the guests had already left. Only a few remained scattered around, more than likely trying to give Mia some privacy while still trying to be there for her family. Knowing they'd probably need their support. After about five minutes I saw the last guest say their goodbyes. I didn't see Mason or Bo anywhere, not even her cousins, just her uncles and her Aunt Lily. The paper had mentioned there would be a luncheon at the Ryder home after the funeral. I assumed it was where everyone headed, needing to get shit ready for the guests. Knowing it would only make Mia even more unsettled.

It was blatantly obvious she was hanging on by a very thin fucking thread. Standing out in the rain, staring at the small casket in the ground. She looked so confused and helpless, so overwhelmed and exhausted. So fucking tiny and frail. As if she hadn't slept since the last time she was in my arms. Laying in my bed at the safe house. Giving me hope that maybe in the back of her mind, in the dark place where she had imprisoned my existence, she might have missed me, too.

The nights had been the fucking hardest for me. Lying in bed wide awake with nothing but darkness all around me. Yearning to have her in my arms, pressed up against me. Mostly, missing the way I could kiss her whenever I wanted, smelling her addicting fucking scent of vanilla mixed with plain ol' Mia.

As much as I tried to stay busy, too consumed with revenge, she was never far from my thoughts. Neither were her words from the night she fucking finished me off.

"Baby—"

"Don't call me that... Who are you? You're scaring me... Where am I?"

"Jesus Christ, babe—"

"Let go of me... I don't even know you... Get out of here... Now!"

Those were the last words I heard come out of Mia's mouth before her mom and McGraw walked back into the hospital room. She calmed down as soon as she saw them, evidently knowing who they were. I stood there in a state of shock, realizing it was just *me* she didn't recognize.

I shook off the memory as I sat on my bike in the rain at the cemetery, watching from afar. Wanting to remember everything about this moment. The way her hair blew in the wind, the way her small frame tried to keep it together. Except, I could physically feel the way she was breaking apart inside. She was no longer the girl with the big, bright smile or the contagious fucking laugh. She was as empty as I was, alone and lost. For the first time since we met, we were now one and the same. Making me hate myself even more for that. Maddie may have been the one they were putting to ground that day, but Mia was already ten feet under.

Both because of me.

All I had left was my memory of the girl who used to fucking love me.

I got off my bike, removed my gun and cut and threw them on the seat, not giving a fuck it was raining. I lit up a cigarette, needing to stop my mind from going fucking stir crazy. Maybe that was why I didn't see it, when I should have known. I should have felt it or expected it. I could have been better prepared. I could have handled things differently.

Now I'll never fucking know.

I inhaled a long, hard drag from my cig before gazing back up at Mia. Never imagining what I would see. I never thought it would come to this, or maybe I had and just chose to fucking ignore it.

Pretend like it wasn't there.

My core sank, my chest heaved, and I felt my face suddenly pale. "The fuck?" I whispered to myself, knowing that this would be the moment where I would no longer be able to pretend.

Watching it unfold right in front of me.

Noah come up behind Mia, murmuring something in her ear, causing her body to lay lax against his. Sending my mind spiraling down a road to nowhere that I knew would end here.

"This is from me to you. So you can always remember me. I'll always remember you. Okay? That's my courage patch."

Noah didn't waver, turning her to face him. Grabbing onto the sides of her face, he started to brush away her tears with his thumbs. Mia softly smiled at him like she used to smile at me, instantly melting into his touch.

Did she remember him but not me?

"How many tattoos do you have?"

"Too many to count."

She softly smiled. "I can count them. I mean... if you wanted to know how many you had, I could count them for you."

Noah smiled back at her, holding her pretty face tighter in his grasp. He leaned in and kissed her forehead, causing Mia's breath to hitch and her lips to part.

Did she always feel this way for him and me?

Ends Here

"I wanted to see you, okay? That's all. I saw you from the window inside. I haven't seen you in a really long time, over a year actually. I missed you."

"Gonna be fuckin' gorgeous one day, that's for damn sure. Slayin' hearts. Boys linin' up out the door for you. Your old man knows it, too. It's why he keeps you under lock and key. Doesn't want to end up behind bars for beatin' ass. Don't blame him either. You'll meet a cocky little shit who'll promise you the world. You ain't even gonna remember me."

Her breathing hitched and her lips parted. "I'll always remember you."

Noah pulled away, putting some distance between them. Without giving it a second thought, Mia threw her arms around him as if all she needed was him.

Did she ever need me?

"Can I write you?"

"Write me?"

"You know, with a pen and paper. Like pen pals. I'll write you. You write me back. So you know you have a friend waiting for you when you come back home."

"We'll see, yeah?"

"Yeah."

I stood and she threw her arms around my waist, like she never wanted to let me go.

Mia tucked her head into his chest, and Noah wrapped his arms securely around her, holding her tighter against him. Shielding her face from the rain. He kissed the top of her head like she had been his all along. Picking up her off the ground, making their bodies becoming one.

Did I ever fucking exist for her?

"Wha—" I threw her over my shoulder, walking toward the lake.

"Wait! What are you doing? This isn't fair! You're bigger than me! NO! I don't want to go in there, Creed! I'm wearing a pretty dress! Please!"

"Beggin' won't work in this situation, Pippin. Shoulda' thought of that before you decided you wanted to go to war with a soldier. I don't lose."

"I'm sorry! I was just playing! Put me down! Please!"

"Alright, only cuz you asked so nicely." I threw her into the lake.

They finally pulled away from each other with tears streaming down their faces. Staring intently into each other's eyes like they've always loved each other. Like she was yearning for him to kiss her.

Did she ever really love me?

"All I wanted was for him to kiss me! To experience what every other girl has already done! You took that away from me, you asshole! You had no right! You ruined my fairy-tale ending!"

We stared intently in each other's eyes before I kissed her, murmuring against my lips, "Gave you your first kiss, now stop fuckin' bitchin'."

I leaned forward, placing my hands against my bike, needing the support to hold me up. Bowing my head, about to lose my shit. I shut my eyes trying to reel in my fury, feeling like I just took several goddamn bullets to my fucking heart.

"I love you, Creed. I've always loved you."

I felt a solitary tear slide down my face as I let my mind and body go to the dark place inside of me, where I'd lived all my fucking life. I don't know how long I stood there with my heart pounding, my ears ringing. Bleeding the fuck out. Not saying a word, not moving a muscle. Frozen in fucking place. Fighting back the compelling need to hit something.

Or more like *someone.*

Out of nowhere, moving on pure instinct, emotion, and feeling, I looked back up. Locking eyes with Mia from across the lawn as if she felt me, too. Noah's back was still turned. He no longer owned her undivided attention.

I did.

He turned around, following her stare. Instantly jerking back when he saw me, hunched over on my bike, fucking waiting. Mia didn't hesitate making her way over to me. Each step more determined than the last. One by one bringing her closer, never once breaking our connection. As much as I wanted to run to her, I couldn't. Her eyes always showed me the truth. She still didn't know who I was, but it didn't mean her heart wouldn't remember.

I owned it.

It belonged to me.

Proving it with her intense stare, answering all my questions and doubt with each step that brought her in front of me.

"You..." she whispered loud enough for me to hear. "You were in my hospital room. How do you... who are you?"

I resisted the urge to pull her into my arms, tell her I loved her, show her how much she meant to me. How much I meant to her. Yearning to just fucking hold her, feel her, fucking love her.

So I simply spoke the truth, "Whoever you want me to be, Pippin, as long as you remember the man."

Her eyes glazed over, it was quick but I saw it. I was still inside her, still a part of her. Mia's mind may not remember me, but her soul did. Deep down she knew who I was, and right then and there I vowed to fucking figure out how to make her come back to me. There was no living without Mia, there never had been for me.

She licked her lips, sucking in her bottom one like she always did when she was thinking about something really hard. "Why do you keep calling me that? My name is Mia."

"Cuz once upon a time, a pigtail wearin' spitfire reminded me of Pippy Longstockin'. Persistent as fuck, but cute as hell."

She tried to hide back a smile, narrowing her eyes at me. "I did that?"

I nodded, wanting to tell her everything, but I didn't want to overwhelm her or worse... scare her away.

"I met ya at the beach when you were just a baby girl. You were always up to no good, even back then. Followin' me around when you knew better not to. Wantin' to be my friend."

"Oh... did we become friends then? Is that how I know you?"

"We became way more than that."

"What do you me—"

"I warned you to stay away from my daughter!" her dad roared, interrupting us. Much to my disapproval.

"Lucas, enough! Please! Enough!" her mom ordered, standing out in front of him. Trying to keep him in place on the sidewalk a few feet away from us.

"What's going on?" Mia asked, frantically shaking her head, looking from me to her parents. "This cannot be happening again! Do you not like any of my friends?"

"Lucas! Just let them be! Maybe it would help bring our daughter's memory back! Please! I am begging you to back off."

"Lucas, she's right!" her Aunt Lily shouted, stepping out in front of them. "God, you can't control this anymore! Mia has no idea who she is! Creed and Noah were a big part of her life before, whether you accept it or not! We all want Mia back, and at this point who cares?! He saved her life! He's the reason—"

"You saved me?" Mia interjected, frowning her face, looking deep into my eyes. Desperately searching for an answer.

I refused to lie to her, so I merely stated, "Somethin' like that."

"Can you please tell me what's going on? I want the truth! Who are you? What are we to each other?"

I was about to open my mouth to tell her everything I needed her to hear. Needed her to know, but I didn't get the chance.

We were no longer alone.

"You want to know the truth, Mia? I'll tell you the fuckin' truth!" Noah called out, coming out of nowhere, bringing everyone's attention over to him as he stepped in between Mia and me.

"Noah…" I warned, cocking my head to the side.

He callously smiled, grinning, "What, Creed? What are you gonna do? Huh? What can you possibly do that you haven't already fucked up! You see, Mia, I used to love him, too. What's not to love, right? My big, protective brother always there for me no matter what."

"I still am."

"Bullshit! The only thing people need protection from is you! All you do is fuck everythin' up, takin' lives that don't even fuckin' belong to you! Everythin' you touch is tainted, includin' Mia!"

"Don't do this… ain't the time or the place," I gritted out, shaking my head. Working my hands into fists.

He stepped back, throwing his arms out at his sides. "Come at me, bro! I don't give a fuck about what you think! They need to know! She needs to know! What kind of man and brother… you really are."

"Everythin' I've ever done has been for you, you little shit. I'd fuckin' sacrifice my life to save your sorry ass. Jealousy don't suit ya, baby brother! She was never yours! Now walk the fuck away!"

"You think this is about Mia? Oh… Creed, you think you fuckin' know me so well! This ain't got shit to do with her! This is about you and me! Been waitin' for this for a long fuckin' time!"

Her uncles walked up, hearing all the commotion. Standing next to her parents'. Their eyes all glued to the scene unfolding in front of them. No one said a word, not even Mia. She stepped aside, away from us, watching with a fascinated regard. Waiting for all her questions to be answered, but I never wanted it to happen like this.

Never like fucking this.

"Noah, then you take it up with me! Alone! Not here! You handle your business with me, man to fuckin' man! Yeah?"

"Why? You scared of the truth? It don't matter, her family already fuckin' hates you! And *your* girl… she don't even know who you are! And thank Christ for that! You're nothin' but a selfish prick! Always have been!"

"Ain't gonna tell you again, Noah…"

He laughed off my threat. "Was it for me when you went and played G.I. Fuckin' Joe or for Autumn? The same girl that died cuz of you… pushed her away like you did with Mia. Except, it *actually* cost Autumn her life!"

Mia gasped beside me, placing her hand over her heart.

"Mia, it's not—"

"Why don't you go introduce them, Creed?! Her memorial is only about hundred fuckin' feet from our daughter's!"

I was over to him in one stride, getting right up into his face. "You don't know shit about shit, motherfucker."

He didn't cower down, if anything he stood taller. "I know about the drunk ass mother you left me with and the piece of shit father who couldn't keep his dick in his pants! For what?! So you could play the hero for once in your fuckin' life! Give me a break… Autumn would have never been there had it not been for you… you didn't join the military for her! You did it to clear your own fuckin' conscience! How'd it work out for you? Huh? Feel better? Did pretendin' like you weren't the cause of everyone's demise do it for you?!" he scoffed out, eyeing me up and down with a menacing glare.

"Wanna know what was really fun? All the times I had to help get Ma to bed after she passed out in her own fuckin' puke! Pops didn't give a flyin' fuck about her! It only left me! How about all the times I thought she drank herself to death cuz she wouldn't fuckin' move! Havin' to make her puke so she wouldn't die of alcohol poison! What other times do you want me to tell you about, Creed? I got hundreds of them just like those. I'm sure these nice folks would love to hear about the scum their daughter's been fuckin'. Let's show them the real man behind the cut. The fuckin' murderer!"

"That's enough!" I ordered through a clenched jaw.

"What? Truth fuckin hurts, don't it, brother? But I'm just gettin' started. Hey, McGraw, you hearin' all this?!" he hollered, nodding behind him.

I stepped back, away from him and took a deep breath. Remembering we weren't alone.

"Where you goin'? Turnin' your back on your brother again? On your fuckin' family?" He shoved me, but I didn't waver. "It's too late for that, you son of a bitch! We ain't brothers anymore!" He pushed me again, harder that time. "Our blood died the day you murdered my daughter, you piece of shit! But it should have died the day you murdered our brother!"

My fist collided with his face before he got the last word out. His head whooshed back, taking half of his body with him.

Mia gasped, backing further away from both of us. I didn't know if it was because of everything he just confessed or she was just trying to get out of the line of fire. Knowing it wasn't going to end here. Her dad ran over to her before I could give it more thought. Grabbing her arm, he pulled her away.

"Fuck," I breathed out, seeing Noah stumbling around, shaking it off.

It was the first time I ever hit my brother. It was a kneejerk reaction from him provoking me. He wanted me to hit him, and I would learn soon enough why.

Spitting blood onto the pavement, he growled, "It's on, motherfucker." Charging me, ramming his shoulder into my torso. Taking me to the ground. My back skidded across the wet assault beneath me, but I was prepared for it and instantly fought back. Ignoring the sting and burn.

"Don't wanna fight you, you fuck! Calm down!"

He straddled me, grabbing ahold of the front of my shirt, clocking me in the face. "I'll calm down after I knock you the fuck out!"

We wrestled around for a few minutes, each of us trying to gain the upper hand on the other. Elbows, fists, and legs flew everywhere, intermingling together as we threw down. I heard the women screaming and yelling for their husbands to do something, but none of the boys would interfere. Not that I expected them to. They were probably hoping we'd just take each other out. Save them from getting their hands dirty, wanting to do it themselves.

Noah whaled me in the face, letting out all the years of pent-up anger and resentment toward me, but I knew he was really just hitting me for his daughter. Which was why I wasn't fighting back as hard as I could have, mostly defending myself from his aggravated assault. I got on top of him, getting a few hits to his face.

He punched me in the gut right where I had been shot one too many fucking times, causing me to fall to the side. Using the momentum of his punch, he flipped me over, locking me in with his weight. I immediately guarded my face, but it didn't matter. He nailed his fists into my ribs, my stomach, getting another few good hits to the side of my face, too.

"Fucking a!" I roared, blocking another blow.

He didn't let up, tugging at my shirt, ripping it off. "Fuck you! Fight back, you bitch!"

I finally did, hitting him in the face, in the stomach, and then again in ribs. Over this bullshit. He peeled over while I staggered to my feet, thinking it was done. We were both panting heavily, sweating profusely with nothing but blood and rain dripping off our bodies and faces. Our eyes never wavered from one another, wild and brazen, taking each other in. He regained his composure, standing up straight. Loosening his tie and pulling his tucked shirt out from his pants, bringing it up to his face. Using it to wipe the blood running into his eye from the open gash above his brow. His chest heaved as he threw off his tie, ripping open his bloody collared shirt. Throwing it to the side, too.

It was then I realized it wasn't over.

It was far from fucking over.

171

He pushed off the ground and came at me full force. Swinging, punching, kicking, hitting me all over. I fought back, throwing him onto the wet pavement with a thud, knocking the wind out of him. Hovering above him, beating his body and face in. Seeing nothing but fucking red as my bloody fists pounded in to him over and over again.

"This what you wanted, you little shit?!" I roared, hitting him again.

"Jesus! Please, Dad! Uncle Dylan! Uncle Jacob! Uncle Austin! Please! Somebody do something! They're going to kill each other! Please!" I heard Mia beg in a terrified voice.

I immediately stopped mid-punch, pushed off Noah, barely being able to stagger back up to my feet. My body swayed, my head throbbed. Pain radiated everywhere. Noah wasn't any better. Groaning into the ground, spitting up more blood, holding onto his side. I continued to forcefully pant, trying to get my heart from pounding out of my chest. Hastily wiping the blood from my face with the back of my hand. Blinking through the mist and haze before I threw my hand down to help him up. He looked at it, contemplating my offer. Deciding at the last second to grab ahold of it and pull me into his awaiting fist. Catching me off guard, he got a few more hits into my face and torso.

It was then her uncles and dad pulled us off each other. Needing two of them on each of us to separate our bodies and hold us back.

Noah's face was void of any emotion. For the first time I didn't recognize the man staring back at me.

He was no longer my brother.

Looking at me with nothing but disgust in his eyes, he sneered, "Might as well keep him like that," Nodding toward McGraw who was still holding my arms behind my back. "He's the one who took Mia! He's not the fuckin' hero! He's the reason she was fuckin' missin'! He had her the whole fuckin' time!"

Before McGraw's hold could tighten on me, I broke away. My hand instantly reached down into his holster, pulling out his gun and clicked off the safety. He instinctively grabbed ahold of my arm, trying to wrestle it out of my hands. When a single shot fired into the air.

"NO!" Mia screamed, her mom and aunt holding her back. Ducking to the ground.

McGraw let go, jumping back with his arms in the air, surrendering. Knowing I wasn't fucking around. Aiming the gun directly at all them, only having seconds to haul ass before they would take me in. I would never hurt her family, but they didn't have to know that.

"This ain't over," McGraw threatened, eyeing me and then his gun.

I nodded, knowing he couldn't have been closer to the fucking truth. I quickly backed away, never taking my eyes or the gun off them as I jumped onto my bike. Throwing back the throttle, the engine roared to life.

"You won't get away with this!" her dad yelled. "I will hunt you down and fucking kill you myself if I have to!"

I wanted to look back at Mia one last time, needing to see her face for just one second, knowing in my heart...

I may never see her again.

I didn't.

I couldn't.

Too terrified to see the look on her face, showing her the man I always tried to hide. I took off like a bat out of hell instead, chucking McGraw's gun into the bushes furthest away from them.

The war didn't end here. It was only the beginning. I would get to the bottom of the truth that cost me my entire life, even if it meant...

I could die in the process.

Mia

"How does that make you feel?"

"Have I told you how much I hate it when you ask that, Dr. Garcia."

"And yet after three months of coming to see me, you still know I have to ask," my therapist chuckled.

Two days a week I sat on a comfortable leather sofa and poured my heart out to a complete stranger. We talked about anything and everything. Sometimes she just listened, and other times she'd ask questions. Trying to stir the empty holes in my memory into submission. Erupt something, anything from the months I was held captive. Wanting to trigger an emotion to open the floodgates and drown me with the truths of who I was.

My parents' sat in on the first few sessions, but Doctor Garcia quickly put an end to that. My dad's outbursts earned him a seat in the waiting room more often than not. So eventually he was banned. The doctor felt that their presence wasn't helping with my healing process. If anything it was possibly making it worse.

"It makes me feel confused," I simply replied.

"Have you seen him?"

"No. Not since I found out the truth. You know how it went down, Doctor. We've spoken about it several times."

"Let's talk about it again."

I sighed. "I knew you were going to say that."

She nodded, waiting for me to continue.

"I don't know who he is... I don't remember him. All I know is what I've been told or what I've seen. His name is Creed, and his brother's name is Noah. I still don't know what Creed and I were to each other, but from what I've gathered, he was very important to me. I guess we were important to each other... One night I ended up at his MC clubhouse and got knocked up by Noah, which is what my parents' have told me. Kick to a few months later... I ended up getting taken by Creed, but I still don't know why or where I was. From what my parents' have said, I guess there was a shootout where I was shot in the back and..." I bowed my head, fidgeting with the hem of my dress. "They had to perform an emergency C-Section. My baby was only seven months and didn't make it. Creed took me to the hospital after... and now... we're here," I relayed, shaking my head. "Jesus, that just sounded like a soap opera."

She chuckled, "A bit, but trust me. I've heard worse."

"I bet."

"Does recalling those events stir any memories or emotions?"

I shrugged. "Yes, but not in the sense that you want. It stirs feelings from the fight I witnessed between them. It was so raw and real. So much pent-up anger, I felt every word, every hit, hurting right along with them. I know Noah blames Creed for the loss of our baby girl. He's told me how he feels."

"Do you believe him?"

"Yes and no. I don't think it was intentional or malicious on Creed's part. I think it just happened and they did what could under the circumstances."

"Now why do you think that? You don't know this man. He's a complete stranger to you."

"Something in my heart tells me not to be afraid of him. Here's the thing, Doctor, from the second I saw Noah, I felt a connection with him and that was before I knew he was the father of my baby. The same goes for Creed. When I saw him at the cemetery, I didn't even realize I was walking toward him until I was standing in front of him. It was like being pulled by a string he was controlling. Luring me right to him. Then when we spoke, I could see it in his eyes, hear it in his voice... he loves me. And not in the 'I love you, I love you, too,' kind of way. It's in the 'You're my person, my lobster, my everything,' and that alone tells me that what we had was true," I sincerely expressed for the first time. Feeling like an elephant had been lifted off my chest.

"Do you want to remember him?"

"I don't know. I think about him a lot… more than I probably should," I nervously laughed. "Sometimes I think it's because I want him to tell me what happened. Give me some closure. Confront him to ask why he took me… and then other times I think it's from missing him. That's what confuses me the most, Doctor. How can I miss a man I don't remember?"

"Our mind and hearts are two different organs, Mia. Just because you don't remember your memories, doesn't mean you can't recall your emotions. The deep feelings may be coming from your core, reminding you of happier times.

"That's deep, Doc."

"Let's walk through how you felt witnessing the burial."

"We have been through this already. Out of everything you ask me to recall, for some reason that is the hardest."

"It's because I'm making you tap into those raw emotions. Pulling them forward in your mind so you can heal. You may not want to relive it, but it will eventually prove that you shared a bond as a mother to your baby girl, which can trigger so much, Mia. Do me a favor and close your eyes."

I did.

"Now go back to that point in time and tell me what you feel."

I took a deep breath, knowing that this was going to hurt. "Okay, I'm standing in the rain…" My mind drifted off, telling the story for me.

I watched with stone-cold eyes as the shiny white casket was lowered into the earth's soil. The heavens were weeping right along with me, raindrops seeping into my black jacket.

Burning my core.

Little by little.

Deeper and deeper.

Until darkness surrounded me, until all eyes were only staring at me. I could feel their eagerness, like a noose around my neck. Waiting for me to react, waiting for me to break down, just waiting for me to do something.

Anything.

I tried to pretend I wasn't there. I tried to imagine that my life hadn't been changed in a matter of seconds. That my world hadn't been turned upside down in the span of a few hours. That everything I wanted to believe in wasn't truly...

A lie.

It also cost me the love of my life. The person I watched being buried deep into the ground, six feet under, where I would never see them again.

Not one smile.

Not one I love you.

My eyes fluttered open when I realized I had tears streaming down my cheeks. I leaned forward grabbing a tissue off the table, wiping away the emotions I tried so hard to forget.

"Continue, please," Dr. Garcia said in a sincere tone. "This is good."

"For who?"

"You."

I closed my eyes again, picking up where I left off.

"I suddenly felt Noah behind me. Everything about him hurt. His scent, his aura, especially his love for me. *For us.*"

"I'm sorry. I'm so fuckin' sorry," he voiced in a tone that was filled with nothing but pain and remorse. *His guilt was so thick, so consuming, I could feel it engulfing me, making it hard to breathe.*

My life ended before it ever had a chance...

To begin.

While I stared at the gray granite tombstone, etched with the last name...

Jameson.

"How does Noah fit into this?" She pulled me away from my memories. Away from my sadness, grateful to be pulled back to reality.

"I mean... he's been there for me. He came and talked to my parents'. Asking their permission for us to hang out. I still can't believe the day he showed up at my house unannounced, a few days after the altercation. All bruised and cut up, asking to speak to my parents alone. They went out on the patio, shutting the sliding glass door behind them, but that didn't stop me from eavesdropping. I hopped up on the kitchen counter and slid the window open a crack so I could listen."

"If it weren't for my wife, you wouldn't be in my house. You have ten minutes before I kick your ass out," Dad ordered in a harsh tone.

"Sir, first I want to apologize for my behavior at the cemetery. That ain't right, what I did... I'm sorry."

"Let's cut the bullshit. Why you really here? You're now down to eight minutes."

"Lucas..." Mom reprimanded, making me smile.

"I came here wantin' to ask your permission to hang out with Mia, sir," Noah declared, making me jerk back. Almost falling off the counter from the sudden movement.

"This is what you're wasting my time for?"

"Oh my God, Lucas! Give the man a chance."

"Look what happened last time we let Mia out... Ended up knocked up by this little shit, and apparently screwing his brother on the side... It's not fucking happening, Alex. Not anymore. We're done here."

I winced, hearing my dad say such hurtful things. He hadn't talked that way to me. At least not recently.

"Sir, it ain't like that. Things are different now. I left the MC behind. I wanna fresh start with my life. Make somethin' of myself. I'm not askin' to date your daughter. I just want to hang out with her. Be her friend. Maybe help her, ya know?"

"What—"

"I agree, Lucas," Mom interrupted him. *"He has a good point. I want my Mia back... And I'm willing to try anything to make that happen. I know you are, too. So please, put your stubbornness aside for our daughter. She's not a child anymore. We can't keep treating her like one. He didn't have to come here to ask for permission, but he did, out of respect for you. That means something to me and I know it woul,d mean something to you, if you let it."*

"Half-Pint, the answer is no. I don't want to lose her again."

"She's already lost! Let Noah help. Jesus, Lucas... you were far from perfect at their age. I don't need to remind you what you were like. Mia doesn't even come close to how you behaved! Noah may not be the man we thought she might end up with, but the same can be said about you! After everything you put me through, my family

still gave you a chance. You owe it to your daughter to help her get better. Do you understand me?"

No one spoke for what felt like forever, until finally my dad yelled, "Fine! But if you lay one hand on Mia, touch her in any way. I will hunt you down and it won't end fucking pretty. You hear?"

"Yes, sir. Thank you."

"Even after what we all witnessed and heard that day from Creed and Noah's fight, my dad reluctantly agreed but it was more my mom's doing. She hopes it will help me remember. I think my dad is just grateful to know the truth behind my disappearance because of Noah. I mean, after Creed took off that day, it was bad.... I mean really bad. I think my dad might also respect the fact that Noah came to him and asked, even though I know he would never admit it."

Dr. Garcia nodded again. "How do you feel about Noah? You've been hanging out with him a lot. Do you ask him questions?"

"I like Noah. I haven't asked him anything about what I don't remember, yet."

"Why? You know he has answers."

"I just... I mean... I don't feel like I disappoint Noah, like I do everyone else. Like he's happy that I don't remember him. It's almost like we can start over with a friendship, and I think he likes that as much as I do. I know if I ask him, he'd answer, but a part of me is scared to know what he would say. It's obvious he hates his brother... I don't know how sincere he may be about the subject, and I guess I don't want it to confuse everything even more."

"Has Creed tried to reach out to you?"

I shook my head. "He'd be stupid if he did. Between my uncles and my dad, they've made it their mission to get him out of hiding. The reward money alone is insane. Uncle Dylan has a warrant out for his arrest, and I wouldn't be surprised if he alerted people on the other side of the world about it. I think I'd prefer Creed to be brought in before my dad found him. I'm pretty sure Dad would be the one who ends up in jail for murder."

"I know, Mia. It's why your parents', mostly your dad, aren't allowed in on our sessions anymore. He's very protective over you. I could see that from the second I shook his hand at the hospital. At first, I thought it was from you missing, him just being worried. Then I realized it's something that I think you may have struggled with before. Holding on tight to the leash they have on you. Every parent raises his or her kids differently. I'm not saying the way they raised you is wrong, but I think it's good that they're giving you some space now. You need it. You're going to be an adult soon, and they're not going to be able to shelter you forever."

"Yeah, the last few weeks they've actually let me leave the house with Noah. I got my Jeep back, I guess they found it abandoned at the train station not too long after I went missing. Since I was returned safe and there was no circumstantial evidence found in it, I got it back. It's been awesome to drive by myself, go to the store, the library, the mall. Sometimes I need to clear my head, so I just drive around, aimlessly… I've ended up at those train tracks a few times. Enjoying the quiet privacy," I shared, thinking about the peace those tracks bring me. "But one thing I do miss is being around people my age. Being homeschooled by my mom is starting to take its toll. I guess it's just exhausting to feel like I was perfect in their eyes before and now I'm not. Even though I still look the same, I don't feel same anymore, Doctor. I'm scared that even if my memories come back, I still won't want to be that girl. It's what terrifies me the most."

"Let's not think about that now, you need to concentrate on taking life one day at a time. In the meantime, between our sessions I want you to write in this." She turned around and pulled a notebook off her desk, handing it to me. "Anytime you remember something, you feel anything, whether it's a trigger or a dream, I want you to write it in there. Consider it your homework. You bring your notebook to our sessions, and we can talk about what you've written down. Makes sense?"

"Yes."

"Okay, great. You did good today, Mia. It will get easier, I promise. Same time next week?"

"Yes. Thank you, Doctor."

I walked out of her office, feeling better. I always did when I left our sessions. There was something about being able to talk to her with no judgment, which made it easy for me to speak the truth.

I looked up when the elevator door dinged, letting me know I was in the parking garage of her office.

"Noah," I announced, not surprised he was standing in front of me.

He did this sometimes. Show up after my sessions were done. As if he knew I needed someone to take my mind off everything that was discussed in therapy.

"Hey, pretty girl. I thought I'd take you to dinner and then maybe a movie. If you're up for it?"

"Yeah! I'd love that. Umm... you want to drive my Jeep?"

He chuckled, knowing I didn't want to go on the back of his bike. I wasn't sure why, it just felt wrong. I chalked it up to being nervous about being on a motorcycle.

"So how was your day?"

"Better now," he rasped, bumping his shoulder into mine before he threw his arm around my neck. Pulling me into his side.

I liked the way he felt, so warm and cozy. Winter officially kicked in, and we were experiencing our first cold front in Oak Island. I smiled, leaning into his embrace. Enjoying the feel of being wrapped in his arm.

Once we got to my Jeep, he opened the passenger door for me, grabbing ahold of my keys. I put my seatbelt on and pulled out my cell phone that my parents' had recovered, from the center console. Needing to call my mom to tell her I was going to dinner and a movie with Noah. Knowing she'd worry if I wasn't home right after therapy.

1 new text message

I clicked over the screen, expecting it to be her or my dad. Checking in on me like they always did after therapy.

"I know you probably don't wanna hear from me, but needed ya to know... I miss you, babe." – Unknown Number

"You alright over there?" Noah asked, glancing over at me.

I quickly clicked off the screen. "Yeah, just texting my mom."

He nodded, appeased with my answer. Focusing back on the road.

I thought about the text message for the rest of the night, not having to guess who it was from.

I knew it was Creed.

And for some reason, it gave me comfort. Not only because he was alive and hopefully well, but because...

He missed me.

"Makes no fuckin' sense, Creed. You know it and so do I," Diesel argued, sitting across from me on his couch.

I took a deep breath, hunched over in the chair with my elbows placed on my knees. My head bowed with my hands out in front of me. Taking in everything he was saying. It had been three months since I last saw Mia, or Noah for that matter. I went into hiding the second I rode out of the cemetery parking lot, leaving my whole world behind. Making up some bullshit lie about how McGraw figured out I took Mia and why I looked beat to shit, knowing what would happen if they found out Noah fucked me over. Devil's Rejects made me disappear until they could calm the shit storm Noah brought on. I was like a caged fucking dog while my old man sent everyone on what seemed like a wild fucking goose chase.

McGraw issued warrants to search all the brothers' houses. Any property that had our names on it, anything that could lead him to me. Threatening the MC with the consequences of aiding and abetting a fugitive. He had each one of their asses sitting back in that interrogation room, trying to get to the bottom of what the fuck really happened. Cross-examining their stories for any loopholes. Comparing their alibis to the ones they gave since day one, knowing nothing had changed in what they claimed went down with Mia's disappearance. Noah was the only one who threw my ass under the fucking bus, McGraw had no circumstantial evidence against them. He couldn't hold him.

I would be lying if I said I wasn't shocked as shit that McGraw didn't tell them his source was my brother. Not using Noah as bait to get them to talk. All I knew was that Noah hadn't dragged the MC name or their involvement in Mia's disappearance through the mud. Just mine. It didn't mean I wasn't fucking waiting for the other shoe to drop. My hands were tied, I couldn't rat out my baby brother, even though he pretty much turned my ass into the pigs.

Delivering my balls to McGraw on a silver fucking platter. The MC would have crucified Noah for turning his back on not only a brother, but also his VP. There was no way in hell I would ever allow that to happen. At the end of the day, it didn't matter, though. He turned his prospect cut in the day after our fight. Standing up to Pops, letting him know that things were different now, he was different. Our old man didn't even put two and two together on why Noah looked exactly how I fucking did. Beat up to shit. I guess he was too consumed with trying to make this problem go away. Noah walked out of the clubhouse that day and hadn't returned since. At least that's what Diesel and Ma told me.

Ma knew I was in hiding, she knew what went down between Noah and me. She was our mother, I didn't expect her to take sides. Especially since Noah had been staying at her new place by the beach. Not far from Mia's mom's restaurant. She officially left my fucking cheating bastard of a father. I wasn't surprised in the least. Their marriage had been over for fucking decades. Only difference now, it was on paper.

Stacey and Laura helped her buy the four-bedroom, three bathroom colonial home set back from the beach. She told me I was welcome to come home anytime I wanted, stating there was plenty of room for Noah and me to live under the same roof with her. It was why she bought such a big house. We'd always have a home and bed to sleep in, no matter what. She even gave me a key. I just think she hated being alone. I knew it hurt her, knowing her sons were fighting against each other. When all she wanted was for us to stay united and have one another's backs. We were the only family we had, and she reminded us of that often.

"I know I left that fuckin' disc Martinez gave me under the mattress in my room at the goddamn clubhouse. I hid it there the day I had to report back to base."

"I already told you! I tore apart your fuckin' room! It's not there!"

"Then someone fuckin' found it and stole it!" I abruptly stood, pacing around the room. "It's my fuckin' fault. I should have checked that disc fuckin' months ago, but I had to report back for duty. Then Mia got knocked up, then the fuckin' shootout and puttin' her into hidin'. It's been one thing after a fuckin' another. I was goin' to check it the day Martinez sent that text message, but I hauled fuckin' ass over to Ma's house cuz of their fuckin' dinner! Thank God for that or Ma and Mia could be dead."

"We've been lookin' in the wrong places, pointin' fingers at the wrong fuckin' people. When we shoulda' been lookin' at our own. And this just fuckin' proves it! You didn't look at that disc cuz you didn't think it had one fuckin' thing to do with this! I followed your orders and our fuckin' Prez's, cuz I knew you had a shitload on your plate with Mia. Which is why you weren't thinkin' straight. Tryin' to keep her safe. I get that. Which is why we gotta talk, now."

"So fuckin' talk. Ain't goin' anywhere. I'm listenin'."

He didn't falter. "Think about it… from the second your old man took Mia and brought her to the clubhouse, he had you by your fuckin' sack, and you know it. Why would he just take her? Huh? Not tell any of us? How did he even know where to find her? Why look like the fuckin' hero? When he should have been fuckin' fightin' by our sides? For his goddamn club?! He don't give a shit about her! He's proven that time and time again. He did it to have your loyalty when he don't fuckin' deserve it. That shootout was bullshit in the first place! Why come to your house?! A home you're rarely at and your father hasn't stepped foot in for who the fuck knows how long. That was personal, it didn't have shit to do with our MC."

I narrowed my eyes at him, cocking my head to the side.

"You know it, Creed! It was a setup, bro. So was that ambush at the safe house."

"Naw, that was my fuck up. I let her outside, knowin' it would lead to no fuckin' good."

"I call bullshit! Even Doc smelled a fuckin' traitor that night. That's what Prez wants you to think! That safe house has been in our MC since before we were fuckin' born. He was waitin' for you to slip up, do somethin' that would give reasonin' for a shit storm. Not to mention that safe house was out in butt fuckin' Egypt! No one would be able to find that place. Can't even stumble upon it, unless you already knew it was there. All this shit started at that first meetin' when he shot Striker in the fuckin' head all those years ago. A man who's been his best friend since they were kids, is all of a sudden a fuckin' traitor? No fuckin' way… eat my ass and suck my cock. That's some bullshit right there."

My mind immediately started reeling with everything he just said, mainly because it made so much fucking sense. Every last bit of it.

"This ain't got shit to do with territory, with Sinners Rejoice, with nothin' that concerns the Devil's Rejects. It's about your old man! It's been about him since day fuckin' one! He wants us to think it's the MC. And he knows we'll believe it cuz he lives and breathes it... until it comes down to savin' his own fuckin' ass! And it's not just about him. It's about you, too! We just need to figure out what the fuck he's hidin'. And who stole that fuckin' disc. It will clear your name from spendin' life behind bars and possibly throw in our Prez instead."

"Jesus Christ... you're right. You're so fuckin' right."

"It's go time, motherfucker. You're in hidin' now, perfect time to find out the truth. No one will suspect anythin'. We ride together, and we fuckin' die together, brother. I'll be right there by your side. Just need to figure out where to start."

"I know where. Suit up, Diesel. We're goin' to fuckin' Hell."

And he was known as...

El Santo.

I never thought it would take three fucking months to get a meeting with El Santo. I had never met the motherfucker, but that didn't mean I didn't know who the fuck he was. Everyone knew him by reputation, but only a hand full of people knew the man behind the name. Especially the corrupt.

Men just like me, but far fucking worse.

Diesel and I pulled up to the underground club around midnight, parking our truck in the shadiest fucking area of Miami. We'd been on the road for eleven and a half hours, only stopping for food and gas. Pissing on the side of the road when need be. We couldn't risk me being seen since I was still in hiding.

The bouncer eyed me up and down, from my combat boots to my cut, to my fucking leather jacket. "We don't accept your kind here," he sneered, making me want to knock his goddamn teeth out.

I cocked my head to the side, gritting out, "We were fuckin' invited."

"By who?"

"Your boss, motherfucker. So how 'bout ya let us through."

His eyes went to my cut, talking into his earpiece, "Creed." He glanced over at Diesel's cut, stating his name over the earpiece next. Moments later he narrowed his eyes at me, nodding for us to go in.

I smiled. "Fuck you very much," I gritted out as we walked by him, purposely bumping into his shoulder.

The club was huge and packed with people. Making it hard for us to even get by without having to wait a few seconds for the crowds to separate. The further we got into the place, the worse it got. The music was pounding through the speakers surrounding us, vibrating through to my core as we tried to make our way over to the back doors. Bodies ground up against Diesel and me, random chicks trying to wrap their arms around our waists, pulling us deeper into the mass of people. The place was obviously exceeding capacity, filled to the fucking brim. Everyone dressed to the nines. Beautiful people just getting their night started. Moving to the beat of the house music blaring above the crowds.

Everything from the flashing lights to the neon strobes, strumming around every corner. There were plush couches along the perimeter with tables stacked with open bottles of Moet and other expensive alcohol. The already fucked up people were dancing their asses off. Eyes closed with their head's leaning back facing the ceiling, letting the melody of the music take over them.

I instantly knew that drugs flowed in this place as much as the booze did.

I didn't give a fuck about any of it. I wasn't there to fucking party, and from the looks of it, this wasn't even the goddamn main event. This was just a cover up for what was behind door number two and possibly fucking three or four. The bouncers let us right in, not asking who we were again. Our names already approved to enter the exclusive fucked up private party. Not one soul could ever get past those doors unless they personally knew El Santo. There wasn't anything he didn't know, including who we were. It was the way he protected himself. The motherfucker was a deviant mastermind. Having everything and anything at his disposal at any point in time. It came along with his world, his territory.

His legal fucking rights.

We continued our descent to our final destination, walking down a long, narrow hallway that was nearly pitch black. Leading to another door, another dimension. Another fucking world.

But this wasn't a club, at least not any kind I'd ever been to.

As soon as the double doors opened, I swear I could feel the demons oozing out, hovering all around us. Waiting to fucking drag us under. They called this place Hell. The rules were anything fucking goes. From sex to drugs, to gambling, to fucking murder—these black walls had seen it all. This was where the elite of the corrupt partied since they could get away with anything. Sex trafficking, prostitution, drug smuggling, slavery, BDSM. You name it, it was there.

It made me sick to my fucking stomach, watching the girls who were tied up, bound and gagged. Some for pleasure, but most for fucking pain.

This was a man's world, end of fucking story.

"Creed Jameson," a woman's voice purred from behind me. I turned around, locking eyes with a blonde whose tits were on full display. "Follow me, boys. He's waiting for you. They all are."

I nodded to Diesel, and we both followed the busty chick toward the back. Leading to yet another fucking hallway with another set of fucking double doors.

Anonymity was the key purpose of this club.

She opened the doors, nodding for us to go through. My hand never strayed far from my gun, prepared for anything, expecting it all. Not knowing what the fuck we were walking into. It could easily have been a setup for all we knew. From what I heard, El Santo was a sadistic motherfucker. A cruel bastard who thrived on pain, pussy, and power. He'd put a bullet in your head just because he was fucking bored. He had no sanctity or value for anything or anyone. Nothing was sacred to him. He respected nothing.

He didn't have to.

He was the best prosecuting attorney in the nation. They called him El Santo for all the good he did around the world. The man could literally get away with murder.

And he did.

All the fucking time.

"You got some brass fucking balls, requesting a meeting with me when you're a wanted fucking man," El Santo challenged in a thick Spanish accent, sitting at the end of the narrow, wooden conference table. Leaning back in his chair. His hands resting behind his head.

His intense, menacing brown eyes were narrowed in, focused solely on me as if Diesel hadn't even walked in the room beside me. His long, dark curly hair that came down to his chin was wild and crazy, hanging along his pretty boy fucking face. He was dressed like he'd just stepped out of the courtroom which he probably had. His black suit jacket was placed on the back of his chair, leaving him in a gray collared shirt with a black vest and matching black tie that hung loosely around his neck. Except that wasn't what caught my attention.

It was the bloody rolled up sleeves he was sporting like he just beat the fuck out of someone or killed them. I'd put my money on both. His gun holsters were still securely strapped to his sides, but his two Glocks were missing. They were sitting right on the table in front of him.

Pointing straight at us.

"Please, by all means, gentlemen. Mi casa es su casa. Take a fucking seat," he added, nodding to the empty chairs on the other end of the table. Directly in the line of fire with the barrels of his guns.

There were two other men sitting next to him, one on each side. The man to the right was Benjamin Robinson, but everyone knew him as *Bossman*. He was a notorious mobster who recently spent some time in the slammer. Was sentenced to life in prison until he escaped, killing a shit ton of guards on his way out.

Supposedly he had some sort of involvement with Martinez and coincidently was indicted right after his murder. He was wearing his signature ball cap with his hair tied back in a ponytail. Dressed in a plain white shirt and a pair dark jeans. I couldn't help but stare at his ink. It was an ocean inspired sleeve on his left arm. The detail was unreal, I was tempted to ask for his artists digits, but I thought it was wiser to keep it business like. Rumor has it that the man loved the water, owned a fuck load of boats that trafficked drugs all over the border. I wasn't surprised he was in Miami.

I also wasn't surprised he was sitting beside El Santo. I'm sure he had something to do with his "escape."

"Who invited the white guy?" I taunted, nodding to Bossman. We'd done business a few times. I liked him. He was a laid back, zero fucks given kinda guy. He didn't talk much, but when he did it was always a smart ass fucking response.

He snidely smiled, scoffing out, "Your mom when she was sucking my cock last night."

I chuckled, "Good to see you out, man."

189

"Good to be seen."

I didn't recognize the other man sitting to El Santo's left. I imagined it was one of his bodyguards judging by his stature and the way he was looking at us. Ready to take us the fuck out if needed. He was wearing a black suit and wire in his ear.

"Let's cut the bullshit, shall we? To what do I owe the honor of your presence, Mr. Jameson?" El Santo chimed in.

"Creed," I simply stated.

"I wasn't aware we were on a first name basis. You can call me Mr. Montero. You haven't even earned the right to shake my goddamn hand, yet."

"Just to sit in your presence then?"

"No. To answer my fucking questions. I'm known for having very little patience, Mr. Jameson. Would you like to test that fucking theory?"

"With all due respect, *Damien*…"

He grinned, arching an eyebrow.

"We asked for a meetin' wit' you. Not your fuckin' entourage, yeah?"

"And here I thought we were all becoming friends now."

"Friends is a term I use loosely."

"You're coming into my territory, making demands? You really are just a stupid biker, eh?"

"Says the man who took the meetin'."

He laughed, big and throaty. Grabbing his gun off the table and pointing at me. "I fucking like you! And because of that, I'm going to excuse your shitty manners, and not shoot you in the goddamn leg. You're welcome. With that being said, what the fuck do you want?"

I nodded to his gun, silently ordering him to get it the hell out of my face.

"Bikers…" he dramatically breathed out, laying his Glock back on the table in front of him. But still pointing it at me. "They have no fucking respect for authority. You have five minutes before my hand gets cold and I get trigger happy."

"What do you know 'bout my father?" I asked, knowing I wasn't going to win this battle.

"What do I know about him or what do I have on him? See what I did there?" He leaned forward, placing his elbows on the table. "Learn to ask the right fucking questions to get the answers you need."

"I thought we were cuttin' the bullshit. You know exactly what I fuckin' mean. You help me, and I'll help you. Now, those are words you fuckin' understand, yeah?" I mocked, leaning into the table mirroring his posture. "You tell me what you got on my old man, and I'll get you the fuckin' evidence ya need to lock his ass away behind bars, for good."

He smiled, leaning back into his leather chair. No doubt, understanding my proposal.

"You're up for District Attorney, yeah? Breakin' news... 'El Santo, Damien Montero, brings down yet another notorious outlaw. MC President, Jameson of the Devil's Rejects, who has been wanted by the FBI for decades. Evidence found, making him liable for the innocent lives he's taken and other crimes punishable by the United States judicial system," I proposed in a serious tone, glancing over at Diesel. "What do ya think, bro? Sounds like a fuckin' promotion to me."

"I'd bet my Harley it was, and you know how much I love her," he retorted, only looking at Damien, who was glaring at us like we just handed him a golden fucking ticket.

"So... what do you know 'bout my father?" I cocked my head to the side. "Am I askin' the right question, now?"

"Leave us," Damien ordered in a harsh tone to his men.

They did as they were told. Bossman nodded over to me before he walked past us, followed by the suit. Damien didn't falter, standing up from his chair, walking over to the makeshift bar in the corner of the room. Pouring three glasses of bourbon, setting them down in front of us. He sat sideways at the edge of the table, taking a long swig from his glass before slamming it down on the table when he was done.

Bringing his fingers up to his mouth like he was contemplating what to say next. "Have you ever wondered why your Prez and Martinez *are* friends?" he questioned, emphasizing the word are.

I jerked back, stunned by his response.

"Hmm… I know you hate the motherfucker, but I've come to miss him. Things were a lot more entertaining when he was *alive*. Especially between your old man and him."

"The fuck?"

"You said you wanted to know what I knew about your father. Not what I had on him. There's your fucking answer. Now get the fuck out."

"You ain't given me shit."

"I've given you plenty. I'm a prosecuting attorney for fuck sake. Can't put words in your mouth. Won't hold up in fucking court," he taunted, grinning.

"It's up to you to find what I need and then we'll both get what we want. Entendido?"

I stood and walked over to the door, having enough of his goddamn bullshit.

"Oh, and, Creed?"

I spun to face him.

"Don't you ever disrespect me, again. Next time I'll blow your fucking balls off."

And with that, I left. Knowing he could tell me what I needed to know, but he wanted to fuck with me, maybe have me prove myself worthy to him. Who the hell knew… He was just another fucked up son of a bitch.

When we got back to the truck, my cell phone pinged with a text. I never expected to read the words that I did on the screen.

"It's Mia. She's gone missing, again. We can't find her or your brother. Neither one of them answered their phones. Please tell me you didn't have anything to do with this." — Ma

My heart fucking dropped, and for some reason, I dialed the first number that came to mind.

Leo.

Fully aware that Martinez…

Was alive.

Mia

Six months had come and gone since I was found, and still no sign of my memory. Although I started having more intense flashes sparks of emotion when it came to certain things. It mostly happened when I was around Noah. Like he would do or say something, and I swear whatever it was had happened before. Almost like déjà vu. Dr. Garcia said there was a good chance that I had or I was developing romantic feelings toward him. The emotions he sparked within me could seem familiar, even though they were new.

But I swear it was so much more than that.

I began having dreams about being gunned down about a month ago, stumbling around in a daze before falling down an endless black hole, landing in strong arms. Then it would warp into losing my baby. Each one hazier than the last, making it hard to put the pieces of the memory puzzle back together. Decipher what I was actually seeing in my dreams, versus what I was feeling in the nightmare. It was all-consuming, almost unbearable some nights. I'd wake up in pure panic and sweat, sitting up in my bed, panting. Remembering what my mind wanted me to forget. Then I'd lie back in bed and hug my pillow, pressing it tight against my body. Immediately feeling comfort as if I was embracing an actual person.

Which didn't make any sense.

Sometimes it felt like I was going crazy, my mind battling within itself. It was hard to feel so much and not remember why it was there to begin with. How overpowering it was to experience such deep sentiments and not know if they were old or new. Real or imaginary.

I was extremely grateful that one thing had returned to normal though. I was allowed to go back to school to finish my junior year with my classmates. Even though there were only a few months left till summer vacation. I remember walking down the hall my first day back, terrified of the looks and whispers I was sure I'd receive, but it was the opposite. I was welcomed back with open arms. I even ran into my friend, Jill, who surprisingly I kind of remembered. We talked for a while over lunch, agreeing to get together for a mall date since prom season was approaching fast.

I was nervous to approach my parents' about ditching the homeschooling, but with the help of my therapist, it was a little easier. I caught up with everything I had missed while I was gone and was actually ahead in most of my classes. I guess I had my mom to thank for that since she had been home schooling me since I found out I was pregnant, saying it was easier on everyone that way.

My parents' were reluctant at first, afraid it would be a setback in my recovery. Not realizing I had yet to really take any steps forward. I was beyond relieved when they finally agreed, nonetheless.

Noah and I celebrated that night at the beach.

"I hated school. Dropped out when I was fifteen," he shared, *looking out at the ocean.*

"Well... it's never too late to try again. A lot can change in five years."

"Mia, it ain't normal that you want to go back to school, pretty girl," he chuckled, *trying to reach for me.*

I pulled away. "You just gave me a backhanded compliment. You don't get to cuddle."

"Cuddlin'? That what we doin'?"

I shrugged. "I don't know. What do you think we're doing?"

He grinned. "Somethin' I've been wantin' to do with you for as long as I can remember."

"Which is?"

"Be wit' you."

"You are with me."

"Am I?"

"We're together right now."

"We've been together almost every day."

"I know," I giggled. "You're a stage five clinger."

He laughed, big and throaty. Lunging for me, grabbing a hold of my waist before I could get away. He didn't hesitate, picking me up off the sand as if I weighed nothing. Throwing me over his shoulder, holding onto the back of my knees to lock me in place.

"Hey! This isn't fair! You're bigger than me!" I shouted, pressing my hands on his back to look up and see where we were going.

He was walking toward the water.

"No! It's nighttime! I could get eaten by sharks!" I squealed, trying to break loose. I instantly started tickling under his arms, making him fall to his knees, laying me down in the sand.

My breathing hitched when I realized he was now hovering above me. His face only a few inches away from mine. There was something about the moment that seemed so familiar to me, stirring all sort of emotions all over again.

"I wanna kiss you," he whispered out of nowhere.

"So, kiss me."

His eyes narrowed in on my face, going from my lips back up to my eyes. "Not gonna kiss you until I know for sure you're mine." With that, he stood, leaving me wanting, needing to feel his lips on mine.

The next day he surprised me with his enrollment papers to get his GED. Saying I made him want to be a better man. I think he just wanted brownie points with me, to be honest. Either way, I was proud of him.

It had been over a month since I'd gone back to school, and things were going great. My classmates treated me the same, knowing my current condition as well as the school and teachers. Most of them I remembered, but some I didn't have any idea who they were. It was easy to fall into a normal routine again, not feeling like I was struggling one bit. Even smiling more often than not. If anything for the first time since I got back, it felt natural. I recalled being a good student in the past, so that was probably why it was simple to fall back into my schoolwork and classes. It was definitely the breath of fresh air I needed.

Noah and I spent every second we could with each other. Learning something new about one another with each passing day. What made him happy, what made him smile, what made him laugh his ass off. It was interesting to peel back the different layers that made Noah who he was.

A man I think I was completely falling for.

The more time I spent with him, the more I wanted to be around him. He made me feel safe, secure, wanted. No longer the lonely girl trapped in the purgatory of her mind. He brought light back into my life, stifling the darkness. At least when he was with me. His presence alone comforted me more than anyone else's, but I often wondered if that would be the case if someone else were here, too.

I hadn't received any more texts from Creed after the first one three months ago. Chalking it up to the fact that I never replied. I didn't know what was the right or wrong thing to say, so I left it alone. I kept it saved on my phone, pulling it up whenever I was feeling lonely. Typing out a message, only to delete it right away. I couldn't even tell you how many times my finger hovered over the send button. Thoughts of him never drifted from my mind, especially when I was with Noah.

My therapist said it was probably from the two of them being so similar to one another. My brain was picking up on things that reminded me of Creed. Plus, my mind knew they were brothers, and that could play a huge factor on its own. I prayed every night Creed was safe. Looking up at the stars, laying on the lounger on my balcony. Writing in the notebook Dr. Garcia gave me to keep track of my feelings. Half the time I didn't even realize I was doing it, and that alone felt so unexpectedly familiar to me. As if it wasn't the first time I had done so.

"Whatcha thinkin' about over there?" Noah asked, glancing at me while he drove my Jeep.

"Where are we going?" I replied, blowing off his question.

"It's a surprise, pretty girl."

He loved to surprise me with all sorts of stuff anytime he could, which happened too often. Bringing me flowers every few weeks, replacing the others that had died, became part of his routine. Attaching little cards that had simple swoon-worthy sentiments on them like, 'Hey good lookin',' or 'These reminded me of you. Hope they remind you of me.' Always signed, 'Have a great day, beautiful,' — A messy heart, Noah. Stirring all sorts of emotions out of me.

"Awe! Come on, give me a hint!"

"Alright... you're gonna need to close your eyes when I tell you to."

I unexpectedly jerked back.

"What?" He grinned. "You don't think I'm kidnappin' you, do you?"

"Can't kidnap what's already yours," I murmured, too low for him to hear.

"Wha—"

I shook it off, shyly smiling. "I can't wait."

"You okay?"

"Yeah... I just spaced out for a second."

"You remember somethin'?"

"No. I don't think so. I swear... my head is just... I don't even know. It doesn't matter. I'm just excited for my surprise, so hurry up already," I laughed, trying to play it off that I was fine, when I wasn't.

"Mia, you know if you ever wanna ask me anythin' about the past. I'll always be honest with you."

"Noah..." I looked over at him, taking a deep breath. "What if I don't want to know? Like what if I don't want to remember?" I had never told anyone this besides Dr. Garcia.

He smiled, reaching for my hand. Bringing it over to his mouth to softly kiss it. "Then I'd be the luckiest fuckin' bastard in the world."

I smiled, not wanting to know what he meant by that statement. Again, I was too afraid to hear the answer. He held my hand the rest of the way, sitting pretty on his thigh. Rubbing his fingers back and forth on the palm of my hand. Sending delightful shivers through my body. Noah was always touching me in one way or another. At times it was subtle, like placing his arm on the back of my chair, rubbing my shoulder with his thumb. Or when we were having a casual conversation, he would play with the ends of my hair. Listening to every word that came out of my mouth with an intense regard.

Making me miss his touch when we weren't together. Especially at night, when I felt there should be a presence, but didn't understand why.

I went over to his house a few times, spending hours hanging out with him and his mom. Laughing our asses off at all the stories she told me about Noah when he was a little boy. I never asked him when his mom finally got sober. Not wanting to dig up past memories, just like he didn't want to uncover mine. She didn't seem like the woman he threw back in Creed's face at all. She seemed so loving, caring, a woman with a big heart. Still bringing me the same sense of comfort she had so many months ago. Almost like a second mom.

We had a bond like I had known her forever. Plus, she made the best apple pie. She'd usually sit at the dining room table drinking her coffee, while Noah and I sat on the couch flipping through channels on the TV. He would snuggle me close and rub the back of my neck, right at the hairline. Making me relax into his side. I would often catch the look on his mom's face out the corner of my eye as if she was torn between her sons. Needing to say something to me, but it never came out.

"Close 'em eyes," Noah ordered, pulling me away from my thoughts.

"This isn't like a sexual thing, right? Because I don't know how I feel about that," I sarcastically stated, wiggling my eyebrows. Trying to stifle a laugh.

"If it were sexual, you'd be wearin' a blindfold and possibly some handcuffs. Now, close 'em eyes."

I chuckled and did as I was told, impatiently waiting for what was to come. A few minutes later he parked my Jeep.

"Can I open them now?"

"No. I'll be back. Won't take long. Do not open your eyes."

I sat there fidgeting with the seam of my dress, anticipating his returned. Trying to ignore the fluttering feeling that was suddenly consuming my belly. A familiar, yet unfamiliar sensation Noah had inflicted more and more these days. The passenger door to the Jeep flew open, I yelped from the sudden intrusion but instantly calmed when I felt his touch.

"Relax, pretty girl. It's just me," he whispered near my ear, once again stirring my emotions. He grabbed my hand, turning me in the seat to face him. Letting me go and stepping away. "You can open them now."

I did. "Oh my God!" I exclaimed, looking at the pink surfboard in his grasp. The words, "Pretty Girl" written in white lettering across it.

"I had this custom made for you. It should be perfect for your size and weight."

"Noah… when I told you that my board didn't fit me anymore, I wasn't saying for you to buy me one. That's a *Channel Islands* surfboard, it must have cost you a small fortune."

"Don't you worry your pretty little head over that. You're worth every penny and then some," he replied, smiling. "You said you remembered how to surf, but ya haven't been hittin' the waves cuz you didn't have a board that fits. So, I got one for you. I wanna watch you kick ass out there in the water." He nodded to the ocean. "Drove us all the way over to Ocean Island Beach, the forecast predicted the best waves here today."

"Wow. I don't know what to say, but thank you so much. It's beautiful." Without any thought, I jumped out of my Jeep and wrapped my arms around his neck, squeezing him tight.

"You're fuckin' beautiful," he murmured in my ear before I pulled away.

I smiled, looking around the beach. "I don't have a bathing suit. I guess we could find a shop around here."

"Took care of that, too." He opened the back door of my Jeep, pulling out a gray bag that had towels, sunscreen, and a new pink bikini for me.

Instantly bringing back those reoccurring feelings by seeing the bag and its contents.

"I see a running theme here. You like the color pink, Noah?" I teased, smirking at him. Holding up the bathing suit.

"You love pink. It's your favorite color."

"Oh…"

"Will you wear it for me? So I can see a big part of your world."

I nodded, feeling as though this had happened before. All of it seemed so familiar. The ocean, the surfboard, and the pink bikini all

199

hit me at once. I shook off the plaguing thoughts, not wanting to ruin the moment. It was such an amazingly sweet gesture that he put a lot of thought into. The last thing I wanted to do was ruin it.

I changed in the restroom at the beach, noticing immediately that the bikini left very little to the imagination. I was grateful it at least covered my faint C-section scar. The only reminder I had of my pregnancy. Other than that, I didn't look or feel like I was ever pregnant. Noah and I hadn't spoken about our baby girl since we laid her to rest six months ago. Neither one of us had breached the subject, not even one time. I think we were both scared to bring it up, afraid it would make it too real. Both of us pretending it never happened were easier.

A piece of each of our hearts was buried with her that day. But she was not forgotten, I had the daily reminder every time I looked at myself in the mirror. One day my mom had noticed me looking at the scar while I was laying out by the pool. Rubbing my fingers against the taut skin. Before she could question me about it, I simply asked her if she could find me a cream that would help take the scar away.

Hoping if it was out of sight, it would be out of my mind, too. I turned my face away from her as soon as the question left my lips, not wanting to see the look on her face. She made an appointment for me at a cosmetology center a few days later. After a few sessions of laser treatments, it's barely noticeable anymore. You couldn't see it unless you knew it was there.

I thought it would make it easier on me.

It didn't…

It made it harder.

I told Dr. Garcia that I felt ashamed, as if I was trying to wipe away the evidence of her existence, like she was never growing inside of me. She told me that I was just trying to cope the only way I knew how. Even though it didn't make me feel any better, it helped.

"Hey, pretty girl. What's takin' you so long, I'm gettin' old here." Noah pounded his fist on the steel door, making me laugh. "Don't make me come in there. Bring that cute little ass of yours out here," he hollered.

I shook my head, taking a deep breath before opening the door.

Ends Here

The expression on Noah's face and the glare in his eyes when I walked out of the bathroom wearing the bikini was enough to push away all my looming fears. The ones I knew I'd never get rid of. He eyed me with a predatory regard, taking in every last inch of my sun-kissed skin. Making me feel nervous for a whole set of new reasons.

"Jesus Christ," he breathed out. "You're even more breathtakin' than I remember."

I blushed, peering down at the ground, shuffling my feet in the sand. I heard him chuckle as he made his way over to me. Stopping when we were inches apart, wrapping his arm around me. Pulling me into the side of his torso where I willingly went, loving the feel of him against me. He kissed the top of my head, and we walked down to the shore together. Grabbing my new surfboard on the way.

I spent most of the day in the water, riding the waves, becoming one with the ocean. Getting lost in my happy place I hadn't visited in I couldn't remember how long. It was just like riding a bike, you never forget how to do it. There was nothing in the world that could compare to the feeling of the ocean breeze and salt water hitting your face when you paddled out. I loved feeling like I had never left. This was me doing something I loved. Every time I'd look back at the shoreline, there was Noah smiling.

Watching me.

I went to hang out with him a few times, but he was adamant that I go back in the ocean. Threatening to pick me up over his shoulder and carry me out there like a barbarian. Throwing me to the sharks. He reassured me he was having the best time just sitting there. Being a part of my world for once. Getting a glimpse of how life should be. It was well into the afternoon by the time I was done for the day. My body physically spent, barely being able to drag my board up to the sand. As soon as I walked up to where Noah had been sitting all day, I noticed there was a spread of food with drinks on a blanket.

"Did you make us a picnic?" I asked with tears forming in my eyes.

For some reason the gesture was too much for me to take.

"I did. Thought you could learn some of your favorite foods and drinks again."

I struggled like hell to let go of the emotion that suddenly coursed through me. I had spent hours thinking about the connection we shared, the intensity of it. The way he looked at me, the way he spoke to me, the way he listened. Every smile, every laugh, every word that fell from his lips, meant something.

It didn't matter how big or how small.

It was there.

Etching its way into my heart where it felt like it had always been.

We spent the rest of the afternoon eating, playing like kids in the sand, talking and enjoying each other's company. Getting to know one another just a little bit more. Before I knew it, we were laying down on the blanket, my head resting in the crevice of his arm. Watching the sun go down. Listening intently to the lull of the waves as they brushed up onto the sand. I closed my eyes, never wanting the day to end.

"Mia." Noah shook me, stirring me awake.

"Hmm…"

"You gotta wake up. We passed out. It's after one in the morning. Your parents' must be flippin' the fuck out."

"What?" I sat up, brushing the sleep out of my eyes.

"Here, check your phone. I bet it's been blowin' up. Mine was."

I grabbed it out of his hands. He was right, there were over fifty missed phone calls from my parents', Mason, Bo, not to mention my uncles and an endless stream of text messages. At least ten from an unknown number, but I pushed it aside needing to call home.

"Shit," I panicked, instantly hitting the call back button on my house number.

"Mia!" my mom yelled into the receiver in a distraught tone. "Please tell me you're okay!" she cried.

"Momma! I'm fine! I swear… I'm so sorry. We came to the beach, the fresh air, all the food we ate… I surfed all day. We just fell asleep in the sand watching the sun go down."

"Mia, oh my God! Do you have any idea what we've been going through! What on earth were you thinking?! How could you be so careless?!"

"I know, I know. I had my phone on silent. Noah did, too. Please don't be mad… it was an accident. I would never want to put you guys through anything like that again. I'm so sorry," I honestly spoke, pacing back and forth in front of Noah who was busy checking his voicemails. I faintly heard a familiar voice before the screaming started again on mine.

"Lucas, calm down!"

"Give me the fucking phone!" I heard my dad say on the other end.

"Not until you calm down! They fell asleep—"

"Fell asleep?! What the fuck were they doing in a bed?!"

"Mia! Come home right now!" Mom ordered.

I nodded even though she couldn't see me. "Okay, we're at Ocean Island Beach so I'll be home in like an hour. I'm so sorry, Momma," I repeated, feeling like I'd let them down again. "I'll have Noah drive faster—"

"No! Drive the speed limit. We will talk when you get home, young lady. You tell Noah goodnight. Do you understand me?"

"Yes."

"Good. Text me when you're in your Jeep."

"I will. Bye." I hung up.

"Fuck... damn it, I fucked up. I'm sorry, Mia."

"It's not your fault. We just fell asleep. I think you put us in a food coma," I said, trying to make him laugh but failing miserably.

"They're never gonna let me see you again." He hurried, picking everything up to leave.

"No. Relax. It will be fine. Please don't let this ruin today. It's been the best day I've had since I woke up in that hospital. Being here with you. It meant everything." I grabbed his arm to stop him, looking deep into his eyes. Showing him I spoke the truth.

He smiled, his worry lessening.

"Thank you, Noah. For everything. Honest."

"Come on, let's get you home."

We rode in silence for most of the drive back to my house. Both of us lost in our own thoughts. I wanted to scroll through my messages to read a few in particular, but couldn't will my thumb to swipe it open. So, I placed it on my seat next to me, staring out the window instead. Thinking about all the amazing things Noah had done for me that day. Resisting the urge to tell him to stop a few streets away from my house, because for the first time since we started hanging out.

I wanted to kiss him and tell him that...

I was falling for him.

Prom night was finally here, and I couldn't be more excited to get dressed up to the nines and just be a normal teenage girl. Not the fragile, broken, scared one who didn't remember who she was. My mom insisted on renting a limo and going all out for it. Saying something about it being an important night in a young girl's life. I remember the day Noah showed up after one of my therapy sessions, holding a dozen pink roses, and a balloon that read, 'Will you marry me?' with a big X through the 'marry me' words. Replaced with 'Go to prom with me?' in black permanent marker in his chicken scratch handwriting.

"Oh my God! You're too much!" I laughed, taking in the image of the tall, muscular man covered in ink. Holding a bunch of pink flowers in his arms.

"That a yes?"

"Did my momma put you up to this?"

"Don't know what you're talkin' about, pretty girl, but I do need an answer?"

"Fine," I breathed out an exaggerated breath. *"I'll go to prom with you. Only because I know you didn't go to yours, and I feel bad for you."*

He busted out laughing.

It took a few weeks for my parents' to get over the incident at the beach. I think it helped that Noah was adamant on coming inside with me that night. Wanting to explain and apologize for scaring the shit out of them. I could see it in my dad's eyes when Noah was talking, he respected the hell out of him for having the balls to come in and face them. Knowing he could have lost his life.

I didn't even want to go in and face them.

They didn't ground me or anything, but they definitely made it clear not to ever do that to them again. I said my goodbyes to Noah and headed to bed, tossing and turning most of the night until I finally gave in. Grabbing my phone off my nightstand, I swiped over the screen and opened the text messages from the unknown number.

8:07 PM "Ma just called me! Where are you?! Answer me! Please tell me where you are!"

9:00 PM "Pippin, I ain't fuckin' around. Are you okay?"

9:30 PM "I know you don't want to talk to me. Just give me a yes or no."

10:15 PM "I just need to know you're okay... Please, babe!"

11:00 PM "GODDAMN IT, MIA! I asked you a question. Expectin' a fuckin' answer!"

11:10 PM "I don't give a fuck if you're with Noah. Just tell me you're alright!"

11:30 PM I need you, babe. I've never needed anyone like I need you. Please let me know you're okay."

12:10 AM Mia, please...

12:46 AM "Pippin, I'm hangin' on by a fuckin' thread! DON'T MAKE ME COME FIND YOU!"

1:05 AM "Baby, please... don't do this to me. I love you. Just tell me you're okay."

1:20 AM "Ma let me know you're alright. Hope you had a great day surfin'. I miss the fuck out of you. Prayin' one day you'll miss me, too."

I read the last text message and before thinking twice about, I typed out, *"Sometimes I feel like I already do."* And hit send.

He never replied, which brought on more unexplained heartache. More confusion. More questions and no answers. I would be lying if I said I wasn't disappointed with his lack of response. I read each text message probably a hundred times over the last month. Memorizing each and every word. Pouring my heart out on the pages of my notebook that I'm sure Dr. Garcia would have a field day with at our next session.

"Mia Pia, you look beautiful," Mom announced as I walked into the living room, doing a little twirl in place.

I was wearing a light-yellow strapless gown that hugged my curves perfectly, subtly flowing out down by my knees. My hair was curled and tied to the left side of my head, with a few strands of hair framing my face. Mom helped me with my makeup, going heavy on the eyes with dark black eyeliner and thick mascara. Some blush and a soft shade of nude for my lips.

"Wow, Mia... you look... Jesus... when did you grow up?" Mason asked, eyeing me up and down.

He was home for a few weeks before having to go back overseas. I hadn't seen him much, probably too busy kissing Giselle's ass. She hated him or at least that's what she said the last time I asked her about him a few days ago. Mason said he came over to hang out with Bo, but I knew he was lying. I'm almost positive Dad told him to stop by so they could both scare the shit out of Noah. Poor guy probably already saw it, coming given the history we apparently all shared.

Bo was sitting on the couch playing his Xbox, glancing over at me from the television. "Look nice, Mia. Make sure to let Noah know that if he touches you, I'll break his fuckin' fingers."

"Bo Savan Ryder!" Mom reprimanded, lightly backhanding him in the head. Glaring at my father who was hiding the proud look on his face from Bo's threat. "You watch your mouth!"

Bo shrugged, turning his attention back to his game again. My mom just placed her hands on her hips and shook her head.

"Be home after the dance," Dad ordered, bringing my attention to him.

"Dad... come on. It's prom," I simply stated.

"Exactly. Be home after prom. I know what happens at those things, Mia. And because of that, you should be grateful you're even going."

"Momma..." I eyed her.

"Lucas, give your daughter a break. Even I was allowed to stay out past curfew on my prom night. Remember you took me, but you ended up ruining that, too," she snidely smiled.

He pushed off the wall, walking over to her. Pulling her tight against his chest. Whispering something in her ear, causing her to immediately start blushing.

"Ugh..." I spewed, locking eyes with Mason who looked just as disgusted as I did. Even after all these years and everything us kids put them through, my parents' were still very much in love. Giving me a glimmer of hope for my future.

I was looking in the foyer mirror, reapplying my lipstick when the doorbell rang shortly after five. My dad beat me to the door with Mason and Bo in tow. They exchanged words I couldn't hear, but the look on Noah's face when they finally let him enter the house said it wasn't too pretty.

He looked so handsome, wearing a tuxedo with accents that matched my gown.

"You look beautiful," Noah praised, kissing my cheek. Handing me a white orchid corsage.

"You don't look too bad yourself," I boasted as he helped me with my corsage and then I helped him with his boutonniere.

After taking way too many pictures and Mom crying one too many times, we were able to leave. My dad and brothers never stopped warning Noah through their glares.

"Come on." He placed his hand on the hollow of my back, spreading a warm heat throughout my entire body. Guiding me toward the limo where the driver opened the door for us. Noah helped me step in, sliding in behind me and closing the door.

We talked about nothing in particular on the drive to the restaurant. Both of us wrapped up in each other's stares. Our eyes spoke volumes. We went to a nice Italian restaurant in town before the dance, having an intimate dinner, which was amazing. It didn't take long until we were walking through the doors of the banquet hall that hosted my prom. Decorations were everywhere, representing the 1920's theme we all voted on in school. They went on for miles, as did the crowd. There wasn't a place in the room that wasn't covered in some sort of streamer, confetti, or balloon.

We took a traditional prom picture with the photographer, but I didn't get a chance to look at it since Noah immediately placed it in the pocket of his tuxedo jacket. He grabbed my hand, and I didn't give it any more thought, I followed him into the ballroom. Stopping to hug a few people I knew along the way. We hung out like we always had, laughing and loving each other's company. When the song "Broken" by Seether came blaring through the speakers, Noah grabbed my hand and led me to the dance floor.

Molding me close to his body, pulling me tighter into his strong, muscular frame. Guiding my arms up around his neck like he wanted no space between us. He wrapped his arm's around me, proving my point. I laid my cheek on his chest, and he placed his chin on top of my head.

"I thought you didn't dance." I smiled, peering up into his eyes.

"I never said that. Ma was into all that romantic shit growin' up. She used to make me dance with her all the time."

I leaned my face into his chest again, frowning. I could have sworn he told me he didn't dance. It was around the chorus of the song when something felt different. He felt different. The mood changed drastically between us as the lyrics of the song intensified. The conflicting emotions came tumbling down on me, crippling me in ways it never had before. There was something about this song that pained me, and I couldn't comprehend or figure out why.

I suddenly needed some fresh air, a moment to myself. I waited until the song was over and grabbed my phone from my clutch.

"My mom's called a few times. I'm going to step outside and call her back," I lied, hoping he wouldn't notice.

He nodded. "Gonna go say what's up to the DJ. I know him. I'll be over there."

"Okay." I backed away from him and left, making my way out to the terrace in the back of the hall.

The second I stepped outside I took a long, deep breath. Feeling as though I couldn't breathe. I leaned against the railing, trying to distract myself by looking at all the city lights and the soft glow it gave everything around me. Normally this view would have me awestruck and at peace, but I couldn't stop the emotions that were wreaking havoc on my mind.

And then just like that it unexpectedly changed again…

I felt him behind me.

"You're there, aren't you?" I whispered, my heart pounding against my chest.

"You wishin' I was?" he countered in a husky, masculine tone.

Why did that simple response strike such a chord inside of me?
"You shouldn't be here."

"That's where you're wrong."

I heard the lock click over on the double doors, followed by his footsteps that brought him closer to where I stood. My breathing hitched as soon as I felt him come up behind my trembling frame. I didn't turn around, I didn't move, afraid if I did he'd disappear like he was just a figment of my imagination. My mind once again playing tricks on me.

I closed my eyes, waiting for I don't know what. Feeling his heat burning into me more and more with each step that brought him closer to me. We weren't even touching, yet I still felt him all over. His hands, his lips, his love. He leaned in just inches away, letting his breath brush against my ear. Causing shivers to course through me and my knees to buckle.

I wrapped my arms around my stomach, trying to hold in the emotions that threatened to spill, revealing my truths. I knew he noticed. There was no way he couldn't have felt the effect he had on me. Even though I had no idea who he was.

He consumed me with his presence, so when he was gone. When he wasn't around me. When we weren't together.

I would miss him.

His touch.

His aura.

His love for me.

"There's nowhere else I'd rather be, than here wit' you, Pippin."

"There's a warrant out for your arrest. If someone saw you—"

"Fuck 'em."

I swallowed hard, not knowing what to say or what to do. I should have left, but I couldn't get my feet to move.

"You're all that matters. Always have been and always will be."

I licked my lips, my mouth suddenly becoming dry. My head spun in a whirlwind of feelings. Battling with my heart to move or to stay grounded. Wanting to turn and face the man who was still a mystery to me, but before I could, his actions made the decision for me. My eyes followed the movement of his strong arms as they came around my body. Skimming the sides of my ribs to place his hands on the railing out in front of me.

Caging me in against his body, his scent, his ink.

His truths...

Engulfing me in nothing but his warmth, his love, and devotion.

Comforting and tormenting me in ways I never thought possible.

It was loud.

It was maddening.

It was everything.

The closer he got to me, the more I wanted to feel him against my body. Yearning to be touched in a way that something told me only he could soothe me. I could sense he wanted to put his hands on me, needing to feel my silky skin under his calloused fingers, but he was taking it slow. Testing the fire, not wanting to get burned.

"I don't even remember you," I whispered, my chest firmly rising and falling with each word that escaped my lips.

"Yes, you do. My blood runs through your veins. I'll always be inside of you. Be a part of you."

I jerked back, confused. "What?"

"In here," he emphasized, placing his hand on my overly active heart, causing me to jump from his sudden touch. I could feel him grinning, knowing he was the cause of the rapid rhythm beating against the palm of his hand. "My blood is runnin' through your veins, Mia. Ya feel me?" he questioned, removing his hand and taking my heart with it. "Since I'm Type O, a universal donor, Doc took my blood weeks before the shootout. Knowin' you were comin' close to your due date, he wanted to be prepared just in case you went into labor and needed it. Left it in the fridge for you. It was my blood that saved your life."

I had no words. He rendered me speechless. All I had were emotions threatening to spill out any second. The floodgates opened, letting out everything I held in so deeply. Tears began to stream down my face, falling to the ground with my heart. His hand started moving slowly up my arm, grazing my skin with only the tips of his fingers as if he was testing my boundaries. What he could and couldn't get away with.

Holding me in his arms like I was his entire world.

I was feeling so much.

Yet not nearly enough.

He made his way toward my shoulder and then down my back. I didn't say one word, terrified he would stop his descent. His control over me would fade.

I sucked in a breath when I felt him lower the halter on my back. His lips casually moved from my ear to where his fingers were placed. Softly, gently letting his lips linger on the scar from the bullet I took in my back.

Rasping, "I'm so fuckin' sorry," in a devastated tone I'd never forget.

He pulled away just enough to trail soft kisses up toward the side of my neck. It was then that I couldn't take it any longer. It was then that it became too much. His words were killing me, but his touch was destroying me.

I abruptly turned around, slightly pushing him away. His eyes told me he wanted to say so much, though nothing came out.

So I simply stated, speaking with conviction, "I'm falling for Noah. It's always been him, Creed."

Breaking his heart into a million pieces. Possibly next to mine.

"You're full of shit, and you know it."

Her eyes widened not expecting my reply, giving her the courage to ask, "Why did you take me?"

"To protect you."

"From what?"

"That's what I'm tryin' to figure out."

"How did you know I was here?"

"I got my ways."

"Aren't you worried about ending up in prison? All I have to do is scream, and this terrace will be swarming with people who would stop at nothing to turn you in. My dad made sure of that with the reward money he has for your head."

"I'd give 'em my fuckin' balls to spend just a few minutes with you. You're worth it, Pippin," I honestly spoke, caressing her cheek with the back of my fingers. Grinning, I challenged, "Besides you were never much of a screamer, why start now?"

I immediately saw it, her eyes glazed over and her pupils dilated. Stunned by my brazen response. It wasn't quite the reaction I wanted, but it was a step in the right direction. I leaned over again, caging her in with my arms. Resting my forehead on hers.

"There's my girl…" I pulled her hair away from her face to stare intently into her bright blue eyes.

That did it to me every time.

There was so much emotion behind her gaze. I knew they mirrored mine, there was no need for words. Our eyes spoke for themselves as I took her face between my hands and caressed the sides of her cheeks with my thumbs.

My thoughts.

My words.

They all seemed to be fucking intertwine with one another. Pushing and pulling like a game of tug of war.

The music changed over to the song she played for me on our first official date at the safe house. Bringing me back to a happier time, hearing her soulful voice belt out the words, pouring her heart out to me. The music wasn't very loud out on the terrace, but it was enough to hear the melody.

Without thinking twice about it I smiled, gliding my hands to her neck, slowly descending down her body to grab hold of her hand. I stepped back, bringing her with me, instantly twirling her around in a circle like a ballerina. Looking at her in the way I always had. Forgetting for just one second that things weren't normal and she wasn't mine.

I pulled her close to my body, bringing her into my chest. Fitting her body perfectly into my hold, I started to slow dance for the very first time in my life.

"What do you want from me?" she whispered, peering into my chest. I lifted her chin so I could once again look into her beautiful eyes.

"Everythin'," I simply stated, wiping away the tears from her cheeks.

"Noah is inside, Creed. Did you know that? Your brother's right inside."

"Don't mean shit to me, Mia. I wouldn't give a fuck if he was standin' behind me with a fuckin' gun to my back. I needed to see you. Hold you... fuckin' feel you. And it's takin' everythin' in me, not to fuckin' kiss you right now and remind you who the fuck you belong to," I declared.

"I can't... I don't even know what to say to you."

"It don't matter. I own you, Pippin. I claimed you. Even gave you my cut. Remember the patches? The property of Creed? Any of that a trigger to you? No one can come between our love, not even your fuckin' mind. I'll spend the rest of my life remindin' you what you mean to me if I have to. Ain't lettin' you go. I will always, always fuckin' love you. And no one can take that away from me. Not even you."

Her lips started quivering, unable to form words. I kissed her forehead, resisting the urge to claim every last inch of skin. I knew I shouldn't have been there, but I had to see her. It had been way too fucking long.

"Can't you see, babe... my heart is fuckin' bleedin' out for you," I repeated the same exact words she said to me on Giselle's balcony all those years ago. When I tried to push her away.

One of my biggest regrets in my life. Everything could have been different if I had just let her in.

"I know you love me, but I don't remember you, Creed. I know that hurts you, and even though I don't know who you are... it kills me to be the cause of your pain. How does that make sense? It's like my mind is playing with my heart and vice versa. There are times where I swear I miss you, but that doesn't change the fact that I don't know you. How can that be?"

"I'm your lobster."

She smiled, knowing what I was talking about. At least she remembered that.

"I want to know what happened the night I was shot. Can you tell me? The night I lost my baby girl?"

"Mia... please... not now."

"I don't remember being pregnant, but I have this scar. This daily reminder of something I have no recollection of. I feel like I'm the worst human being on the planet. How can a mother forget her own baby?"

"I promise. I swear to ya, I'll tell you everythin' one day, but can't do it right now."

"Why?"

"Cuz I can't lose you again."

"You don't have me now."

"You're in my arms, yeah? I'll take you any way I fuckin' can."

Her face frowned as she pulled away from me. Breaking our connection. Shaking her head. "I wasn't lying when I told you before. I am falling for Noah. He's inside waiting for me. He's the only one who has been there for me this entire time. I can't do this to him. I won't. I owe it to our daughter to see where our relationship goes. I'm sorry, Creed, but I'm not yours anymore. I'm his."

Her words gutted me, leaving me there bleeding as she turned around and started to walk back toward the double doors.

"Pippin," I called out, stopping her dead in her tracks. I was over to her in three strides, turning her to face me. "I know you'll remember me, and when ya do, you'll need this." I handed her the key to our house, kissing her forehead one last time. Hating the fact that I didn't know when I would see her again. "Come back to me. I'll be there waitin'."

I walked away from her that night, leaving her with my brother. Praying that it wouldn't be...

Forever.

Mia

It was the annual Oak Island Fourth of July Fair weekend. Where anyone and everyone came to our small town from all over just to experience the biggest festival around. I remembered it was my favorite time of the year, having fond memories of being at the events with my family. Always kicking Uncle Jacob's ass at all the carnival games. I was very competitive when it came to winning another huge stuffed animal I didn't need.

"Jesus Christ, Mia! Can you let me win a game?" Noah chuckled, bringing my attention to him.

"Nope. It's not in my nature," I giggled as he came up behind me, wrapping his arms around my waist to kiss the side of my neck.

"How am I supposed to impress you if you keep kickin' my ass?"

I turned around to face him, draping my arms around his neck. "I can think of tons of ways."

"Is that right?"

"Oh yes. I am almost positive there's one way you can impress me, and it involves your lips."

His eyes widened, smiling. "Why, Mia Ryder, are you gettin' ballsy with me?"

"One of us has to."

Two months had gone by since my prom. School had officially let out, and I was on summer vacation. Ready to let loose before my senior year started in August. Nothing had really changed as far as my memory was concerned, I still attended therapy twice a week like clockwork, no closer to the truth. Noah and mine's relationship was growing with each passing day, but we had yet to do anything but flirt or cuddle, with some small kisses to the forehead and cheek. That was it. I made it my mission to stop thinking about Creed and focus on Noah. At least he was there, I hadn't seen or heard from Creed since that night.

Which made it easier to give Noah my undivided attention.

For me at least.

"Pretty girl, I already told ya… ain't kissin' you, touchin' you, doin' anythin' wit' you until I know you're only mine. But trust me, Mia… it don't mean I don't wanna feel you under me again more than anythin'."

My lips parted. "Noah, I am—"

"You stupid motherfucker!" I heard someone roar from behind me, making me immediately turn around.

Noah instantly placed me behind him. Viciously peering at the man in front of us. I'd never seen that look on his face before, and it actually scared me a little.

"Don't fuckin' start, old man. Get on your bike and get the fuck out of our faces!"

The man took a huge gulp of the whiskey bottle firmly in his grasp, pointing it at Noah when he was done. "Come on, Rebel. I know it's your favorite drink. Where's my boy, huh? The man I fuckin' raised. Not this pussy-whipped bitch standin' in front of me," he slurred, stumbling all around.

"Who is that?" I asked Noah, looking up at him. His menacing stare never left the man swaying in front of us.

"I'm his father! The man who gave him fuckin' life. He don't talk about me? That's a shame. Spent all my life raisin' my boys fuckin' right. And look what happens… they both fall for a two-bit whore who's spread her legs and has gotten on her fuckin' knees for both of 'em."

I gasped when Noah abruptly pushed me back, getting right up in his father's face. "You miserable fuck!" He punched him, knocking him sideways into the brick wall. "You don't ever! EVER! Fuckin' talk about her like that again! Or I swear I'll fuckin' put you to ground!"

"Who the fuck you think you are?!" He went at Noah, but a few other men wearing the same cuts he was sporting grabbed ahold of him, tugging him back as he went crazy in their grasps. "You're nothin' without me! Nothin' without this club! I gave you everythin'! Fuckin' everythin', you piece of fuckin' shit! You'll be back! I'll make you get on your knees like your fuckin' bitch and beg me to let you in again! Do you understand me?!"

Noah shook his head, disgusted with the scene unfolding in front of us. He grabbed my hand, pulling me toward him.

"I ain't your son. You ain't my father. You never fuckin' were! Go drink somewhere and crash your fuckin' bike. Do everyone some good if you just fuckin' died."

"Noah," I breathed out, glaring at him.

We locked eyes.

"Come on." He tugged me toward him, and we left.

Neither one of us said a word as we made our way down to the beach. I could tell he was lost in his own thoughts, trying to calm himself from the altercation. I never wanted to know what he was thinking more than I did at that moment. Wanting him to confide in me, open up, and let out all the pent-up anger I knew he was holding in. Though I didn't want to pry, it was obvious he was upset and hurting.

He sat down in the sand, pulling me beside him. Sitting with his knees up and his arms placed over them, looking out at the ocean. Reluctant to look at me.

I opened my mouth to say something, but nothing came out. I didn't have to wait long until he was the one to break the silence between us.

"Never wanted you to see me like that again," he said out of nowhere. "Promised myself I'd never let you witness what you saw the day of our baby girl's funeral. I was fuckin' ashamed of what I did. Not about fighin' with Creed, about doin' it near her gravesite. I was no better than my father, and I fuckin' hated myself for that."

I placed my hand on his shoulder in a comforting gesture. "It's alright."

"No it ain't, Mia. I keep fuckin' up with you. And it's the last thing I wanna do. I want you to like me. Fuck…" He bowed his head. "I want you to love me," he murmured, looking over in my direction with his head still bowed. "Cuz, I do. I love you, Mia. I've loved you since the moment I laid eyes on you. I may not have known it then, but I know it now. I know you don't remember me or us, but I think you feel it. In here." He placed his hand over my heart, and just like that it brought back memories of Creed when he did and said the same thing to me at prom. Erupting a flood of emotions back. Each brothers feelings intertwining, intermixing with each other, causing a whole new level of confusion to wash over me, but I quickly pushed it away.

Wanting to stay in the here and now with Noah.

"I'm sorry if this scares you, but I can't hold it in any longer. I wanted you to be the mother of my kid. Jesus…I still fuckin' do."

My eyes watered with tears as I took in all the words he was professing to me, all the emotions pouring out of his heart and soul and into mine.

"I'm so fuckin' in love with you…" he added in a soft, gentle, almost painful tone.

Which nearly broke my heart to hear. Tears started to fall down the sides of my face, unable to hold them back any longer. He didn't think twice about it, he grabbed under my arms and carried me over to him, making me straddle his thighs. Caging me in, holding my cheeks between his hands. Kissing all over my face to wipe my tears away with his lips.

"Please, baby… say somethin'…"

I peered deep into his eyes, resting my forehead on his and spoke with conviction, "I'm yours, Noah. It's only you."

He didn't falter, gripping onto the back of my neck, kissing me.

Devouring me.

Taking his time, savoring my taste as if he never wanted to stop. His lips parted, beckoning mine to follow, and they did. We kissed for what felt like hours, but I knew it was only minutes. He wrapped his arms around my torso, lowering me back until I felt the sand beneath me. Laying his body on top of mine.

He wanted me.

He needed me.

My mind was scrambled with thoughts and emotions I couldn't control, label, or even begin to understand. It was one giant clusterfuck of feelings. I tried to ignore them all, but they were as consuming as the feeling of his body on top of mine.

I put my arms around his neck as he pushed me further into the sand, kissing me deeper, harder, and with more determination. Something told me this wasn't the first time he had kissed me like this. My chest rose and fell faster and faster with every slip of his tongue. With every deep breath I took, with each caress of his fingers along my face, with each groan that escaped his mouth and with each moan that left mine.

I felt his heartbeat pounding against my chest. Mimicking my own. They were beating together in a rapid rhythm, dancing with pleasure, mixed with a little bit of pain.

He kissed me one last time. Letting his lips linger for a few seconds longer before pulling away. I instantly felt the loss of our heated kiss when he set his forehead on mine. Our heavy panting was the only thing that could be heard over the waves crashing into the shore as we laid there in the sand, trying to calm our breathing. He pushed the hair away from my face to stare deep into my eyes. Wanting to stay lost in each other's minds.

His hands framed around my face, kissing me again with the same intensity and passion, but slower, more delicate this time. Less frantic and desperate. We stayed like that for I don't know how long, just kissing. Completely engulfed in one another.

As much as I loved the feeling of his lips, his body, his heart next to mine. There was something deep inside of me that was still hurt and pained. A dreaded, uncomfortable feeling that repeatedly stabbed me right in my core. I desperately tried to push it away, but it was permanently attached to me. As if my heart didn't even belong to me anymore.

Because it was owned by someone else.

The time we had been waiting for had finally arrived. This was our one and only chance to raid the clubhouse for the missing disc undetected. It was the annual Fourth of July fair weekend in Oak

Island where people from all over came to celebrate and enjoy the biggest display of fireworks in the country. Everyone's attention would be focused on the event and not what's going down on the outskirts of town. Our MC and other chapters from all over the state of North Carolina rallied up together and made their presence known at the festival for all to see. It had been a tradition for generations, one I knew my old man fucking loved and wouldn't fucking pass up.

It had been three months since we had a word with Damien at his underground club in Miami. We still hadn't figured out jack shit about what we needed to know. The pieces of the puzzle were still scattered everywhere, and Damien's cryptic information made no fucking sense at all. Other than revealing that Martinez was indeed alive, we had nothing to go on. The only place we hadn't searched for the disc was the one place I left for last.

The compound.

Only problem was we couldn't do it with Pops around. Hence the reason we waited fucking over ninety whole days for this one night. We knew the motherfucker hid everything conspicuously in his room. There had to be something there. Anything that could point us in the right direction to find the evidence we needed to put an end to everything.

We hid the truck in the woods about a half a mile up the road from the clubhouse, preferring to tread on foot just in case someone showed back up early. We waited, bunkered down in the woods, out of sight until we saw them ride out toward the fair, all sporting their colors with fucking pride. The Prez knew Diesel was with me most of the time since I was technically still in hiding. I needed backup in case more shit hit the fan. Diesel and I breached the property just after eleven at night. Getting in unseen, dodging the fucking security cameras to get to the control panel. I knew how to fuck with the cameras and security system my father had installed after the shootout.

The cheap bastard didn't get anything high-tech. It was easy to mess with the setup, so we could be undetected. I went in through the back while Diesel walked in through the front, just in case there were any stragglers or club whores left behind. It would look suspicious if he was sneaking in like I was. The brothers knew I couldn't step foot on the compound, it would be too careless to put the club in jeopardy if for some reason the cops found out.

"Everyone's gone," he announced, nodding to me to come in through the sliders. "We got less than a few hours to find what we need. Don't wanna push our luck, who the fuck knows how long your old man will stay out at the fair. I guess it depends on how much Jack they have."

I nodded, grabbing the hidden key for his room before making our way down the hall and up a set of stairs to his private quarters. Hoping Christa, Pop's whore, wasn't there since we didn't see her on the back of his bike. We stopped in front of his door and listened for a second, making sure the coast was clear. It didn't surprise either one of us that the door was fucking locked.

We spent the next two hours searching hell and high water for any sort of clue. From the walls to the floors, even the goddamn ceiling. Rummaging through drawers, cabinets, and shelves, coming up empty. On the verge of tearing the fucking room apart, trashing it just to find where he hid Martinez's disc. But we didn't, wanting it to look like no one had been there.

The last thing we needed was for him to figure out we were fucking on to him. It would start new problems we didn't have time for.

"Fuck!" I yelled, frustrated we weren't finding what we needed. Sitting my ass in the recliner in his room, trying not to think about how many bitches sucked his cock while he was sitting in it.

I grabbed my phone out from my back pocket and pulled up the picture that Martinez sent me months ago. I had probably looked at the goddamn photo hundreds of fucking times, still feeling as though I was missing something of importance. The photo was aged, worn, and fucked up, so it was hard to make out his face.

"Creed," Diesel called out, bringing my attention to him. "Since when does your old man listen to classical music?"

"What?" I asked, cocking my head to the side.

He nodded toward his C.D. case in the corner of the room. My eyes narrowed in on the shelf, finding the case he was talking about almost instantly. It stuck out like a fucking sore thumb.

I lunged off the recliner and was over to the shelving unit in three strides. Grabbing ahold of the C.D. in question, opening it before it was even fully in my grasp.

"Hell yes." I held up the contents, smiling so fucking wide when I realized it was Martinez's disc.

"Help me grab all the fuckin' C.D.'s out of the cases. I don't give a fuck if he notices."

We grabbed every last one, throwing them in the bag we had with us, noticing several were not music, but possible files. After making sure everything was back in place, we hauled ass out of there just in the nick of time. Hearing the roar of bikes in the distance as we sped away, with hopefully the truth in the bag.

I knew Diesel was trying not to speed on the way back to his house, as anxious as I was to get to the bottom of everything. Have some sort of closure and fucking justice for all parties involved.

He grabbed his laptop off the coffee table, hurrying into the kitchen. Clearing the contents of the counter off with one swipe of his arm. Sending beer bottles clinking to the floor, setting up shop for the long night we had ahead of us. I wouldn't sleep until I had answers. Laying all the discs out, I inserted Martinez's first. Never in a million fucking years did I expect what I would find. Each C.D. solved another piece of the puzzle.

Except I never thought it would lead to another road where we all might not make it out...

Alive.

Summer vacation came to an end way too quickly. I missed being able to hang out with Noah all day, every day at the beach, surfing, sunbathing, kissing. There was a lot of kissing. My senior year of high school had started, and my eighteenth birthday had come and gone. I was officially and legally an adult. I think my dad was a little sad about that fact, no longer his little girl. Especially when I joked with him, saying he could no longer tell me what I could and couldn't do. Earning my mom a *control your daughter* kind of glare.

We celebrated by having dinner and cake at my house. Surrounded by my family and Noah, only missing Mason who went back overseas to once again fight for our country. Giselle showed up with her new boyfriend, who didn't seem like her typical type. Polar opposite of my brother. I could tell Uncle Dylan didn't like the man very much, staring him down with a killer look in his eyes. Waiting for him to make one wrong move.

I immediately wondered if my brother knew what she was up to. Knowing it wasn't going to go over well if and when he found out. I felt bad for the poor guy, but I also didn't want to see my brother end up in jail for taking him out. There was definitely a shit storm brewing, and for the first time in a while, I wasn't the cause. I had to be grateful for the small miracles.

Everyone belted out, singing happy birthday to me, telling me to make a wish and blow out my candles. For some reason, at that exact moment, I thought about a penny, which didn't make any sense. You'd think that feeling would have become a natural reaction for me by now, but it didn't. Not even after all this time.

After filling up on my homemade cake my mom made, I opened a ton of gifts. Getting jewelry, a new laptop, some clothes and a bunch of gift cards. I couldn't wait to go shopping. It was a great way to say goodbye to seventeen and welcome eighteen with open arms. Spending my birthday with all the people I loved and wanted to be with the most.

Noah gave me a beautiful necklace with a heart-shaped pendant made of diamonds. Saying as soon as he saw it, he had to get it for me. That nothing was as pretty as I was but this came close. We were exclusively in a relationship, spending every waking hour together.

The first time he called me his girl was in front of my mom and dad. We were messing around in the pool while my parents' grilled out. They didn't say anything, but I did see my dad corner Noah in the kitchen, through the sliding glass door later that evening. It appeared they were having a heated conversation, although I didn't hear what it was about. I imagined it was his typical threats, which Noah had become more than accustomed to.

Since I turned eighteen, they weren't on my ass as much as they used to be. I didn't have a curfew anymore. I could come and go as I pleased. I could stay out at friends' houses as long as I communicated where I was and what we were doing. I knew they weren't stupid. I'm sure they assumed I was staying with Noah, but they never called me out. I think a part of them started to like him and possibly even trust him. He kept me safe, and I was happy. Which was ultimately all they ever wanted for me.

Even though my life had changed, my memories had yet to return. It had been almost a year since I was found, and no closer to the truth that was barricaded in my mind. The case of my disappearance was still open but had become stagnant. Creed was still on the run, and my uncle and dad were still chasing him. I knew they'd never stop.

To be honest, the more time that went on, the more I realized my memory might never return. At that point, I think I started to become fine with that intuition.

It was what it was.

My therapist and I began talking about the future, instead of living in the past. I had to start thinking about college and all that came along with that. With my help, Noah passed his GED with flying colors. His ma was so proud, watching her baby receive his certificate. We spent hours upon hours getting him ready for it. He didn't give himself enough credit, he was extremely bright when he put his mind to something. Most of the time I had to bribe him with pervy favors. Like if he got this answer right I would take off my shirt, or if he got it wrong he wouldn't be able to kiss me for an hour.

It motivated him in the right direction for the most part, although it just led to us making out more often than not.

We hadn't had sex yet, and he hadn't pushed me to do anything I wasn't ready for or comfortable with. He was being patient with me, and I thought that was super sweet of him. We could spend hours just making out, lying together, letting our hands roam. He'd touch me under my clothes testing my boundaries, but he never took it any further. As far as I knew, it kept him satisfied just being able to feel me and love me in that way for now.

I hadn't seen or heard from Creed since my prom, over five months ago. That all changed when my phone dinged at midnight on my birthday, scaring the shit out of me. An unknown number lit up my dark room like a beacon in the night, calling for me to answer.

I swiped the screen over, reading his simple message, *"Happy birthday, Pippin. Don't forget to make a wish."*

His words made me smile, but that quickly faded as did the light on my phone. I worked so hard to keep him out of my mind, and every time I thought he was gone, he'd make his way back in. Almost like he sensed I was moving on. Other than that night, it was like he dropped off the face of the earth. I debated on texting him back more often than not, just to know he was alright. Also, resisting the urge several times to ask his ma if she'd heard from him, afraid of the response I'd get.

There were times when I would catch myself thinking about him, hoping he was safe. Praying he was alive. Holding the key he gave me tight in my grasp. Trying to figure out why my mind wouldn't bring him back, and I had yet to fully grasp that question.

"Whatcha thinkin' about over there?" Noah probed, walking back into his living room with popcorn in his hands. Ready to play the movie.

His mom went away for the weekend with some of her girlfriends. Saying something about it being long over do. Noah had suspected that she was seeing someone and just didn't want him to know. Probably too nervous, thinking about how he would react to the news. Fearing for the guy's life.

To be honest, I would be, too. I wouldn't be surprised if she was dating again, she was beautiful. Inside and out. I knew Noah still held onto the resentment he had toward her, and I'm sure she knew it as well. Even though there was bitterness on his end, I knew he loved her, and she loved him more than anything. Proving that every day. Their relationship was amazing for mother and son. I think over time his anger for what she put him through would fade. I hoped it would be the same for his brother, too.

Noah never talked about Creed, and I never brought him up, either. His mom didn't even mention him around me. Which made me think she knew more about where he was than she let on.

"You always bite your lip when you're deep in thought," he remarked, once again pulling me away from my thoughts.

"Is there anything you don't notice?"

"Not when it comes to you."

I smirked, grabbing some popcorn out of the bowl as he took a seat beside me. "I was thinking about my Jeep if you must know. Thanks for picking me up in your mom's car tonight. My Jeep should be out of the shop tomorrow morning. Can you take me to pick it up?"

He raised an eyebrow, grinning. "That mean you spendin' the night?"

I shrugged, smiling. "It depends. Did you rent a man movie? If I have to sit through another violent or bloody film, there better be some hot ass guys."

"Why? You got one sittin' right here."

"Really?" I looked around the room and then back to him. "Where?"

He put the popcorn on the coffee table and grabbed my foot, tugging me to him. Making me squeal and giggle all at the same time.

"You're lucky you're so fuckin' pretty," he rasped, laying on top of me.

"What about my awesome witty comebacks?"

"What about them?"

My mouth dropped open. "That's not nice."

"Someone wasn't bein' very nice a few minutes ago," he retorted, kissing along my neck. His facial hair was inflicting all sorts of feelings in my core.

"Don't hate because you're not funny!" I giggled, angling my head down so he couldn't get into the crevice.

"Now I ain't funny? I'm fuckin' funny!"

"Oh yeah, fuckin' hilarious. You ain't fuckin' funny," I mocked him, using the way he talks.

"Don't say fuckin'… sounds too dirty comin' out of somethin' so sweet."

"Awe! That was so sweet! But you're not the boss of me! I can say whatever I want! Fuckin', fuckin', fuckin', fuck!"

He chuckled when he realized I wasn't going to let up and let him at my neck, so he lifted my dress instead. Blowing raspberries all over my belly, causing me to thrash around like a crazy person.

"Who's fuckin' funny now?"

"Definitely not you! I'm only laughing cause you're torturing me!" I accidentally kicked the popcorn off the table, sending it flying everywhere.

He continued his assault, tickling my sides for I don't know how long when he suddenly just stopped, catching me off guard. I caught my breath for a few seconds before I leaned up on my elbows to see what he was doing. Instantly jerking back, realizing his eyes were dead set on my faint C-section scar that could only be seen if you knew it was there.

The same one I still stared at all the time.

I froze in place, not knowing what to say or do. We had yet to breach the subject about the past, pretending as if it never existed to begin with. When he moved his hand, I stopped breathing. Knowing exactly what he was about to do. His fingers lightly touched along the faded memory of the day I was still so terrified and overwhelmed to remember. Although, the tips of his fingers were barely grazing my skin, that didn't stop me from feeling the sensation all over.

Especially stabbing at my heart.

"Her name was Madison, we were goin' to call her Maddie for short," he said so low I could barely hear him. As if he was no longer in the present with me, he was somewhere else entirely stuck in the past. Lost in his own mind. "She was beautiful, Mia. I'd never seen anythin' more beautiful in all my life." His eyes filled with tears. It was the first time I saw him so vulnerable since her funeral. So exposed and so raw.

"You got to meet her?" I asked in the same low monotone he was speaking in.

"No. By the time I made it back, she was already gone." His mind was reeling. I could see it clear as day, the visions playing out in front of him. "She was so fuckin' tiny. Her body fit right in my palms," he paused, looking down at his hands like she was still in them. "She had your lips and round face, your complexion, too." I watched as tears streamed down his cheeks, feeling so helpless. He didn't bother wiping them away, too consumed with what he was telling me. As if he was there with her and not here with me. "She had my black hair, though. Her skin was so fuckin' soft, and she smelled like nothin' I'd ever breathed in before. She was so fuckin' perfect. I loved her immediately. Didn't think I could ever love somethin' so much until that moment. Except, maybe you."

I sucked in air, taking in everything he was saying, reliving it through his eyes. Not noticing I'd been crying right along with him until a tear fell to my lips.

"I dream about her all the time. Thinkin' about somethin' that will never be. You see, Mia, your purgatory is the fact that you don't remember anythin'… mine is the fact that I do."

"Noah…" I whispered, my voice breaking.

"I don't want you to remember. I pray every night that you don't. Cuz I know the day you do, you'll fuckin' hate me. Just as much as I hate myself for not savin' our baby girl."

I grimaced, his words too much for me to bear. I sat up, taking him along with me, straddling his lap. It was my turn to wipe away his tears. Using my lips, my fingers, wanting to take away his pain and sorrow.

"I could never hate you," I murmured, caressing all over his face. Silently praying he would believe me.

There wasn't an inch of me that didn't ache for him, that didn't want him. I craved his touch now, more than ever before. I licked my lips, needing the moisture to soothe the burn his words and breath caused against my mouth. His eyes followed the simple gesture of my tongue.

"It's not your fault. It's no one's fault. I may not remember what happened, but I know in my heart who you are and what you mean to me. You can't keep blaming yourself for something you had no control over. You didn't pull the trigger. You would never hurt me. I know that without my memory. Do you understand me?"

He pulled back a little, narrowing his eyes at me. Searching my face for I don't know what. He just nodded, answering my question as he reached up to sweep my hair away from my face, never letting his eyes waver from mine. I didn't hesitate, leaning in and kissing him. Wanting and needing to take away his memory of that day, knowing in my heart it wouldn't matter, it would always haunt him. I felt as though it was the least I could do to try.

Allowing my touch to speak for itself.

In a matter of minutes, our kiss turned into something else entirely. Something we both wanted but had yet to make happen.

"Pretty girl," he rasped, against my mouth. "What are you doin'?" Feeling the urgency of my lips claiming his.

"I want you," I simply stated in between kisses. Not wanting to stop comforting him, even if it was just for a second.

"Mia…" he groaned in a husky, torn tone. Waiting for me to say the words he desperately yearned to hear.

"Please… Take me to bed. I'm yours."

He abruptly stood, carrying me up with him like I weighed nothing, wrapping my legs around his waist. Roughly smacking my ass, causing me to yelp. He carried me into his bedroom where he laid me down on the bed, hovering his huge frame over mine.

Looking deep into my eyes, he breathed out, "Are you sure?"

"Yes." I sat up enough to take my dress off, discarding it on the floor. Leaving me topless and exposed, wearing only my panties.

I knew he had seen me naked before, but right now, it felt like the first time all over again. I was so nervous laying there, waiting for him to do what he pleased with me. My heart beat at an uneven rate, threatening to erupt from my chest. Maybe it was the predatory look on his face or the fact that I had just seen another side to him. It also could have been from knowing I was going to touch him, feel him, and see him in ways I didn't remember experiencing with this man.

"You're so goddamn beautiful," he praised with a sincere tone, standing above me at the edge of the bed. Pulling his shirt over his head, revealing his hard, toned, muscular body, covered in nothing but art.

It was then that I saw it, the name Maddie tattooed in small cursive lettering over his heart.

"When did you do that?"

"The day after she died."

"How is this the first time I'm noticing it?"

"You weren't lookin' for it before."

His eyes shifted, taking in every last inch of my body as if it was the first time he was really getting a good look at me.

"Spread your legs for me, baby."

I timidly obeyed, willing my already shaking legs to move. Opening them, anxiously waiting for what I knew was to come. He released a loud growl that escaped from the back of his throat, adding fuel to the flames already burning inside me. Grabbing onto my thighs, he pulled me to the edge of the mattress and sank down on his knees.

I rapidly closed my eyes, and the familiar uncomfortable feeling returned with a vengeance. I was finding it hard to breathe as he kissed and licked his way up my thighs. Not understanding why the intimacy of what he was about to do felt so wrong. I bit my lip, pleading with my mind to let me go, let me live in the moment right here, right now with him. Enjoy the sensations his mouth would stir inside of me.

"Mia," he muttered, making me look down at him. "Can I taste you? You wouldn't let me before, but fuck, baby... I need to. I'm fuckin' starvin'."

His words struck a chord deep inside of me, mimicking the way I was feeling. And I wasn't referring to the filthy things he said, but to the fact that this was the first time he would be doing this…

Is that why it felt wrong? Because I didn't let him before? Why didn't I let him?

I nodded, unable to speak. Forcefully pushing away the sentiments as best as I could.

My head fell back the second I felt his tongue on me. The closeness of his mouth to my most private area was a feeling that had me grabbing the sheets in a frenzy, and he'd barely even started to touch me. I expected him to be rough, but he was being so gentle, taking his time to devour me. Making me wet for him and only him.

"Oh God," I whimpered in pleasure.

He growled, returning his tongue to my heat. Lapping at me, eating me like I was his favorite meal. Making me go crazy with passion and desire while I battled the unrelenting feelings raging war in my head. They were merciless and unforgiving.

He sucked on my clit harder, side-to-side, causing me to scream out his name in ecstasy. Within seconds he was making me come over and over again, plunging his tongue in and out of me. Using his thumb to work my clit, sending me further and further over the edge till I was free falling, leaving behind everything my mind was adamant on showing me.

I shook the entire time as he let me ride out my orgasm against his lips. Only releasing me when I was done and couldn't take anymore. He kissed his way up my body, stopping when he was just above my faint scar. Causing tears to threaten my eyes when I felt his lips brush against it, letting them linger for what felt like hours but was really just seconds. Before continuing his descent up to my breasts.

With one hand, he grabbed the back of my neck, keeping me close to his body. Exactly where he wanted me. I moaned when his lips crashed into mine, bucking my hips off the bed, arching my back. Silently requesting him to keep going. He smiled against my mouth, pleased by my subtle request. Ready to give me what he wanted, what he craved, what he had been waiting for. Kissing me long and hard, he reached over to his nightstand drawer and pulled out a condom. Never once breaking our connection.

My shaking hands moved hastily to his belt, undoing it as fast as I could. Moving to unbutton his jeans next. Using my feet to help him slide them down, along with his boxers. He chuckled, taking in the expression on my face when I saw his hard cock jut free. I bit my lip as he rolled the condom down his shaft and into place. Crawling his way back up my body when he was done. He caged me in with his arms around my face, gripping the back of my neck again, not wanting to lose our connection.

"Don't close your eyes, baby. I wanna look into them as I make love to you."

I kept my eyes open, my mind and heart battling against each other to close them. His hold tightened on my neck as he angled his dick into my opening with his other hand. Gently starting to thrust inside of me, resting his forehead on mine, causing our mouths to part in sync from the feeling of becoming one.

He stopped when he was fully inside of me, just wanting a moment to look into my eyes. To memorize the sensation of him wrapped up in me. My arms went around his neck as he slowly started to thrust in and out, wanting me to get used to his size and girth.

"Fuck, you feel good," he groaned, thrusting harder. "How do you feel this fuckin' good?"

I winced, but he didn't see it, too caught up in the moment, in us. The one I knew he had been waiting for since the first time we did this over a year ago. Everything he was saying was like I'd heard it before, but it wasn't from him.

Was it Creed?

He grabbed my leg, angling it higher. It was much deeper that way, making me clench and tighten around his shaft, which earned me a loud, ravenous growl in return. He never once let up his hold as he continued to move at a hard and fast pace that had me weakening beneath him. Feeling every last inch of him moving in and out of me. Hitting my g-spot perfectly which had me panting, moaning, and screaming all at once. Trying to push through the unease my mind was conjuring up. Struggling to push away the thoughts of someone who wasn't there.

Our bodies were so wrapped up in each other, tangled together on the white sheets.

He kissed me deep and heady, savoring the new sensation of our skin-on-skin contact. I started to move my hips forward as he thrust in. Our bodies moved in time with one another, getting faster and harder with each second that passed.

I was literally trying to fuck Creed out of my mind.

"Fuck," he growled, rotating his hips more demandingly.

I was close to losing it…

My mind.

My heart.

My soul.

My orgasm.

It all intertwined, mixing with the pleasure and the pain. The confusion and the sensations. The want and need.

The past and the present.

And then I couldn't take it anymore.

In one swift motion, I rolled us so I was on top. Needing to be in control of my mind, my heart, and my soul. I couldn't feel him on top of me any longer.

It hurt too damn much.

"I'm going to come," I panted against his mouth.

He gripped the back of my neck, pulling me down on him to look deep in my eyes. Kissing me passionately, sending me over the edge. Taking him right along with me. He hid his face in the nook of my neck, kissing my sweaty skin.

Making a single tear roll down the side of my face when I heard him say, "I love you."

The thought of sleeping for more than a few hours here and there sounded fucking amazing. I couldn't remember the last time I had shut my eyes for longer than what felt like ten fucking minute intervals. Feeling like I was back in the Army, out on missions. There wasn't a part of me that didn't feel like absolute shit.

I pulled out my keys, unlocking the house, and stepping inside. Closing the door behind me. I threw my keys on the table in the foyer, noticing there were a few lights already turned on in the living room, but the house was eerie and silent. I was about to take off my cut when I heard a noise coming from down the main hall. It sounded like muffled voices, followed by some shuffling around.

"The fuck?" I whispered to myself, pulling out my gun from the back of my jeans.

Immediately made my way toward the noise from the other end of the house. Being extra cautious so I wouldn't be heard, no one was supposed to fucking be here. I rounded the corner with my gun held tightly in my grasp, pointing it directly at the floor as I trod lightly down the long, narrow hallway.

It was better to go into the situation like this undetected. Catch the motherfuckers by surprise. Take them the fuck out before they even knew what hit them. It was my life or theirs, and I had always fucking chosen mine.

Over the last three and a half months, it had been one thing after another since Diesel and I uncovered the truth hidden on the discs we recovered from Pop's room. He hadn't said shit about it, so we figured he had yet to figure it out.

As soon as I saw the proof right in front of my goddamn eyes, it was like I had an out of body experience. Shifting through images, documents, the truth that nearly brought me to my fucking knees. I couldn't believe what the fuck I was seeing, swearing my eyes were playing tricks on me, my mind reeling that it took us this fucking long to put the puzzle together. Still needing to find the last piece that would nail the fucking coffin shut.

I owed Martinez more than I ever imagined owing anyone.

Which was what led us to this place and time. Where there was no more evidence to be found, no more roads to go down—it all would end here. The facts were all laid out in front of us. Some had been staring me in the fucking face for years, and I never put two and two together till recently. Involving a hell of a lot more people than just my old man and me. Face after face after face filled Diesel's screen. Stopping on one that that made my blood boil to the point of rage.

Hers.

It was only a matter of time until the truth came out, and the devil and saint would descend upon us. He would be coming for me. If my old man didn't find out first.

I just hoped I could still get to him fucking first.

The next few minutes of my life went down in slow fucking motion, the closer I got to the room where the door was slightly ajar.

More truths.

More facts.

No more fucking lies.

I was suffocating in them. My mind, my sanity, my life—I couldn't take it anymore. My whole body felt like it was giving out on me. Shutting the fuck down. Game over. There were too many emotions happening all at the same fucking time, and I couldn't control any of it. Nothing could have prepared me for what I was about to see, about to feel.

This was the night my life truly fucking ended.

I heard her pant like I was the one touching her.

I heard her moan like I was the one kissing her.

I heard her scream out his name like I was the one fucking her.

Except it wasn't me. It would never be me again.

I stood frozen in place as I watched Noah on top of Mia, *my* fucking girl. Kissing her, holding her—making love to her like she was only his and had never truly been mine. With each thrust he pushed inside of her, I realized I still couldn't see the girl, she could only be heard. I needed to fucking see her to believe it. Holding onto the false hope that maybe this was all him. Or maybe I was mistaken and he was fucking a whore, but I knew Mia's sounds. Her moans, her screams, all of it had been etched into my mind.

My heart.

My fucking soul.

I was one second away from hauling ass inside of his room, throwing him the fuck off of her. One second away from proving I was right and he was wrong. My foot was mid-air moving forward when I saw her suddenly flip him over to get on top of his cock. Riding the shit out of him, looking deep into his eyes. Kissing him like she once kissed me.

It was like watching a car accident, unable to look away. Wanting to fall to my fucking knees and break down right then and there. Each sway of her hips brought me closer to my own demise. I could have busted in there, I could have beaten my baby brother's face in before putting a bullet in his fucking skull. The possibilities were endless. Except, I couldn't move. It was like God had ahold of my ankles, shackling them to the floor, punishing me for all my sins. While the Devil laughed his fucking ass off.

It wasn't until I heard her moan, "I'm going to come," that I wanted to take the gun in my hand and aim it directly at my heart. Pulling the fucking trigger, ending my miserable fucking life with one single bullet.

I finally backed away shaking my head, turning around to leave when I heard Noah say, "I love you." Pulling the goddamn trigger for me.

I went to my room, threw my cut on the bed, and put on a hat and black hoodie. Trying to hide my face and body from anyone who could recognize me. I was still a fucking fugitive, a wanted man on the run with several warrants and rewards out for my arrest. But I didn't give a fuck anymore. I left the house before I did something I would regret for the rest of my life.

Walking to the gas station that was a few blocks away, needing the distraction. I paid cash for the biggest bottle of Jack I could find, strongly gripping it in my hand the whole way back to my mom's house. Taking swig after swig after fucking swig from the bottle. Drowning in the amber liquid, letting it consume my entire being. I went straight to the back porch and sat outside in nothing but darkness. Not ready to face the light which was inside Noah's room. Pushing away the images of Mia fucking my baby brother, but I couldn't.

Now my mind was punishing me for every last sin I committed.

Every last life I took.

Playing the sound of Mia's laughter all around me like a goddamn broken record. Seeing her beautiful face smiling at me. Wishing she was there with me and not in my brother's arms. I had lost her, after everything...

I had still fucking lost her.

I took another swig, welcoming the burn of the fiery liquid with fucking delight. I wanted to forget. I wanted to pretend like the last hour didn't fucking happen. Sitting out in the dark under the full moon. Letting the momentary solace it provided me take over.

I didn't want to feel anything.

I didn't want to remember anything.

I didn't want anything anymore.

But peace.

Knowing I never had any to begin with.

I don't know how much time went by when my phone rang, breaking me out of my trance-like state of emptiness. "Yeah?" I answered.

"You ready for this?" Diesel questioned on the other end.

"As ready as I'll ever fuckin' be."

"You gonna tell your ma everythin'?"

"Ain't sure yet. Gotta few days to figure it out." I took another swig, smacking my lips as it went down. "She don't even know I'm here. No one does."

The only reason I showed up on her doorstep was to let her in on the truth. She had a right to know. Explain to her what was about to go down and what I was going to do with the evidence I found. Not because I needed her blessing.

It was her forgiveness I was after.

"You alright?"

"No," I sternly stated. "Go get some rest. You're gonna fuckin' need it."

Diesel had been my wingman throughout this entire fucking manhunt. I know the endless, sleepless nights had finally run its toll. On both of us.

"You gonna tell Noah?"

I shrugged. "Don't know if I can trust Noah." Especially after what I saw tonight.

"He's still your brother, Creed. I know it don't seem like it now, but he is. He's just hurtin'. Been through a lot these last few years."

"No shit. So have I."

"It's different. You were born into this life. It's all you've ever known and cuz of that, you sheltered your baby brothers the best you could. Not just Noah but Luke, too. Noah didn't see the reality of our world until the day you got on that goddamn bus, leaving one fight to battle another. He had to step up and become a man. You were fuckin' born one."

I took a deep breath, taking in his words, guzzling the bottle now. It was more than half empty by the time I was done.

"I'll be by tomorrow, Creed. Gotta figure out a fuckin' game plan."

I hung up. Leaning back in my chair, taking the last few swigs of whiskey. Trying to focus my attention on the waves of the ocean and not the fucking hurricane that ripped through my heart, leaving nothing but destruction in its wake.

By the time I was finished drowning my fucking sorrows, it was late into the night. I stumbled to my feet realizing I was a lot more drunk than I'd thought. Chucking the empty bottle to the water, going back inside to pass the fuck out. Hoping in my drunken state, my gun wouldn't accidentally meet Noah's fucking balls. Grateful as fuck that my room was on the opposite end of the house, not wanting to hear any more bullshit with them throughout the night.

I staggered into my room, shutting the door behind me. Abruptly stopping dead in my tracks when I saw Mia sitting on the edge of my bed, staring blankly at the inside of my cut that was in her grasp. I blinked a few times, thinking I was imagining things through my drunken haze. Rationalizing it was probably wishful fucking thinking. There was no way she'd be on my bed, in my room, this late at night.

She peered up at me, wide-eyed like she'd just seen a fucking ghost. At that point, I might as well have been one. She didn't see me anymore, eyeing me up and down, taking in the state I was in. I instantly sobered up some, realizing she really was fucking there. Causing me to lean against the door, folding my arms over my chest.

"What the fuck are you doin' in here?" I rasped harsher than I intended. "Shouldn't you be in my brother's bed? You seemed pretty fuckin' cozy in there before."

She winced and didn't even try to hide it.

"What do ya want, Mia?"

Her stare fell to my cut in her hands, peering intently at the inside again. "Were these the patches you were talking about?"

"No."

We locked eyes.

"Those are the ones you gave me. At one time they meant somethin', I guess now they're all fuckin' bullshit."

Her mouth parted. "I gave you all these?"

I nodded. "Every single one ya see on the inside."

"You stitched them in your cut?" She ran her fingers over each one like she was trying to pull some recognition from them.

"From the first one you ever gave me till the last one. I just added to it every time you handed me more."

"Why?" She looked up, confused.

"So I could have you close to me everywhere I went."

"Did I know this before? That you had these on here?"

"No."

She bowed her head again, and it was then I noticed she was wearing nothing but Noah's shirt. Stabbing me in the heart a little bit more.

"Creed—"

"Asked you a question. Expectin' a fuckin' answer. What are you doin' on my bed?" My patience was running very fucking thin.

"I don't know. I couldn't sleep, and I went into the kitchen to get some water… I just… I mean… I ended up here."

"Un-fucking-believable," I breathed out, pissed that she was playing these games with me. When she obviously made her choice. I pushed off the door and was over to her in three strides. "Do you think I'm that fuckin' stupid? What, Mia? Did you come in here cuz baby brother didn't fuck you right? Need a real man's cock inside you? Funny, cuz I never pegged you for bein' a whore."

She gasped. Her eyes widened and her breathing hitched, winded by my response. She didn't falter, standing, throwing my cut on the bed, and leaving without saying another word.

I grabbed her arm before she could even take a step. "Truth hurts, don't it, baby?"

"Let go of me." She used the momentum of my hold to swing back around and slap me across the face. "You don't get to talk to me like that! Ever!"

I touched the side of my face, feeling the sting from her hand. Cocking my head to the side, I spewed, "What, babe? You gonna let him fuck you in the ass, too?"

She raised her hand to slap me again, but I caught it mid-air. "I let you hit me, once... It won't happen again."

She jerked back. Trying to break free from my hold, but it was useless to fight. I wouldn't let her go. "Fuck you! You asshole!"

"Are you shittin' me? I have done nothin' but protect you and fuckin' love you, Mia! And this is how you repay me? By fuckin' my brother! Do you remember anything I said to you at prom? What I fuckin' gave you? What? Did you think I was just goin' to sit by and give you my goddamn blessin'? Waitin' for you while you fuck my brother? Jesus Christ, you want me to hate you?"

"No! Of course not... I'm sorry, okay? I don't remember you! I don't remember our—"

"Bullshit! You wouldn't be in my room, on my bed, in my fuckin' face right now, givin' me shit, if that were true."

She frantically shook her head. "That's not fair."

"You wanna know what's not fair, sweetheart? The fact I just saw you ridin' my brother's cock while you were gettin' off!"

Her chest heaved. "I didn't know you were here. I would have never—"

"You would have never what? Fucked him? Fallin' for him? Let him make love to you? Please, Mia, tell me what you would have never done."

"I love him," she simply stated as if it meant everything when it meant absolutely nothing to me.

Finally making me realize I'd been fighting a war I never had a chance of winning.

"Yeah?" I let her go. "Well, you fuckin' loved me, too. Since you were nine-years-old." I nodded to the door. "Go. Be with my brother. You love him, yeah? Then go be in his bed. Go lay in his arms. Let him kiss you. Touch you. Tell you you're his… And try not to think of me the next time he does it. Unless you want me to put my hands on you and remind you who ya really fuckin' belong to."

She slowly backed away, looking at me one last time before she turned and left. And it took everything inside me not to go after her.

Knowing in my heart.

We ended here.

I called in church.

Except this meeting wouldn't include any of the brothers. It would be just my father, myself, and the fucking truth. It took Diesel and me a few days to get our shit in order and line everything up for doomsday. He made sure no other brothers would be present at the clubhouse for the whole day other than us. The last thing we needed was any distractions, interruptions, or retaliations. This was between my father and me.

Had nothing to do with club business.

After this there would be no second chances, no do-overs, no going back.

It was now or never.

I didn't realize until the next day that my ma not being home actually turned out to be a blessing in disguise. Not from the bullshit I witnessed, which would haunt me forever, but from me saving her a world of pain. Making me realize that she didn't need to know the truth. She'd been through enough and had already moved on with her life. It wouldn't have been fair to drag her into something that, for the most part, had nothing to do with her.

At the end of the day this would be my burden and my burden alone to bear.

The doors opened to the clubhouse conference room just after twelve-thirty in the afternoon, and in walked the fucking Prez. Talking on his cell phone, not paying any mind to where he was and what was going on around him, until he abruptly stopped. His boots crossing the threshold, seeing it was just me filling the large space between us.

Sitting at the head of the table.

In his fucking seat.

He quickly ended his call, narrowing his eyes at me, questioning, "The fuck is goin' on?"

I nodded to the seat on the other end of the rectangular table, ordering him to sit down. He understood my silent demand, closing the door behind him. Cautiously stepping further into the room to take a seat. Each of his steps were cool and calculated, heading straight for the chair that was parallel to mine. His eyes never wavered from my stare as he sat down like he was told.

I was shocked by the fact that he actually listened. Grabbing the gavel, I hit the table three times, announcing church was now in session.

"You scared?"

"Of you?" he challenged, grinning.

"Of the fuckin' truth."

"What truth would that be, son?"

"The truth of how fucked up you really are."

He maliciously smiled, arching an eyebrow. "Like father, like son."

Slowly and deliberately, I shook my head no. "I ain't anythin' like you, motherfucker."

He leaned back into his chair, placing his boots up on the wood table with a loud, hard thud. "That what you think? You're exactly like me. You kill for what you believe in. You protect what's fuckin' yours. You take shit from no one, includin' me. You're a fuckin' Jameson, through and fuckin' through."

"Is that right?" I countered, nodding my head.

"Fuck yeah it is."

I didn't waver, demanding, "We need to have a word." I never took my eyes off of him as I grabbed the files that were sitting on my lap. His eyes immediately went to the manila folders in my grasp. "You want 'em?" I taunted, holding them up in the air. "Or should I make you fuckin' beg for them."

"Fuck you! I don't know what you're tryin' to pull, but how 'bout you cut the pussyfootin' bullshit, and just tell me why the fuck I'm here."

I dropped the folders on the table, sliding them across the polished surface. They stopped right in front of him. "I ain't got a fuckin' death wish like you do."

He jerked back, confused by my declaration. Waiting a few seconds before opening the first file. The one I placed right on top, just for him.

"I gotta know. Did ya really think I wouldn't have figured it out? I just wanna know how fuckin' stupid you really think I am?"

His eyes were glued to the first photo. The realization of what I knew immediately seized over his face. "Where ya get this?" he asked, looking me dead in the eyes.

"In your extensive music collection. Never thought you were the classical music type, Pops."

"Creed, it ain't what it fuckin' looks like."

"A picture is worth a thousand words, so are all those fuckin' documents. So, I'm gonna ask you again... did ya think I wouldn't have fuckin' figured it out? But by all means, keep goin', Prez, there's a ton of incriminatin' evidence, exactly like the contents of that folder. The last envelope, though... that's the one that really fucks with me."

He took in my words, slowly spreading the photos and documents out on the table in front of him. Taking in each and every picture with no remorse or guilt present on his face. I sat back, watching, waiting for a reaction, even though I shouldn't have. I knew he was a heartless bastard, a fucking prick, but I slightly hoped that maybe somewhere deep inside of him, there truly was a man with an underlying conscience.

His face stayed stagnant, proving my suspicions. He really was just a fucking monster.

He grabbed the last document with a photograph clipped to it, the one I had been losing sleep over. The one photo that Martinez really wanted me to have was the one I'd been waiting for my old man to see.

The same one I wanted to fucking kill him for.

"How long?"

He peered up at me through the slits of his eyes, conscious of the fact that he finally had been caught. His moment of truth, probably the first one in his miserable fucking life. There were no more bullshit lies he could spew, the truth was held blatantly in his goddamn hand for me to see.

Angling his chin up in defiance, he snarled, "From the moment she came runnin' into her momma's restaurant, wearin' pigtails and a fuckin' pink baby doll dress."

"You sick fuck!" I slammed my fists on the hard wood, sending my chair flying out from under my body. It took everything in me to restrain the urge to take him the fuck out, right then and there.

He chuckled, eyeing me up and down. "I get a lot more money for little girls than I do for women. She was such a cute fuckin' baby girl. You would know, Creed, she's been followin' you around since the day I wanted to fuckin' take her. Do you remember that day? You were standin' out front with her. If it wasn't for her overprotective fuckin' father, it would have been done already. It didn't help that her uncle is the fuckin' detective that's been on our ass for years." He shrugged, throwing the document and photo back on the table. "So, I had to let it go. Until the moment she stepped foot on this compound and spread her legs for your fuckin' brother. Comin' back six weeks later sayin' she was knocked the fuck up. She's nothin' but a two-bit fuckin' whore! I bet you it wasn't even his fuckin' kid. But…" He deviously smiled, big and wide. "A pretty young girl and a newborn baby," he paused, shaking his head, "now, that's some serious fuckin' bank."

"You motherf—"

He pounded his hand on the table, standing. Pointing at me. "I was doin' it for you! And for your fuckin' brother! Look what she's done to you! To the both of you! Makin' you lose sight of what is really fuckin' important! This goddamn club!" he roared, walking over to me. Getting right up in my face. "What was next, huh?! You tell me that your leavin', too? Turnin' your back on your brothers?! On your fuckin' colors?! Goin' to make a nice life for yourself? Get a house with a fence and a fuckin' dog?! How was that goin' to work, huh? You get to fuck her on Mondays, Wednesdays, and Fridays, and your baby brother gets her all the other days?"

I lunged at him, grabbing him by the throat. Slamming his back into the wall as hard as I could. Knocking the wind out of him, causing a loud gasp of air to escape his mouth.

"How many girls, you piece of shit?! How many fuckin' girls have you trafficked?!" I let go of his throat just enough to where he could speak.

He sucked in the air that I was brutally taken away from him, looking me right in the eyes. He stated, "Too many to fuckin' count."

"So, it was all a setup? The shootouts?" I gritted through a clenched jaw, wanting to choke him the fuck out.

"Yes. Except the first one that took place here, at the clubhouse... that wasn't for Mia," he paused, letting his words sink in. "That was for Autumn. Your other fuckin' whore."

My eyes widened, jerking back, never expecting him to say that.

"You had to play fuckin' hero, and Marcus couldn't grab her. You remember him, right? Sinner's Rejoice were never the threat per se, they were workin' for me. Takin' little girls from their beds at night, snatchin' more at the fuckin' store. All. For. Me. But it don't matter, you ended up killin' Autumn before they could go to New York and fuckin' collect her! It's safe to say that one is on you."

I cocked my arm back, shouting, "You son of a bitch!" clocking in him the face, not once but four times before he even got the last word out, sending his body to the ground with blood gushing from his nose.

He laughed, spitting up crimson onto the ground, trying to hold up his head, pinching his nose. "I didn't think you'd figure out I had Mia so fuckin' fast after the shootout at your ma's! They were almost here! If it weren't for her bleedin' the fuck out, and the stupid motherfuckers that Sinner's hired haulin' ass too fuckin' quick, she would have been fuckin' collected!" he chuckled, leaning his back up against the wall. Wiping the blood from his nose with the back of his hand. "So, I had to wait again... it didn't take long until you fucked up! Shoulda never took her outside, who knew you were such a pussy, makin' her a fuckin' picnic. I gotta say, though... havin' her lose her bastard of a baby and memory, now that's been fuckin' fun to watch!"

"You were the fuckin' traitor!" I kicked him in the stomach as hard as I could. He immediately peeled over to his side. "That's why you suggested the safe house! This has been your obsession all along! You sick motherfucker! I will make you pay for that! Do you hear me?! That was your fuckin' grandbaby, you piece of fuckin' shit!" I kicked him two more times.

My chest heaved, and my eyes burned. All I saw was fucking red. Rage couldn't even come close to describing how I felt in that moment. It took over every last fiber of my being.

"For what?! To make me loyal to you?! That's what this is about! All you want is for me to live and breathe this fuckin' club! Well, I hate this fuckin' club!" I shouted, kicking him three more times.

He groaned, clenching his stomach. Coughing up blood from the blows I was delivering with my boot.

"Get up! Get up, motherfucker, before I fuckin' kill you!"

"Creed, I—"

The double doors to the conference room suddenly flew open, bringing our attention over to *him*. The man I'd been waiting for, showed up just in the nick of time before I ended my father's life. His stare went from me to Pops and back to me again, quickly taking in the scene unfolding in front of his eyes.

"I hate to interrupt this father and son bonding moment, but I got places to be and people to see," Damien announced, walking into the room. Closing the door behind him.

"The fuck is he doin' here?"

He smiled, slamming his briefcase on the table, taking a seat where my old man had been sitting. "I'm slumming it. That's what the fuck I'm doing here. Now, get your ass up off the floor, we got business to discuss." Damien shuffled through all the photos and documents laying out in front of him, even though he was more than familiar with them all. Having stacks of his own and then some at his office.

Pops rolled over onto his side. Holding onto his stomach, trying to keep it together as he picked himself up to his feet. Using the wall for leverage to stand, taking way too fucking long to be upright. He finally stood, hunched over, walking his way back to the table. Sitting in the head seat.

Where he still thought he fucking belonged.

"This her?" Damien asked, holding up the picture of Mia.

I nodded, sitting in one of the seats adjacent to both of them.

"You like them young, eh? Seems like your daddy does, too."

"Fuck you," I scoffed out, glaring at him.

He held up his hands in the air in a surrendering gesture. "No judgment. I'm all for young pussy. It's much tighter that way," he rasped, smiling.

"The fuck is goin' on?" Prez chimed in again, wheezing for air.

"May I?" Damien questioned, glancing at me.

I nodded again.

He placed the picture back down on the table, pulling out a small recorder from the inside of his suit jacket. Setting it up in front of him. Appearing to be the non-corrupt man, the law-abiding citizen everyone knew him to be. His hair was slicked back into a bun, not a strand out of place. His white suit was crisp and clean, not one wrinkle could be seen. He played the educated, clean-cut lawyer well. Even his tone of voice and dialect was different.

He was portraying El Santo now, far from the man I had been negotiating with these last few months. It was like he had two different personalities.

The sinner and the saint.

"Anything that you say in here from this point forward is confidential between all parties present."

"What the fuck does that mean?"

He rolled his eyes, sighing, "It means I'm here to save your sorry fucking ass. I have all the evidence I need to place you behind bars for life. Thanks to your son here." He nodded to me. "Honestly, I don't give a flying fuck if you serve time or not. I want to become District Attorney, so I'm here to make you a deal. You give up every fucking name involved in this fucked up mess. Tell me the information I need to know and sign this plea bargain, which clearly states you're fucking guilty for committing all these crimes. And I'll make sure you don't serve a life sentence at Riker's Island where you'll get fucked in the ass every night by men who will make you bleed just for fun. Now… are those words you understand?"

"You ain't got shit!"

"These files?" He gestured to the evidence on the table. "This ain't shit?" He pulled out more from his briefcase and slid them over to him across the table. "What about these? Those shit, too? What? You need more shit? Because I have plenty of shit back at my office. You just tell me how much shit you need, and I'll make sure you're knee deep in it."

No one said anything for I don't know how long. I knew the wheels were spinning so goddamn fast in his head he could barely keep up. Trying to figure out how he could weasel his way out of this, save his sorry ass.

"I'd take his plea bargain, old man. As much as I'd love to see you rottin' away in prison. Unfortunately, you're still my fuckin' father. I can't bring myself to do that to my mother or Noah, even though you're nothin' but a fuckin' piece of shit. It may have been different if you had actually succeeded with trafficking Mia. So I guess that's your only savin' fuckin' grace. Cuz, see…" I leaned over on the table. "I ain't nothin' like you. I got a fuckin' conscience. And I can't take any more lives, not even fuckin' yours."

My father peered back and forth between us, knowing his end was fucking near.

"Either way, your ass is serving time. It's just up to you to determine how long," Damien added.

"How do I know you ain't lyin'?"

"You got trust issues, Jameson?" He held up the plea bargain. "It's all written here." Sliding that over to him, too. "Oh wait…you can read, right?"

"Fuck you!"

"Eh, I prefer fucking putas. Now pick up the fucking pen and sign."

It didn't take long for my old man to agree, spending the next five hours telling Damien everything he needed to know and then some. I couldn't believe the shady shit he was involved in. It made me sick to my fucking stomach that we were blood and he was my father. He had his hands in a little bit of everything. Things that made human trafficking look like fucking child's play.

I just waited.

Listening to every word. Every confession. Every person he betrayed.

Anticipating when everything was said and done. My moment. Everything I'd been fucking waiting for, pursuing, investigating. All the sleepless nights, all the bullshit I'd gone through. Every life that had been taken.

Mine.

Noah's.

Mia's.

Especially Maddie's.

It all collided together. Except this time, there was no more doubt. No more struggle. No more what ifs.

My time had come to make things right. All I ever wanted led up to this point in time. Where nothing else mattered.

But fucking revenge.

We walked out the back doors of the clubhouse when they were done with his confession. Pops was getting ready to light up a cigarette, smoking one last time before Damien was supposed to take him in. I didn't think twice about it, in one swift movement I grabbed the gun from the back of my old man's jeans and aimed it right at his head.

"The fuck you doin'?" he immediately let out.

"Damien, grab the gun he's hidin' in his boot."

He obliged, pulling the handkerchief out from his suit jacket and bending over. Using it as a barrier between his hand and the gun, he grabbed ahold of the Glock. Placing it in the back of his slacks still using the handkerchief as a barrier between his skin and the gun.

"Grab that shovel over there and fuckin' walk," I ordered, nodding to the shovel behind my father.

He peered over at Damien, waiting for him to interfere. Say something, anything so I would lower my gun.

Damien just shrugged, putting on his sunglasses. "I have what I came for," he let out, holding up his briefcase.

My father's eyes widened, spewing, "You fuckin' played me!"

"WALK!" I roared, pushing my gun into the side of his head.

His chest heaved and his nostrils flared, stepping one foot in front of the other toward the direction I demanded. Eventually figuring out where I was taking him. I followed close behind, remembering everything about that goddamn night.

How thick and suffocating the fog from the rain the day before was. The way the wind blew a cool breeze through the trees, skimming the surface of my overly heated skin. I remembered the sounds of twigs cracking beneath my boots, the noises from the birds and owls, along with whatever else fucking lurked in the woods.

Most of all, I remembered feeling so much fucking hatred for my father. Not giving Luke, his son, a proper burial. Just wanting to throw him in a field along with countless other bodies the club had taken.

I hadn't been back there not one fucking time since the night he made me bury my brother.

Not one fucking time.

Until now.

We stopped when we stood over the exact place where his body lay buried under dirt, rocks, and God knows what else.

Nodding to him, I ordered, "Dig."

"You can't be serious."

"Ain't ever been more serious about anythin' in my fuckin' life! Now fuckin' dig!" I seethed, daring him to defy me.

"You gonna tell Damien over here? How you murdered your brother, huh? What? Wanna a cell by your old man? Is that it?"

"He already knows," I simply retorted. "Don't you see, Prez, this is all part of the plan. I give him what he wants, he gets a promotion. I get immunity for providin' evidence to finally turn your ass in. Make sense now? All the roads comin' together for you?"

Pops shook his head, gripping the shovel tight, grumbling something under his breath. Forcefully driving the blade into the hard ground over and over again. Heaving dirt over his shoulder while Damien and I watched. I kept my emotions in check. Trying like hell to remain calm the closer he got to digging up my brother's grave. Until all that could be seen was a giant hole in the dirt along with the black body bag that held Luke's remains.

"There! There's your fuckin' brother! Tell him how sorry you are again! Forget you're the reason he's in the ground?" he sadistically mocked.

"Bring him up here!" I demanded, looking only at him.

He did as he was told, placing the bag of bones next to me. "We done now? This the family reunion you wanted, Creed?" He was about to jump out from the hole, but I had other plans for him. I cocked back the chamber, making him jerk back in place. "What the fuck you think you doin'?"

"What I shoulda done a long fuckin' time ago," I simply stated.

He put his hands up in the air, surrendering, stepping further into the makeshift grave. "You don't got to do this… I'm already goin' to prison!"

"Prison is too fuckin' good for you!"

"Damien! What the fuck?! You gonna stand there and watch him—"

"I don't like to involve myself in family disputes. I'm not that kind of attorney. It wouldn't be my place," he sarcastically interrupted in his serious *El Santo* tone. "I already told you, I have what I came for. It doesn't matter if I bring you in, dead or alive. I solved the case. Not to mention all the names and evidence you provided. By the way, thank you for that, but in my honest opinion…" He smiled. "Justice is always served better on the fucking streets."

"You piece of shit!" My father spit at him, peering back at me with a vicious glare. "How the fuck is this happening? How the fuck did you even find out?!"

"That was all—"

"Me." All eyes went to the man dressed in an expensive fucking suit, casually walking out from the woods like he just appeared out of thin air.

All the blood drained from my father's face, immediately turning pale as if he was looking at a goddamn ghost and in a way…

El Diablo was.

"What the fuck are you doing here?" Damien questioned, arching an eyebrow.

He wasn't in on this part of the plan. I only did it for Martinez. I gained nothing with him being there.

But I owed it to him.

"I heard you were missing me. So I came just to see you," Martinez rasped, standing beside me. Making Damien chuckle and shake his head.

"You're... the papers... I thought... you... were dead..." Pops stuttered, still staring only at him with petrified eyes. An expression I'd never seen before.

"You can't believe everything you read, Jameson," Martinez relayed, grinning. "The news and the papers are always exaggerating shit."

"Now ya scared, Prez?" I mocked, smiling. "You wanna have a little bedtime story before you go to sleep for good?"

He swallowed hard, his eyes couldn't focus on one of us for very long before moving onto to the next.

"You see, Martinez handed me a disc, and I hid it under the mattress of my bed when I reported back to base. When Diesel went to find it, it was gone. Fast forward to a few months ago, and it miraculously showed up in your C.D. collection. Funny how that is, yeah?"

"That—"

"He texted me a photo the day of the shootout of my mother, your wife, sittin' on another man's lap. But you probably already knew that... seein' as the shootout was that night. Needed to distract me, yeah? Get me away from her? Why do you think he chose that picture?"

"Creed—"

Martinez stepped forward, rendering him speechless. Crouching down in front of the makeshift grave, trying to get as close as he could to my dad's face, wanting to look him in the eyes. "I may be a lot of things, but I don't fuck with women and children. You know how these things go, Jameson. People talk, especially fucking criminals. There isn't anything I don't ever know. When I learned about your involvement, I saw an opportunity, and I took it. Seeing as it involved my niece's friend's daughter. And family has always come first to me. No matter what."

"The photo was so old, it was hard to make out it was Striker's lap she was sittin' on, but that wasn't what Martinez wanted me see... It was the fact that the picture was taken in Mia's mom's restaurant, a pigtail faintly in the background. I didn't figure that out until I saw what you wanted to do with *my* girl... Now, the rest of the fuckin' files you had," I breathed out, pursing my lips and shaking my head.

"The pictures of a woman bein' fuckin' gunned down? Now, that! That was helluva fuckin' surprise! Why did ya hold onto that for? Souvenirs? You sick fuck! I didn't even realize who the woman was until I saw a written agreement on another document, statin' you murder his wife and he'll deliver the sex traffikn' to you on a silver fuckin' platter... Mind-fuckin'-blowin'! But you do have trust issues, yeah? Why else would you leave a fuckin' paper trail? It just took one phone call to Leo, one fuckin' call lettin' him know I knew who killed Martinez's mom, and the next day this motherfucker was at Diesel's door. Not gonna lie, it took us a minute to figure it all out. To make it work so everyone would walk away satisfied. But here we are..." I paused to let it all sink in. Needing him to understand every last word that came out of my mouth.

"The question is, Prez," I eyed him, "did you know Martinez was gettin' close to the truth? Or did you just kill Striker cuz he was the only one who knew what really happened? Since he was there with you. Or did you just put a hole in his head cuz he was fuckin' your wife?"

"You—"

"I asked ya a question, expectin' a fuckin' answer," I interrupted my father, not wanting to hear any more of his bullshit lies.

It was the first time I had ever seen pure fear cross my father's face, realizing that he was really going to fucking die. Never expecting it to come from the hands of his own firstborn son.

His fucking prodigy.

"Look me in the eyes, motherfucker," Martinez ordered, leaning forward, closer to his face. He didn't falter. "I promised my mother the day she died in my arms. The day that you and your biker trash murdered her... I would find the pieces of shit who put her there and make them pay. And as you know, Jameson. I am a man of my fucking word."

"Ya got any last fuckin' words, Prez?" I baited.

"Please, don't—"

"On second thought." Cocking my gun to the side, I locked eyes with my father for a split second. Needing him to know it was me who put him to ground. "I don't give a fuck." I pulled the trigger.

His brains blew out from the back of his head, splattering all over the dirt before his body fell back into the deep, dark hole with a hard, loud thud. Mimicking the sound of Luke's body the night he just threw him in there like he was taking out the fucking trash. Time just seemed to stand still, nothing moving, including me. While Martinez and I battled our demons for a whole different set of reasons.

There was an unfamiliar feeling lingering in the air, burning into my senses. Where it would forever be etched in my skin. Except this memory would be the first one that would never, ever, fucking haunt me.

I was the first to break the silence, whispering, "Ashes to ashes, dust to dust, and all that fuckin' shit."

Martinez spit in the grave before standing up, walking back over to us. Once again the cool, calm, collected man he'd always been.

"Well... that was entertaining," Damien proclaimed, bringing our attention to him.

Martinez grinned, taking him in. "He just murdered your promotion. How the fuck you going to explain that?"

It was Damien's turn to smirk, cocking his head to side. He pulled out Pops' gun from the back of his slacks with the handkerchief wrapped around the grip, and aimed the barrel right into his own shoulder.

He didn't hesitate, pulling the trigger. "Mierda!" he shouted, chucking the gun to the ground. Immediately holding onto his bullet wound while blood gushed out all over his white suit. "Murdered?" he repeated, mocking Martinez. Letting out a big, throaty laugh as more blood seeped through his fingers. "All Creed did was save my fucking life," he simply stated. "Clean up this mess so I can call it in." With that, he turned, walking back toward the clubhouse like nothing ever happened.

It was then I realized this man would do anything to get what he wants, including shooting himself to fucking prove it.

"Damien!" I called out after him, making him turn to face me once again. "Everyone know you're a corrupt motherfucker?"

He arched an eyebrow, smiling. Nodding to me. "Not to anyone who matters. I'm just a fucking Saint."

Martinez took off shortly after that, going back to whatever hole he crawled out of, with closure. Diesel showed up with all the brothers in tow. He spent the entire day at his house, showing them all the proof of what their Prez had been involved in. How much he compromised the club, our brotherhood, our fucking pack. Proving to them that he didn't give a shit about anyone but himself. They didn't ask questions after they learned what he was trying to do with Mia. Already fully aware that what I did was necessary.

Knowing they would have done the same fucking thing had it been one of their ol' ladies.

And we always protected our own.

As much as I wanted to bury my old man in that grave, we couldn't. We made the scene look exactly the way Damien said it was, which didn't take very long. The club had always been good at staging shit, it was one of the things we did best. Diesel made sure to take Luke's remains with him so I could give him a proper burial, finally laying my brother's soul to rest peacefully.

McGraw was one of the first people to walk into the clubhouse, followed by an endless amount of other pigs marching to his beat. Following him in line. I sat in the corner in the back of the game room and watched as he and Damien exchanged words after the ambulance had patched up his bullet wound. He took off moments later, going straight to wherever he needed to go to get everything in order for Prez's case.

McGraw immediately made his way toward me when he was done with Damien. Before he could even say a word to me, I handed him the file of everything that had to do with Mia. I knew Damien gave him most of the rundown prior to leaving, but I just wanted to slam the nail in the fucking coffin. And have no more bullshit and animosity between us.

"Make sure you let her daddy know, yeah?"

He peered up at me through the slits of his eyes, nodding when he was done looking over the folder. "This doesn't change the fact you're an outlaw," he emphasized, staring at the 1% patch on my cut.

I didn't hesitate, ripping it off, throwing it to the floor between us. I stood. "Not anymore. Not ever again."

He narrowed his eyes at me as I turned around, gazing at all the brothers who had just watched me resign my colors.

"I'm done wit' this fuckin' club. You wanna ride by a man who follows the law… then follow me out. Ya feel me?"

Ends Here

My father wasn't the only one that I put to ground that day.
VP of the Devil's Rejects, Creed Jameson...
Was, too.

"How do you feel about that, Mia?" Dr. Garcia asked.

"I don't know."

She gave me a look that I was more than familiar with. Making me roll my eyes and take a deep breath. "I guess I just never expected my mind to flip a switch like that. I mean… Uncle Dylan said he was a free man now. I'm torn about all the stuff I learned involving their dad and me. I'd only met the man in passing a couple of times, but I was targeted by him even before that. It upsets me that I don't even get to ask him why…"

It had been three months since their dad had been killed and I had learned the truth. My family contemplated whether to tell me or not, but it was national news. There was no hiding the truth when it was plastered all over the T.V. and newspapers. Learning the truth was harder than I'd ever imagined.

"It makes me sick to my stomach, knowing what could have happened if his plans had succeeded. Knowing I would have been sold to some sick person, most likey tortured and forced into slavery is a sombering thought. The intent behind his actions is a tough pill to swallow. Before now, I never knew such a disgusting world existed. And I almost fell victim to it," I paused, reining in my plaguing thoughts. My poor parents are beside themselves. My mom said that my dad tried to meet up with Creed to apologize and thank him, but hasn't found where he's staying. If that's not irony, I don't know what is. I can only imagine what Creed must be feeling.

Finding all this horrible secrets and taking his own father's life must be weighing heavy on his shoulders. I know Noah is having a hard time with it. Not that his father is dead, but that he wanted to kidnap me."

She nodded. "It's a lot to take in. Do you feel better now that you know the truth?"

"I do."

"You don't sound very convincing, Mia."

"I'm just torn."

"With the news? Or with Creed and Noah?"

"Wow, Doc, you're not making it easy for me today, huh?" I nervously chuckled.

"Well?"

"I know Creed was the one who technically kidnapped me, but he was just trying to protect me. I know that now. Everyone does. But the shootout, me getting shot, Maddie... that wasn't his fault. It was his father's. For almost a year Creed was on the run, in hiding, trying to get to the bottom of the truth. For me. That changes things, Dr. Garcia. I know I still don't remember him, but it doesn't change the fact that he truly was my hero this entire time. Not the villain everyone portrayed him as. He was the good guy. I never thought of him as a bad person, he just made bad things happen and bad decisions."

"How does that make you feel? Does it tap into the memories at all?"

"Here's the thing, it's been over a year since I lost my memory. Every day since I woke up in that hospital, I feel like I remember something, but it doesn't present itself to me like a memory. It's just a feeling in my gut, deep within me. I have no idea how that even makes sense, but the feelings are getting more and more intense as time goes on. I may not remember Creed, but you were right, Doctor, he's been right here since the beginning... in my heart. Has been since day one."

"What about Noah?"

"I love Noah. I honestly do. That's why I'm torn, Doc. The Mia I was in the past is madly in love with Creed, and the Mia I am now is in love with Noah. Except, learning all these things that Creed has done for me… Makes me think, this Mia, the woman I am now. Loves him too, and maybe she never stopped."

"There could be worse things than loving two men, sweetie."

"Not if one of them gets hurt."

"Have you seen Creed?"

"You know I haven't. Not since that night at his mom's. The very same night he saw us. The same night he was brutal and nasty to me. Which in a way I guess I deserved. I know he was hurting and drunk, and I don't blame him for that. The crazy thing is, even though he was deliberately being cruel to me, he never once stopped saying that I was his. That he loved me. That I belonged to him. His love always spoke through the pain. The pain I caused the man who's done nothing but protect me."

"Have you and Noah discussed this?"

"No. What am I supposed to say to him? He didn't do anything wrong. He's been nothing short of amazing to me. He's been there as a friend, a boyfriend, and a lover. I can't imagine my life without him in it."

"But you can with Creed?"

"I can, but only because I haven't spent any time with him since the shooting. I know I would feel different if he became my friend, but I don't think we could ever just be friends. At least not for him, and the last thing I want to do is hurt him any more than I already have."

"How about Maddie? How has it been since you and Noah finally talked about her?"

"I have a better sense of understanding the love I had for her, and it makes me feel less like a horrible mother. I also think it has given Noah and me a bit of closure. We don't talk about her, but it doesn't feel like there's a huge elephant in the room anymore. I also know that if I wanted to talk about her, he would listen and vice versa."

She nodded. "What would happen if you woke up tomorrow and remembered, Mia? If suddenly your memory was back. Do you think it would still be Noah?"

My eyes widened, biting my lower lip. I shrugged, not knowing how to answer.

"Then I think that's what you need to figure out. Because that one day, sweetie, could be tomorrow."

"Yeah…" I whispered.

She flipped through my notebook, paying particular attention to some of my last entries. "I think the answers have been in front of you all along, Mia," she said, closing it and handing it back to me.

"What do you mean?"

"I see a pattern happening on those pages. Your homework is to take some time for yourself, and read through your thoughts in that notebook, alright? Same time next week, okay?"

I nodded. She ended our session, leaving me with a lot to think about. When I exited the elevator, Noah was patiently waiting for me in the parking garage like always.

"Hey, pretty girl," he greeted, kissing me and pulling me into his arms.

"Hey, yourself," I teased, smiling.

"Guess what today is?"

"If you say something sexual, I'm going to hit you," I giggled, pulling away.

"Get your mind out of the gutter!" he chuckled, grabbing my hand and kissing it. Leading me out of the garage. "I know my cock is good to you and all, but you gotta give the man a break sometimes."

My mouth dropped open. "Oh my God! You're the one who wants to live on top of me."

"Really? Says the girl who's on top most of the time."

I looked down at the ground, not wanting him to see the expression on my face. I was scared it would give away why I wanted to be on top. Why I needed to be. "So, what is today then?" I asked, changing the subject.

"Today is the day you ride on the back of my bike."

I shook my head, glancing at the side of his face. "Nope. Not happening."

"Oh, it's happenin'." He picked me up off the ground, throwing me over his shoulder before I even saw it coming.

"You can't do this every time you don't get your way!"

"Try and stop me, Mia."

I struggled against him, laughing the entire time as he walked us to the back of the huge building, to the alleyway where he had parked his bike and there were no other vehicles.

"It's time for you to meet my other girl. She's gettin' her feelings hurt since I don't ride her as much as you ride me."

I smacked his back, making him chuckle.

"You're gonna sit your pretty little ass on my bike for a minute, so you can get used to the feelin' of somethin' so big between your legs. Wait, you should already be used to it cuz of me."

I smacked him again.

He clutched onto my waist, sliding me down his hard, muscular body. Making me straddle his waist as he straddled his bike, placing me on his lap. Our innocent encounter turned into something else entirely different when he yanked me closer. Molding us into one person and kissing me as if his life depended on it. I moaned into his mouth, and he groaned into mine as he suddenly fisted my hair at the nook of my neck. His other hand drifted down the side of my breast to the seam of my panties, under my dress. He slid them over, gliding his fingers into my wet folds.

I swallowed hard. "Noah… someone could walk back here."

"Fuck, you're so wet. I did this to you. Me," he growled, continuing to work my clit. Ignoring my fear, seducing me to keep going. He swiftly pushed me back, and I placed my hands on the gas tank for support.

My head was spinning, my heart was racing, my core was throbbing. I leaned forward to kiss him, but he tore my hair back harder. Wanting me to stay right where I was, spread wide open for him on his bike.

I couldn't stop it.

I couldn't stop this.

My mind and my heart wouldn't let me, colliding into one.

He wanted to watch me fall over the edge, needing to feel me deep in his soul. Never once stopping his assault on my core, rubbing me back and forth, causing my body to shudder and my hips to rock, taking what he was giving.

His lips parted like he was feeling everything I was when all he was doing was watching me come apart. For him and only him. His fingers worked me over, finding my g-spot, creating this longing, this intensity, this mind-blowing explosion all over my body. My back arched over the gas tank, my dress riding up, exposing his sweet torture. Allowing him to go faster and harder.

My heart continuing to beat rapidly, hammering in my head, and making me feel dizzy.

Lightheaded.

Overwhelmed by everything that was suddenly happening. Feeling as if I was being mentally torn in two directions.

His.

Ours.

My mind was in overdrive, putting up one hell of a fight with my heart.

He roughly jerked my hair back to look into my eyes and spoke with conviction, "You're fuckin' mine. I claimed you."

When our eyes locked together, it was all over, feeling his thumb manipulate my nub as his fingers continued to rub my sweet spot.

Bringing me right to the edge of the ledge, on the tips of my toes, about to free fall when I heard the horn from the train at noon sounding off a few blocks away. Pulling me back to the here and now. Getting louder and louder, ready to barrel through town, taking my heart away with it. I shook off the sudden unease and tried to focus on Noah's touch, shoving away my feelings I told Doc about.

This moment, it was truly the end for me.

Right then and there like a wave washing me to shore with Noah's hands pulling me under.

I unlocked the door, stepping inside my place. Throwing the keys on the entry table before making my way inside. It had been five months since I took care of business, putting my father to ground. Finally walking away from the MC, free to do whatever the fuck I wanted.

Completely out from under his control for the first time in my life.

The press had a fucking field day with the news of what supposedly went down at the compound. The story Damien pulled out of his ass was nothing but pure and utter fucking genius. I quickly realized he really was good at what he did, especially all the illegal shit. Which would definitely earn him the death sentence by the law's standards if he ever got found out. Even without my help, it wouldn't have been long before he became District Attorney, like he was now. The corrupt motherfucker was all over the news, shaking hands with the top fucking dogs from all around the world. Painting the picture of the man everyone knew as El Santo, doing what he does best—serving justice.

He portrayed me as the knight in shining fucking armor. Mia Ryder's hero. I couldn't leave my house without getting hounded by reporters. All wanting an interview with the man who took down the President of the Devil's Rejects. The fact it was his son who did so made it even better tabloid gossip. I couldn't even turn on the T.V.

without seeing our faces plastered all over the screen. Making me miss her that much more.

About a week after the incident, I made arrangements to have Luke's remains buried at Oakdale Cemetery next to Autumn's memorial. Giving my ma the closure she needed, knowing that her baby boy was now truly resting in peace.

She didn't say much about what happened, other than thank you when I handed her Luke's medallion at the memorial. Pulling me into a tight hug with tears running down her cheeks. She didn't any ask questions, probably because she already knew all the answers. She was still briefed by Leo, preparing for my father's case with Damien. It was standard protocol to question all parties involved, just to go through the motions. They even brought Noah in.

I saw my brother at Ma's house a few days after we took down my old man, and everything was already headline news. I had gone into my room to pack up some of my shit that Ma had brought over from the old house. Wanting to take it back with me to my place.

"Hey," Noah greeted, leaning against the doorframe to my room with his arms crossed over his chest.

I nodded at him, grabbing the dogtags Autumn had made for me from my nightstand. Throwing it in one of my bags on the bed. I hadn't worn it in years, but I couldn't part with it. Autumn would always have a special place in my heart. She was my best friend.

"Can't believe you still got that," he added. "I remember when you mailed it to me from overseas while you were playin' G.I. fuckin' Joe. Askin' me to put in your room for you."

"Probably the only letter you ever read of mine."

"I read them all, Creed. Every last one. Most of them I read so many fuckin' times that I started to memorize them. I may have resented you, but I needed to know you were okay. Make sure you were alive. I had to, you're my big brother."

I glanced over at him, surprised by his revelation.

"You were the only family I had left at that point. Couldn't lose you, too."

"Ya never wrote me back. If it wasn't for Pippin, wouldn't have ever gotten any mail."

"She's a good girl."

"You'd know," I sternly said. "She's yours now."

He slowly nodded his head with a flicker of something in his eyes that I couldn't make out or begin to understand. But he continued before I could give it anymore thought.

"I couldn't bring myself to write you back," he voiced, changing the subject. Walking over to sit on the edge of my bed, leaning his elbows on his knees. His eyes never wavered, following me as I went around the room, collecting all my shit. It was like he was truly looking at me for the first time since I was discharged from the Army.

Seeing his brother.

Not his enemy.

"I was fuckin' pissed at you for leavin' me behind. To take care of all the bullshit that had suddenly become my life. I hated you. Mostly cuz I knew you coulda died over there, leavin' me really fuckin' alone. Not given me a chance to even say goodbye to you before I woulda had to walk up to your grave. Exactly like I did with my daughter," he shared, immediately making me stop what I was doing to look at him.

"Yeah, I was fuckin' livid with you, Creed, letting it happenin' on your watch. The brother who had done nothin' but protect me for most of my childhood, couldn't do the same for my daughter. It brought back all those feelings I went through when you were gone, just pourin' fuckin' salt to my already bleedin' wounds." He took a long, deep, sturdy breath, composing his thoughts before adding, "I know it wasn't your fault, alright? If I would have been in that situation... havin' to choose... I probably would have chosen Mia, too. And that was the hardest pill to fuckin' swallow cuz that baby girl was actually my kid."

I didn't know what to say, so I didn't say anything. I just stood there in a state of shock.

"And that alone made me feel like I'm no different than our fuckin' father. When I don't wanna be nothin' like him."

"You ain't, Noah. I ain't either. And it's taken me a really long fuckin' time to realize that. Ya feel me?"

He nodded, his eyes glossy, blinking away his unshed tears. "When you enlisted. You didn't even ask me how I felt about you leavin'. Not one fuckin' word to me about it. I find out while you and Pops were kickin' each other's asses which seems to be a runnin' theme with our fuckin' family," he chuckled, trying to lighten the mood. "You made me feel like I didn't fuckin' matter to you anymore. When I went through my whole life feelin' like you were the only one who ever made me feel like I did matter to someone."

I shook my head, blindsided. "Gotta shitty way of fuckin' showin' it, Noah."

"I'm a Jameson, right?"

I scoffed out, grabbing a few more things from the drawers, throwing them in my bags. Hurrying around the space, gathering more shit so I could leave. "The fuck you want?" I finally asked, knowing he didn't come in my room for an afternoon fucking special where I'd tell him it was perfectly okay to continue loving and fucking my girl.

He knew me better than that.

"All I wanted was to tell ya was that we'll always be brothers, Creed. Don't matter how many times we kick each other's asses. We're blood."

"No shit," I rasped, eyeing him. "I love ya, Noah, but I don't have to fuckin' like ya. And right now, that ain't nothin' but the truth."

He nodded, understanding. Throwing me the shirt that was on my bed. "Pops ended up bein' more fucked up than I ever thought, huh? Thanks for takin' care of that. Findin' out the truth and all that shit."

"Didn't do it for you. She's my girl, baby brother. Been my fuckin' girl for as long as I can remember. No matter how many times you fuck her, tell her you love her, take her to bed—don't change the fact that she's always gonna be mine." I grabbed my bags off the bed, walking over the threshold to leave. I halted not looking back at him, addressing what I needed him to hear, "Shit happens. It's life. You take care of her, treat her right like she fuckin' deserves, yeah?"

"Always."

I nodded. "You better or you'll fuckin' answer to me." And with that I left, never once looking back.

I made my way to the kitchen, opening the double sliding doors to the back patio. Letting the ocean breeze sweep through the house. I came to love the salty smell in the air as much as the scent of vanilla, both reminding me of who I lost. It didn't get any easier as time went on, if anything it only got fucking harder.

I grabbed a beer from my fridge, needing it after a long day at the garage. I had opened a motorcycle shop in downtown South Port, in a prime location where most of the local bikers hung out. Business was booming, for only being open for two months. Diesel and a couple other brothers worked for me. It was the only thing that kept my mind occupied. All I'd ever known were guns and bikes. It only made sense to start making money off it. It was easy to rent the space and get my business going. I never spent much of what I had earned throughout my four years in the military. Getting paid extra money for every deployment, risking my fucking life for everyone else's. It was the only good that came out of being shipped overseas all those times.

Plus, I still had most of the money I received from doing all the illegal shit for the Devil's Rejects. At the end of the day, something bad turned into something good. I donated a chunk of that money to Polarins, an organization dedicated to fighting against human trafficking, in Mia's name. Figuring it was the least I could do with the corrupt cash.

For the first time in my life, I was making some sweet ass choppers, living and making decisions on my own. I was on the straight and narrow. Finally free of the demons that I thought would haunt me forever, but something, someone, was always missing.

Devil's Rejects became non-existent, or at least our chapter did, right after Prez fell six feet under and I resigned as VP. No one wanted to be associated with the name that was now tainted with bad blood around our parts. I was in the process of getting another club in order, taking my time setting it up the way I wanted it to run. The brotherhood of the MC was all I'd ever known. We had a bond that I didn't want to give up. I was just done with the illegal bullshit. Especially the bloodshed. I never wanted to be a 1%er in the first place, but it came with the territory I was born into. My new MC would cater to the true definition of a motorcycle club.

Family.

I finished my beer, throwing it in the trash. Warming myself something up for dinner. Hadn't eaten all damn day, I was fucking starving. It was easy to get caught up in what I loved doing. Work became my distraction. Something to fill up my time and the void in my heart. The shop was all I had now. I spent more hours there than I did at home. Too many memories of what could have been floated around the big space, taunting me.

Especially at night when I would lay in bed alone, wishing Mia was wrapped around me. I couldn't bring myself to sell our house, even though it hurt every time I walked in the goddamn door. Knowing I wouldn't see Mia's beautiful face greeting me.

Not a day, an hour, or a motherfucking second went by that I didn't think about her. Hoping she was happy, even if it was my brother's doing. She deserved all that and more.

Sometimes Diesel would drag my ass up to the bars with him, trying to score some pussy. I never had a problem getting fucking laid, but I honestly had no interest in it. Women in general. I was fine being on my own, knowing that at one point in my life I at least had *my* girl. I knew what love was, and a huge part of me didn't want to give that up. Often skipping out early, much to Diesel's disappointment. Hounding me, saying I had turned into a lovesick fucking pussy.

I threw my dirty dish in the sink, deciding to wash it later. Wanting to take a shower first, needing to wash away all the dirt and grime. I was over being fucking filthy. I just wanted to let the hot water run down my sore muscles for a few minutes. The daily manual labor taking me a minute to get used to. I tried not to think of Mia as I walked down the hallway toward my room, instantly noticing the adjacent door that I kept closed all the time was slightly ajar.

And then it suddenly hit me, running into a brick wall of her smell. Her scent. Wrapped all around me. Suffocating and engulfing me exactly the way it used to.

Damn, she still smelled so fucking good.

The closer I got to the room, the stronger her scent lingered until there were no more steps for me to take. Bringing me face to face with Mia. She didn't see me, too consumed and lost in her own mind as she sat in the rocking chair in the corner of the room. The magazines I had brought from the safe house placed on her lap, but that wasn't what had my undivided attention.

It was the photo she held tightly in her grasp. A picture no one had ever seen, not even me after that night.

One that could make or break her.

The next few seconds played out in slow motion as I watched her lift the photo to her pouty lips and whisper, "I'm so sorry, Maddie. I love and miss you so much."

Her expression filled with pain and emotion as tears streamed down her beautiful face, void of anything but remorse spewing out of her. Her voice laced with nothing but hurt and sorrow.

Hitting me all at once where it hurt *me* the most.

My heart.

One right after the other. The truth wasn't over yet. At least not…

Ours.

"Pippin," I called out, bringing her tear-stained face up to look at me.

My eyes widened and my mouth parted, sucking in air. Peering deep into her big blue eyes that always did it to me. Showing me everything I needed to hear. To know. I knew exactly who was staring back at me.

My lips were moving, questioning in a tone I didn't recognize, "How long, Mia?" It felt like my question echoed off the walls and straight into our fucking hearts.

She bit her lip, fully aware of what I was asking. Of what I meant. Of what I wanted to know, desperately needing to hear it fall from her mouth since the moment she woke up in that hospital bed.

Broken and lost.

I had waited.

For her.

My girl.

I didn't hesitate, asking again. Making myself more clear so there wouldn't be any more bullshit between us.

I spewed, "How long have you had your memory back?"

Mia

I unlocked the door, stepping inside our house before I even knew what I was doing. Not giving myself the chance to change my mind. I debated on actually going through with this for the past two months. Not sure if I could handle all the emotions and feelings I knew would come from stepping over the invisible line of our relationship. Continuing to battle my heart over my mind.

I didn't see his bike outside, so I knew he was at his shop. It was the talk of the town, even making the local papers. Stating, *Military veteran and reformed biker outlaw was now a law-abiding citizen.* Building one of a kind motorcycles from scratch. Bringing people in from all over just to see his next creation at his new shop downtown named, *Pippin's.* I couldn't have been more proud of him. Always knowing he was capable of so damn much. Never giving himself enough credit for anything in life.

I walked through our house for the first time, taking it all in. From the furniture we picked out together, to all the photos on the walls. I had no idea he had purchased any of this, yet. He never told me, never let me know what he had planned. It was all dreams, fantasizing about the day we could finally be together. I couldn't believe my eyes, seeing the life we talked about and planned for behind all these walls.

Our future.

I knew the layout of the house because he showed me the blueprints, wanting me to be just as excited as he was about the home he purchased for us.

For our family.

Including a baby girl who wasn't *his*.

My feet gravitated toward the room closest to ours as if I was being pulled by a string. Reeling me into the unknown. I didn't fight it. I went willingly, not sure what to expect, but needing to find out nonetheless. Nothing would stop my feet from moving toward the room we had designed the most out of the entire house. Spending hours upon hours looking through magazines and catalogs, wanting to make it absolutely perfect for her.

"Oh my God," I breathed out, stopping dead in my tracks when I was standing in front of the room that was supposed to be Maddie's nursery.

Exactly the way we wanted to decorate it, from the color of the walls to the crib, the accents, and changing table, even the scattered stuffed animals strategically placed around the room. There wasn't one thing that we didn't pick out together that wasn't already in the nursery.

I couldn't breathe.

I couldn't move.

I could barely even stand.

My eyes pooled with tears, taking in the memories flooding my mind. Each one unfolding in front of me, playing out one by one as I made my way around the room. My fingers lightly skimming across everything, needing to make sure it was real and not a figment of my imagination.

My healing mind playing tricks on me.

"Pippin, baby girl's room cannot just be pink," Creed spoke, turning the page as we laid against the headboard on his bed.

I turned the page back and circled the light pink rocking chair that he blew over. "Why? Pink is the best color in the world, and it's not even the same pink, it's a totally different shade."

"I like this one." He pointed to the white rocker next to mine, taking the marker out of my hand and circling it.

"White is so boring!"

"How 'bout we buy the white chair and you can pick out one of those fluffy, pointless, fuckin' pillows you seem to love to put on it."

I bit my lip, smirking. "Fine."

He smiled and crossed out the pink chair with a big black X.

My fingers gently glided along the soft bedding in the crib.

"I like all this princess shit," Creed stated, circling the pink and white bedding with tiaras and castles. "You're my fuckin' queen, and she'll be my princess."

I kissed him, straddling his lap, beaming. "I love you, too."

I opened one of the drawers, seeing all the magazines and catalogs he had brought me throughout the weeks of my pregnancy. I reached in grabbing them, revealing something I never in a million years thought he had kept.

Fresh tears filled my eyes as I took in the two stacks of envelopes, rubber banded together. The first stack I instantly recognized, they were the letters I had written him during his years in the Army. The ones that all went unanswered. I always thought he had thrown them away, but that didn't stop me from sending one every chance I got, wanting him to know someone back home was thinking about him. Praying for him.

But mostly just waiting for him to come home.

Each one was opened, crinkled, and torn like he had read them a thousand times. Memorizing all my words that I had written only for him.

It was the second set of envelopes which really caught my attention. They were all sealed with stamps, addressed to Miss Mia Ryder, AKA Pippin in his barely legible handwriting.

I smiled through my tears that were falling full force at that point. So many emotions were rushing over me, overwhelming me in the best possible way. He wrote me a letter for every one I sent him, replying to all my questions, all my thoughts, all my love for him.

I grabbed everything from the drawer, bringing it over to the rocking chair with me, taking a seat in the place that would have contained all our happy memories of the baby girl we lost. I imagined what it would have felt like to actually rock Maddie right here, in my arms as I stared at her adoringly.

"I can't wait to see you in that rocker, babe, holdin' baby girl," Creed rasped, getting down on his knees to kiss my belly.

I turned a few more pages, laughing at some of the ridiculous things Creed had circled like the onesies that said, 'I love my daddy and his tattoos,' or 'If I look funny it's because my daddy dressed me' and my personal favorite, 'My daddy owns a gun, any questions?' He always thought of Maddie as his own. No matter what.

I flipped a few more pages when I suddenly stopped. My heart started pounding out of my chest, my ears began to ring, echoing all around the room when I saw there was a picture of Maddie and me placed in between the pages.

I gasped, my shaking hand instantly went up to my mouth in shock of what was in front of my eyes. "Oh my God," I whispered to myself.

My eyes immediately filled with more tears. There was no controlling them from pouring out of me like a stream running down a mountain side. Cascading along my cheeks to the magazines below. Shedding every last tear I had pent up since the day I woke up in that hospital bed.

I never got see what she looked like.

I never got to hold her.

I never got to feel her skin against mine.

But I did...

She was laying on my chest with her tiny little face turned toward the camera. And what looked like Creed's tattooed hand holding her securely in place. Both our eyes were closed as if we were just sleeping. Peaceful as one. She looked exactly how Noah described her for me. My finger unconsciously started to trace her little button nose and tiny fingers that were lying on my chest next to her face.

She was so precious, so delicate, so beautiful. My heart ached from how full of love it was for this baby girl. Meeting her for the first time through this picture. Wanting to touch her, feel her, love her unconditionally, but I couldn't because she was gone. All I had left were the memories of being pregnant, feeling her inside of me, and now... this photo.

Portraying a mother and daughter content in each other's arms.

"I'm so sorry, Maddie. I love and miss you so much," I wept, mourning the loss of my baby girl and all that could have been. Staring at my precious daughter, smiling through my despair.

And then, out of nowhere, I suddenly felt *him* in the room like I had at prom.

"Pippin?"

With every last emotion, feeling, sentiment, memory pouring out of me, I peered up and looked him in the eyes. Knowing he already knew the truth because he had always felt me, too.

Our connection was alive and thriving all around us as if my memory was never gone to begin with. Right along with our love and the all the years of turmoil and passion, of lost times and heartache.

Of all the roads that led us to nowhere which finally would end here.

He visibly took a deep breath, murmuring, "How long Mia?" Gazing deep into my eyes, looking at *his* girl.

The one he never gave up hope would come back to him.

Me.

A war was raging in his eyes, but for the first time since I woke up, it wasn't for me because he knew I was already there.

With him.

His internal battle took place right in front of me like he wanted to hold me in his arms and never let me go. Except things were different now.

I was different.

And so was he.

We weren't the same people we had been before, and I think that was what scared him more than anything. Maybe realizing that just because I was his.

Didn't mean I still might not also be Noah's.

The serious expression on his face captivated me in the same way it always had. Which only added to the plaguing emotions that were placed in between us.

"How long have you had your memory back?" he elaborated, yearning to know how long it had been since I remembered him and our love.

"Two months, give or take."

He jerked back like I had hit him, and in a way, I probably had.

"It didn't come back all at once," I added, hoping it would calm him.

"How?"

I shook my head, not wanting him to know. It would hurt him too much.

"How?" he repeated in a stern tone I was more than familiar with. Fighting a battle I knew I wouldn't win.

"Creed, please… it doesn't—"

"Ain't gonna ask you again, Mia."

"Noah carried me onto his bike," I simply stated, not wanting to go into more detail.

He grimaced, didn't even try to hide it. Proving my intuition right. I knew him just as much as he knew me. That was just the way we were and always had been.

"It was the first time I had been on it, I could never do it. Why do you think that is?"

"Cuz on *my* bike, I made you mine. Claimin' you for the first time."

"I—"

"Did he fuck you on it, too?"

It was my turn to jerk back, even though I expected him to ask me that. It was why I didn't want to tell him, but it still hurt to hear.

"I just wanna know what made ya remember me. Was it the fact that you were on another man's bike when you only belong on the back of mine… or the fact that he made you come again when it shoulda been me? Simple question, Mia."

"Yes and yes. That what you want to hear, Creed? Make you feel better that you know now?" I paused, letting my questions sink in. "But it was his words that really put things into perspective for me."

"And what were those?"

"That he *claimed* me and that I was *his*."

"Are you, Pippin? Are you really his now? That what you came to tell me? Stab that knife a little deeper in my fuckin' heart, watch me bleed out for you? Again."

"I don't know why I'm here, okay? One minute I'm walking on the beach, the next I'm walking into this house... our house."

"Is that right? Took you two goddamn months to find your way home? Did I not mean anythin' to you?"

"That's not fair..."

"Life ain't fuckin' fair. Trust me, I would fuckin' know." He turned, breaking our connection. Running his hands through his hair in a frustrated gesture, pacing the room.

I honestly didn't know what to expect out of this, but that didn't stop me from having to come here. Needing to tell him. Even if it hurt both of us.

Instead, I held up the photo of Maddie and me, needing my own answers. "And this?"

He glanced over, shifting his eyes from me to the photo. Contemplating what to say, "She was still alive when I laid her on your chest, Pippin. Needed ya to know just cuz you were knocked out, don't mean you weren't there."

My lips trembled, taking in his words. Recalling all the times I told him I couldn't wait to be the first person to hold her. Place her on my chest and tell her how much I loved her. How much I wanted her, waiting impatiently for this moment. The one where she was finally here, in my arms. With me.

"Thank you. Thank you so much for taking this. If it wasn't for this picture, I wouldn't ever know what she looked like," I wept, looking at it once again.

I heard him walking toward me, stopping when we were about a foot apart. He crouched down in front of me, grabbing the stack of envelopes on my lap. "You found my letters."

I nodded, locking eyes with him again.

"I was gonna give them to you the first night we slept in our bed. Here, in our new home. The place I made perfect for you. For us. I wanted all of this to be a surprise," he shared, opening his arms, gesturing around the room. "Every time I came back from the safe house... I'd spend a few hours here wit' Ma. She helped me buy everythin', put it together. Waitin' for furniture to be delivered when I couldn't be here. You were always wit' me, Mia. No matter where I went, where I've gone, what I've seen and what I've done... you have never not been wit' me. You've always been my home."

"I know," I murmured loud enough for him to hear.

"What happens now?"

"I honestly don't know. I came here because I couldn't ignore it any longer. Never expecting any of this, though."

"Then what, huh? You leave? Go back to him? That how this works?"

"How long have you lived here, Creed? Has it been this entire time?" I questioned, needing to know.

He shook his head no. "After…" His face fell, taking a deep breath. Holding his head in between his hands. "I couldn't after what happened. It was all set—

the house, the nursery, all of it. For you. The last time I stepped foot in this place was when I left that photo in the magazine. Hadn't been back until a few months ago. I needed to move on, but I couldn't sell this house. I didn't even wanna."

My hand subconsciously went through his hair, wanting to comfort him any way I could. He leaned into my embrace, placing his cheek on my lap as I continued to softly caress him.

"I still don't know what to do wit' this room. Ain't ever been in here till now," he breathed out, his voice barely above a whisper.

He stirred beneath my touch, peering up at me. Searching my face for I don't know what before suddenly wrapping his arms around my waist. Bringing me down to the ground with him. Setting me down on his lap, holding me as close as he could to his heart. I willingly went, wanting, needing to feel his arms around me, too. The strong arms that enveloped me, protected me, and carried me countless times.

The same arms that used to push me away and let me go.

"I fuckin' love you, Mia. I fuckin' love you so much," he spoke, his voice breaking. "I'm sorry, babe. I'm so fuckin' sorry. Please tell me you know that… I would never—"

I looked up, placing my fingers against his lips. "I know, Creed. I knew that even when I didn't remember you. No doubt that you loved her. Did everything you could for her when I couldn't."

The look on his face would have brought me to my knees, had I not already been on the floor with him.

He placed his hands on the sides of my face, bringing me closer to him, but not nearly close enough. "I can't lose you again, baby. I just got ya back. Tell me you're here for me. Tell me you choose me. Please…"

Ends Here

My heart was breaking right along with his. Piece by piece fell to the floor between us, knowing it would never be whole again. "He loves me, and I love—"

"You may love him, Pippin, but you're not in love wit' me. You've been in love wit' me for most of your life. I own you, babe. You know it as much as I do. You wouldn't be here if you didn't. Why you doin' this to me? *Us*, Mia."

My chest rose and descended with each word that fell from his lips. His face mere inches away from mine, I felt him everywhere and all at once. His scent, his body, his eyes, his mouth, even though the only thing that touched me was his hands.

"Tell me you don't love me. Tell me you don't wish it were me who held you in their arms. Tell me you don't want me to kiss you right now, yeah? Touch you, take you to our bed and make sweet fuckin' love to all night long, until there isn't an inch of your skin I haven't kissed, licked, or touched. Tell me you don't feel *me*," he whimpered, placing his hand over my heart, "here."

"Creed," I whispered in a voice I didn't recognize. Trying to reel in my feelings, hide the fact that he still had an effect on me. After all this time.

"Tell me any of that, and I swear I'll leave you alone, cuz at the end of the day… All I ever wanted was for you to be happy, and if that's not wit' me, then at least I have the memory of the love of my fuckin' life." He placed his forehead on mine, bringing his hands up to frame my face again. "Say the words, babe," he groaned in a tone that made my stomach flutter and my body warm.

His mouth so close to mine that I could feel him breathe on me. The smell of cigarettes and mint took over my senses. As if he was testing me, he licked his lips slowly, provoking me.

Proving that he was right.

I shut my eyes. I had to. The realization was too hard to admit, and I knew he could see it in my gaze.

He knew me.

"Creed," I panted, my breathing mimicking his. "Please…"

"Please what, baby?" he rasped as if he was hanging on by a thread. Waiting for me to say the magic words that would set both of us free.

"Please… let me go. I'm not the same girl you hold so dear to your heart. I may remember now, but that doesn't change the fact that the girl you claimed… died a little at that house in the woods. And not even your touch, your love, your faith can bring her back. I'm just so confused. A part of me wants to jump right into your arms and tell you to never let me go. Your Pippin. The other part, the girl fighting the waves trying to stay afloat, tells me to turn left, right into Noah's embrace. It's like a train wreck waiting to happen. Both sets of tracks cross, coming together at some point, colliding with my heart. I'm sorry. I know that's not what you want to hear, but it's the truth. I can't do this to Noah, not like this. He's been nothing but there for me while you've been… gone."

"Baby, you know why I was gone. Woulda never left you if I didn't have to."

"I know. But that doesn't change the fact that he's been here. With me. Throughout everything my mind has gone through. And I do love him, Creed. It may not be as powerful or as strong as my feelings for you… but it's there. Inside of me. You both are. You have my past, and he has my present. I'm just so confused on who has my future."

He nodded, shuddering like a bucket of cold water had been poured down his body, never expecting me to say that. His hands instantly dropped, releasing my face. He stood, looking down at me with glossy eyes, struggling to step away. To walk away from the love we once shared. Making me feel the loss of his warmth, his love, his everything.

The damage was already done, and the look on his face made me question what I just did.

I stood, going right for him, but he backed away as if my touch would burn him. "Creed…

"I can't do this wit' ya anymore. It's fuckin' killin' me."

I forced back the tears that wanted to escape, feeling like I was dying right along with him.

"I love you more than anythin' in this world, Pippin."

Tears streamed down my face, so overwhelmed with so many emotions. Trying so hard to keep them at bay. I wiped away the tears from my face feeling like he'd just ripped out my heart and stomped all over it. I couldn't fucking breathe.

I nodded, unable to form words, but it didn't matter because there was nothing left to say. We said everything that mattered. I turned to leave, but he instantly grabbed my hand, pulling me back into his arms. Finding myself sobbing against his chest, soaking his white cotton shirt with nothing but my insecurities as his strong arms wrapped around me. I felt him cry, too.

"Jesus Christ, you're my everythin'. You'll always be my everythin'. The little girl who fuckin' saved me from myself more times than I count. The same one who made me realize what love was, what havin' the love of a good woman felt like. I never deserved you, baby, but God, I don't fuckin' care. Please..." he begged in a tone I had never heard from him before.

"I love you, too, Creed, and I always will," I cried as he held me tighter, knowing he needed to hear me say those words. He'd been waiting for the last year and a half to hear.

I stayed there in his arms, both of us knowing this might truly be our end. Our final goodbye. I pulled away first, and he wiped away all my tears, kissing along my face for the last time. Battling not to kiss me on my lips. I sucked in air that wasn't available for the taking. His arms fell to his sides, releasing me. Leaving me completely empty as I made my way toward the door, trying like hell not to look back at his broken expression.

"Pippin," he called out as I walked out the door.

I stopped, waiting on pins and needles for what he was going to say.

"I've been wishin' for you all my fuckin' life."

His words were too much. I needed to escape, run away, and get out of the house before all my walls caved. Our house that was supposed to be nothing but happy times.

"I'm sorry," I said one last time. And left.

Even though...

It nearly killed me.

Mia

"Mia, you listenin'?" Noah asked, pulling me away from my thoughts.

"Hmm..." I replied, looking up at him from my laptop. I had been aimlessly staring at my freshman class schedule for I don't know how long. I would be attending The University of North Carolina, Wilmington campus in a few short weeks. So I wanted to be prepared for my first official day as a college student.

I graduated from high school three months ago, surrounded by my friends and family, and of course Noah. My parents' went all out with a huge party in their backyard. Decked out in my class colors, balloons, and streamers. The works. I swear the whole graduating class was in attendance, people hanging out everywhere, swimming and eating barbecue.

Though I often found myself searching the crowd for a certain tall, broody, tattooed man who would stick out like a sore thumb at a party like this. I knew my mom had mailed an invite to his shop a few days before the event. Thinking he'd like to see me graduate or tell me congratulations. He didn't show up to the ceremony, but that didn't stop me from hoping he'd come by the party for at least a few minutes.

"He's not here, sweetheart."

I turned around to see Noah's mom standing behind me in the kitchen. All the other guests were mingling outside. "Yeah he is, didn't you see him? He's kind of hard to miss," I nervously chuckled when she caught me once again looking around the crowd of people for him.

"Not Noah, Mia. My other boy."

I winced. "How did you know I was looking for Creed?"

"Honey, I have never seen you look at anyone the way you do him. Even after everything that had happened, you still get this gleam in your eyes, and your face lights up like Christmas with the mere mention of his name."

"I think you've been reading too many romance novels, Diane."

We both laughed.

She stepped toward me, caressing the side of my face in a motherly gesture. "Sweetheart, call it woman or even mother intuition, but I know you're torn between them, and you have been since Maddie's funeral. I love my boys more than anything in this world, Mia. Noah's a good man, and I would hate to see him get hurt, but stringing him along is far worse than letting him go, darlin'. Your heart has always belonged to Creed."

I swallowed hard, biting my lip.

"I remember all the times you'd come over and sit with Noah on my couch. I wanted to pull you to the side so many times and tell you, but I couldn't do that to my son. It wasn't my place. Now things are different. You got your memory back, and it's time for you to be honest with yourself. The longer you're with Noah, the more you're hurting him, and I can't stand by and watch that happen. Not anymore. I love you like you were my own, and it doesn't surprise me in the least that both my boys are in love with you. You're a good girl, either one of them would be lucky to have you. It's time to do right by them and you."

I just nodded, taking in all she was saying. Knowing in my heart she was right. "I love him, Diane. I also need you to know that I love Noah, too."

"I know, sweetie. But loving someone and being in love with them are two totally different things. Don't make the same mistakes I did. I married the man I loved and left the one I was in love with behind. For the same reason you're holding on to Noah, not wanting to hurt him. Jameson wasn't always the cruel, vicious bastard he became. Money and power did that to him. I'll never regret my choice to be with him because he gave me three beautiful, loving

boys, and I wouldn't change that for anything or anyone. But you always have a choice, Mia. Don't let anyone make you feel like you don't."

"Did you hurt him? The other man... The one you were in love with?"

She took a deep breath, looking down at the ground for a few seconds before peering back up at me with anguish written all over her face. "I did. Especially after I married Jameson. I never wanted to be that woman who cheated on her husband, but it happened. For decades. My heart wouldn't let me forget him, and in the end, it cost him his life."

I jerked back with wide eyes. "Did—"

"Can't change the past, but you can change your future," she interrupted, pulling me into a tight hug. "Anyway, I'm going to head out. I just wanted you to know that I'm here for you, no matter what. No judgment."

I hugged her back, so grateful to have her in my life.

"You go and enjoy your party, ya hear?" She smiled, pulling away. "Congratulations, sweet girl!" She gave me one last sweet smile, then turned and left.

Leaving me with so much more to think about, in ways I hadn't before.

Creed never made it to my graduation party after all. I guess I couldn't blame him. We hadn't talked or seen each other since that day at the beach house almost five months ago. Not even in passing. It wasn't from lack of trying, often going out of my way past his shop. Hoping one day I'd see him. I knew he was avoiding me after I left him broken in Maddie's nursery. Trust me, if I could avoid myself, I probably would have, too. I was the true definition of a hot mess. Conflicted, knowing no matter what, someone was going to end up getting hurt.

And I started to think it might possibly be me.

It pained me, not to have him there. All he used to talk about was how he couldn't wait until I graduated. He would be standing in the crowd, proud as fuck of his girl.

His words, not mine.

It didn't come as a shock to anyone that I decided to stay in Oak Island for college. It had always been my home. I applied to several colleges out of state and got accepted into every last one of them, including my dad's alma mater, Ohio State. Part of me contemplated running away. Starting fresh. Leaving behind the two men who were playing tug of war with my heart.

But in the end, I believed I'd find my way eventually. I just didn't know which direction I would turn in. It was best to stay close to home, face the facts and move forward.

Or so I told myself.

In the back of my mind, I knew I didn't want to be far away from Creed. Already had spent way too many years apart, as it was. At that point, I'd take him any way I could. Even if it meant just seeing him in passing. I'd take an occasional nod of the head in my direction, a wave of his hand, or a hello to escape his lips. Praying that he wouldn't just ignore me like he did when I was a little girl. When I had to watch him get off his bike with another girl on the back. Pretending as if he didn't know me, like I never existed in his world.

I couldn't bear that again.

Noah and me were sitting on the couch in his new apartment. That happened to be right above the mechanic shop he was now employed at, not far from Creed's business downtown. I had to drive by it every time I came to see him. There was no avoiding it. It was like the whole situation was just mocking me.

"What's up with you lately, pretty girl?"

"Nothing." I shook my head, my gaze still glued to the screen of my laptop in front of me. "Why do you keep asking me that?"

"Cuz you keep lyin' to me."

"I'm not lying. Why would I lie?"

"I wouldn't know, Mia. Cuz you've shut down on me."

"What?" I replied, taken back. Finally looking up at him, catching me off guard with his eyes, dark and brazen.

"You gonna tell me what's wrong? Cuz I can't make it better if I don't know, baby."

"I have no idea what you're talking about," I simply stated, shutting my computer. About to stand up, but was stopped me short when he grabbed my hand.

"Don't walk away from me, we ain't done."

I jerked my arm away. "Obviously, I don't want to talk about this. I'm fine. Promise."

He cocked his head to the side, narrowing his eyes at me. "Is this about your memory? Cuz God knows we haven't talked 'bout it since it miraculously reappeared."

I didn't know what to say, so I didn't say anything at all.

He leaned back into the couch again, slowly nodding his head. The realization quickly took over the expression on his face. "So… this really is about your memory? Or should I say Creed?"

I winced, hearing his name. I couldn't help myself, it was quick, but he still saw it.

He shook his head, running his hands through his hair in a frustrated gesture. "I fuckin' knew it. I knew once your memory came back it would be all over for me. For us."

"I didn't say that. You're putting words in my mouth."

"You don't have to. It's written all over your face. Has been since everythin' started coming back to you. I've been tryin' to ignore it. Pretend like it isn't there, like I don't see it. Fuck… even been tellin' myself you're just tired or overwhelmed, it's why we haven't been havin' sex. You barely even let me touch you."

"I let you touch me, Noah."

"When? When was the last time you really let me touch you? Huh? I know." He sternly nodded. "When I fucked you on my bike."

I gasped from the vulgarity of his words.

"Don't look so surprised, Mia. I'm not that fuckin' stupid."

"I never said you were."

"You're takin' me for a fool now. Why you playin' me? After everythin' we have been through, have I ever made you feel like you couldn't be honest wit' me?"

"No," I softly spoke.

"I love you, but you already know that. I tell you all the time. You feel it in your heart when the words come out of my mouth. It's the sincerity in my voice. My touch when I feel you beneath me. You consume me."

"I know. I love you, too."

"But that don't mean you're in love with me, does it?"

"I'm here, aren't I?"

He shook his head, scoffing out, "That's your answer? Jesus, you can't even say it to me."

I sat back on the couch, closer to him. "Please, just drop it, okay?"

"No. I can't just drop it, Mia. That how you think this works? I continue to pretend you wanna be with me when you really want to be with him."

"That's not true. You're my best friend. I don't wanna lose you."

"You also don't wanna hurt me, but don't you realize you're hurtin' me right now? You been hurtin' me for months. Your indifference fuckin' shatters me, cuz I know it ain't you. I felt you, baby. Your heart, your touch, your fuckin' words. I had you, and now I fuckin' lost you, haven't I?"

I bowed my head, feeling ashamed. "I'm just confused... it will pass, and we will be good again, promise," I swiftly lied, the words feeling so foreign leaving my mouth.

"Not as long as he's around."

"That's not fair! You know how much I love you. It's been you for almost two years!"

"Well, it's been him for longer than that. Just admit it." He leaned forward, sitting on the edge of the couch. His elbows placed on his knees. "If you wouldn't have lost your memory, we wouldn't have been together. This would have never happened between us."

"You don't know tha—"

"The fuck I don't!" he roared, his hands connecting with the coffee table as he yelled, making me scoot away from him. "You fuckin' him? Is that what's going on? Feelin' guilty or somethin'?"

"No! I can't believe you just asked me that!" I shouted back, abruptly standing to leave. Hastily shoving everything into my backpack, then heading straight for the door. No longer wanting to have this conversation with him.

He was over to it in three strides, blocking my way. "I'm sorry, babe. I didn't mean to scare you." He instantly pulled me into his arms, and I reluctantly went. "I have been rackin' my mind, tryin' to figure out what I did wrong? What he has that I don't? How I could step up my game, be everythin' you need in a man. I got us this apartment. I know it ain't big, but it's a home. I got a job so I could take care of you. I love you so fuckin' much, it kills me inside." He pulled away, needing to look into my eyes. "I thought we would be together forever. Get married. Try for another baby. Maybe have a few more after that. Fuckin' grow old together," he paused, trying to reel in his emotions, but it was pointless. The hurt was evident his voice. His heart was bleeding out in front of me, too. "You don't want that, do you? At least not with me, right?"

"Noah... I... I'm just so confused and overwhelmed. I don't know what the right or wrong answer is. I have been worrying myself sick, these last four months. You have no idea what it is like to have years of emotions come pouring back into your life as if they were never gone. Except, now they're full force. Mixing in with the way I feel about you in my heart. I feel every touch, every look, everything that I used to know when it came to Creed. It all came rushing back. But there is no doubt in my mind that I love you, too. You have to believe me!" I stressed with tears suddenly falling down the sides of my face. "You have been my rock, my best friend, and one of the best things that have ever happened to me. And I will never be able to thank you enough for that. I'm so sorry, Noah. You have no idea... how sorry I am," I wept, letting the tears flow loosely now. "I never wanted to hurt you. I can't imagine my life without you in it. I love you so much..."

"But?"

"But... my heart is telling me... it's not you." My lips trembled. My heart ached for him. "I have been in love with Creed since I was nine-years-old. And as much as I want to tell my heart it's wrong, I don't think it is." More tears spilled down my face, waiting for him to say something, anything. To yell and scream at me. To tell me he hates me and that he will never forgive me for this.

I deserved it all.

"So what now? I just watch you run off into the sunset with my brother? Pretend I never fuckin' loved you? Never felt you beneath me? Never kissed your lips? And heard you say you love me, too? What, Mia? The fuck you want me to do? Cuz I can't keep doin' this. Lookin' into your eyes, seein' it's not me you want. Keep fuckin' you, knowing that when you're on top of me, it's cuz you're tryin' to stop thinking of him," he choked out, his eyes glossy and torn.

"Please... Noah," I begged for I don't know what.

"You know I'm right. So, who's it goin' to be? Huh? Him or me?"

"Noah, I'm so sorry. I never meant to hurt you," I simply repeated, staring into the depths of his soul. Needing him to understand and believe me. "But I can't keep lying to myself, and I can't keep stringing you along… when my heart belongs to another man. It's always been his since day one. I just lost my way and couldn't remember that. But I will never regret being with you. Having you in my life is the only thing that kept me going when all I wanted to do was die right along with Maddie. You saved me."

He took a deep breath as tears streamed down his face. Mimicking mine. Our emotions mirroring one another.

"Can I kiss you just one last time, please? Pretend that you're still mine before I have to say goodbye to you. Knowing that you're going back to him. Leaving me with nothing but my heart dying for you."

I fervently nodded.

He didn't waver, grabbing ahold of my face and kissing me like his life depended on it. Putting every emotion, every feeling, every last part of himself into our last kiss.

It would go down as the sweetest, saddest kiss of my life.

He leaned his forehead against mine, still peering deep into my eyes. "I'll always love you, Mia Ryder."

I nodded, murmuring, "I know. I'll always love you, too."

And I would.

I found myself going to the train tracks more often than not. The same place that used to torment me, had now become another spot that reminded me of her. Out of all the places we'd been together, this one was the closest to my heart. Clearly aware of the reason, this was where she became mine.

I shook off the sentiment, slowly letting the smoke seep from my nose and lips, savoring the taste of the nicotine that coursed through me. Sitting under the same tree in the open field, waiting for the twelve o'clock train to pass through town. I left Diesel in charge at the shop, running out to grab lunch, and yet here I was.

The one place that now gave me peace.

Trust me, the irony was not lost on me.

It had been six months since I last saw Mia. Nothing had really changed in my life. Same shit, just a different day. I was working so damn much, drowning myself in hours upon hours of custom builds at the shop. Sometimes showing up before sunrise and leaving well after midnight, if not later. It was easier that way.

Plain and simple.

There were times where I thought I saw her, felt her, rapidly turning around to find her, only to realize very fucking quickly it was just wishful thinking. My mind playing games that I had no interest in participating in. Especially after learning that she and Noah weren't together anymore. They hadn't been for three months, according to Ma. By the look on her face, she was waiting for me to run out the door of her house and go claim what had always been mine.

I didn't.

I couldn't do it anymore.

It hurt too fucking much.

Every day that went by was another day without her. Another day where I didn't see her, hold her, kiss her, fucking love her...

Another day that she didn't come to me. And God fucking help me that was all I wanted. I needed *her* to come back to me like I needed air to breathe. I couldn't keep fighting for her if she didn't want me. No longer being able to take the rejection. I was raging a war within myself. Debating whether to go after her or hold my ground. As much as I wanted to, the desire to have her choose me won in the end.

Which was probably why I started spending so much time at these goddamn train tracks, feeling as though I had really lost her for good. She'd moved on, and maybe it was time for me to do the same. I would mourn the loss of her for the rest of my fucking life.

Mia Ryder was a woman to love.

And... fuck did I still love her.

More so now than ever before.

"What are ya doin' here?" I suddenly found myself asking, unable to turn around. Knowing exactly who was behind me. Except this time, I knew it was real.

I felt her.

"I went by the house, and your bike wasn't in the driveway. Then I drove by your shop, and it wasn't in the parking lot, either. I don't know why but I knew you'd be here, so I came to find you."

After all this time.

She was finally there.

The moment I waited over three goddamn months for. Standing behind me, waiting for me to acknowledge she existed. That she was still part of my world. When a small breeze brushed through the open field, bathing me in nothing but her scent. The smell of vanilla overpowered my senses. I would be lying if I said I wasn't fucking terrified to turn around and find she was never there. My mind playing tricks on me once again, wishing for someone who would never come.

Before I could ask her why, I heard her walking in my direction until she took a seat right beside me. Glancing at the side of my face, waiting for me to say something else. Anything else. Instead, I took another drag of my cigarette, inhaling it long and deep. Trying to calm my overly beating heart. Keeping my emotions in check.

"I spent the last three months trying to get my life back in order, Creed. It was such a mess. I was such a mess. I needed a minute to be myself, to figure things out. Find who I was and what I wanted to be," Mia revealed, never taking her eyes off the side of my face.

"You miss Noah, Pippin?"

"Yes, but not in the sense that you think. I've spoken to him a few times, both of us checking in on each other. I hope one day we can put all this aside and become friends, again. I hate that he's not in my life anymore, but I had to let him go."

"Why is that?"

"Because he wasn't the man I'm in love with. The man I've never stopped being in love with. The man who owns my heart, body, and soul. The same one who's sitting right in front of me, but won't look in my direction because he's scared I'll disappear." She slowly crawled her way in front of me, sitting up on her knees. Staring straight into my eyes. She leaned forward and grabbed hold of the sides of my face, her lips inches away from mine. Adding, "I'm here, Creed. It took me a long time to get here. But I'm here nonetheless. For *you*. I can't say I chose you because there's never been a choice to make. It was always you… ya feel me?" She shyly smiled, throwing my line back at me.

I couldn't control it, as much as I wanted to, narrowing my eyes at her, I spewed, "What makes you think I even want ya anymore?"

Her eyes widened and her lips parted, not expecting me to say that.

"I asked you a question. Expectin' a fuckin' answer, Mia."

Her hands dropped from my face into her lap, defeated. A look of pure hurt crossed her eyes that were now glossy. It wasn't my intention to cause her any pain, but she needed to know I wasn't some fucking dog that would sit and roll over on her demand. Just because she was finally ready, didn't mean I was quite there yet. Of course, I fucking wanted her. I had been waiting for her to come back to me for as long as I can remember.

She surprised me when she said, "I don't know, but I'm calling bullshit. I know you love me, still. I can feel it every damn day like no time has passed between us at all. I'm not expecting you to forgive me today, but I hope you can find me in your heart again. I never left, I was just hiding for a really long time."

"Is that right?"

She nodded. "Let me make it up to you. Let me back in, and I will never leave again. You're stuck with me now, Creed Jameson."

Her breathing hitched, and her eyes dilated when I suddenly wrapped my arms around her. Lifting her tiny frame onto my thighs. All it would take was for me to kiss her, bite that goddamn bottom lip that had me hard just staring at it.

I. Needed. Her.

I was about to get lost in the moment and do exactly that, but the horn from the train blared nearby, breaking our connection.

With wide eyes she watched as every last car blew by with the breeze, not knowing what trains meant to me. The horn sounded three more times into the afternoon air as it clinked along the old tracks. All I did was watch her. I wanted to remember everything about that moment. The way she looked, the way she felt, but mostly the way she made me fucking feel. Searing and scarring me in ways I never wanted to recover from.

I heard the last car squeal down the tracks. "Pippin," I rasped, bringing her attention back to me.

My fingers ran up her arms, stopping when I reached her face. Brushing along her cheeks with my thumbs, I finally got to trace her pouty fucking lips like I wanted to for the last two and half years. Trailing them down to the back of her neck, pulling her closer to me, as close as she could get.

"I fuckin' love you. I won't lose you again," I paused, searching her expression. "For the first time in my life, I watched a train go by, and I didn't want to haul ass on it." Her eyebrows lowered as I peered deep into her eyes, confessing my truths. Placing my lips close to hers, I murmured, "Marry me." I didn't give her a chance to reply.

No longer being able to restrain myself, I crashed my mouth onto hers. Clutching harder onto the sides of my face, biting her goddamn bottom lip exactly the way I had fantasized moments ago. My tongue found hers. The slightest feel of her drove me over the edge, and all we were doing was kissing. I couldn't fucking wait to have my hands on her, my cock in her. Our tongues continued to move in sync with one another, colliding, afflicting, and penetrating deep into my soul. Where she fucking belonged.

I kissed her one last time, letting my lips linger for a few more seconds. Resting my forehead against hers, breathing profusely. My hands clutched the sides of her face with my eyes still closed as well. Needing a moment to take her in. To take all of this in.

I felt her smile against my mouth and whisper, "Yes."

My eyes instantly opened, and for the first time since she woke up in that hospital bed, I saw my future.

She pressed her hands against my chest, swallowing hard, peeking up at me through her lashes. "Take me home. Now."

I didn't have to be told twice.

My hands fell to her ass, gripping it tight, picking her up in one swift motion as I got to my feet. Causing her skirt to ride up her thighs, making her straddle my waist as I walked us back toward my bike. Bringing back all the memories of the first time I did this, consuming the both of us. My senses were heightened, taking in the scent of her all around me, plunging my tongue deep into my mouth. Unable to get enough of her.

The taste of her was all around me.

I straddled my bike with her now on my lap, yanking her closer, molding us into one person and claiming her like I did all those years ago.

I groaned into her mouth, "As much as I wanna fuck you on my bike again, I wanna break your pussy in our bed even more. Haven't been with anyone else since you."

Her mouth dropped open, caught off guard by my confession.

"Need to fuck you, babe. Claim you again. Then I'll take my time wit' you. Make sweet fuckin' love to you all night long." Kissing her one last time, I reluctantly placed her on the seat behind me.

She tried to hide the fact that she was beaming, but it was spread clear across her face, so she put my helmet on instead. Hoping I wouldn't notice. I threw back the throttle and rode with my girl on the back of my bike.

Ends Here

Where she always fucking belonged.

I couldn't believe he asked me to marry him, a random question that came out of nowhere. One minute I thought he was rejecting me, and the next he was asking me to be his wife. To spend eternity with him, making up for lost times.

Starting *now*.

It was all I ever wanted. He was all I ever wanted. We were lobsters that got lost at sea, but made their way back to each other. It didn't take long for him to pull up in our driveway, speeding to get me home and into bed. The second he kicked out his kickstand, I threw the helmet off and maneuvered my way onto his lap again.

In his arms.

"I want you," I moaned into his ear, kissing all along the side of his neck.

He growled, carrying me off the bike with my legs wrapped around his waist and my arms around his neck. The second his lips touched mine he growled again, parting them. Beckoning me to the same.

I did.

His hands were all over me. He couldn't decide where he wanted to touch me the most. I leaned into every touch, every sensation, every single filthy word that fell from his mouth. Anything he had to offer, I would take. He was mine. I was loving the thrill of what was to come, reaching for his belt before he even had the front door open. Knowing we were giving our new neighbors one hell of a show. I didn't care.

I wanted him.

I needed him.

Every last part of him.

He eagerly moved his hips against my hands as I worked his button and zipper. Unable to get them off fast enough. Pulling out his long, thick cock, aggressively and urgently stroking it up and down while he opened the door.

"Fuck, Mia…" he breathed into my mouth, rushing in and kicking it closed behind us. Slamming it shut.

He walked us down the hallway as best as he could, but our ravenous bodies had taken control. My back hitting a few walls, sending picture frames flying to the floor beneath us. We were both spiraling in a frenzy from the feel of our mouths and bodies colliding. It didn't matter how big of a mess we were making, just needing to get there as fast as possible.

He laid me on the edge of the bed, standing, hovering above me. Our mouth's attacking one another's while he pushed me down into the mattress. Taking what we both had been wanting.

What we needed.

Each other.

He tore open my blouse, sending buttons flying everywhere, crashing onto the floor with a ting sound. Not wanting to break our connection, not even for a minute. My bra was off within seconds, finally feeling his strong, callused hands roughly kneading my breasts as he sucked and licked all around my nipples. Causing my back to arch off the bed. Making me grip onto his neck, wanting him closer, and yet he still wasn't nearly close enough.

I never stopped stroking his cock, licking my lips. Imagining I could taste him on my tongue. He roughly ripped off my skirt and panties like he couldn't get them off fast enough.

"I want to fuck you with my tongue," he breathlessly urged, immediately placing his face in between my thighs.

I didn't even have time to blink before his tongue was pushing into my folds, swirling it into my opening.

"Oh, God," I panted as he placed my thighs onto his shoulders. Angling my clit in a way that made me go mad with need.

My hands instantly went into his hair, tugging and pulling. Gripping onto it with every lick to my core. Watching as his face was buried in my most sacred area.

As if reading my mind, he opened his eyes to look up at me as he sucked my clit into his mouth. Instantly moving his head in a side-to-side motion, followed by a back and forth rhythm.

"Ah!" I yelled out, trying to catch my bearings. Releasing his cock, unable to focus. My chest heaved with every precise manipulation of his skilled tongue and lips. His mouth literally eating me alive. I watched him push two fingers into my wet heat, causing my legs to shake. Which only enticed him to finger-fuck me harder and lick me faster. Bringing me so close to the edge of ecstasy.

About to have the most intense orgasm of my life.

Through hooded eyes, I saw him start stroking his cock, thinking it was still one of hottest things I'd ever seen. He looked so primal and heady, moving his hand up and down. Making me yearn for it to be inside of me. That was my undoing. I came so hard, my eyes rolled to the back of my head. My back arched off the bed, again. My hands fisted in the sheets. I swear I saw nothing but stars.

I didn't even have a minute to recover before he was pulling his shirt over his head, kicking off his boots and pants. Throwing them onto the floor without so much as a second thought. He scooted me onto the center of our bed, the one we picked out together. It warmed my heart and soothed my soul, creating a throbbing need to have him claim me on it.

I couldn't wait any longer.

"Please…" I begged, swaying my hips against his cock as he grinned above me.

"Wanna piece of me?" he baited, and I readily nodded my head. My body tingled all over. Sending spasms straight down to my very being.

"I want your… that." I nodded to it, blushing.

"Say it, Pippin. Wanna hear filthy shit come out of that sweet lil' mouth of yours. Tell me…" He grabbed onto his dick again, stroking it, accentuating his abs and V muscles. "Tell me you want my cock."

My eyes dilated, reaching for his shaft, but he intercepted had my hands pinned above my head, locking them in place by my wrists before I even saw it coming.

"Let me hear you say the words," he whispered, kissing my lips.

"Please… I want your cock," I repeated just for him.

He didn't falter, in one swift thrust he was deep inside of me.

"Shit!" I instantly yelled out, causing him to suddenly freeze. "I'm not on the pill, Creed!"

"Yeah?" He relaxed, slowly thrusting in and out of me, savoring the moment. Making me inadvertently moan. "That mean you only ever gone raw wit' me?"

"Yes…"

"Good."

"But, I could get—"

"Shhh…" he ordered in between kissing me. "No shit, I know."

I smirked, kissing him deeper and faster. He thrust into me harder and more demanding, his balls drenched from my wetness. Making me come so hard.

"That's it, baby… just like that… squeeze my fuckin' cock with your sweet, tight pussy. I ain't ever get enough of."

The slapping sound of our skin-on-skin contact echoed in the room. My body shuddered. No one could ever touch me like he could, and I knew that from the moment he first put his hands on me.

I was his.

He didn't stop, his hands moved to the sides of my face, caging me in with his arms. Feeling the weight of him on top of me as he continued to thrust in and out. Exactly how I wanted him to. I tried to keep his pace, barely finishing one release before another would hit.

"Keep comin' on my cock, baby. Take what's fuckin' yours."

"Creed…." I purred, breathless and gasping for air. Climaxing so intensely and long down his shaft, feeling like I couldn't stop coming.

He made this roaring sound from deep within his chest as we both came together. Panting profusely, trying to catch our bearings while he placed kisses all over my face, still not pulling out from deep inside me.

"I love you."

He looked deep into my eyes and spoke with conviction, "I fuckin' love you, too, babe. You're mine."

We spent the entire day just like that, making love, wrapped up in each other. Ready for the future that included marriage and possibly…

A baby.

I grabbed my throbbing head before I even opened my eyes, moaning in pain.

"You alright, babe?" Creed asked, nuzzling against my neck while he wrapped his arm around my waist. Tugging me closer to him on our bed.

It had been six months since we got married and almost nine months since we got back together. We didn't waste any time on getting hitched, having a small, intimate wedding out by the lake near my Uncle Austin's house. It was just family and close friends. Mason was Creed's Best Man, though I knew he wanted it to be his brother. Who never showed up. Mason and my dad both took the news of Creed and me much better than I had anticipated. I think after everything was said and done, they were both just beyond grateful for what he did for me.

Finding out the truth and putting an end to the danger.

Literally.

Giselle was my Maid of Honor, looking gorgeous in her soft pink dress. Although she said she wanted nothing to do with my brother, it didn't seem that way to me. Creed said something about him walking in on them in some sort of compromising position. Whatever that meant. Last she told me, she was still dating that guy she brought to my birthday party. I knew Mason would always be head over heels in love with her, who knew what would come of them. Only time could tell.

Noah and Creed still weren't talking, which was probably why he didn't show up. Not that we expected him to. He did send a gift and a card with his mom, though. We hadn't spoken since Creed and I got back together. I was giving him the space he obviously needed, even though it still hurt me that I was the cause of his pain. His mom told me he was doing fine. Her boy was strong, and at the end of the day…

All he wanted was for me to be happy.

And I was.

We said our vows under the willow tree, Creed found me at all those years ago. Swinging on my rope swing and fighting in the water. Which he threatened to throw me in, wedding dress and all, but my momma quickly put an end to that. Saying it would ruin my perfect gown, not to mention my hair and makeup that took hours to perfect.

Our wedding was the best day of my life.

"Mia Alexandra Ryder, I promise to always take care of you. Love you. Cherish you. Treat you like the queen you are in my life. For now and forever. And each day in between." He leaned in, kissing me. Murmuring, *"And I fuckin' love you."*

"Ugh, please don't move me. I might throw up on you," I declared, my eyes fluttering open. Adjusting to the bright sun cascading into our bedroom from the sliding glass doors.

He chuckled, laying soft kisses along my collarbone and then down to my chest. "Shouldn't have drunk so much last night."

"I'm never drinking again."

He took my nipple into his mouth while he fondled my other breast. "You got the most perfect tits," he groaned, continuing his assault.

I didn't even remember coming home after the initiation party for Creed's new End of the Road MC. He had finally opened the doors with all his brothers. Most of them used to be Devil's Rejects while others were new members.

"Creed?" I called out, looking down at him. "Am I naked?"

"Yeah."

"Did we have sex last night?"

He grinned up at me. "Yeah."

My eyes widened. "Oh my God! I blacked out and you still had sex with me?!"

"Yeah." He nodded as if it was totally normal.

"Did I even wake up?"

He shrugged, still grinning. "Your pussy got wet when I finger fucked you, and you made some noise here and there. That's all that matters."

My mouth dropped open.

"What? I'm a man, Pippin. You were grindin' your sweet, little ass on my cock all night. Bein' fuckin' adorable with your sloppy drunk ass. Took fuckin' care of you. Not to mention when we got home, I had to carry your ass inside, cuz you passed the fuck out on the cab ride back. Laid you down on the bed, got ya some water, and made ya take some pain pills. Which apparently didn't help since you still feel like shit. Imagine if I hadn't made you take 'em, though." He smiled, starting to kiss along my collarbone again. "I took your clothes off and went to shower. When I came back you pulled all the sheets off you, your ass and pussy were perched up in the air. So I fuckin' took what's mine. Considered it my reward for bein' such an amazin' fuckin' husband."

"Unbelievable," I breathed out, shaking my head. You literally had sex with me while I was passed out."

"What?" he scoffed out. "You pissed that you missed out on my cock? You want some of me?"

I rolled my eyes. "I'll throw up on you. That's not a threat, it's a promise," I mocked, trying to stifle a laugh.

"Naw, don't you know that orgasms make everythin' better," he said in a husky tone, his lips kissing their way down my body.

"Next, are you going to tell me that if we don't have sex your balls are going to fall off? Because I'm not fourteen anymore, I know that can't happen now."

"Who said anythin' about sex? I'm fuckin' starvin', babe, wanna swallow you for breakfast. You gonna feed me, baby?"

I didn't have time to answer before his tongue spread me open.

"Mmm..." I moaned, my eyes closing. Rolling to the back of my head for a whole different set of reasons.

"I want a baby girl," he rasped, making me smile big and wide. He always did this, putting it out in the universe like it would magically come true.

"This isn't the way to make that happen," I sassed, as he sucked my clit into his mouth, moving his head side to side. "Ah…"

He gently bit down, and I squirmed. Pushing two fingers inside of me, causing my back to arch off the mattress. Hitting my sweet spot while he devoured me with his mouth.

"That feel good?"

My breathing hitched, and my legs trembled.

"Yeah?" He pushed harder and sucked faster.

It didn't take long till my legs tightened so hard around his head, come running all the way down his face. He didn't let up, savoring the taste of me against his tongue, swallowing all my juices like I was his favorite meal. He kissed my clit one last time and made his way back up my body, wiping my come from his mouth with the back of his arm. Only stopping when he was fully on top of me. Caging me in.

"Feel better?"

"Maybe."

"I always take care of my girl."

"Are you trying to get in right now?"

"Depends." He kissed my lips. "You gonna let me in?"

"I'm surprised you're asking. Considering you took what you wanted last night."

"I take what I want every night and mornin' too, but I'm tryin' to be a gentlemen cuz you ain't feelin' good."

"You? A gentlemen?" I teased. "Oh, come on… you're a lot of things, but a gentleman definitely isn't one of them. More like barbarian and part caveman maybe."

"Is that right?" he rasped, positioning his dick at my entrance, and in one thrust he was balls deep inside of me.

I sucked in air while his lips parted against mine. "Do you feel me inside you?" he growled into my mouth.

"Yes," I panted, trying to keep my eyes open for him, knowing he loved it when I did.

"I wanna make a baby girl with you."

I beamed. "We could be makin' one right now."

He paused, taking in my words. Cocking his head to the side, waiting for me to continue.

"I'm ovulating so—"

He slammed into me, shoving his tongue into my mouth. Angling my leg higher on his side, trying to get as deep as he could. Roughly taking what was his. Our mouths never stopped kissing, even though we were both panting profusely, desperately trying to cling onto every sensation of our skin-on-skin contact.

I felt myself start to come apart, and he was right there with me. Always so in tune with my body, knowing it better than I did. He thrust in one last time and came deep inside of me. Planting his seed, hoping it would grow. Not moving for one single second once he was done.

"There's my girl," he growled into my mouth. "You gonna give me a baby girl, yeah?"

I smirked. "Not up to me. I just bake it. You're the one who needs to put something in my oven."

In one swift motion, he flipped me over so I was now on top of him. His cock still deep inside of me never once pulling out. "I'll spend all day puttin' my seed inside of you. It's where it fuckin' belongs."

And he did.

When Mia finally made her way back to me, I never in a million years thought I'd ask her to marry me right then and there. It just randomly flew out of my mouth, like saying I love you. I had zero regrets, though. It was the best thing I had ever fucking said.

I needed to do right by her, and by that it meant I needed to ask her old man for permission to marry his daughter. Even though I technically did it ass backward, asking her first instead of him. That was our little secret in the heat of the moment. He didn't have to know that. I prayed to God that it would go over well. I figured this way he wouldn't give me too much shit when I moved her clothes out of her room that weekend. I was over the bullshit of not having her in my bed every night. We had missed so much time together, I planned on making up every last minute with my cock, in our bed.

At that point, we had been back together for about a month. They knew about us, and to my utter disbelief, they were okay with our relationship.

"Come in," her dad announced after I knocked on the door to his office at their house.

Mia was in class all morning. I waited until I knew she wouldn't be around. We said we were going to tell them together when the time was right, but I wanted to make sure she knew I respected her parents. That things were different now.

That I was different.

Her mom let me right in, grinning like a damn fool the entire time as if she knew what I was coming there to do. Stating that he was in his office before I even asked where he was.

I opened the door and walked inside, abruptly stopping when I saw him cleaning his gun on his desk. I didn't even know he had a gun, but fuck did I respected him a hell of a lot more for what he was trying to do. Showing me we weren't that different from one another. I would have done the same fucking thing if a man like me was coming to ask for my baby girl's hand in marriage, too.

"Nice piece." I nodded to his 9mm Glock, taking a seat in one of the chairs in front of his desk.

"I have three more just like it."

I hid back a smile.

"I know why you're here, Creed."

"Figured you would."

"What makes you think you're good enough to be her husband and my son-in-law?"

"Cuz I love her. I'd do anythin' for her. Includin' gettin' your blessin' cuz I know it would mean everythin' to her."

"Don't think just because I might let you marry her that you'll be able to get rid of me. I'll always protect my baby girl. You hurt her. You so much as make her cry, I won't think twice about shooting off your balls. That goes for any of my future grandbabies as well."

"I'd never hurt her or my family, sir. Mia has always been my life," I simply stated, looking him in the eyes, so he knew I spoke the truth.

He nodded, leaning back into his chair. "Don't think you're ever going to call me Dad. It's Mr. Ryder or sir to you. Understood?"

"This mean I got your blessin' to make Mia my wife?"

"She has to say yes, Creed. Until then, I'll hold onto the hope that you won't be my son-in-law," he said with a hint of a smile on his face.

"She won't say no."

"You think so?"

"I wouldn't let her."

He narrowed his eyes at me, taking a good long look at my face. "For reasons I may never understand, my wife fucking likes you. Alex has always been a hopeless romantic, and she thinks you're good for our daughter. That is the only reason I'll give you my blessing. Not because I fucking like you. We clear?"

I nodded again. "Thank you, sir."

"Good. Now get out of my office before I change my mind."

I chuckled and leaned over to shake his hand. He looked down at my gesture, hesitating before taking it for the first time... respecting the hell out of me, too.

"Oh, and, Creed," he announced, making me turn back and look at him. "One day, I'll thank you for saving my daughter's life."

I smiled. "Lookin' forward to that day, sir."

"Whatcha thinkin' about over there?" Mia asked, pulling me away from my thoughts, six weeks later.

"Babe, don't play with me. What's it say?"

She put her finger up to her lips. "Oh, whatever do you mean? What does what say? Was I supposed to be doing something? I don't remember."

"Pippin..." I warned. "Asked you a fuckin' question. Expectin' an answer."

"See, here's the problem, Creed Jameson."

"Oh, we got fuckin' problems now, Mia Jameson?"

She smirked. "Yes. We need to have a word."

I laughed, big and throaty. I couldn't help it. She was too fucking adorable for her own good. She smiled, all proud of herself as she made her way toward me. Straddling my lap on the couch and wrapping her arms around my neck.

"I don't want my baby's—"

"Our *babies*," I corrected, gripping onto her waist. Letting her know I wanted more than one. Wanting a house full of kids, running around driving us fucking crazy, but loving the shit out them regardless.

"Yes. That. Our babies. I don't want their first words to be shit, fuck, goddamn it, motherfucker, son of a bitch, bullshit, and... well, the list is endless when it comes to your filthy, dirty mouth."

I kissed her lips. "I thought you loved my filthy, dirty mouth, especially when it's fuckin' yo—"

She placed her hands over my lips again, silencing me. "And you just proved my point. So, I think you need to start watching how you speak and what you say."

"Is that right? Now, why is that?"

"Because..." She pulled out a stick from her back pocket. I didn't realize it had been there or I would have pulled it out myself when she walked out of the bathroom.

"Babe... you're testin' my fuckin' patience."

"What do you think a baby is going to do?" She turned the stick so I could see the word clearly written across the screen. "Seeing as you're going to be a daddy."

I smiled, immediately grabbing onto the sides of her face. Bringing her closer to me to kiss her pouty fucking lips. My heart was so full I could barely see straight, the emotion coursing through my veins was almost as crippling as the news itself. We'd been trying to make a baby girl for the last nine months and nothing. Her doctor reassured us that she was perfectly fine. I didn't want to lose hope, but it was starting to take its toll on me that she wasn't getting pregnant. I never let her see that side of me, though. Knowing that she wanted a baby just as much as I did.

"Mia, I'm really gonna be a daddy?" I asked, needing to hear her say the words.

She nodded. "I took four pregnancy tests. This is the only one I brought out here to show you. They all came out positive the second I peed on them. I'm pretty sure the answer is a yes, but I still need to confirm with the doctor."

I kissed her again, long and hard. My cock throbbed to be inside her. "I fuckin' love you, baby." Turning us sideways on the sofa, I leaned her back into the cushion. Kissing her all over her face.

Ends Here

I had everything I ever wanted and more.

My wife.

My baby.

My family.

My life was finally complete, and I owed it all to a little girl wearing pigtails and a pink baby doll dress. Who stole my heart when she was nine-years-old.

Before I even knew what I was doing, I lifted her dress and kissed her stomach, whispering, "I already love you so much, baby girl. You and your momma are my world."

"How do you know it's a girl? It could be a boy."

"I wanna name her Harley."

She smiled, and it lit up her entire beautiful face. "Harley it is."

"Did you hear that, Harley? You're gonna have your momma's bright blue eyes and her pouty lips that are goin' to be too big for your round face. And her button little nose, too."

"You're making me sound like a Gremlin," she giggled as I rubbed all over her belly.

"You're fuckin' gorgeous, and our baby girl will be, too. Hopefully, you have my good sense, cuz I still don't know how your momma chose me," I said to her stomach. "But damn do I thank God for it every day."

"You're gonna make me cry."

"No fuckin' cryin'," I let out, causing her to shriek and shudder as I started tickling the sides of her stomach with my hands. Using my beard to attack her neck.

"This isn't fair!" she shouted, thrashing around through a fit of laughter.

"What?" I taunted. "What's not fair, babe? Can't hear ya. You're gonna have—"

The doorbell rang, interrupting us.

"Fuck off! We're busy!"

"Creed!" She slapped my arm. "You better hope they didn't hear you. What if that's my parents' or your momma? Go answer the door!"

I groaned, irritated that I had to go take care of whoever was out front. When all I wanted to do was spend the rest of the afternoon inside my wife. Talking to our baby girl.

I opened the door. "This better be fuckin' import—" I jerked back as soon as I came face to face with the last person I ever expected to show up on my doorstep.

"Noah," I greeted, shocked as shit by the sudden turn of events.

"Hey." He nodded to me. "Was in the neighborhood. Thought I'd stop by and see how you were doin'. See how both of you were doin'."

I stepped aside, gesturing for him to come in. He did, following behind me as I made my way back to the living room. The expression on Mia's face mirrored mine.

"Noah," she muttered with wide eyes, taking him in.

"Hey, Mia," he replied, peering at her in a way I hadn't expected. Like family.

She stood, walking over to him. Pulling him into a tight hug. "It's so good to see you." I knew she was missing him. She hadn't seen or heard from him in a long ass time. Even after everything that happened, she held out hope that they could be friends.

He hugged her back, slightly smiling. "Good to see you, too." Pulling away, eyeing me. "Good to see the both of you... Heard you had a beautiful wedding. Sorry I missed it."

"We missed you there. How are you? What are you up to these days?"

"I'm good. Been travelin' a bit. Nothin' too crazy."

"Oh, where are my manners. Would you like something to drink?"

"Sure, I'll take a beer."

"Okay. You want one, too?"

I nodded, unable to form any words yet. Still completely taken aback that my baby brother was in my house. A place he had never been before. Not that I didn't want him there, I just never thought it would actually happen. Figured seeing Mia and me together might be too much to handle. But here he was, and I was grateful regardless. I gestured to the couch before I sat down, placing my elbows on my knees. Rubbing the back of my neck.

"How's the shop? Heard all sorts of good shit about it. Ma's proud as fuck, can't say I ain't either."

"Thanks, bro. Business is good. Life is good. Always thinkin' about you, though. You stickin' around town for awhile?"

"Yeah, I'm back. Just needed a little time away, clear my head, ya know?"

Mia walked back in the room with our beers and water for herself. Giving me a stern look when she handed me the bottle, with her back turned to Noah.

Mouthing, "Don't." Gesturing to her stomach.

I pulled her down on my lap. "What was that, babe? Tell Noah he's gonna be an uncle in nine months?"

"Creed!" she scolded, smacking my arm.

"What?" I looked over at Noah, expecting to see a hurt look on his face. But seeing the exact opposite.

His eyes went back and forth between us not knowing who to focus on more. He smiled, nodding his head to me. "That's great, you two. I'm happy for you. Honest. I am. Need some fuckin' kids in our family. Did you tell Ma, yet?"

"Naw, just found out ourselves."

"Well, I'm honored to be the first to know. Can't wait to be an uncle. Expect me to spoil the shit out of them, too," he stated in a sincere tone before adding, "Rumor has it you opened up your own club, yeah? Well, that's actually why I'm here. I came back to be your VP."

I smiled. I couldn't help it. "Yeah?"

"Fuck yeah."

And just like that...

Some things never changed.

Especially when it was your goddamn blood.

EPILOGUE

Mia

"But, Momma, I don't wanna wear the black bathin' suit!" Harley argued, folding her arms over her chest. Cocking her hip out to the side. "It ain't pretty. I wanna wear the pink bikini. Please, Momma, please!" she begged in the cutest baby voice.

"You don't *want to* wear the black bathing suit. *It's not* pretty. You *want to* wear the pink bikini," I corrected, emphasizing the right dialect.

She tilted her head to the side, looking at me like I was crazy. "Well, my daddy don't talk like that."

I laughed, shaking my head at her as we stood in her room. I swear she was five going on twenty-one.

"I'll tell you what. I'll work on your daddy with letting you wear the pink bikini, okay? I promise. I think the pink bikini is much prettier, too, baby girl. But for today you have to wear the black bathing suit."

She sighed. "Fine." She rolled her eyes, walking over to me so I could help her change. "But, Momma, why do Daddy let you wear the pink bikini? When he says you belong to him, too," she asked, scratching her little head when we were done.

She was too smart for her own good.

"Cuz, Daddy, will beat some asses if anyone so much as looks at Momma the wrong way," Creed chimed in, holding our two-year-old son, Luke, in his arms.

"Creed... mouth!" I reprimanded, now shaking my head at him. I swear I had three kids already.

Harley, Luke, *and* my husband.

He kissed Luke on the cheek before handing him over to me. Leaning forward to kiss my swollen belly. "How's my boy in there?"

"Kicking, moving around, driving me crazy. Much like his father."

"Pippin, don't hold him too long. You gotta enough weight on your tiny frame with that belly. Don't want ya to strain yourself."

"I'm fine," I replied, kissing all over my little man's face.

"Momma, I think the next baby after that one should be a sister, not another brother."

"Another one? Who says I'm having another one?"

"Daddy." She innocently shrugged, trying to put her shoe on the wrong foot. "He says he wants ta keep ya barefoot and pregnant in da kitchen, makin' his food, cuz that's where you belong. Momma, I thinks that's a good idea, cuz I like when you make my food, too."

"Oh my God, Creed! What are you teaching my daughter?!"

He proudly smiled with a gleam in his eyes, pulling me in for a kiss. "Our daughter," he corrected.

"Babe, she's going to think that's okay," I whispered low so she couldn't hear. Knowing it was useless because she could hear everything, but I had to at least try. "What are you going to do when her boyfriend says that to her?"

He narrowed his eyes at me, arching an eyebrow. "First off, ain't gonna be a boyfriend. Got my guns for a reason. And most importantly." He glanced over at Harley. "Baby girl, cover your ears."

She did, smiling and giggling. Knowing exactly why she had to take cover them.

"Any boy comes near her, I'll break his fuckin' legs and that's if I don't put him to fuckin' ground first."

"Creed!"

"What?" He grinned, looking at me with a mischievous glare. "She can't hear. Can you, baby?"

She giggled louder. Making me laugh right along with her.

This was my family.

The loves of my life.

And I wouldn't have it any other way.

"You ready, baby girl?"

She eagerly nodded, grabbing onto her pink backpack. "Daddy, can you helps me? I can't reach it." She stood on the tips of her toes with her little arms up high, trying to get her cut from her closet. I had it custom made for her, the back read, *Property of my Daddy.*

I grabbed it down for her, and she immediately put one arm through the hole of the vest while I helped with the other.

"How do I look?" She smiled, posing for me with her huge sunglasses on her head like she was grown. Reminding me so damn much of her mother.

She looked just like her, exactly how I wanted. My son, Luke, on the other hand, was all me. Much to Mia's distress, saying she could only imagine what kind of trouble he would get into. Especially with the ladies. Making me proud as fuck my boy would divide and conquer just like his father. Already molding him to love bikes and women. All the baby girls followed him around on the playground. Causing Mia to only worry about him more.

"Beautiful, baby. Just like your momma." She grabbed my hand, and I kissed Mia one last time.

"I'll be right behind you guys. Going to get little man dressed, and I'll meet you at the clubhouse. I won't be long. Drive carefully please."

"Always." Baby girl took my hand and led me out of her room and to my bike. I placed her on the seat, grabbing her helmet from the garage.

"Daddy, when I gonna get to drive this bike?"

I snapped her helmet into place, patting her head to see if she was ready.

She looked up, smirking. "Come on, Daddy! Let's ride."

I chuckled, putting on my own helmet and getting on my bike behind her. Wrapping my arm securely around her waist, bringing her close to my chest. "You can drive when you can tie your own shoes."

She happily nodded, putting her hands on the gas tank in front of her just like I taught her. Ready for the ride down to the clubhouse. Baby girl loved my bike just as much as her momma did, riding around with me with bystanders all looking over at her, pointing. Saying how cute she was with her little girl cut that matched my Prez cut. She was the talk of Mia's mommy group that she took her to. Saying she needed to learn how to socialize or some shit. My baby girl didn't need to socialize with any fucking boys, and I made sure to tell the facility that.

Pulling up to the clubhouse, I cut the engine and got off my bike. Taking off my helmet, then helping Harley with hers. She handed me her hairbands from her pocket, patiently waiting for me to do her hair. I put it back in pigtails the best I could like I did every time. They weren't nearly as perfect as what Mia did, but Harley always said she loved mine more.

"Unkey Noah!" Harley shouted, running over to him as soon as I put her on the ground. Running as fast as her chubby little legs could move.

"Baby girl," he greeted, immediately picking her up and throwing her onto his shoulders.

She wrapped her tiny little arms around his neck, laying her face on the top of his head. Hugging him tight with her eyes closed. She adored her uncle, she was attached to everyone, but Noah held a special place in her heart. They had a bond, probably because he was just another person who let her get away with anything. Always giving her what she wanted before she even batted an eye.

"Everyone's already inside. What took you so long?" he asked, nodding to me.

I grinned, and he rolled his eyes. "Harley, cover your ears," he ordered, making her fall into a fit of giggles. She had the most adorable fucking laugh, making us laugh right along with her. "Jesus Christ, bro. Let your ol' lady breathe. She's already knocked up. Don't need somethin' else inside of her," he chuckled.

"Gotta take it when I can with a whole bunch of cock blockers runnin' around."

We both laughed.

It didn't take long for Mia to show up with Luke. I grabbed my boy from her arms, giving her the what the fuck look for carrying him again. To this day my woman never fucking listened to me. But goddamn did she make me hard as fuck, walking in wearing her Property of Creed cut. Her mom grabbed him out of my arms, kissing all over his face. Talking to him in that baby gibberish I couldn't stand. My boy was a man, not baby girl, but I wouldn't argue with her about it. My ma did the same thing, so it didn't do me any good to try to change it.

Everyone was at the clubhouse for the family barbecue we had every Sunday. It had become my favorite day of the week. The brothers would bring their families, the kids would bring their friends. I built a new warehouse on some land out in the country, not far from our house. It had the works with a pool, acres of land for the kids to all play on with their four wheelers and dirt bikes, and whatever the fuck else they brought over. I even installed a jungle gym playground in the back as a Christmas present for Harley. The look on her face when she saw it was all the thanks I needed. Although, her momma took care of thanking me for her later that night. Which was how we ended up with my new boy in her belly.

I had my one baby girl, all I wanted were boys now. Someone needed to kick some ass and watch her back. I knew they'd make me proud.

Her family and I were on good terms for the most part, other than being a pain in the ass in-laws. Her uncles and old man were possibly considering getting custom choppers of their own and joining the club. End of the Road was nothing like Devil's Rejects. Never would be. It was all about family, so if they wanted to ride by me, I'd fucking love it.

My life was about my wife, my kids, my brothers, my whole family. The way it always should have been.

"Pippin," I whispered into Mia's ear, coming up behind her while she was cleaning vegetables in the sink. Wrapping my arms around her belly, feeling my boy bouncing around. My hands slipping under her shirt, wanting to feel her smooth, silky skin against my fingertips. "How you so smell so fuckin' good all the time?" I groaned, skimming toward her tits that were fucking huge.

You couldn't even tell she was pregnant from behind. She was all belly like with all her pregnancies.

"Creed," she giggled, hiding her neck. "Babe, how does a pregnant woman turn you on this much? I'm huge."

"You're fuckin' perfect. Come on, baby, let me in. We can go into our suite, tell everyone you needed a minute to lay down... with my face in between your legs."

"Creed! Go! You're up to no good! Go play with Harley."

"But I wanna play with you."

She squirmed out of my embrace. "Later, you're lettin' me in or I'll just fuckin' take it," I warned, grinning at her.

"Oh my God! You're insatiable."

I walked out back, shooting the shit with the boys, her uncles, and old man. Throwing back some beers while we grilled out. Mia walked out sometime later, wrapping her arms around my waist.

"Who's that?" I asked, nodding to the car that had just pulled up.

She looked in my direction. "That's just Giselle and her on and off again boyfriend or something... I don't know. I can never keep up with her anymore."

"Mason know?"

She shrugged. "He's about to."

Giselle stepped out of the car, and I never imagined the man who would be following her.

"Mia!" She wrapped her into a hug, pulling away and touching her belly. "I swear you're so lucky! You're the cutest pregnant woman in the world. It's not fair," Giselle stated, but my eyes were locked with the man stepping up in front of me. Giselle looked back and forth between us. "I don't have to introduce you, do I?" she teased. "You guys are more than familiar with each other."

He cocked his head to the side, muttering, "Creed."

I nodded, breathing out, "Fuckin' Damien."

M. Robinson

For Creed and Mia.
It's only the beginning for...
Damien Montero, El Santo
(Next is a Spin-off Standalone Contemporary Romance of Damien Montero's Story)

Releasing August 29, 2017
Amazon Pre-Order Coming Soon
Pre-Order Available on i-Books, Nook and Kobo

Made in the USA
Lexington, KY
26 December 2017